BEYOND CHANCE,
BEYOND TIME,
BEYOND FORGETTING . . .

The 18th-century journal of a young man's tragic love affair . . . The four-hundred-year-old portrait of a beautiful woman, inexplicably familiar . . .

Wealthy jet-setter Andrew Moffat is led to the ruined walls of an 18th-century castle by what seems an alluring series of coincidences. But once inside those haunted walls, he discovers it was destiny that lured him to Nonsuch Palace—to begin a journey deep into the past, to vanquish an evil which has twice destroyed him . . . to consummate a love he has found and lost throughout the centuries, but which he means to have and to hold for all eternity . . . .

"A lovely, lovely book."
—Dorothy Eden

"A gripping experience."
—Sidney Sheldon

THE NONSUCH LURE

MARY LUKE

A BERKLEY MEDALLION BOOK
published by
BERKLEY PUBLISHING CORPORATION

Published by arrangement with
Coward, McCann & Geoghegan, Inc.

Coward, McCann & Geoghegan, Inc.
200 Madison Avenue
New York, N. Y. 10016

Library of Congress Catalog Card Number: 76-12605
SBN 425-03552-2

BERKLEY MEDALLION BOOKS are published by
Berkley Publishing Corporation
200 Madison Avenue
New York, N. Y. 10016

BERKLEY MEDALLION BOOK ® TM 757,375

Printed in the United States of America

Berkley Medallion Edition, NOVEMBER, 1977

For Claire M. Smith

and

Patricia B. Soliman

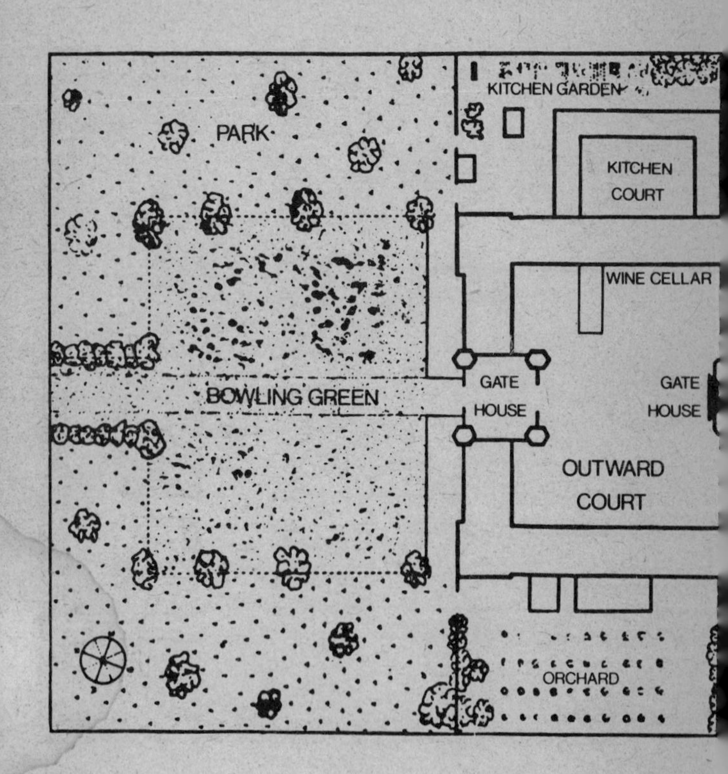

KITCHEN GARDEN
PARK
KITCHEN
COURT
WINE CELLAR
GATE
HOUSE
BOWLING GREEN
GATE
HOUSE
OUTWARD
COURT
ORCHARD

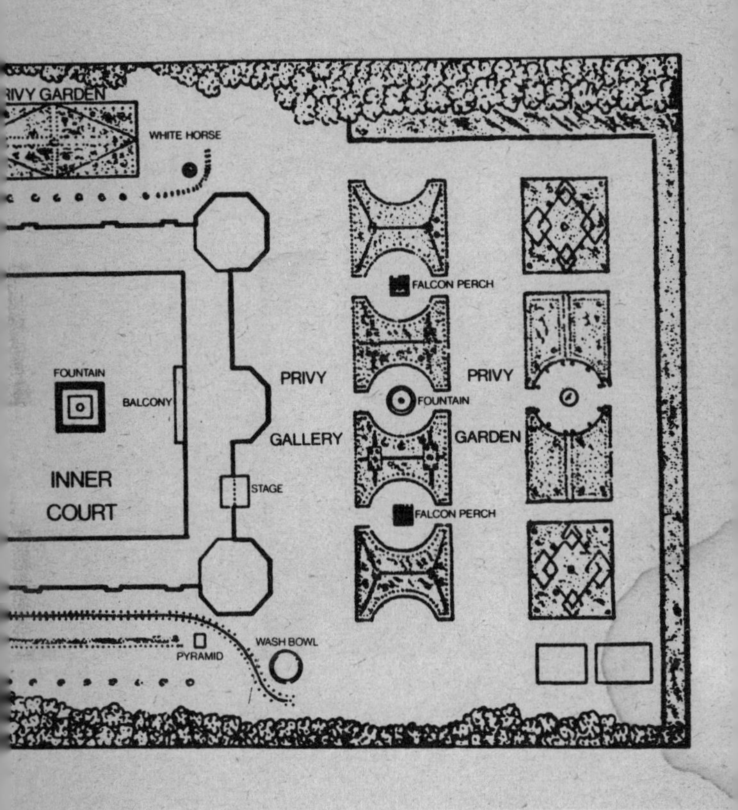
RIVY GARDEN
WHITE HORSE
FOUNTAIN
BALCONY
INNER COURT
PRIVY GALLERY
STAGE
FALCON PERCH
FOUNTAIN
FALCON PERCH
PRIVY GARDEN
PYRAMID
WASH BOWL

Nonsuch, a royal retreat, in a place formerly called Cuddington, a very healthful situation, chosen by King Henry VIII for his pleasure and retirement, and built by him with an excess of magnificence and elegance even to ostentation; one would imagine everything that architecture can perform to have been employed in this one work. There are everywhere so many statues that seem to breathe, so many miracles of consummate art, so many casts that rival even the perfection of Roman antiquity, that it may well claim and justify its name of Nonsuch, being without an equal; or, as the poet sung,

This, which no equal has in art or fame,
Britons deservedly do Nonsuch name.

—*The Travels of Paul Hentzner,* 1598

NOTE

The inspiration for this book was a visit several years ago to Nonsuch Park near Ewell in Surrey. There the late John Dent, author of *The Quest for Nonsuch*, told me the story of the Cuddington family, Richard and Elizabeth, whose lands were confiscated by King Henry VIII in order that he might build a palace "as there would be none such in the land."

In 1959, during what he called his "Nonsuch Summer," John Dent was closely involved in the actual excavation of the old Tudor Palace. In his book, he recounted the eviction of the Cuddington family, the destruction of their home, the church, the village and nearby Merton Priory.

Upon these facts I have peopled Nonsuch Palace with fictitious characters and events. Set against a solid historical background, they have given me pleasure in my own "Nonsuch Summer."

MARY M. LUKE

Summer, 1975
Ridgefield, Connecticut

Andrew

Chapter One

The tall man swung his briefcase from overhead, eager to leave the big jet. He hoped there would be no long wait for luggage, for he was anxious to begin the search that had brought him to London. As he followed the passengers toward the exit, he wondered at the quiet elation that always accompanied a return to England. His work had taken him all over the world; he was comfortable in most of its largest cities. Yet the sight of England—whether approaching its incredible green from the sky or gliding silently through the Solent by ship—always inspired a jubilant sense of homecoming and pleasure.

Andrew remembered someone once telling him that everyone on earth had a spiritual home—some one place where they were part of the environment and functioned more satisfactorily than any other. It could be a Norwegian fjord, a hill town in India or the colonial simplicity of a New England village. For Andrew it had always been England. Yet he'd have hesitated to confide the feeling to anyone. It didn't fit the sophisticated image of a distinguished author, lecturer and world traveler, one trained as an architect whose own private fortune allowed him the privilege of evaluating buildings instead of erecting them. Such a belief might seem naïve and would hardly enhance the solid reputation of the architectural connoisseur who wrote so vividly of the wonders of the Kremlin, the Colosseum and Versailles.

Even the crowded traffic of Earls Court and the dull mediocrity of the Cromwell Road did nothing to lessen his delight at the prospect of more than a month in London. Passing the great red pile of Harrods, as the cab swung toward Hyde Park Corner, turning down Grosvenor Place toward

Buckingham Palace, Andrew felt the excitement of the ordinary tourist. It was late afternoon, and the area around the graceful iron gates of the palace was almost deserted. He noted the taut standard signifying that Majesty was in residence and then settled back to enjoy the pleasing prospect of the long straight vista down the Mall. His trained eye savored its symmetry and form, even as the artist in him appreciated the luxurious green and the bright scarlet tulips of St. James's Park. He wondered—not for the first time—at the translucence of the air over the towers of Whitehall lying just ahead, their pale washed stone fringed at the bottom by the park trees.

At Charing Cross, the busy intersection before the Strand, Andrew gathered together coat and briefcase as the driver slowed to look for the number. He could almost read the man's thoughts: an American with an authoritative air, wearing well-cut clothes and carrying good luggage should really be destined for the Savoy Hotel up ahead, not an obscure number which Andrew insisted was a small residential hotel. "If 'tis, 'tis news to me, guv'nor," the man had said, "and I bin drivin' a long enough time, 'tis true. . . ."

The cab slowed to a crawl. Just ahead, Andrew saw an old building, its faded stone mottled and dirt-begrimed, set back several feet from the pavement. "That must be it, driver. . . ." He pointed, overlooking the man's disdainful sniff, as he pulled to a stop. It was. A small plaque, CUDDINGTON HOUSE. NUMBER 18 IN THE STRAND, was affixed to a door oddly out of keeping with the building's façade. Andrew tipped the driver generously to atone for the man's disillusionment; the sight of the note brought him from the cab to pile Andrew's luggage at the door. To the right, an electric sign, TEAS, flicked on and off in a window. Hardly prepossessing and possibly a real fleabag, Andrew thought, which may just serve me right for indulging myself in this extravagant whim. Forget the feather bed, down quilt, newly laid fire, proper English tea and breakfast—such civilized amenities were fast disappearing from other better hotels as the traditional English servant passed from the scene.

Inside, however, was a pleasant surprise. The lobby was unusually large and filled with those wicker pieces so dear to

English hearts. Yet here and there older, more substantial pieces filled in: a japanned cabinet, highly glossed to a deep ebony sheen, an octagonal table atop a magnificent acanthus leaf base, holding a lamp of dubious origin, fringed and balled. Pastel paintings on delicate rice paper, filled with the feathery strokes of the Oriental artist, hung over the sofa, its chintz so faded the pattern was indiscernible. The once-magnificent rug was threadbare and in spots revealed portions of what appeared to be a stone floor. There was insufficient light from the undersized windows; consequently everything was dim, almost dark in the corners. Even the electric bulbs were too weak to be effective.

A pleasant-faced woman behind the desk welcomed him. As he signed the surprisingly thick register, she asked, "Were you recommended by a friend, sir?"

Andrew hesitated. "Well, not exactly. No, not a friend. But I heard about Number 18 in the States."

"Well, it makes no matter. We ask only because, you see, we *do* get many recommendations from people who've stayed here, and it makes it more friendly if we know who sent you."

An older man emerged from the room behind the counter. Nearly bald, he had the pallor of one continually indoors. He wore a frayed black coat over a paunch, baggy trousers and a pair of well-worn bedroom slippers.

"My husband"—the woman gestured—"he'll take you up to your room. We've given you a front room, sir, which I hope won't be too noisy. But the Strand does quiet down somewhat at night and over the weekend, you know. 'Tis all we have anyway."

Andrew followed the man to the lift—small even by English standards. He scorned Andrew's offer of help with the luggage, insisting he could get it all in if just left alone. As suitcases wobbled precariously atop each other, he strained at the rope that, after three mighty tugs, sent the lift soaring upward with surprising ease. Andrew helped unload the luggage, and at the end of the hall the man threw open a door.

The room was larger than Andrew had expected, with the same unusual contrast in furnishings as downstairs. There was a hint of lost grandeur in its spaciousness, in the intricately carved plaster ceiling, now so begrimed the design was difficult to see. The walls weren't contemporary with the ceiling; Andrew had the feeling the originals would have been carved plaster, too. And the floors, covered with several rugs of uncertain derivation, were no more than thirty or forty years old. A wide bed, unbelievably canopied in balled and fringed maroon velour, was against one wall. Andrew had seen similar beds in museums and exclusive country houses around the world. A nondescript night table and lamp were at the side. To the right of the windows—and up here their width and thick embrasures were in proportion to the room—a handsome cabinet, cleverly converted, served as a bureau. An Edwardian armoire stood in the corner, a faded counterpart of many turned out by the thousands fifty years before. A serviceable sink and towel rack were near the door, and as the man left, he pointed to the bathroom several doors down the hall.

It might have been worse. Andrew went to the window. The glass was very old, even wavy in spots; it had to be the original. He cast a professional eye over the outside stonework. *Mullioned*, by God. He opened the window and felt appreciatively of the rough old stone. Something tugged at his mind as he gazed into the Strand below. Across the way the soaring splendor of the Shell-Mex building pointed heavenward, one of the few taller buildings the English had done well, most being graceless travesties of the worst being put up in the States. The Shell-Mex fronted on the Embankment, hiding the Thames from view.

The late-afternoon sun was fast disappearing, glinting on the sloping roofs of the Embankment buildings. At the end of Hungerford Bridge on the opposite side of the Thames was the square cube of the Royal Festival Hall. Traffic roared along the Embankment below, and through the trees Andrew could just glimpse Cleopatra's Needle—an incongruity from a desert land that, over the past century, had mellowed into part of the river scene. The windows of the Houses of Parliament were aflame with the lessening rays of the sun, and behind them was the roseate tip of Westminster Abbey. Opposite the Houses of Parliament the small red jewel of Lambeth Palace was doll-like beside the greater mass of St.

Thomas's Hospital, which hid the palace gardens from view.

Looking in the opposite direction, Andrew blessed the good fortune that had halted the great London Fire of 1666 at the Temple, only a few steps away to the north. The original city of the Romans, the Conqueror, the Plantagenets, Tudors and Stuarts hadn't survived. Only the Tower, parts of the Temple and a few isolated buildings dated back earlier than the late seventeenth century. But Westminster Hall, over by the Houses of Parliament, had been built by William Rufus, a son of the Conqueror, about 1090; the Abbey itself was even older. Andrew didn't consider himself a historian, but his work had given him access to many facts he might not ordinarily have acquired.

He was engrossed in the scene when a knock on the door revealed the lady from behind the counter. She carried a tray with a teapot and cup and some generous slices of bread, meat and cake. " 'Tis Sunday, sir, and you'll have to walk to Piccadilly to find anything open, and you'll still not be finding anything as good as this." She set the tray down on top of the bureau. "Did you find everything all right, sir?"

Andrew eyed the tea; he was hungrier than he'd thought. "This is very kind of you, Mrs. . . ."

"Caudle, sir, Rosa Caudle and Harry's my husband." She looked around the room. "This is one of the nicest. We usually save it for Americans; they like the bed and the view"—she waved to the windows—"such as it is since *that* monster went up. . . ." The Shell-Mex was obviously no favorite of Mrs. Caudle's. "As a girl I can remember being able to see the river from here. Ever so pretty on a fine day it was, sir, and prettier inside Cuddington House, too, more light and all."

"Then you've been here since you were a girl?" Andrew laid some meat between the buttered bread. "You've always lived here, Mrs. Caudle?"

"Ever since I can remember, sir. You see, I was a Cuddington before I married Harry. The Cuddingtons have lived here since the place was built, and that's *hundreds* of years ago—it's all down in papers we have in the safe. I think it's one of the oldest places in the Strand, sir. The Americans always seem to like that part. There's a history of the place printed in the lounge, sir, if you'd like to read it. Just leave the tray outside the door when you're finished, sir.'' And Rosa Caudle was gone from the room before Andrew could frame another question. There were so many he wished to ask.

Well, it all fits the story so far, he thought, lighting a cigarette and relaxing against the pillows under the faded grandeur of the canopy. Checking into Cuddington House, Number 18 in the Strand, had been the first step in solving the mystery that had so unaccountably gripped him since the discovery he'd made in Williamsburg. He'd come to England direct from the little Virginia city, where he'd spent several months working on the restored or reconstructed buildings that had played such an important part in America's early history.

Following the completion of his work in Williamsburg, Andrew had planned a month's vacation with married friends in Vermont whose little guesthouse had more than once provided a welcome retreat. It was just at that time he'd noticed an obscure item in a Washington newspaper reporting that the Palace of Nonsuch in Surrey would soon be excavated.

When he was a child, Andrew's parents, cultivated and knowledgeable travelers, had been guests at the stately pile of Lord something-or-other near the village of Ewell. One afternoon a serving girl had been directed to take the eight-year-old Andrew to play in Nonsuch Park. He'd been entranced. It was summer, and the great park—so vast and open to a child more familiar with the confines of New York's Central Park—had stretched before him, an endless expanse of green grass and trees. He'd flown his kite, eaten the generous picnic the girl had brought and listened to the soughing of the trees that grew to great heights. In the early dusk they'd walked down a long tree-lined drive through the park gates,and the girl—whose every feature was still clear in his memory, though he'd long since forgotten her name—had told him that once a magnificent palace had occupied the site, a palace built by Henry VIII for his queen. Unfortunately, she couldn't remember which one. Henry had stayed at Nonsuch, and so had his children; it was a favorite of the great Elizabeth. The girl didn't know what happened to the palace, but the surrounding park had been kept open to the public. In the intervening years Andrew had often driven by car or traveled by train in the general vicinity. Passing signs reading NONSUCH PARK, he remembered the intelligent maid who'd cared enough to stimulate a small boy's imagination—and he cursed the lack of time prohibiting a grown-up visit.

The news story had set Andrew to thinking of substituting England for Vermont. With any luck, he might see the excavations; he might, with his professional background and knowledge, even be able to help. When he mentioned the possibility to his secretary, Miss Dabney—whose idea of a proper vacation was more likely the Club Méditeranee—her response was an expressive shrug. Several friends reacted similarly when Andrew mentioned Nonsuch, noting with amusement that he didn't usually involve himself in anything so whimsically trivial. He, cheerfully, agreed.

Livia Thomas was no exception. She worked for Colonial Williamsburg as an art expert, with sixteenth- and seventeenth-century England her special province. Much of the art, architecture and general construction of eighteenth-century Williamsburg was a direct derivation of those periods. She'd been invaluable to Andrew, who preferred not to employ a permanent assistant. Livia had been much taken with him and, in his months in Williamsburg, had endeavored in every way she knew—and some of the ways were mighty impressive, he now admitted—to see that she became more permanent than an assistant. In the end she'd found, as countless others before her, that the lure of a new assignment was sufficient for Andrew to disentangle himself—he was always the gentleman, he hoped—from any emotional encumbrances.

If asked, Andrew Moffatt couldn't have explained why, in his late thirties, he was unmarried, with no serious romantic involvement. His parents had been very happy together. They'd rarely been apart, and when his father died unexpectedly in his fifties, his mother—in seeming good health—had followed him within a year. It had left Andrew, at twenty-five, with a well-nigh limitless future before him, thanks to his good education and propensity for hard work, his assured architectural expertise, all buttressed by a healthy, well-administered trust fund. His tall, rangy good looks had made him the target of women of all ages, sizes, colors and creeds. Along the way he'd taken what was freely offered, being careful that no emotional entanglement would hinder his leaving—as he always knew he would. Oddly, few begrudged such treatment, recognizing they had unexpectedly captured a *rara avis*. Instead, they remained flattered by his attention, accepting that the affair would be short-lived. Andrew could, in almost every major city of the world, have phoned an Old Friend. She would have been eager to see him, even willing to revive their romance, knowing that at the end he would leave.

As far as he was concerned, his life-style left nothing to be desired. A pied-à-terre in New York held a few of his things: his books, the good porcelains from his parents, his out-of-season clothes and his important papers. Everything else traveled with him. He'd trained himself to sleep on short flights as well as long ones, to hire the finest in chauffeured cars, always to have first-class accommodations. Since travel was an integral part of his work, he'd long ago decided to enjoy it. He'd achieved a solid fame in his field and had enjoyed every step of the way. He wasn't given to idle whims or hurried decisions, and the curious sense of urgency that made him forgo a New England vacation with old and dear companions for the opportunity to see the remains of an ancient Tudor palace had puzzled him as much as it had amused others.

In short, he was here in England, but he was not sure just why.

During those last few weeks in Williamsburg he might easily have changed his mind. Common sense told him he could obtain full reports, complete with photographs, of the excavations through his professional contacts. Livia continued charming, applying subtle pressure for him to stay. The Virginia countryside in late spring was as beautiful and relaxing as the comfortable Vermont hilltop. Yet remembrance of that English park and its vanished stately palace recurred daily. Indeed, he might still be there at Williamsburg if it hadn't been for that momentous day he found the book he now referred to as Julian's *Journal*.

Artifacts—broken shards of glass, ceramic pottery, bent ironwork, moldering pieces of wood—were constantly being turned up. Any new digging or cleaning of existing Williamsburg foundations uncovered buckets of debris that went to the restoration workshops for any information they might give on colonial life.

But Andrew's discovery hadn't come from the earth; it had come from a very respectable bookstore in the shopping complex just outside the restored area. The proprietor had asked Andrew to autograph copies of his latest book on architectural finds from the caves of Indians who'd inhabited the great American southwest thousands of years ago. Andrew had browsed among the current best-sellers, selected a few paperbacks against his next air trip and paused briefly in front of a locked glass-door cabinet. It contained matched sets handsomely bound in leather, as well as single volumes in various sizes—all undeniably old. One book caught his attention simply because it was smaller than and not as rich-looking as the rest. Out of sheer curiosity, he asked the proprietor if he might see it.

He riffled the pages idly, attempting to sort out from the fine, clear handwriting who had written the book and what it was about. The flyleaf bore the inscription "*Julian Cushing. My Journal. Williamsburg, 1699 and England 1700*." Not really old, Andrew noted, a little more than two hundred and fifty years ago, and undoubtedly the tired reminiscences of an old codger who'd taken the Grand Tour. He was about to return it to the shelf when a sentence leaped from the page: "I am hoping soon to go to Nonsuch. It will be a fitting reward for the vile trip on the ocean. If it had not been for the portrait, I would never have come this far. . . ."

Andrew had been startled and later puzzled by his reaction. He felt an intense inner excitement, and it seemed only to increase as he turned the pages. The feeling was difficult to explain. It wasn't an expensive or rare volume—more the type a man of modest means might have purchased to record the passage of his days. Hundreds of years ago, Andrew knew, everyone who could read and write had kept a journal. The modern-day diary satisfied, in briefer form, the same need to record one's daily activities. But journals were never numbered daily as modern diaries were, and the writer could go on at length, dating the time himself. One entry might contain innumerable pages of the writer's musings, as well as the affairs of the day. Other days might contain, as Julian Cushing had written, "Nothing." He had also, Andrew noted, skipped a day or two whenever presumably little occurred to merit even the abrupt "Nothing."

Still the sense of excitement stayed with him, so he'd bought the journal, returning to show it to Livia Thomas. She pronounced it genuine enough, but whether Julian Cushing had lived a life sufficiently interesting to merit its price, only a thorough reading would show. Andrew resolved to find out that evening.

He'd read the book with a concentration part curiosity, part exhiliaration and an odd compelling acuity to which he could put no name. It was unusual, to say the least, that this unknown and seemingly very ordinary young man should, more than two hundred and fifty years ago, when one did not undertake such a journey casually, have been so passionately inquisitive about Nonsuch Palace that he'd crossed the sea to view its ruins. Just as he, Andrew Moffat, was now contemplating crossing the sea (but not a "vile trip," he hoped) to see whatever they'd unearthed of it. He returned to the paragraph mentioning the portrait. How fortunate Julian was to have seen a portrait of Nonsuch! Andrew was familiar with the only existing sketches or pictures. Extensive as several of them were, they still showed frustratingly little of what the interior of the great structure must have been like.

Now, months later, recollection of the *Journal* caused Andrew to rummage through a suitcase, and he thumbed the pages of the book, looking for Julian's comments on his arrival. There they were on page 42. He lit another cigarette, leaned back against the bed pillows and read:

"I am very pleased with my Reception here. Being greatly fatigued with the discomfort of my passage, I remained overnight at Dover. Today by horse to London and to Cuddington House in the Strand which had been so highly recommended to me as it was the home of my friend, James Cuddington. It is a most gracious Structure, one of the sights of the Strand, being of more recent construction which is in pleasant contrast with the Dire condition of many of those older mansions of the nobility along the River. The furnishings are very handsome, being family pieces so Miss Rosa Cuddington, who lives here now, told me.

Some of them have remained in the house since its Construction. I am in a fair room facing the River—the view is most Gratifying and the air remarkably Restorative.

At tea (which is a new drink only now becoming available to other than the Aristocracy due to its price—which I found most Pleasing), I told Miss Cuddington of the Portrait which has become so Dear to me, and at length we removed the coverings which had withstood extremely well the punishment of the crossing. I also told her of my Desire to see the portrait returned to its owners. I can only hope I withheld my Passion from her gaze. She is a very Perceptive Woman.

And so tomorrow I go to Nonsuch. It promises to be a glorious morning. I am to travel with Miss Cuddington who has also arranged for me to stay at Sparwefeld Farm in the park near Nonsuch, which the Cuddington family own. She was very impressed with the portrait's beauty and said I would find things little changed at Sparwefeld—it is near enough to the palace site and she said the ruins are indeed more Extensive than I had been led to believe—or hoped."

And then, maddeningly, under the next day, an abrupt "Nothing."

It was this "nothing" when he'd expected so much that most intrigued Andrew. Even more remarkable was the disparity in the entries after Julian's arrival in England, compared to what had gone before. In Williamsburg his writing had been unselfconscious and free. Julian had been unassumingly honest, noting his day-to-day activities, recording his reactions as well. The pages were cluttered with little philosophies and homilies Andrew had found touching. His arrival in England had been much as he'd expected, although the crossing seemed to have been unusually severe. Julian seemed pleased with Cuddington House and with Miss Rosa Cuddington, to whom he'd shown the Nonsuch portrait. She'd even sent him to a family residence near the old palace. He'd felt great anticipation for viewing the ruins the next day. Then, under that date, "Nothing." Exasperating and somehow mysterious—it seemed as though once he'd seen Nonsuch, Julian was somehow reluctant to convey too much to his *Journal*.

The enigmatic "Nothing" had gnawed at Andrew. His attention and curiosity were thoroughly aroused, and he decided then and there to visit the excavation site. However, he'd never expected to find Cuddington House, Number 18 in the Strand, still in existence. Familiar as he was with London, the small, shabby structure, now captive between two office buildings, had simply gone unnoticed. In the travel agency at Williamsburg, while he waited for a clerk to process his airline ticket, he'd thumbed through some travel literature. A brochure, featuring "Places to Stay—the Offbeat, the Unusual," listed Cuddington House. "Popular with Americans for its highly convenient location, this venerable old structure is already over 400 years old. It has been dispensing old-fashioned hospitality to the public since the early 1800s. Mrs. R. Caudle, Prop."

Andrew couldn't believe the coincidence: that the same lodgings where Julian Cushing had stayed more than two hundred fifty years before should still be available and that he should so casually have learned of their existence. Number 18 in the Strand. Four hundred years old. Wavy floors and things that go bump in the night. Bathrooms a half mile away. Dust under the bureau and flypaper hanging from the ceiling. No telephone. Gray-haired schoolteachers in sneakers, and balding, bookish scholars, complete with umbrella, or wispy effeminate young men on culture kicks. That's what he'd find at Number 18, and it would serve him right.

Yet the desire to see Cuddington House—to take advantage of that incredible coincidence—was overwhelming. Common sense told him to head straight for his London favorite, the Connaught. But common sense seemed to have deserted him the moment he thought of visiting a field of Surrey ruins. So caution (and the Connaught) were hastily abandoned, as Andrew requested the agency to make reservations at Cuddington House. If he were going to follow in Julian Cushing's footsteps, he might as well go the whole route. He left the agency thinking he'd have only himself—and Julian—to blame if the journey became the crashing bore his friends predicted.

He looked now at the remainder of the *Journal*—about fifty-five additional pages. He'd read them all thoroughly. Julian Cushing's life in the opening passages had been quite simple and yet, by the standards of that time, probably a comfortable and certainly a fortunate one. The boy—he seemed to be about twenty years old when he began his entries—had some income from a small Jamestown plantation left by his late father. Evidently, it wasn't enough to support him as he wished to live—as a gentleman and a learned one at that. Julian seemed at one time to have considered the church as a career but, for reasons not given, had become interested in the building of the new town of Williamsburg. Jamestown had previously been the capital of Virginia. In 1699 the State House had burned, and a new and more desirable site, Middle Plantation, between the York and James rivers, some seven miles away, was chosen as the new capital. It was renamed Williamsburg in honor of William III. The new college at the end of the Duke of Gloucester Street was also named after the English monarchs, William and Mary. Early in 1700 Julian seemed to be a teacher there on a part-time basis while also serving as a tutor—probably a "gentleman's" way of supplementing a small income.

The *Journal* was full of his daily activities:

"*November 4, 1699*: To a Muster at the Village Green in honor of the King's birthday and an Agreeable Evening at Marriot's Ordinary following the Musick which was most Pleasant. There was much discussion of the Design for the new Capitol which will be at the end of the Duke of Gloucester Street a mile away from the College. There are many Persons of repute who wish it elsewhere."

On another occasion, in late December of the same year:

"Master James Cuddington has kindly invited me to Partake of the Christmas merriment at his house in Francis Street. Planning goes forward for the Town Gaol and the Powder Magazine. The Streets are being layd out quite straightly using the old Roman grid. It has been decided to put the Capitol at the end of the Duke of Gloucester Street."

Several days later, the entry was more personal, allowing a glimpse of Julian Cushing's personality:

"Services were held at the little church and were most beautiful and I felt a great Solemnity which I often find when at Prayer. A surcease and a great longing which is most puzzling, but which does not remain Longe. Master Cuddington had a fine Feaste and there were gifts for all, including the servants which are all black and very kindly does Master Cuddington treate them, is not always the case. I am minded of the Poor conditions of some of the Jamestown plantations. There will be many blacks here at Williamsburg, for there is a great Lacke of other help and much building will commence soon. It is now all in Planning form."

The elaborate entries were interspersed by an occasional "Nothing." A dull wet Sunday? An anticipated event that disappointed? Andrew wondered. There was very little about Julian's work as tutor or teacher; apparently, he'd considered it boring. And who was the Cuddington who'd gone to America? Andrew couldn't recall the name from his work at

Williamsburg where most houses bore the names of their original owners.

But the *Journal* seemed to come suddenly alive when Julian discovered what he called "the Portrait," and there was no question but that he'd become virtually obsessed with it. He referred to it constantly: "A rare find of such Beauty which set in me such a longing for Nonsuch." Or, "Master Cuddington tells me the Portrait is from Nonsuch—would that I could see the original in all beauty and grace!" Shortly afterward Julian seemed to have somehow acquired the funds for the journey to England, but his references to Nonsuch puzzled Andrew, for the palace was a ruin by the time Julian had crossed the sea. Yet even that hadn't deterred the young colonial, whose obsession with the portrait seemed such an odd contrast with the sensible and somewhat pragmatic young man of the early pages. Even as, Andrew had to admit, the ruins were not deterring *him* either. Actually, he'd see only excavated ruins. Julian would have seen the remains of buildings still above the ground.

Returning to the *Journal*, Andrew examined the inside pages near the binding carefully to see if any pages had been torn out. It was inconceivable that Julian would record no thought or impression of Nonsuch. Yet, several days after noting his excitement at seeing the palace, Julian had made only the cryptic entry: "We went today to the Ruins for the fourth time. If the Lure is there, we mean to find it, for C. says it has to be there still. . . ."

Lure? What was the lure of Nonsuch—what did it mean to Julian Cushing? The entry seemed to indicate the Lure was a physical thing, not an appeal to the emotions. The lure of the Tudor palace had brought him across the sea, and viewing the ruins had apparently not abated his infatuation with the place. Yet there seemed to be something more. And, whatever it was, clearly Julian did not feel confident in noting it in his *Journal*.

The outside light was fading from the room, and Andrew made a mental note to ask Mrs. Caudle for stronger bulbs for his lamp. Now the repleteness of her tea and his concentration on Julian Cushing's neat handwriting made him realize his weariness. He laid the *Journal* on the bedside table, put the tray outside the door as Mrs. Caudle had asked and unpacked. Early retirement would help diminish any lingering effects of jet lag, and tomorrow he'd hire a car, drive to Ewell and see Nonsuch Park and the excavations.

His last conscious thought after turning out the light was the remembrance of a small boy running with a kite over grass so smooth and green he could not believe it real. He was running toward a great palace which he knew hadn't been there then, but perhaps now—somewhere in the future—he might be able to get a glimpse of what it had been in all its glory.

Chapter Two

The lobby of Cuddington House was warm with sunshine when Andrew emerged from the lift early the next morning. He'd slept well and was eager to be under way. Walking toward the desk, he found his attention caught by the pleasant contrast with the previous afternoon, when he'd been the only one about and everything had appeared dim and dark. Now people passed with pleasant greetings toward the dining room. The lobby's early-morning brightness was emphasized by bouquets of simple garden flowers on tables and desks, spots of color in the clear, lambent light. Harry, Rosa's husband, had just finished vacuuming, and the red, gold and black carpet appeared burnished in the sunlight. There was a homelike serenity to the room that was very appealing. No canned music floated from its four corners—no radio or television blared from the lounge. Only the muted roar of traffic outside and a delightful sense of isolation and privacy within. A few guests sat in the wicker chairs reading the morning *Times*. They were a comfortable-looking lot, and not a gray-haired schoolteacher in sneakers among them; just ordinary travelers who seemed much at home in Cuddington House.

Rosa Caudle was at the desk, and Andrew asked if she'd arrange for a car he might drive to Ewell, where he hoped to see the Nonsuch Palace excavations.

"Ewell, sir?" Rosa's tone was disapproving and she thought for a moment. "Ewell's very near, sir, and the excavations aren't far away. A train would be much quicker and cheaper, too, a car being so dear and all. If you don't mind my saying so, sir, a train would be better—it's only about twenty minutes."

Andrew had savored the idea of driving south into Surrey, but his hostess was probably right. So, asking her to look up a convenient train, he said he'd return after breakfast and, strolling to the dining room, noticed the plaque Rosa had mentioned the previous day. It was handsomely printed, longer than he thought, and he stopped, thinking to skim through, for it might give the name of the architect of this remarkable old house. After a few lines, he found himself so engrossed he went back to the beginning and read it carefully:

A History of Cuddington House
No. 18 in the Strand

"Cuddington House may well be the oldest surviving structure in the Strand. It was erected by Sir Richard Cuddington, Bart., in the year 1520, being completed the day King Henry VIII and Queen Catherine of Aragon left for France for the Field of Cloth of Gold. They passed by the house from the Tower of London en route to Dover.

At the time, Cuddington House in the Strand, as it was called, was quite innovative. The northern side of the Strand was largely unbuilt because the great episcopal mansions of the church hierarchy such as Worcester, Essex, York, Durham and Salisbury, occupied the opposite or south side. They fronted directly on the River Thames and were approached for the most part by water stairs. Their courtyards backed onto the Strand, and many of their gardens or orchards were on the opposite side of the street. Therefore, when Sir Richard Cuddington elected to build on this site, his decision was considered novel.

Cuddington House was also remarkable in that it largely dispensed with the medieval façade. Its design incorporated many of the properties later associated with the classical Renaissance period. Security was no longer a problem, and wide windows, handsome staircases, double doorways, inside drains and a generous number of chimneys were becoming more popular.

Upon the death of Sir Richard in 1530, Cuddington

House was occupied by James Cuddington, the second son. Richard, the elder son, inherited the title and the vast Cuddington holdings in Surrey, near Ewell, property which was confiscated by Henry VIII in 1536. The king demolished the village of Cuddington, the manor house, the church and Merton Priory and erected on the site the renowned Palace of Nonsuch, which stood until 1682, when it was torn down by the Duchess of Cleveland, the notorious Barbara Villiers, the mistress of Charles II, to pay her gambling debts. In exchange for the Surrey property, Sir Richard Cuddington was given the manor of Ixworth in Suffolk, where he died in 1567 and where his descendants still live today.

Cuddington House was the birthplace of Sir James' son, Richard, who was to become the well-known Tudor artist. It was also the residence for a time of Bartholomew Penn, a student of Hans Holbein, who immortalised the Tudor monarchs and many of their court. Penn was the husband of Chloe Cuddington, a granddaughter of the builder. She and her young husband were great favorites at the court of Elizabeth I.

Cuddingtin House was a private residence until 1842. It survived the Great Fire and the attempts of later owners to sell it for a more fashionable residence, a difficulty which increased with the years as the Strand became a more commercial thoroughfare. In 1730 a mistress of George II was lodged in Cuddington House while heirs of the late baronet fought over its disposition. The royal mistress brought several of her friends to the house, and when the court case was settled, the owners decided to make it an inn. It was run on an informal basis, mostly for the convenience of court ladies and gentlemen [*a nice touch that*, thought Andrew] for several years, and when Queen Victoria came to the throne, the owner, a spinster lady, Miss Chloe Cuddington, remodelled the building to take in paying guests from the public.

In 1933, the premises were thoroughly modernised, and it is, substantially, the building the visitor sees today."

Well, by God, a royal bordello. That's an unexpected bit, he thought, and they hadn't balked at including it either! And since Rosa Caudle had said she was a Cuddington, there was even a baronet in the old girl's ancestry. 1520 and on. Henry VIII and the Field of Cloth of Gold. Cardinal Wolsey and Sir Thomas More. Mary, Edward and Elizabeth Tudor and that passel of six queens who had died, were divorced or beheaded, who had spent their married lives—some of them very brief, he remembered—trying to give their husband an heir to the Tudor throne. All had seen this house in its prime, as had Raleigh, Essex and the first Stuart king. Even William Shakespeare must have passed it often. Had they all regarded it as unique for their time as the plaque implied?

The paragraph that interested him most—so much so he read it twice—was the one noting that it was the Cuddington family who'd owned the vast lands King Henry had confiscated so he might build Nonsuch. What arrogance! To annex a whole village, wipe out a church, a priory and a manor house so a residence might be built to make hunting more convenient. Was that the reason Henry had taken Cuddington? The plaque made no mention of the cause; he looked again to be sure. Yet that *must* be the explanation—it was odd he should think of a motive when one wasn't even noted.

He also reread the paragraph referring to James Cuddington. Julian had mentioned a gentleman of that name in Williamsburg. It had been a James Cuddington who'd provided that holiday "merriment" Julian had shared. It must have been one of Rosa Caudle's ancestors—a descendant of the man who'd built this very house—who had emigrated to Williamsburg a hundred or so years after Henry had built his palace.

It was all very confusing and exciting, and Andrew mulled it over a few moments later while enjoying what he privately considered one of the world's vanishing wonders: a traditional English breakfast. Strawberries and cream, eggs and fried mushrooms, a plate of hot muffins—and cold toast in the British manner. Small vats of sweet butter and a choice of several preserves, marmalades, jams and jellies were already on the table. And everything was accompanied by several cups of steaming China tea, brewed to the turn.

Andrew glanced around the room, wondering if it had been used for dining when Julian Cushing was visiting. Probably not—Julian would have eaten in the Great Hall outside with the family or gone to a nearby pub or inn for his breakfast of ale, meat and bread. "Victuals" he'd have called them. Odd the name should pop into his head. The room that now served as the dining room faced away from the busy Strand and would, in Julian's day, undoubtedly have looked out on a garden or courtyard bright with sunshine. Now it was hedged in and windowless. At its back there was probably a dank alleyway where trash was collected, with an entrance for the help.

Finishing his tea, he reflected on the coincidences of Julian and himself both coming to England because of a ruined palace—of both staying in the same lodgings and being taken care of by women who'd borne the same name and served in the same role. He wondered what Mrs. Caudle would think if he were to tell her the story.

She was waiting at the desk, train schedule in hand. Transportation ran very frequently, she said. Andrew realized they were probably commuter trains, bringing workers to London in the morning and spewing them out at night. He really would have preferred a car, but his hostess was explaining about the train. She seemed unusually pink and breathless. She leaned toward him and said, "Sir, please don't think me forward. I asked Harry, and he said it would be all right, you being a gentleman and all." She stopped, a bit unclear as to just what to say to this nice good-looking young man.

There was a long moment's silence as she grew pinker before Andrew, relishing a confusion he found endearing, rescued her, "Tell me what, Mrs. Caudle?"

"About Sparrow Field Farm, sir. It's our place. Where Harry and me will retire one day. It's at Nonsuch—well, not exactly, but very nearby." Again confusion reigned, and she gripped the counter determinedly, ready to give it another try. "It's a house a little way from where Nonsuch Palace used to be, sir."

"You have a house there?"

Andrew's question brought forth one of Rosa Caudle's broadest smiles. "It's a house quite near where the palace used to be. We stay there whenever we can get away. We went there last week to see the excavating and things."

"And it belongs to you and your husband?" This was getting better every moment. Fancy old Harry and Rosa having a house near Nonsuch Park!

"Oh, sir, it's been in the family forever! It's older than Nonsuch!" She smiled again, more relaxed. And then, fearful she might have sounded too grand: "Of course, it's not a *big* place, sir. Not nearly as large as it once was. And there's not nearly the land around that used to belong to the house. But Sparrow Field is still there, and a farmer watches over it for us when we're up here. He gets the produce from the kitchen garden and his lodging for his wages—what we don't use here, that is." And she gestured vaguely in the direction of the dining room.

Andrew now understood the wondrous simplicity of his breakfast—all from a country garden only twenty minutes away by train. All served in a Tudor showplace, much changed, but still maintained and obviously cherished by the same family. And all because he'd picked up a fifty-dollar *Journal* and a travel brochure. Rosa interrupted his reverie. "And so I asked Harry if it would be proper for me to tell you if you went to Nonsuch by train—and you'd pass Sparrow Field on the way, sir—*if*, after you've seen the ruins—and they can be pretty dusty and tiring—well, you may want a washup and a pot o' tea, and you can get them at Sparrow Field. And that's what I asked Harry!" She finished triumphantly in a flurry and blushed another shade of pink.

Andrew thought maybe he'd fallen in love. Julian had called his Rosa Cuddington a "very Perceptive Woman." Andrew now labeled his "the Artless Charmer." He would indeed look in at Sparrow Field, he said and, thanking her and bidding her good-bye, walked on through the lobby. Sparrow Field. The name seemed familiar. Then he remembered. In his *Journal*, Julian had written that Miss Cuddington had arranged for him to stay at Sparwefeld Farm in the park near Nonsuch which the Cuddington family owned. Could Sparwefeld and Sparrow Field be one and the same? If so, it was yet one more link in what was fast becoming a remarkable chain of similarities. Then the clock on the stairway landing chimed the hour, and he hurried on. He didn't want to miss his train.

Sitting in the comfortable first-class carriage, Andrew rummaged in his briefcase for some Xeroxed sheets Miss Dabney had made for him. They were brief extracts from the writings of the British antiquarian William Camden and were valuable for the description of Nonsuch Palace as it appeared some forty years after its completion. In delightful Tudor English and spelling, Andrew read:

> "About four miles from the Tamis within the Country, Nonesuch, a retiring place of the Princes putteth downe, and surpasseth all other houses round about; which the most magnificent Prince, King Henrie, the Eighth, in a very healthful place called Cuddington before, selected for his owne delight and ease, and built with so very great sumpteousnesse and rare workmanship, that it aspireth to the very top of ostentation for show; so as a man may thinke, that all the skill of Architecture is in this one peece of works bestowed, and heaped up together. So many statues and lively images there are in every place, so many wonders of absolute workmanship, and workes seeming to contend with Romane antiquities, that most worthily it may have, and maintaine still this name it hath of Nonsuch. . . ."

Camden was like the many others who'd seen the palace in its prime. All had praised its exquisite beauty in elaborate phraseology that, even allowing for the ostentatious mode of expression fashionable at the time, left little doubt the king had succeeded in erecting a peerless structure. Its fame had spread throughout Europe. Nonsuch became so celebrated that the first place a foreign ambassador invariably wished to see on arriving in England was not the venerable Abbey or the Tower—but glorious Nonsuch Palace.

At Ewell, a half hour later, Andrew asked directions for Nonsuch Park and, walking the pleasant streets of the little

Surrey village, attempted to envision how it might have looked in the sixteenth century. Buildings still in existence could have witnessed the passage of the king and his party returning from a morning hunt. He could picture old Henry coming upon the little village of Cuddington, surrounded by forests full of wildlife, and deciding to appropriate the lot. A priory, a manor house, a church *and* a village. Andrew wondered how he himself would have felt if he'd owned it all—several thousand acres and a half dozen buildings—and had it all wrested from him. It was a fruitless attempt at guessing—everything was too far removed from one's own experiences. And over the centuries there'd been a great change in values. In those days, he remembered, the monarch was much venerated. Richard Cuddington might have been *honored* at the king's action. . . .

So preoccupied was he that he didn't realize he'd left the village behind. Suddenly he was walking on an unpaved road with thick hedgerows on either side. Large stones, moss-covered and deeply embedded in the earth, lay beneath giant sycamores, their boughs dipping and bowing in the midmorning breeze, creating an everchanging pattern of sunlight in his path. The stillness was broken only by the cawing of birds.

To his left, a team of dun-colored oxen, led by a man in heavy stained work clothes, tediously plodded through the field. The birds were diving into the furrowed earth, picking up seeds, worms and larvae. Up ahead, the sound wafted from a large tree where other birds had taken possession, chattering and talking to each other, darting from the branches to the ground below. Andrew had never seen so many birds at one time. He stopped to watch. The bottom of the tree was hidden by a red-brick wall that followed the line of the road. The birds were diving from the tree to something inside the wall, then triumphantly returning to the green lushness of the boughs.

Arriving at the gate, he looked into the enclosed courtyard to see what was proving such an attraction. A grizzled old man sat on a bench under the tree, out of the sunlight that streamed on the path leading from the street. The path followed in a beautiful circle, ending at the front door of a substantial farmhouse at the far end of the courtyard. Clumps of rhododendrons, day lilies and fuchsias softened the outline of the building that looked remarkably fresh in an area where most had taken on the soft patina of age. To one side of the house a corner of a garden was just barely visible, an oasis of green planting, interspersed with rose bushes, phlox and hydrangeas enclosed by a wall magnificent with honeysuckle and wisteria. An old spaniel padded from behind the house to the shade of the garden's largest tree, an imposing beech, and settled himself at its base. He disdained to watch the old man, who sat with a large cloth bag in his hand and, muttering and calling, was throwing seed out to the birds. Some came close to him; others, more daring, lit briefly on his shoulder or atop his greasy cap until he impatiently brushed them away, muttering even louder.

It was a charming scene, reminding Andrew of those hordes of kindly citizens he'd watched in many of the world's parks as they gathered daily to feed the birds and squirrels. The man sat squarely on the bench, his feet shod in leather sandals. He wore a short faded coat and pants of some rough material; they seemed banded or tied at the knee. Andrew could not make out his features, as his cap was pulled down on his head. The man's voice was crooning and soft, and he flung the seed with an agility belying his age. He fitted perfectly into his surroundings, blending with the solid substance of the farmhouse in the background. Rather grand for a farmhouse, Andrew thought, as he reluctantly left the scene, reflecting what a perfect painting it would make.

At the end of the unpaved road he joined the main thoroughfare. There were the signs: NONSUCH EXCAVATIONS —STRAIGHT AHEAD. The area seemed busier and more alive than back at the farmhouse. Trucks and automobiles sped by, filled with what he assumed were site workers. Few were sightseers. Undoubtedly, the weekend would have been prime time for visitors, and he hoped this early on a Monday morning he'd be able to observe the work without the distracting presence of too many tourists.

He followed in the wake of the trucks, entering the park through a wrought-iron gate. It seemed familiar, and when he saw the long treelined drive just ahead, Andrew realized this must be the very gate he and that serving girl had passed through almost a quarter of a century before. In every direction he could see, there was no other line of trees ending in a gate.

There were a few workers in the trenches, and as he stood above them, everything professional in Andrew reacted to what he saw. There it was—spread out before him—the excavations of a royal dwelling from Tudor times. A palace that had so intrigued him as a child its spell had lain dormant for nearly twenty-five years. Even the tents, the huts for equipment and portable vans at one far end of the field, could not detract from the joy of the moment. He'd been right to come.

Looking off to the distance, he found Nonsuch Park even more impressive than he remembered. To the south the land fell away in a gentle slope. Off to the east were dark clumps of beech, oak and elm—the remains of the vast forest that had once covered the whole site. Nonsuch lay at the foot of the North Downs, and in Tudor times much of the land would have been arable with the forest providing protection and cover for pheasant, partridge, foxes, hare and deer. It was still clear and kept open for public use with no dwelling except an old farmhouse to the west. Many of the trees, especially the Spanish chestnut and oak, grew to great heights; they were very old. And for the rest, there was that smooth, incredibly green grass where he'd run and flown his kite. It did not seem very long ago.

From where he stood, the excavations appeared to be near, even possibly on, the very site where he and the girl had picnicked. They'd spread the contents of their basket under the trees on one side of the roadway leading to the gate. From what he could see before him, it appeared that all the while they'd been sitting atop the palace foundations.

Andrew walked toward the eastern rim and, with a professional eye, noted the size and condition of the foundations on which Nonsuch had stood. It had not been as large as Windsor, Greenwich or Richmond or even—by Tudor standards—as large as the homes of several of Henry VIII's more prominent nobles. It had never been intended as a lodging place for the whole court. Instead, it was to be a royal residence—an extravagant one, to be sure—where the king and a few of his companions might seek respite from the affairs of court or hospitality after a long and vigorous hunt. Henry Tudor had had great fondness for Nonsuch and had spared no effort or expense in its ornamentation. Stone from Liège and Caen, Andrew remembered reading from Miss Dabney's notes. Lumber from forests for miles around. Real glass in the windows. The renowned Nicholas Bellin of Modena, a veteran of many of the French king's fancies including the glorious Fountainebleau, headed scores of workers and craftsmen.

The trenches were rapidly filling up. Several workers, obviously student volunteers, were filling wheelbarrows with rubble, decayed roots, broken stone, brick and earth. Farther off, near the southern end, a bulldozer approached a section where other workers waited with barrows and carts to remove the displaced earth.

The sun was beginning to climb higher. Andrew took off his coat and slowly walked along the perimeter. At the remains of the kitchen buildings, he saw small deposits of animal and poultry bones, oyster shells, charcoal and fragments of kitchen utensils lying beside piles of cobbles from the courtyard. A well of surprisingly fresh-looking Caen stone had yielded pieces of rubble—balustrading from the palace and chunks of decoratively carved blocks—that lay piled near other fragments of pottery, pewter and glass.

Adjoining the kitchen block was a cleanly excavated area. Old Henry's wine cellar, a workman told him. When Andrew commented on its size—more than sixty feet in length and eighteen feet at its widest, with walls six feet high—the man told him that over a hundred tons of rubble, including broken bottles and flasks, had been removed before the walls became visible. Stone steps led to the cobbled floor; they interested Andrew so much he asked permission to look at them closer.

He took a small magnifying glass from his briefcase and minutely examined the large blocks of stone that appeared different from the others. No doubt they'd come from some other structure; some contained carvings, some were smooth, some were rough. One even had a Norman roundel, as perfect as the day the carver had laid aside his tools. Some building had obviously been destroyed, and the king's workmen had saved time and expense in using the blocks for constructing the wine cellar. The square joist holes in the walls where the wine racks had stood were clearly evident, and three stone-lined drainage gullies ran down the sides and middle of the cobbled floor to meet in a soakaway in the center. Water had been piped into the cellar for washing vessels and casks—a skillful setup for the early sixteenth century, Andrew thought.

It was obvious from what he could see that the palace had been built around two great courtyards. It was the inner court where the royal apartments were situated that had provided the glory of Nonsuch. Here the four walls were stone at ground level with the second story of timber. But between the timbers, huge white plaster panels, ingeniously decorated with figures of gods and goddesses, cherubs, floral specimens and royal insignia, had been hung. The panels were framed in carved black slate, gilded in portions, and the contrast between the black slate and white plaster figures must have been startling to anyone viewing them for the first time. At the opposite end of the courtyard there had been two five-story octagonal towers, and from ground level to tower top, the walls had been similarly covered with panels featuring life-sized figures in different classical motifs. These magnificent panels and frames had been topped by oversized painted statues of the King's Beasts holding a pennant with the royal badge. Other descriptions of Nonsuch, from those who'd seen it at various times, had mentioned its great fountains, the greenery, arbors, alleys, small ponds and numerous statues—all enclosed by a wall outside of which was the "wilderness." Here the larger trees had been trained to form a canopy for shade, and one later monarch had even kept an aviary.

And here he was, now, looking at all that remained of it.

Leaving the wine cellar, Andrew walked on to the extreme southern end where the foundations of those richly decorated turreted towers were distinct. Here were piles of broken plaster bits that had formed those magnificent panels: here a fragment of an angel's wing, there a Roman gladiator's foot almost nine inches thick. Obviously, they'd been deeply carved. Cherubs, the head of a horse, swags of fruit and flowers and here a piece of painted glass with the letters "et Mon Droit." Andrew pushed a fragment with his foot. All these charming pieces—destroyed to pay the gambling debts of a royal mistress—had been used to fill in the foundations. The Tudor workmen, having taken everything of real value from the site, had doubtless found it easier to dispose of them that way rather than laboriously cart them away. One panel in particular caught Andrew's attention, and he leaned forward to read, in exquisite flowing handwriting, a direction written on what had been, at the time, wet plaster: "*Troisiesme pillier*"—an instruction from one workman to another. Had he left it behind as he went to eat his noonday meal in the shade of nearby trees?

Andrew had walked three-quarters of the foundations, completely immersed in what he saw. It was while near what he later learned was the site of the great fountain in the inner court that he began to feel unsettled. It was nothing at first. A small sense of discomfort attributed to the sun now approaching a noon zenith. He'd been out in the open for more than an hour, concentrating deeply, storing up impressions for notes on the return train ride.

The feeling persisted, though, and the warmth deepened. He loosened his collar and tie and sat down briefly in the shade of the roadway trees. The roadway passed completely through the middle of the palace; part of the excavations were on the other side in the shade. He noticed the trenches were deeper there and, questioning a workman, was told that just the day before, several pits with human remains had been uncovered. They'd been buried several feet deeper than the excavation level. Obviously, they hadn't been disturbed when the palace was built. The graves had been in the crypt of what had been the Church of St. Mary the Virgin at Cuddington—and all the inner court covered the church graveyard. Huge slabs of Reigate stone had sealed the burial pits, and the Tudor workmen had simply built Henry's inner court atop the church foundations. The bodies had remained in place ever since.

Well, thought Andrew, I've heard of and seen moldering bodies before—that's not what's making me queasy. Yet his unease remained. To distract himself, he followed the line the bulldozer was making, admiring the professional delicacy of the operator who skillfully skimmed the smallest amount of earth from the foundations; they'd apparently lain only a few inches below the surface. A laborer told him that plows from the only structure on the field, the old house called Cherry Orchard Farm to the west, had fallen into pits and holes in the earth, and often various artifacts had been turned up by other machines.

Returning to the church site once more, Andrew felt a growing anxiety. The more he blamed the heat and his deep concentration, the more the feeling intensified. Yet he'd visited *hundreds* of excavation sites. Why should this one particular area fill him with an apprehension bordering almost on despair? Just to test himself, he walked off into the trees' deep shadow, emerging in the area of Cherry Orchard Farm, only a few hundred feet away. There some measure of composure returned. He made a few notes and, feeling well again, walked back to the church area.

As he approached, the same sense of heat assailed him. His face felt flushed, and he noticed his hands were trembling. Deliberately, he walked to the very center of where the church had once been. The chancel, covered by Henry's fountain, was a good measuring point, and there he felt a numbing, hot anxiety and a searing sense of foreboding that nearly overwhelmed him. Shocked and ill, he walked shakily back into the shade and leaned against a tree. In a few minutes his trembling ceased, yet he was bathed in perspiration that dribbled down his cheeks and onto his shirt. He returned to find his coat and briefcase and sat down, lighting a cigarette to recover from the—the *what*?

Nothing like it had ever happened to him before. It must be a physical reaction, Andrew reasoned, one stronger than he'd anticipated, to viewing the ruins. Yet he'd seen more impressive excavations than Nonsuch. The weather had never affected him before—some of his work had been in tropical countries. And, he forced himself to the truth, his foreboding occurred nowhere but in the area where Cuddington Church had once stood.

Why the church?

It was well past one o'clock and he'd planned to lunch there, spending the rest of the afternoon at the excavations and the adjoining park. But now he'd do as his Artless Charmer had suggested and have a washup and a pot of tea at Sparrow Field Farm. Then he'd head back to London, making notes on the way and try to understand what had happened at the ancient church site.

Once more on the road back to Ewell, he asked the first person he saw—a woman pushing a baby carriage—the direction to Sparrow Field Farm.

"You can't miss it, sir." She was obliging as she jiggled the carriage to keep her youngster quiet. "Just stay on this road, and it's to the left behind a large wall. There's a car park opposite for the stores on the Ewell side. . . ." And she motioned in the general direction of the way he'd come.

Andrew thanked her, bewildered. He'd passed no parking lot or "stores on the Ewell side" while walking to Nonsuch Park. Merely an old farmhouse with a man feeding birds in the courtyard. And he certainly hadn't passed Sparrow Field Farm or he'd have known it, he was sure. There was no other farmhouse there.

He walked briskly for about ten minutes before he saw the parking lot ahead. He was happy to note his composure had returned, and even though it was midday, he didn't feel overly warm and had donned his coat. There was the lot, just as the woman had said, and there were the back entrances to the stores fronting on Ewell's main street. But where was the farmhouse? Andrew was annoyed with himself. Obviously he'd originally taken a different route, for the path had taken him past a farmhouse and a field where a farmer was busily plowing. Path. *That* was it—he needed to find an unpaved path—where in front of him was nothing but macadam as far as he could see. And that was directly into the village of Ewell itself.

Well, there was no path in sight. He looked in every direction. Small houses he didn't remember were everywhere. Neat little dwellings, each with its own garden plot in front and a garage to one side. The houses became more numerous as he approached the near end of the parking lot, then there was an open space and the beginning of a brick wall. Elated, he hurried forward, for he recognized the wall. It's *my* brick wall!—he almost shouted the news aloud—and *that's* where I'll find the farmhouse and I'll ask the old man the way to Sparrow Field Farm.

He followed along the wall and came to the opening. Hurrying inside, he stopped, thunderstruck, and felt again that strong sense of anxiety. There *was* no farmhouse in sight. The huge tree and the house, the beautiful circular drive, had disappeared as if wiped away in a few hours by a giant hand. In its place was an open field with grass badly in need of cutting. Here and there lay farm implements, some rusting from disuse. A ramshackle lean-to built against the wall held several smaller tools and a tractor stood nearby. Apparently it had been in recent use, for a pair of gloves and a bandanna were still on the seat. Some distance away, a small square building, its steeply pitched roof seemingly out of proportion to the building's height, sat in a graceless enclosure behind which there appeared to be a garden. Several large trees, well pruned and lush, bordered on the house, the one tidy note in the whole scene.

Andrew picked his way over the rusting farm implements, along a path miry in spots that seemed to draw every winged insect in the area. Nearer the farmhouse, the ground appeared neater. The path was cobbled, and the shrubs and hedges surrounding the lawn were trimmed and clipped. He was, he realized now, approaching from the back. Surely the front would reveal the garden area he'd seen.

A tall man, followed by a black and white dog, came out the back door. Clad in working clothes, he was undoubtedly the farmer. He stopped a moment, wiped his mouth with his hand, then stooped to pat the dog. Andrew called to him. "Hello! I'm looking for Sparrow Field Farm. Is this it?" His shout brought the dog on the run. The farmer waved Andrew forward. The dog ran up to sniff, then, disappointed, ran off in the opposite direction.

"Good morning," Andrew said. "I'm looking for Sparrow Field—Mrs. Caudle sent me."

The farmer doffed his cap. "Yessir, this be Sparrow Field and Mrs. Caudle telephoned you might be cummin' by . . . you be Mr. Moffatt?"

Andrew was relieved, and he realized now, for the first time, how his experience at Nonsuch had rattled him. Farmhouses disappearing and parking lots springing up in their place all in a matter of hours! It was nice to have normality return in the form of a dog, telephone messages and a pleasant farmer.

"I'm Mr. Moffatt." Andrew realized he'd only disconcert the man by offering his hand, so he plunged right in. "Mrs. Caudle said I might use the farm for a wash and maybe some refreshment. I've been over to the excavations."

"Blasted mess they be causin' over there—blessed nuisance, they be. Can't leave anything decently buried as the Lord meant it." The farmer was clearly no student of history. "Go right in, sir, the wife's just clearin' up the lunch. I has to get back to me work."

Andrew thanked him and opened the back door. The kitchen was cool—the blessed coolness born of thick walls and overhanging trees. A woman of indeterminate age, in a shapeless dress, was clearing the table. "Hello, I'm Mr. Moffatt, ma'am. Mrs. Caudle telephoned about me."

"Oh, sir, do come in." The woman was pretty in a faded way, her hair pulled back in a bun that gave her features a sharpness they didn't deserve. But her smile was welcoming, and she motioned him to the bathroom. "Go right in there, sir. I've put fresh towels out against your comin'. Mrs. Caudle will be glad you stopped by, sir. . . ."

Ten minutes later, refreshed and at ease, Andrew was taking his hostess at her word to "tuck right in" and more than doing justice to a plate of ham and hot biscuits, carrots and peas. "Right out of the garden, they be, sir. You'll be gettin' more at Cuddington House as my man will take some up to Lunnon a day or two maybe," she said pleasantly as she did the dishes in the old stone sink. "You've been to the excavations, sir?"

"I have and found them most interesting." Andrew noted the woman—he wished she'd give her name—start to say something, then decide against it. "I had quite a walk this morning, actually." He lit a cigarette and helped himself to another cup of tea.

"Did you, sir? You came by train, Mrs. Caudle said."

"Yes, I walked from the station, through the village and right on to Nonsuch Park." Andrew chose his words carefully. "I came right by here but seemed to have missed the place the first time."

"Well, it's easy to do, sir, the house is set so far back from the street—and actually, it's only the backyard where we keep the farmin' stuff. . . ." She gestured out to where he could see her husband tackling a bit of rank grass he'd stepped through a little while ago.

"Actually, I didn't notice the place at all." Andrew waited, then thought, hell, I'll never find out otherwise. "But there was something else there."

"Sir?" The woman raised a dripping hand in query. "Something else?"

"Well, I know it seems strange, ma'am, but yes, I walked along the wall and saw a lot of birds coming out of a tree. I know this sounds peculiar, but there were a great, great many of them. There was an old man plowing in a field across the way. You probably think the sun played tricks with my imagination. Maybe it did!" Andrew gulped at his tea. It had been a mistake, and she was probably taking him for a fool and be glad to be rid of him. He might as well play the gentleman, finish and leave, so she could clean up. Would she go out and tell her husband about the crazy American who'd seen a tree and a plowman right over near the Ewell car park? Andrew could imagine how they'd laugh, and the farmer would probably say it wouldn't surprise him—anyone interested in excavations must have a lot of fancies!

"And there was an old man sittin' there feedin' the birds?" The woman's voice was ordinary; she might have been asking him the time of day.

"Why, yes!" Andrew's relief was intense. He hadn't seen a mirage—he must have confused the directions. There *was* a house and a garden and a tree with lots of birds! And it was probably one of their old friends who fed them each day. "How did you know?" he asked.

The woman dried the last dish, wiped her hands and came over and sat down opposite Andrew. She brought a clean cup and poured herself some tea. She was very quiet. Andrew could see she was sorting out her thoughts, trying to pick her words carefully. She wasn't as simple as he'd imagined.

"Now, sir, don't think me daft, but I think you've seen the ghost." She laughed merrily. "You're not the first one, though, so don't let it bother you." She was obviously enjoying the effect.

"A ghost? A ghost of what, in God's name?"

"Well, sir, it's a long story." The woman settled down. Andrew sensed she'd told it before. "Yes, it's a long story. You see, the Cuddingtons used to live over there." She pointed in the direction where Andrew had seen the house. "What you saw was the manor house where Sir Richard and Elizabeth Cuddington lived. The old man feeding the birds was Domino, their gardener."

"Sir Richard was the owner of all the land. . . ." Andrew started to say, but she was ahead of him.

"Sir Richard owned *everything* around here, sir. The village was named after his family. They'd been here for hunnerds and hunnerds of years. That was their manor house, the garden was where old Domino worked. And this place, Sparrow Field, was where Domino lived. It was the gardener's cottage. It was smaller then. This is the original kitchen, and there were only one or two rooms. Domino slept upstairs in a loft over the byre where he kept a few cattle for himself and a few of his farmin' tools." She stopped, wondering if she was going too fast. "When the Cuddingtons had to leave, because the king took their land, why, then, sir, they gave this cottage to Domino, for he was too old to go wherever they went."

"To Suffolk, I think." Andrew tried to recall from the plaque.

"Well, wherever they went, Domino didn't go. He stayed here in this very cottage, sir, until he died. Then it went back to the Cuddingtons, and later on some of them from Lunnon came down here and lived here, too. They even built it up a bit, but it's not like it was. It's always been in the family, sir, and now Mrs. Rosa and Mr. Harry are the last ones—they have no children. I don't know what'll become of it, sir, when they die. Me and my man worry about it, sometimes.

The town'll just tear it down and build some more o' them matchboxes on it.'' And she gestured contemptuously in the direction of the houses he'd passed.

Andrew was stunned. He sat with his tea growing cold and thought, well, my God, I've never seen a ghost before. Yet the picture was as clear in his mind as if he'd seen it minutes before. The old man crooning to his birds as he flung seed and impatiently brushing them from his cap and shoulder.

''And so Domino often sits out there, y'see, and sometimes people see him.'' The woman's voice interrupted his thoughts. ''His cottage was called Sparwefeld at the time, sir—it had something to do with birds, sparrows, I guess. He was a great one with them and fed them a lot, so they stayed in the neighborhood. Anyway, many people have seen the manor house and old Domino feeding his birds. So you see, sir, it's nothing to worry about—although I guess it can give you a turn to come back and look for it and then it isn't there anymore!'' She smiled a comforting smile and offered him more tea.

Andrew declined the tea and asked, ''May I see the front of the house, ma'am?''

''Of course, sir. Mrs. Caudle said to make you feel right at home. She's taken a real likin' to you, sir. She doesn't often send people here.'' The lady led the way from the kitchen into a living room that reminded Andrew instantly of the lobby of Cuddington House. It had undoubtedly been added on to from the original size, but even so, it had been a long time ago. Hadn't Rosa Caudle said Sparrow Field was older than Nonsuch? Then it had to be almost five hundred years old. The room had that same odd contrast in furniture. Two sofas on opposite sides of the fireplace were no more than thirty or forty years old. But the trestle table between them, cut down from its original size, was pure Tudor as was the refectory table against the stone wall. The farmer's wife had filled a large white porcelain pitcher with garden flowers, and their color brought the whole room to life. Several portraits, Elizabethan he was sure, lined the walls and he went to look at them. *My God, Holbeins* . . . but they couldn't be. He looked for a signature—there it was in the corner, ''*B. Penn*.'' He stood back and admired the paintings; they were the best imitation Holbein he'd ever seen. He'd have sworn they were genuine. B. Penn, whoever you are, you are damned clever, he thought.

His attention was drawn by the farmer's wife opening the front door—a massive piece, heavily carved from a single slab. Studded with huge nails, it creaked loudly as she opened it. He felt a little cheated in not being left to examine the room more fully, but the woman was good to give him this much of her time. He smiled gratefully as they stepped out into the sunlight. There was a great difference between the front and back of Sparrow Field Farm. The front lawn was neatly clipped, and a sundial in the center was surrounded by borders of marigolds, petunias and alyssum. The dial was too large and ornate for the lawn. He went some distance away and, gazing back at the farmhouse thought: five hundred years old and still looking tremendous. He saw why the pitch of the roof seemed out of proportion. Over the years the earth had built up to well over a foot around the building's base. That one foot made all the difference. To the right was a small arbor with a plaque in the form of a domino—a large plank, painted black with white dots. The dots spelled "Domino's Garden." Fascinated, Andrew walked through the arbor into a good-sized area enclosed by a wooden fence. In contrast with the unkempt backyard, the garden of Sparrow Field was tidy, with rows of vegetables straight as soldiers and not a weed in sight. This was obviously where the farmer and his wife spent a good deal of time. One whole end was given to roses and larkspur, and even from where he stood their fragrance was heavy in the midday heat. Nearer the kitchen end was the herb garden with a fountain in its center—waterless and as out of place as the sundial. There were several rows of spinning aluminum disks to keep the birds away. The sight made him remember the old man feeding the sparrows. How ironical that hundreds of years later birds were unwelcome in Domino's garden.

Andrew returned to the woman waiting on the porch. "It's all lovely, ma'am. I'll tell Mrs. Caudle how kind you've been. And thank you for explaining about—explaining about. . . ."

"Oh, sir, that was just old Domino. Mrs. Caudle knows

the story. I think she saw the same thing when she was younger, although Mr. Harry never has. I've never seen it, and neither has my husband. Seems like strangers mostly see it instead of those who've lived here all their lives." The thought seemed to rankle; she pursed her lips. "But 'twas only the old man and his birds, so don't let it upset ye. That was his garden you saw—not the one for the manor house, of course, just the one he kept for himself. We like to keep it nice, as you can see."

A half hour later, returning to London, Andrew saw the whole experience as farfetched and ridiculous. He knew Rosa Caudle would ask about the excavations and her farm. His problem now was how to tell his Artless Charmer that Nonsuch had made him physically ill and at her farm he'd seen the ghost of a man dead more than four hundred years.

Chapter Three

Back in town, Andrew stopped at the London Museum to see the famed models of old London before the Great Fire of 1666. Tiny landscapes, riverside scenes, houses, bridges, gardens, trees, the Abbey—all meticulously reconstructed in lifelike miniatures—occupied several glass cases. He was primarily interested in old London Bridge. In medieval days the bridge had been lined on both sides with houses and shops, and one building was traditionally believed to have been modeled after Nonsuch Palace. Andrew recognized it at once. Called Nonsuch House, it stood proudly in the center, turrets, towers and pennants intact. The famous plaster panels, carved and ornate, surrounded by the black slate frames, were all accurately reproduced and compressed into such a small size that Andrew marveled at the builder's skill. Several structures, such as Nonsuch House and farther, near the southern end of the bridge, the exquisite gemlike Chapel of St. Thomas à Becket, spanned the bridge, with archways for traffic.

Rosa Caudle was nowhere in sight when he arrived at Cuddington House. Andrew left word for her to contact him and then, once in his room, went to work. He had long trained himself to record his immediate impressions, and after sorting his notes, he dictated into a tape recorder everything he'd experienced at Nonsuch. After some deliberation he also included a description of what he called his "time slip" at Sparrow Field Farm. He could visualize Miss Dabney's reaction as she transcribed the tapes.

He then made a detailed architectural rendering of the manor house as he remembered it and was dictating an accounting of the farmer's wife's conversation when the telephone rang.

It was Rosa Caudle, and she sounded troubled. "I spoke with Mrs. Williams at the farm, sir. She said you'd had a bit of an adventure. Was everything all right, sir? Did you find everything you expected?"

Andrew replied that yes, he'd had an adventure, and that's what he'd like to talk to her about. It was nothing to be worried about, he assured Rosa, sensing her apprehension. Yes, Mrs. Williams had been most kind. But there were several things he'd like to discuss and he asked if she'd join him for tea in the lounge.

There was a moment's silence. Clearly, guests didn't often invite their landlady for tea. She probably thinks I have some complaint, Andrew thought and assured her he only wished to take a little of her time. Would she meet him in half an hour? Rosa agreed, yet sounded reluctant and thoughtful as she hung up.

She was at the table waiting when Andrew appeared a half hour later, briefcase in hand. She'd changed her dress and wore one of those incredible flowered hats so dear to the English lady's heart. Yet her face was concerned as she watched him approach. Andrew tried to set her at ease.

"You *are* good to come, Mrs. Caudle." He smiled. "I hope I'm not interrupting your routine." He shook her hand and was pleased to see the beautiful pink spread across her face. "Your woman took very good care of me at Sparrow Field today. It's a lovely place—I envy you and your husband."

Rosa appeared to unbend. "Harry's at the desk, sir. He told me to take my time. I told him you'd had an experience, as Mrs. Williams said, and we both wanted to be sure it was nothing we'd done. Was the train all right, sir?"

Again, Andrew assured Rosa that everything she'd suggested—including the visit to Sparrow Field—had been fine. There was a moment's diversion as they ordered tea. Then Andrew decided to plunge right in. If he dawdled and tried to draw her out, he'd only succeed in confusing Rosa, and that was the *last* thing he wanted to do. She was too kind, too guileless for him to play games. And so he told her, step by step, of his trip to Ewell. Of his walk from the station, through the village, of wondering about old Henry VIII riding through after the hunt and of how he'd seen a plowman with oxen tilling a field on one side, while down the road, there was a flock of birds behind a wall. . . .

"Mr. Moffatt, you *saw* the birds?" Rosa's voice was incredulous, and she set her teacup down nervously. "What else did you see?"

"I'd like *you* to tell me what I saw, please, Mrs. Caudle." Andrew smiled, and his voice was kind. "It's important to me." He poured the tea carefully, trying to appear calm. It would be wise to have Mrs. Williams' story confirmed.

Rosa looked out the window for a moment. She's wondering what to say, he thought. This has been a surprise for her. Perhaps it was unfair to spring it on her so suddenly.

"You saw an old man feeding the birds—they were all over him," she said quietly, "and he kept brushing them away and throwing seed out to them all the while. And he talked to them. . . . And it was very quiet. Then an old dog came out of the house in the back and went to lie down under the tree. It was all very lovely."

"That's it, exactly." Andrew was relieved. They'd seen the same thing. She'd even recalled the dog which, he now remembered, he'd not mentioned to the farmer's wife at all. "And when did *you* first see it, Mrs. Caudle?" He tried to sound matter-of-fact and helped himself to a generous slice of seedcake.

Rosa sighed—she was more relaxed now that the "adventure" had been explained. "Once when I was very little and again about four or five years ago." She sipped her tea, grateful the awkwardness was over. "When I was small, there was quite a ruckus about it, sir, for people thought I was telling lies, when I went to find the man and the birds again. But then someone in the village said they'd seen the same thing, and my parents had to believe me. Not that they ever liked it, though!" She laughed pleasantly. "They'd never seen it themselves, y'see. But over the years I discovered quite a few people have seen it, though many of them don't like to talk of it for fear of being made the fool. It can come upon anyone at any time."

"And the second time?"

"The second time I was hurrying down the village steeet, not even thinking about Domino—that's the old man's name, sir: I don't know whether Mrs. Williams told you. Well, I was just hurrying to get back to Sparrow Field, and when I turned in at the back gate, there it was again. It had been nearly twenty-five years since the first time, so I stood very still and looked carefully."

"And what happened?" Andrew poured them both another cup of tea. He was intensely interested and Rosa was unselfconsciously realistic. At the same time he couldn't help thinking, how many people in this room, gorging themselves on sandwiches, tea, tarts and cake, are so placidly discussing a four-hundred-year-old event they've witnessed—and doing it as calmly as if remarking on the weather?

"Just the same thing, sir. Old Domino sitting there in the sun. Feeding the birds. The dog came out and lay down. The house—oh, sir, wasn't the house beautiful! That was the old Cuddington house—where the man who built this house was born, you know." Rosa's smile deepened, and again that exquisite pink flooded her face. But there was no confusion—only a quiet pride. "It *was* a beautiful house, wasn't it?"

Andrew drew the pencil sketch from his briefcase. "This is as I saw it." He set the drawing between them on the table.

"That's it!" Rosa's voice was excited. "That's it exactly—oh, sir, you've made it lovely."

"It was a beautiful house, Mrs. Caudle." He watched as she savored the details. "Certainly the people who built it—and who built Cuddington House—had excellent taste. But I'd like to know a little more, and you may be able to help. How did the vision appear? You see, I walked away, on toward the excavations. But I'm sure you didn't walk away—not the second time."

"No. I didn't. I stayed right there, hardly daring to breathe, looking at the flowers and the house. Oh, it's all still so real! I almost wanted to walk right over to the old man, but I didn't. I wasn't scared, not really, but I knew that actually, the house and the old man were truly not there . . . and if I went in and they disappeared, then *I* might disappear, too!" She laughed, and Andrew joined in.

"Well, sir," she finished, "it finally just faded away. I think I stayed there watching for maybe four or five minutes . . . and then the whole picture began to darken. Like it does on the telly sometime when they're going to change a scene. It began to darken, it began to waver a bit—like if you had a camera pointed at it and you jiggled the camera a little—and then, suddenly, there was just old Sparrow Field's backyard and the Williamses' dog coming toward me." She brushed a crumb from the tablecloth and said quietly, "I hated to have it go."

Andrew was silent, oddly moved. Both he and this woman had shared an extraordinary experience and one which, coupled with his extreme reaction at the church site, had profoundly affected him. She'd told him everything she knew and was probably eager to relieve Harry at the desk so he might have his tea. But Andrew was reluctant to part with the one person who'd shared some of the same adventure. In the back of his mind was the desire to tell her why he'd come to England. He didn't think she'd laugh, and for some unexplainable reason, he felt sure she might even be able to help. So, for the next half hour, while they enjoyed another pot of hot tea, Andrew told Rosa Caudle everything. Of his childhood visit to Nonsuch Park and hearing the story of the palace. Of roaming the world over with his parents and later in his professional capacity. He took the newspaper clipping about the Nonsuch excavations out and read it to her, explaining how eager he'd been to see them. He recalled the day he'd purchased Julian Cushing's *Journal*, thinking he might read more of Nonsuch from Julian's travels, and he told her how disappointed—and intrigued—he was by Julian's omission of anything concerning the palace.

For a reason he found difficult to analyze, he didn't tell her about his unpleasant reaction at the site of Cuddington Church. It was still vivid in his mind, but he could think of no plausible explanation, and he didn't want to bewilder Rosa. He was giving her a good deal to think about as it was. He mentioned the casual way he'd learned of Cuddington House at the travel agency and how it had been a Miss Rosa Cuddington to whom Julian had come in *his* time for lodging. And how she'd sent him to Sparwefeld.

When he finished, he was encouraged to see that—far from being bewildered—Rosa Caudle was deeply attentive. "Well, sir, if you don't mind my saying so, there are a good many coincidences, aren't there? That particular Rosa Cuddington I *do* happen to know about, because she was the first of that name in the family. The Cuddingtons have always been great ones for names, sir. There are always Richards, Jameses, Elizabeths, Chloes and Rosas. But Julian's Rosa, *she* was the first, I know."

"And the James Cuddington who went to America and lived at Williamsburg and was Julian's friend?"

"Well, now him I wouldn't know about at all. I never knew there *was* a Cuddington who'd gone to America. If it was a James, then he was the second son, for Richards were always first sons, especially when there was a title to inherit, and Jameses were always second."

"What especially intrigues me, Mrs. Caudle, is this." Andrew took the *Journal* from his briefcase and leafed through the pages. "Julian Cushing was to go to Nonsuch. He went, not once, but several times, but never wrote a thing about the visits. *Nothing*. That's exactly what he writes on the days he went there—'Nothing.' Yet he's vividly descriptive of everything else. And he mentions a portrait of Nonsuch—not once, but several times. He'd first seen it at Williamsburg. You see, here it is. 'A rare find of such Beauty which set in me such a longing for Nonsuch.' And here, later on, 'Master Cuddington tells me the portrait is from Nonsuch.' " Then he found the paragraph describing the moment when Julian and Rosa Caudle's ancestress had unwrapped the portrait that had crossed the sea with Julian, and he'd written, "I also told her of my Desire to see the portrait returned to its owners. I can only hope I withheld my Passion from her gaze."

Andrew put the *Journal* aside and asked Rosa, "Do you ever remember hearing about—or did your family ever own—a portrait of the palace which Julian Cushing apparently returned to the original owner?"

"Well, sir"—Rosa's voice was matter-of-fact—"I myself don't remember any portrait of Nonsuch. I find Mr. Cushing's remarks very confusing. He could hardly return a portrait of the palace to its original owner in 1700—was that the year, sir? The original owner was King Henry, and he'd been dead a long time! If it was returned to *any* Cuddington, it would still be in the house or at Sparrow Field—or else, sold long ago. I'm afraid a great deal has been sold over the years. The Cuddington fortunes were never the same after the king took so much of their land. That's why the London house was remodeled to take in guests. We could never have kept it otherwise."

Andrew read aloud from Julian's *Journal*. " 'Would that I could see the original in all beauty and grace.' " He set the book aside again. "Clearly, the boy was obsessed with seeing Nonsuch, yet I've always found it confusing that he must have known what he'd see when he arrived here could only be ruins. It would hardly have looked like the original of the portrait."

Rosa remained silent as he read, a faraway look in her eyes. Then she leaned conspiratorially across the table and said quietly, "Sir, did you ever stop to think that perhaps it was *not* a portrait of Nonsuch that Mr. Cushing was so taken with?"

"But he says so right here in the *Journal*!"

Rosa looked dubious. "I think you've *assumed* that, sir. You've read all the parts to me, and he never *says* it's a portrait of Nonsuch he's so blasted daft about. He talked of the 'original' and 'bringing it back to Nonsuch.' Maybe it originally came from the palace. Maybe it did. But *I* don't think it's a portrait of the palace."

"Well, then, what is it?"

"I think it's a portrait . . . of a . . . woman. . . ." Rosa was very definite now. "Oh, sir, think! No young man—I don't care if he lived a couple of hundred years ago—no young man is going to fall in love with a palace. He might have been truly interested in Nonsuch, but he came across the sea, I am sure, because of a woman—not a lot of ruins."

Andrew's thoughts were racing—this was something he'd never considered. Julian's comment about "hoping to go to

Nonsuch'' and mentioning the portrait directly afterward had led him to believe the boy was bewitched by the old palace. He leafed through the places in the *Journal* he'd marked with bits of paper, rereading the paragraphs with Rosa's theory in mind. He looked up, saw her somewhat self-satisfied smile, read a bit more, then closed the book with a bang. ''I'll be damned. . . .''

Rosa laughed merrily, clasping her hands, and he joined in. ''You're absolutely right. Of course, it must have been a woman. I wonder who in God's name it could have been?''

Again, Risa leaned toward him and spoke almost in a whisper. ''Now, Mr. Moffatt, I'm *sure* it's a woman he's writing about. No young man would get that worked up over a palace, no matter how he longed to see it.'' She was silent, pondering the idea. ''Yes, it *had* to be a woman. I wonder . . . . Sir, you're going to think me crazy, but I—I think—yes, I'm sure—I *know* the portrait he wrote about.''

Andrew gazed at his Artless Charmer in amazement—and admiration. ''But, Mrs. Caudle, how could you know?''

Rosa was already on her feet, impatiently brushing crumbs from her lap. ''Oh, sir, do come!'' She was excited. ''Do come at once. I think I know the portrait he meant. And what's more''—she tugged at his arm, and again that deep pink edged her kindly features—''I think I know where it is.''

Moments later Rosa was explaining to a patient husband that she was going to show Mr. Moffatt the attic. Resignedly, Harry Caudle handed her a large key ring containing a dozen keys or more and waved her away. At the lift, Rosa instructed one of the waiters to bring Mr. Harry his tea at the desk. Then she and Andrew were on their way to the top of Cuddington House.

They emerged on the third floor. There were only three floors, Andrew knew from the building's façade. He was momentarily mystified when Rosa opened a door at the end of the hall and, in the dim light, he could see another flight of stairs. His companion was silent, puffing a little with her exertions, her flowered hat askew. ''Now, sir, it's going to be a bit dusty and dark up there, but we always leave a torch or two right here on the steps.'' She handed one to Andrew, took one herself and closed the door behind them. In silence, they climbed the few steps to the attic.

It could hardly be called a room. Light from one window at the far end revealed a large expanse of vaulted space. Andrew could stand upright only in the center of the area running the length of the house. Rosa snapped on an electric light here and there, and with the aid of his flashlight he could see the handsome ceiling and thick oak beams with heavily carved bosses at each end. It was the original ceiling of the floor below. In the unfortunate "remodeling" of a hundred years before, some Cuddington had resolved on a way to get himself storage space, building the false ceiling for the floor below. This space might even, at one time, have been used as servants' quarters.

It was now, obviously, the repository for centuries of Cuddington castoffs. Trunks, suitcases, valises, eighteenth-century portmanteaus were cheek by jowl with an array of old Gladstone bags and an army rucksack, vintage 1916. The Cuddingtons had been a well-traveled lot. An old pith helmet lay in a basket filled with canteens and hip flasks; there was even a small cask that might once have held a good brandy atop a shabby Vuitton trunk. Above the luggage, mounted heads of antelope, tiger and gazelle gazed eternally into the gloom. Yellowing photographs of hunting parties, weekend shooting matches at country estates, peopled with buxom ladies and proper Victorian gentlemen, their guns held jauntily or displaying trophies, lined one wall. A broken chandelier, really a beauty, was spread out on a moth-eaten blanket on the floor, its pendants glimmering briefly as the flashlight's beam lingered on them.

One Cuddington had obviously been to India, for there were several boxes of dulled Indian brassware piled against a broken folding screen of great delicacy. Overhead, hung against an oak beam, was a sword—broken and tarnished—the memento, perhaps, of a seventeenth-century Cuddington who'd cut a swath at the Stuart court? Or had it belonged to one of the gentlemen who visited the house when the rooms below had been used in the pursuit of illicit love?

On the other side were the larger pieces. Two lyre-shaped

music tables, one with a lamp, its iridescent glass broken in several places, caught Andrew's attention. They were eighteenth-century—he'd seen their counterparts many times at Williamsburg. Two high-backed armchairs in faded and torn raspberry and mulberry velvet, trimmed with a silver almost black with age, looked even older. A doll's house in Palladian design caught his fancy. Pedimented and porticoed, it was a small gem—the birthday present of an indulgent father to a Cuddington child? There were dozens of walking sticks, some with yellowed ivory handles, propped in a broken umbrella stand of Oriental design. Nearby was an old hip bath. How many young maids had hurried up Cuddington House stairs with cans of hot water to fill *that* monster? A slate blackboard stood on an easel in one corner; neatly arranged on shelves were rows of books—children's books, devoted to the sea victories of Nelson and Wellington, gardening books, a history of King Arthur and several small velvet-bound volumes with clasps, probably locked and useless.

The whole space needed a good going over, Andrew thought. There must be dozens of valuable items in here, and the Caudles, so used to seeing them, doubtless didn't realize what a treasure trove they owned. Some weren't beyond repair; he'd seen many things in worse shape beautifully restored in the Williamsburg workshops.

"It's over here, sir. You'll have to help, I'm afraid." Rosa's voice came from behind the room's largest object, a large oaken armoire from which half a door was missing.

Andrew apologized profusely. Fascinated with the objects around him, he'd all but forgotten Rosa. She was tugging at something wrapped in heavy cloth, tied with a stout yellow piece of what appeared to be hemp. He helped her carry it from behind the screen, and together they brushed the dust from the covering.

"It's impossible to see up here, sir. Do you think we might take it downstairs where the light is better?"

Nodding, Andrew picked up one end. It was heavier than he thought; the frame must be pure oak. He wondered if it might not be too much for Rosa. "Just straight ahead and down the stairs—careful going down, sir." She didn't seem to mind the weight. "We'll take it right to our rooms, if you don't mind."

Once down the stairs, Rosa directed him around a corner. "Just at the end of the hall at the back, Mr. Moffatt," she said. Andrew was surprised at her agility. Rosa was a large woman, plump and nicely rounded. Yet she moved the portrait with a skill indicating many hours of arranging and rearranging hotel furniture. She rummaged in her purse for the keys, opened the door, and together they propped the picture against the wall.

The Caudles' quarters were cramped. Two rooms—obviously too small for guests, yet such as might have once been used by servants—were dark until Rosa switched on a lamp. She'd attempted to make them homelike and cheerful. Family photographs, vacation souvenirs and other mementos filled a table. The furniture was shabby—cast off from the guests' rooms, but not yet ready for the attic. Everything was neat and clean, with fresh scarves on bureau and table. An improbable dried flower arrangement and seashells stood on the mantel of a fireplace much too large and elaborate for the small room. This room and others on the floor had probably been partitioned off from what was once a large and spacious hall; the fireplace would then have been in proper proportion.

"We won't get much light in here, sir, but at least we'll have some privacy." Rosa had removed her hat, smoothed her hair and opened the desk, looking for scissors. Her face was flushed from her exertions and excitement.

"Mrs. Caudle, you're extremely kind to go to so much trouble." Andrew felt guilty. "If I'd known that frame was so heavy, we could have arranged for someone else to move it." He took the scissors and cut the hemp carefully. The cloth covering was linen or a heavy muslin, and the twine yellow with age. "How long has the portrait been up there?"

"Well, sir, I can't be sure, but at least twenty years. Oh, I do hope it's all right!" Rosa was obviously hopeful she hadn't led him on a wild-goose chase. "It used to hang over the fireplace here in this room. I always remember it being here when I was a little girl. It's very old, sir, and Harry and I thought it would be safer up in the attic. So we wrapped it up good and secure, as you can see. We found the covering and hemp in an old box in the attic; I think they'd been used to cover this portrait before. Harry and I thought it a bit too fine for this room the way it is now. At one time, you see, all the rooms and the outside hall were really one large space—that's what it was like in the old days, sir."

A musty smell permeated the room as they carefully unwrapped the cloth from the frame. Andrew wondered if such protection had been necessary; any dampness in the cloth would only result in mold and ultimate deterioration of the picture. But the cloth was bone-dry, and, he remembered, so was the attic. This wasn't the kind of a house with a roof that leaked—it was probably as intact as the day it was built.

"The light is going to be poor to see this as it should be seen." Rosa was apologetic. Her voice shook slightly from excitement. "I remember it as very beautiful, and it will be nice to see it again. There we are, sir. Now stand back as far as you can."

Andrew could only go to the fireplace a few feet away, and he watched as the last of the covering dropped from the portrait. Rosa was right; the picture needed viewing from many more feet away, but this would have to do. She turned the frame slightly so he could look at it directly and everything came into focus.

The impact was tremendous. The room, Rosa Caudle, everything disappeared for Andrew the moment his eyes met those of a young girl, certainly no more than eighteen or nineteen, in medieval dress. She was an incredible beauty, and the artist had caught every nuance of her loveliness. Her hair was an extraordinary silver. Nearly white in its blondness, it seemed a halo for the strong, square face. Every feature had been lovingly fashioned and was alive with a vividness that almost leaped from the canvas. As a contrast with the pale skin and silver hair, the girl's eyes were deepset and gray with strong-winged, delicately arched black brows. Her chin was square with a deep cleft. It lent a sobriety to her expression belied by the gentle humor in her eyes—they were expressive and intelligent and framed in the darkest lashes Andrew had ever seen.

Andrew felt himself almost lifted from the room as though he were there in the picture with the girl. She was seated in a heavily carved gilt chair, her hands folded and relaxed in her lap. Her gown was simple, a delicate shade of peach, its square neckline trimmed with ermine, beautifully rendered so one could almost feel its sleekness. A tiny cap of peach velvet, bordered with ornate scrollwork and pearls, covered a small portion of her fair hair; a golden circlet, from which a heavy diamond and pearl pendant hung, was clasped around her neck. The folds of her gown fell to the floor, almost covering the peach velvet sandals peeping from beneath its hem.

Andrew wrenched his eyes from the figure to study the background. It was remarkable. He was certain it was a Holbein, although he could recall no other work of that distinguished portrayer of the Tudors that showed such perspective. The artist had seated his subject in the center of a room that seemed altogether familiar. It was sunlit, bright and spacious. At one end was a long mullioned window, and through that—a very unusual treatment—he could see a river and the corner end of an old stone building. The artist had reproduced a complete Tudor room—obviously the very one in which the young girl was sitting. A splendid Oriental rug on the floor was vividly patterned, each color superbly distinct and glowing in the sun's rays. At the far end was a handsome fireplace faced in what looked like Sienese marble, and over the mantel was a large portrait. That was innovative for the time, Andrew recognized—a portrait within a portrait.

He went closer to observe it. It was of an imposing square building, that also seemed familiar, of pale washed stone, its gleaming windows framed on the inside with opulent green velvet. There was even a suggestion of the interior sketched in. Large double doorways opened directly onto the street, and in front was a railing of strong wrought iron. A shield—or more likely a family crest—was set in the center. The small portrait was as detailed as the larger one of which it was a part. The perspective was striking, especially with the river scene outside; the collective impact of the portrait was electrifying.

". . . it *is* nice to see it again and in such good condition." Andrew came out of his reverie to listen to Rosa Caudle.

"And what do you think, sir?" *I am speechless*, Andrew wanted to say. He was astonished—and overwhelmed—by the radiant beauty of the subject. He cleared his throat as he helped Rosa lean the portrait against the wall so she, too, could observe it from a distance. "Who is it?" was all he could think to ask.

"Chloe Cuddington, sir. The granddaughter of the man who built this house. Her father was the one who owned all the land King Henry took. She lived in this house for some time, sir, before she married Bartholomew Penn. He was a very famous artist. It's all in the history down in the lounge, sir. She was a famous beauty at court, too. She painted also, but never was as famous as her husband. He was a student of . . . of. . . ."

"Of Holbein," Andrew finished. *Of course*. That accounted for the pictures he'd seen at Sparrow Field. "B. Penn." They *were* Elizabethan and by a gifted artist every bit as talented as his master.

"That's it, sir. Here, I think there's something on the back. At least there used to be." She went to the portrait to turn it around. Andrew grasped one end, and together they read, in faded old-fashioned handwriting on what looked like parchment now almost brown with age, "Miss Chloe Cuddington. Painted by Bartholomew Penn, later her husband. At Cuddington House in the Strand. London, July, 1536 A.D.."

"It was painted here! Of course!" Andrew went back to look once more. "It was painted in what's now the lobby. There's the same fireplace." The Sienese marble had since disappeared, but the mantel was identical. He was very excited. It was tremendous to see what the ground floor of Cuddington House had looked like before it had been gouged out and scrambled to make a dining room, lounge, lobby and kitchens. "The whole first floor must have been one huge room," he said, "and that's what the view looked like when you could see the river." He pointed to the Thames through the window. "Very different now with the old Shell-Mex."

"And that's what Cuddington House itself looked like on the outside." Rosa pointed to the portrait within a portrait—

the handsome pale structure with the coat of arms in its black railing. "A lot different today, more's the pity."

"More's the pity, indeed," Andrew replied, recognizing why the building seemed so familiar. More than once he'd tried to visualize it as it had been long ago, and now here it was, minutely detailed for him by a superb craftsman. "Mrs. Caudle, you've given me quite a treat!"

"And d'you think this is what Julian Cushing saw? Won't you sit down, sir? You *do* look a bit pale."

Andrew had completely forgotten about Julian Cushing. That girl has bewitched me, he thought. He sat in the chair Rosa indicated and lit a cigarette.

"I'm convinced that's what he saw, Mrs. Caudle," he said. " 'A rare find of such beauty which set in me such a longing,' " he quoted from the *Journal*. "Yes, I'm sure that's what Julian saw. But one thing puzzles me. He mentions returning it to its owners. How did it get to Williamsburg in the first place? That's where he first saw it. He mentioned uncovering it with Miss Rosa Cuddington so she might see it when he arrived in London."

"Well, sir, I think it probably was taken by that James Cuddington to Williamsburg. Now let me see—if he was a James, he was a second son, and it had to be before 1700—right? So it could have been the great-grandson of the James Cuddington who owned this house, sir. He was the second son of the builder, and when the older boy, Richard, inherited the title and the Surrey lands, James got this house. Of course, later the king took all the land, so I guess the one who owned the house ended up better."

"And possibly," Andrew said, "when James Cuddington—who would have been quite an old man in 1699, when Julian first saw the picture—when he knew he'd probably never be going back to England, he was eager to have the portrait returned to the family. And Julian, having fallen in love with the girl in the picture, volunteered to bring it here. But that doesn't explain how the portrait came from Nonsuch as James Cuddington told Julian it had."

"That was probably James Cuddington's fancy, sir. After the Cuddington house was destroyed, the area around Sparwefeld became known as Nonsuch from the palace being there."

"Did the Penns have any children?" Andrew had an inspiration. It was an odd thought and hardly made any sense. But then what had happened over the past twenty-four hours didn't make much sense either. "I mean they might have had a daughter who looked like her mother."

"Well, as to that, I'm sure I don't know." Rosa frowned. "I probably *should* know more about my own family, sir. But truth is, we've always been so busy here and at Sparrow Field. And we always did hear a little o' this and a lot o' that when we were youngsters, and it never seemed important to know any more." She seemed disappointed she couldn't reveal anything further. Then, brightening: "Sir, you might be interested in our family records. I don't know how good they are. But they're down in the safe—and some at Sparrow Field—and there are some up in the attic. We've quite a few letters and journals and things we never destroyed. It seemed a pity to do so as long as we had the room to keep them. You're welcome to look at anything."

Andrew was touched. "Mrs. Caudle, you're very good, indeed, much too kind. You've given me great pleasure by showing me this portrait." Again his eyes met those of the beauty in the heavy gold frame, and he felt an unfamiliar tugging at his heart and mind. He tore his gaze away with an effort. Turning to Rosa, he grasped her hands. "My interest is even greater after seeing that magnificent picture. I *would* like to sift through anything you'll let me see. And now, perhaps, we should go back downstairs. I'm sure your husband is wondering what's happened to you."

He said good-bye to Rosa at his floor and went on toward his room. As he turned the key in the lock, it occurred to him that—once more—Julian's *Journal* had provided another coincidence: together he and Rosa Caudle had unwrapped a portrait, the same as Julian and Rosa Cuddington had done more than two hundred fifty years ago. It was, without any doubt, the same picture. And he had reacted the same: he'd fallen in love with Chloe Cuddington just as Julian had. "And I hope I withheld my passion from her gaze." He smiled at himself as he closed the door.

Chapter Four

Dr. Timothy Hodge lifted the receiver as his secretary had requested on the intercom. It seemed an emergency, she said. He listened for a moment as the voice on the other end called him by his first name. American accent, obviously a friend. The doctor's craggy features broke into a pleased smile, and he leaned back in his chair. "Well, Andrew—Andrew Moffatt! I say, old friend—how are you and what's all this rubbish about an emergency?" For the next few moments he listened, his eyes focused unseeing on the shelves of medical books opposite and then, swiveling in his chair, he gazed thoughtfully out his Sloane Street window at the busy edge of Belgravia. From time to time, as the conversation continued, he turned to make a note, biting his pencil speculatively, engrossed in his friend's words.

"Damnedest thing I ever heard, Andrew," he finally said, "anything like this ever happen to you before?" There followed another few minutes of conversation until, glancing at his appointment pad and watch, he agreed to a one o'clock luncheon. Thoughtfully, he replaced the telephone. Andrew Moffatt was clearly distraught. Cleaning a pipe, he recalled the many years they'd known each other. Their fathers had been old and devoted friends, had attended the same schools and college, served as best man at each other's wedding and had even traveled around the world together. His own parents hadn't been so hell-bent to have him with them as Andrew's had, and he'd been sent early to boarding school. Andrew, on the other hand, had a tutor who accompanied the family whenever a school term coincided with the elder Moffatts' desire to take him along to Bali or for Easter Week in Madrid. Inevitably, the two boys met at vacation time. They'd spent a disastrous summer at an American camp on the shores of what had to be the coldest lake in New Hampshire. There, he recalled, he and Andrew—who could already outswim, outtennis, outsail and outrun anyone else their age or older—had spent the entire summer pooling their allowances for cigarettes, cadging whatever tobacco they could find to roll their own and instructing every willing camper in the fine art of smoking. Following that, there'd been a longish period of less contact; they'd both been either in uniform or doing postgraduate work—he in Edinburgh, while Andrew was somewhere on the other side of the world, digging up civilizations in order to write long and learned architectural treatises on the buildings uncovered. Neither had married. Each had done a fair amount of hell raising, either together or apart. Each, if asked, would have mentioned the other as a valuable and close friend. Timothy was used to receiving telephone calls from Andrew from outlandish places the world over—and just as accustomed to having him turn up in London with little or no warning. He himself rarely left the city, for he'd quickly established a thriving psychiatric practice, a vocation Andrew often joshed him about. "How's supershrink?" was one of his friend's more repeatable greetings.

Timothy's reverie was interrupted as his secretary-nurse ushered in his next patient. He checked the time, for he didn't wish to be late. Andrew had sounded shaken—actually more in need of treatment than the person now coming through the door.

He was already seated at a table at the Empress when Timothy Hodge came in. He rose to shake hands and pummel the doctor affectionately. Yet Timothy's trained eye could detect something he'd rarely seen in Andrew Moffatt: the poor bloke was wound tighter than a spring. One of his friend's greatest charms had always been his relaxed geniality. He rarely took himself seriously. Now, Hodge could see, the man seated opposite—for all his upfront affability—was under terrific stress.

"God, it's good to see you, Tim—and you're fantastic to

see me on such short notice." Andrew lit a cigarette and gave an order for drinks to the waiter. "I really need to talk to you."

"Glad to be of help, Andrew—I'd no idea you were even *in* London! How long have you been here?"

"Only three days, Tim, and I've seen nobody. I haven't called any of our friends, because there were several things I wanted to do before I made any appointments. It's been *some* three days, Tim. God, the things I have to tell you! The whole experience is beginning to get to me. You'll probably think I'm going round the bend. . . . Maybe it's an early symptom of male menopause."

"Christ, Andrew, you're too young for that." Hodge took a gulp of his drink. "Something to do with one of your women—some gorgeous dame finally gotten to you?"

Andrew looked surprised. "Well, in a way—no, not really! At least, not in the way you're thinking. Although there *is* a woman involved . . . but I'll have to tell you about that later. And when I tell you, I think you're going to be convinced I've gone bananas."

Hodge laughed heartily at the Americanism. "Well, get on with it, man. I don't have all day." He smiled encouragingly. "This had *better* be good—"

Andrew cut him off. "Tim, this is nothing funny. I've never been so disturbed—shocked—agitated—you name it. I think you know I'm not the kind to come unhinged easily. Hell, I've been in trouble before—sometimes with women, sometimes with the stupidly arrogant foreign authorities I've had to deal with. I've had my differences with some of my less-than-bright colleagues. I even, at one time, spent several days at loggerheads with my tax accountant! The point is, I've dealt with them all and then not given them another thought. But this—this experience I've had the past few days—has stunned me. Because, you see, I can't find any explanation for it. I've searched and searched—and lost a lot of sleep, I should say—and in the end my thoughts keep coming around to one thing: there's no explanation of which *I* am capable. I'm dealing with something completely outside the sphere of my own experience. So you see, I need your advice."

"Well, you know you can have it, Andrew. There's nothing I wouldn't do to help—if I can." Hodge was impressed in spite of himself. Whatever had gotten to Andrew, it had certainly made him anxious. He wasn't sure that drinking scotch in a fashionable restaurant was the proper environment for treatment, but he could see the drink was visibly relaxing his friend, so he remained silent.

"I'll start at the beginning, Tim, and try to bring you up to date. It's going to sound like a . . . like a—"

"A hodgepodge?" The question recalled a childhood joke, and Andrew laughed—the first spontaneously free mirth Hodge had seen.

"Yes, a real hodgepodge, old buddy." Andrew snuffed out his cigarette, ordered more drinks and said, "Now here's what happened. . . ."

For the next half hour he recalled for Hodge the day he'd seen the Washington newspaper clipping mentioning the Nonsuch excavations; he told of finding Julian's *Journal* and learning of Cuddington House's existence. He recalled the tolerant amusement of his friends when he finally left for England on what they considered an extravagant whim. He described his arrival and his meeting with the Caudles, explaining who they were.

He then told of his journey to Ewell, of seeing the farmhouse on his way to the excavations. He reviewed a little of the palace's history and dwelled descriptively on his reaction at the site of the old church. He told Tim of his effort to find the farmhouse on the return to Ewell, ending up in Sparrow Field's kitchen. He was gratified to see his old friend's deep interest when he got to Mrs. Williams' comment, "Oh, sir, I think you've seen the ghost. . . ." He stopped there. "Not ready to write me off yet, Tim?"

"Of course not—don't be an ass, Andrew—do get on with it!" Clearly, Hodge was impressed, Andrew was relieved to see. Which was fine because he was going to need *all* of his friend's interest and tolerance—both personal and professional—before he was through.

He continued the story—of his visit with Rosa Caudle and the discovery of the portrait. He described it as graphically as he could—the remembrance of Chloe Cuddington's cool, gray stare caused him to stumble. Somewhat apologetically, he said, "Tim, *no* picture has ever affected me like that before. You've got to see it to understand. . . . Believe me, I can understand Julian Cushing's falling in love with it. In fact"—his voice was quiet—"in fact, I think *I've* fallen in love with it myself."

Hodge nodded, obviously nonplussed by Andrew's intensity. He was tempted to make some easy analytical remark—to suggest that loving a picture might be less satisfying but also less risky than the real thing—but, in the face of his friend's candor, thought better of it.

Andrew continued. "Well, this is the hardest part, but bear with me, Tim. All that I've told you happened within the last two days. This morning I decided to go back to Nonsuch just once more because, frankly, that reaction at the church site kept bugging me. I couldn't understand it. Nothing like it has ever happened to me before—it seemed damned stupid, fainthearted, something I couldn't handle. . . . So I went back by train—walked through Ewell—no time slip at Sparrow Field this time—walked straight to the excavations and sat down for a while to look at the pictures I'd brought along." He opened his briefcase and withdrew two glossy prints—reproductions of paintings and sketches of Nonsuch Palace. "This one is by an anonymous Flemish painter about 1620—roughly seventy-five years or so after the palace was complete. Take a look."

He handed Timothy Hodge the print. It was an early-morning scene showing the treelined driveway with the palace viewed in the distance from the northwest. Several early risers were playing a game of bowls outside the gatehouse entrance. Another was about to capture a deer to which several mounted horsemen in late Jacobean dress were giving pursuit. The palace was a mélange of turrets, towers, oriel windows, arched entranceways with lush green trees whose tops were visible over the enclosing brick wall.

"I've seen the original painting"—Timothy handed it back to Andrew—"but I'm damned if I can remember where."

"It's at the Fitzwilliam Museum at Cambridge." Andrew buttered a roll. "Well, what do you think?"

"I'm no authority on Tudor palaces, old man. I leave that bit to you. It's an uncommonly handsome-looking place. A few too many towers and flags waving for my taste, but if this was old Henry Tudor's bag, so be it. Elegant clock tower there in the center."

"Yes—that clock—that *was* Henry's idea, by the way. He had six French workmen imported just to build it. It stood at the entrance to the inner court, which was where the royal apartments were. That was supposedly the most beautiful part of the entire complex. . . . Here's where it was." Andrew pointed to the Privy Gallery. He took another print, a pencil sketch, from his briefcase. "And here's what it looked down on." The sketch showed a formal garden of geometrically precise plots planted with flowers and shrubs arranged in "knots" and enclosed by a miniature fence painted in the Tudor colors, green and white. Among the beds a statue of a prancing white horse reared atop a pedestal. On the opposite side was an ornate obelisk, resplendent with carving. Two large columns—"they were called the 'Falcon Perches,' " said Andrew—were topped with large birds. Water fed into the figures by concealed pipes streamed from their beaks into bowls below. At each end of the Privy Gallery were the two five-story octagonal towers, covered with lifelike white panels and handsomely carved black slate frames.

Timothy's attention was completely caught. " '. . . as there would be none such in the land.' " He repeated the king's words that Andrew had mentioned. "God, it must have been a sight to see. Now where did you say you had that bad experience the first time?"

"It would have been right about here." Andrew took up the picture and ran his finger along the wall. "Here was where the Church of St. Mary the Virgin was located until Henry had the whole area leveled to make way for the palace. There was a large fountain about in the center of the inner court which was built over the site of the chancel, and that's where . . . where. . . ."

"That's where that astonishing reaction got to you," Timothy finished, "so what did you do on the second trip this morning?"

"Well, as I said, I'd decided to test the area again. I'd

given it a lot of thought and concluded that it was very probable some one place might affect a person for any number of reasons. I figured maybe I'd been overtired or too warm when I was there yesterday. So I left my coat and briefcase under a tree and walked back to the same area. The day was overcast and actually a little chilly, so it was unlike the previous visit, when the sun was high and it was very warm."

The waiter arrived with their lunch, and each took a bite or two before Hodge prompted Andrew to continue.

"So I got to the site—I'd planned this for noon since that was about the time I'd been there before. There were very few people around—only one or two. I guess the others were taking a lunch break. I walked very deliberately to the site, not lingering anywhere else, and even before I got there, Tim, I knew I was in trouble."

"What kind of trouble?"

"It's hard to describe. About fifty feet away I began to feel different—unreasonably warm—and by the time I got to the chancel site I was suffused with heat. It was like walking into a red-hot furnace. Perspiration broke out all over my face, arms and shoulders. My shirt clung to my back. I was weak, nauseated, my legs were trembling. Suddenly, *I* was trembling all over, and everything seemed to recede, come back, waver a bit. My God, it was hell." Andrew's voice broke. "Sorry, Tim, but this has really hit me. Even talking about it makes me feel ill all over again. Frankly, it scares the bejesus out of me."

"Well, let's give it a bit of a rest, and here, there's a good chap, polish off the last of my scotch, why don't you? I don't usually have two when I'm going back to the office directly afterwards."

Andrew drained the glass. "Yes, that's better. I won't describe it again except to say that there's nothing in this world that would induce me to go back to that damned spot again. If I were going to meet that old royal bastard, Henry himself, I'd stand him up." He laughed, and Timothy joined in.

"That's quite a tale, Andrew. You know, if it were anyone but you, I'd be very skeptical. Oh, I suppose there might be a good and justifiable medical reason if I wanted to dig deeply, but my first impression would be that the person telling me something like this was fanciful, impressionable, even a bit of a kook. But not *you*. Now tell me"—he pushed his plate away and leaned forward—"what do *you* think it is—or was?"

"I've no idea, Tim, but I do know this. It is a manifest *something*—obviously not material—nothing you can see and, apparently from what I can observe, no one else working there feels a damned thing. Only *me*. There might be others who've reacted the same, but I don't know them. I can only speak for myself. It's *me*. I know this is going to sound melodramatic, but honestly, it almost feels as though there's something waiting there for *me*. I know that sounds berserk. . . ."

"Not at all, Andrew. Don't you remember the ghost stories we used to read at that god-awful camp when we were kids? Ghosts lying in wait for an impressionable someone to come so they could scare them to death? Or else giving them a message from the Great Beyond for someone still living? Or else spooks working out an old grudge against whoever was living in their house? As a matter of fact, I can tell you, there was a lot of sound reasoning or assumption—if not good medical diagnosis—in those old stories. Science today is finally acknowledging there's more to this old earth and its atmosphere than meets the eye. Prestigious universities are dealing with it under any number of unpronounceable names mostly ending in an 'ology.' But what it comes down to is this. They're attempting to explain the unexplainable: the phenomena which have manifested through the centuries—clairvoyance, astral projection, precognition, psychokinesis. Some very big guns, I'm happy to say, are doing a first-rate job."

"Now how does all that affect what happened to me?"

"I'm not saying it explains it, but what I mean is that I think it's all part of an unexplainable package. You had what many would call a supernormal or paranormal experience. Yet it's probably quite normal and would be explainable if we were familiar with the forces behind it and if we only knew how to explain it in terms the layman could understand."

"Then you don't think it's just *me*?"

Hodge understood Andrew's question—and his fear. "No, I don't think it's you, Andrew. I think you encountered some force—some energy—that's brutal and ugly. It's some one thing that you, particularly, are attuned to. The kids today would say your vibrations are right. The vibrations at that church site aren't right, however, and they affect *you* disastrously. The workers are unaffected because they're not on the same wavelength, so to speak. Yet tomorrow another person could go there and be similarly traumatized. It all comes down to how sensitive you are, and you, I know, are a sensitive person."

Andrew was tremendously relieved to know there was even a remote explanation, that Hodge didn't think he was cracking up. Yet there seemed to be more to the situation than Hodge could or would explain.

"I can give you some professional advice, if you wish," Hodge said lightly, "and the price is right—free."

Andrew grinned and waited.

"As your physician, Andrew Moffatt, I'll advise you of one thing. *Stay the hell away from Nonsuch Palace*. There's some malevolence waiting there for you, and it's waited a long time. All those similarities you talk about are a bit too pat to be explained away as coincidences. So there's probably more—much more—to this whole thing than you or I could even imagine or comprehend. Even if we knew the complete story in minute detail, we could absorb only so much, for we have only a mortal mind to accept and deal with that information. And here we're dealing with something immortal—and vastly immoral, too, I think, Andrew. So, old buddy, stay right here in London, and don't set *foot* in the environs of Nonsuch again. I don't think your bête noire can—or will—leave Nonsuch. So good riddance to him—or is it an 'it'? You just stay the hell away, hear? And now are you going to pay this check or am I?"

Andrew walked back to the Strand mulling over Tim's words. It might be the wisest thing to leave Cuddington House and finish his vacation in Vermont, after all. Or he could check into the Connaught for a few days, see his London friends to whom he'd given no thought at all since his arrival, so mesmerized had he been by all the nonsense about Julian Cushing and the Nonsuch excavations. Well, he'd seen the ruins, and they'd affected him in a way he could hardly have foretold. Yet even as he considered other plans, an absurd disappointment and regret lingered; he felt almost as if he were evading a responsibility, leaving some very important business unfinished.

There was an unfamiliar young woman at the desk when he entered Cuddington House. He went directly to his room, glad he didn't yet have to inform his Artless Charmer he was leaving ahead of schedule.

Opening his door, he stood stock still. The little sunlight that could escape the Shell-Mex's shadow usually reached into his room in late afternoon, and it was now almost unnaturally bright. It reflected off the white walls, providing a luminous aura for the object on the opposite wall. There, between the two large mullioned windows, looking perfectly at home, hung the portrait of Chloe Cuddington. Andrew forgot his disappointment and weariness. An incredibly strong magnetism seemed to reach out to enfold him as it had the previous day. Quietly, he closed the door and stopped to look at the portrait as if seeing it for the first time.

In some ways he was. His room was twice as large as Rosa's, and he was at a sufficient distance to admire the striking perspective, as well as the artist's superb craftsmanship. The reflected sunlight bounced off the light walls and acted almost as a spotlight, bringing the sitter vitally alive. The beautiful girl with that extraordinary silvery hair seemed about to grasp the armchair, rise and come toward him. The expressive gray eyes were alight with welcome. He could almost imagine her opening her arms to receive him.

Steady, old boy, you've had enough fantasy for one day, he told himself. There was an envelope placed strategically in the middle of the bed. It was from Rosa Caudle:

"Mr. Moffatt—we hope you won't mind our hanging the portrait in your room. You seemed to enjoy it so, it seemed a shame to return it to the attic right away.

Harry and I thought it looked quite nice in here. The packages inside the desk are from the safe, and I've told the porter to let you look for anything you need in the attic. Harry and I will be at Sparrow Field for the weekend. The girl's name—the one at the desk—is Jennifer; she stays in our rooms when we're away. Ask her for anything you need.

R.C."

Again, Andrew studied the portrait. It was in remarkably good condition. As he walked around the room, the dark-lashed eyes of the lovely Chloe seemed to follow him. He could well understand Julian Cushing's obsession. A boy, probably a lonely one, striving to make a living and a name for himself in the raw newness of a little Virginia town. And on some social occasion or perhaps while acting as a tutor in James Cuddington's home, he'd come upon this picture hanging over a colonial fireplace. Obviously, it had haunted young Julian, and together with his interest in Nonsuch, Chloe's beauty had been sufficiently overwhelming to bring him—as well as the young medieval beauty herself—back to the very house where she had been painted.

With an effort, Andrew withdrew his gaze from the picture and opened the desk. Inside were three old Harrods' shoeboxes filled with papers tied with fine twine, hemp and rubber bands. There were several keys, with labels attached. An envelope of calling cards with the name "James Cuddington" heavily engraved reminded Andrew of the kind his father had carried. Several packages of what appeared to be legal documents were all bound with ribbon. Andrew methodically began to sort them out, then settled himself in the room's one comfortable chair and started to read. He reached for a pencil and pad and made several notes, read extracts from the folded sheets and referred several times to the pictures of Nonsuch in his briefcase. The sunlight faded, and the room became shadowy. He switched on a light, stretched, looked for some time at the portrait of Chloe Cuddington as he smoked a cigarette and then went back to his reading.

It was past midnight when, exhausted and hungry, he put the papers aside. It was too late for room service, and he was in no mood for the several-block walk to the nearest restaurant that would be just on the verge of closing. Supperless, but totally immersed in his thoughts, he undressed for bed. He lay, smoking a last cigarette and looking once more at the portrait. "My dear, you must have been *some* woman," he said aloud, "some woman indeed." He knew as he turned out the light that he was not going into the Connaught or to Vermont. He was going to stay right here in London, probably at Cuddington House, till he'd unraveled the mystery. And at the end—if what he read was correct—he had little doubt that he, too, would meet a Miss Chloe Cuddington, just as Julian Cushing had two hundred and fifty years before.

Chapter Five

On Monday, Rosa Caudle returned to her place behind the desk, and Andrew told her how much he enjoyed having the portrait in his room. He'd spent a good deal of time prowling in her attic on Sunday, he said, and he'd taken several boxes to his room. He hoped that met with her approval—he was being very careful of everything and more than appreciated her indulgence. And soon he might be able to tell her more about Julian Cushing, for he'd learned a good deal about the young man.

"Have you, sir?" Rosa beamed. "Well, I'm glad those old papers and things in the attic are proving useful. And to think of the number of times we've almost thrown them out! Take your time, sir. Harry and I will be glad to be of any help, and we'll just leave the portrait in there until you go—if it's all right with you."

Once outside, Andrew took a taxi to Timothy's Hans Place apartment. His friend had promised to meet him there as soon as he could leave his office. Housekeepers being a thing of the past, Andrew was to get the superintendent to let him in. He tipped the man for the inconvenience, and then, after admiring Hodge's quarters, helped himself to a glass of his host's scotch, settled himself on a comfortable sofa and took from his briefcase some papers and books he'd found in the attic the day before.

He began with one small leather-bound book. It was, he could see from the contents, about two hundred and fifty years old. That would put it back just about in Julian Cushing's time. Its pages were brittle and dry, and the handwriting in the first few was a faded brown. It seemed to be a casual record of the Cuddington family genealogy. Births and deaths were noted, and a few comments included at appropriate points. The handwriting was the same for four or five pages, and then—the writer presumably having died—another person and a different handwriting took over.

The fluid hand at the beginning was typical of the mid-fifteenth century, and the writer had apparently copied his information from older, probably deteriorating records, some of which went back to the thirteenth century. He'd taken great pains to explain that Cotintone, Cudyton, Codington all meant Cuddington—that the name had been spelled differently during the centuries since the first Cuddington landowner was mentioned. That, Andrew was impressed to see, was in the Domesday Survey in 1086. In the following pages the writer noted with quiet satisfaction that one Cuddington had married a sister of the Walter de Merton who became Chancellor of England in 1260 and had later founded Merton College at Oxford. When he died, the chronicler stated with evident pride, he was Bishop of Rochester and had left twenty marks for the poor of Cuddington village.

In the fourteenth century, the writing continued, one Simon de Codynton had become sheriff, building a manor house that had, with its chamber, great hall, pantry, buttery and kitchen, been the wonder of the parish. A very imposing residence for 1350, Andrew knew, when most people of substance were more concerned with security than comfort. That building would have been part of what he'd seen in his "time slip" at Sparrow Field. The next hundred years were detailed descriptions of family squabbles with the common people of Cuddington over the land that, from the villages named, must have encompassed thousands of acres. Within this area was the "common land," where the poor pastured their cattle and planted their crops in individual strips. The name of the land, the chronicler noted, was Sparwefeld. *And*, thought Andrew, as he sipped at his drink, *today Sparwefeld is an ancient farmhouse with an attractive front yard, a tidy garden and scruffy-looking backyard*. Sic transit gloria mundi. . . .

Following the unknown Cuddington who'd recounted the

family's early history, a different handwriting recorded that in 1495 Sir Richard Cuddington's wife, Chloe, had given birth to the son and heir, Richard. Two years later, another boy, James, was born. In 1520 the same writer noted, with lordly satisfaction, that Cuddington House in the Strand had been completed. "And King Henry passed this way in the Straund for France this day."

Those years and the few that followed seemed to have been the peak of Cuddington prosperity. Both boys married young. Richard was barely nineteen when he wed a Miss Elizabeth Darrell of Ewell. "One of the Squire's seven" was written after her name. James had married the following year. Several lines were drawn through two births, indicating, Andrew assumed, that the children were stillborn. However, in 1522, a boy, Richard, had survived. He would have been the one mentioned in the lounge history who became the famous Tudor painter. As for the elder Richard and his bride, Elizabeth, they'd had only one child, born in 1516, a girl named Chloe after her grandmother. *That* was the Chloe Cuddington who had sat for the portrait. Chloe's marriage to Bartholomew Penn in 1536 was duly noted, and after the date, someone in a different script had scribbled, "a great favorite of the Quene."

Three pages later the handwriting changed again. The baronetcy had ping-ponged between the descendants of Richard and James, and childhood mortality being what it was, there were as many stillborn children or those who survived but a short time as there were those who lived. Andrew was amused to see the truth of Rosa Caudle's statement that the family had faithfully stuck with the tradition of naming the eldest son Richard, the second son James—the older daughter was inevitably a Chloe. After that there were a few Rachels, Elizabeths, Charleses, Georges and Henrys. The Richard Cuddington who became the painter had had a passel of children, and it was his great-grandson, James, who'd gone to Williamsburg. His birthdate was recorded in 1630, and he left for America (noted as "the colonies") at the age of twenty, probably when his father died and his older brother had inherited Cuddington House. He would have been nearly seventy when he'd shown Julian the portrait and asked the young man to return it to the family. It had probably formed part of his inheritance.

Through the Georgian and Victorian periods, the Richards, Jameses, Elizabeths and Chloes had lived on in Cuddington House, much as the lounge history had described. There were rarely many children, which was undoubtedly a blessing, for it was apparent that over the years the family fortunes had dwindled even further. Several ladies had remained spinsters, possibly for want of a decent dowry. In 1912 he noted the birth of his Artless Charmer. She had been an only child and named for the Rosa who had been the friend of Julian Cushing.

He had just finished at the date of Rosa's marriage to Harry Caudle in 1930 and the date of a few major restorations to the house when Timothy arrived. He looked at the papers spread on his sofa and said, cheerfully, "Well, Andrew, what have we here?" Peering at some of the books and papers more closely, he laughed, "Looks like you've robbed the British Museum."

"Sit down, Tim. I've got *some* story to tell you. . . . Believe me, you're going to need all your wits about you to understand this, so you'd better have a drink first—here, I'll fix it."

"You seem a lot better than last Friday. Have you stayed away from that blasted place as I asked you to?"

"I haven't been back, but I'm going there soon." Andrew looked at the papers thoughtfully. "Listen, Tim, I think I know what's there."

"Well, what in hell is it—don't keep me waiting!" Hodge sipped his drink. "And how did you find out?"

"It's all here—almost the whole damned story. I've spent the weekend reading everything I could find. There are some missing pieces, but I think—no, I'm pretty sure I've got the basics right. Are you ready?"

"As ready as I'll ever be." Hodge regarded the mess on his sofa. He was happy to see his friend looking more like himself. "Where did you find all that ancient memorabilia?"

Andrew told him how Rosa had hung Chloe's portrait in his room, how she'd left boxes of family records from the safe for him and given him permission to look in the attic. After going through all the records, he'd taken the keys, discovered they fitted several locked trunks, found boxes containing books, papers and old letters and had closeted himself with them till he felt he knew most of what had happened to Julian Cushing.

"There are still some blank spots—and they're important, Tim—I'm not denying that. But what's here really tells us quite a bit." He lit a cigarette and continued. "Julian, as you know, lived in Williamsburg. We have all that information from his *Journal*. He saw the portrait of Chloe Cuddington, became infatuated with it—he was a very impressionable boy, I think. When James Cuddington offered to pay his passage to England if he'd return the portrait to 'its owners'—the family at Cuddington House—Julian leaped at the chance. That, by the way, was not in Julian's *Journal*, but in other papers I found in the attic."

"What kind of papers?" Hodge drew his chair nearer to see what Andrew had in his hand.

"The best kind—diaries. Those days people didn't have our demands on their time, and when they had their leisure moments, there was no car, no theater to speak of and certainly no television. So for entertainment they turned to their diary or journal. It was a calendar of whatever happened to them on a certain day, and many of them used the pages as a sort of psychiatric clearinghouse—they'd confide things to it, for instance, that they'd tell no one else."

"The sort of thing my patients tell me," Hodge volunteered.

"Exactly"—Andrew waved the book—"and this is one of those books. It's the diary of Miss Chloe Cuddington. Not the one in the portrait, of course. She'd been dead for over a hundred years. But there was another Chloe who later lived in Cuddington House, and she, I'm thankful to say, was a very bright well-educated young lady for her time. She kept journals *and* diaries, and it's from her that I got most of my information." Andrew went to his host's well-stocked bar, refilled his glass and went on.

"Apparently, old James Cuddington in Williamsburg knew from communications with his relatives in London that his brother's son had a daughter named Chloe and that *she was the image of the portrait of her ancestress*. Not only were the names passed on, but this particular family characteristic—the almost white-blond hair, the square chin with the deep cleft, that incredibly strong beauty—was a physiological signature that surfaced every generation or so. Actually, it seemed to have been such a distinguishing trait that it was looked for quite early in the Cuddington children. Often a generation or two would pass; then, suddenly, there'd be a child who grew to the image of the girl in the portrait. All this, of course, was known by the James Cuddington in Williamsburg. Whether he mentioned it to Julian or not, I don't know. However, it would account for Rosa's—Rosa Cuddington, that is—for her remark to him that he would find things little changed at Sparwefeld. That's where Chloe lived a good deal of the time—the girl seems to have loved the outdoors and preferred Sparwefeld to Cuddington House. She, too, had some knowledge of Nonsuch that doesn't come through clearly. But after all, I haven't had time to go through all of her diaries thoroughly—not yet."

"What do you mean—had some knowledge about Nonsuch?"

"Well, you must remember that although the palace had ostensibly been pulled down, there were still many ruins aboveground. What the neighboring villagers hadn't pillaged or pilfered would still be standing, I'd think. Rosa Cuddington told Julian the ruins were more extensive than he'd been led to believe. So he went to Sparwefeld—to Sparrow Field of today—to see Nonsuch. It must have been a fantastic moment for him. Yet in his diary, as you remember, all he says of that day is 'Nothing.' Well, here, in Miss Chloe Cuddington's diary, it tells what actually happened:

> "*April 10, 1700*: I went to the ruins for my morning Walk as is my Wont, hoping to paint the part of the Wall which remains with the great tree in the Wilderness hanging over it. The sun often makes this very Beautiful. While setting up my easel, I was reminded of the Lure. Why can't I put this fairy Tale from my Mind? 'Tis only a legend, I am sure. My father once told me

Dr. Dee was a great Fakir for his time; he had even hoodwinked the Quene. . . .

But while I was walking about the ruined buildings, waiting for the sun to strike the right spot, *he* came. . . ."

"And here"—Andrew laughed—"you can see that he—and it was Julian she saw—must have made a great impression, for she has underlined it four times!" He continued reading:

"He introduced himself to me most gracefully as Mr. Julian Cushing of Williamsburg, which is in America. I was very Excited to meet someone from the Colonies—he was sent by my great-uncle James, who must be quite old. Mr. Cushing told me of his deep Interest in Nonsuch, and so I took him on what I called My Grand Tour. I have talked with many Old men in the village who can remember Nonsuch when it was still all standing Together, and they have described what the ruins are, although some of them are so Tall, they need no description. . . ."

"Then there must have been more of it left than one might think," said Hodge, draining his glass and going to the bar to refill it. "Read on, old man."

"As this was Mr. Cushing's first visit, we started near the old Banqueting House and walked through the Wilderness to where I had planned to paint my Tree and Wall. We went on through the kitchen buildings—he being Most Pleasant and Charming. His speech is different—and he says so is Mine—but he speaks truly and well, and we both were at Ease. He told me I greatly resembled a portrait of a relative he has brought back to Cuddington House.

He was very interested in the Wine Cellar, which is so full of stone and waste as can barely be seen at all. The tower bases still have pieces of the panels which were so famous, and I had great Pleasure in explaining to Mr.

Cushing how they had been built and how they looked before being pulled Down.

When the sun had got too High to paint the tree, I directed Mr. Cushing to my Easel and proposed we return to Sparwefeld. A terrible Occurrence followed, for when we came to the Inner Court, Mr. Cushing was taken with a great Sickness. His features were very Red and he sweated much and would have Swooned had I not held him up. . . ."

"Andrew! My God, the same symptoms!" Timothy set his glass down so hard that liquid splashed on the table. "Unbelievable," he muttered as he wiped at the mess.

"Well, they had to be right where I was," said Andrew, looking up from the diary, "right over the chancel in the old church, though of course, they didn't know it, for there were only ruins, no excavations to be seen. Probably at that time some of the cobblestones were still in place. Here's what she says happened next."

"I became so Concerned with Mr. Cushing's condition, I helped him away very quickly. At the tree where my Easel was, he became more Normal—and, in a few moments, felt quite at Ease, though very listless and, I think somewhat fearful—though he did not wish to show it. We went back to Sparwefeld at once, and there was much Humour with Aunt Rosa, who had sent Mr. Cushing to the ruins knowing I would be there. It seems he has brought from the Colonies a portrait of our ancestress, Chloe Cuddington, for whom I was Named. Everyone says we look exactly alike. They think it is quite Remarkable. But I do not wish to be like her. I think her taint has escaped me . . . thanks be to God!"

"Her taint?" Hodge asked. "What was that? Jesus, Andrew, this is beginning to sound like one of those serials on the telly."

Andrew was regarding the diary with a furrowed brow. "That's something that hasn't surfaced yet, but if it's in these pages, believe me, I'm going to find it. You know, Tim, I was really ready to leave London last Friday—all set to look up my friends here, catch some shows, maybe even run down to see a colleague who has a house in Cornwall—and then go on to Vermont for a few weeks. Then I read that bit about Julian Cushing experiencing the same symptoms I did—and at exactly the same place in the ruins. You know, it's like a who-done-it that gets better with every chapter! There are still *boxes* of stuff in the attic—I don't think that family *ever* threw anything away—and Rosa Caudle tells me the Sparrow Field attic's the same. Somehow, I'm sure there's an answer to the whole mystery. I've got the original Chloe Cuddington hanging in my bedroom, too, and you've got to come and see her. She's at the center of this whole story, Tim, I'm convinced of it. Sometimes I even think if I just wait long enough, she'll tell me everything herself." Andrew smiled at Timothy's raised eyebrows.

"I won't read any further from the book right now, Tim, but what happened in essence is that they went back several times. Julian in his own *Journal* says they went back a fourth time to look for the Lure. But they avoided the spot where he'd been ill, and as long as they did, there was no trouble. His Chloe apparently believed something called the Lure was there—and what the Lure is, I haven't the faintest idea. But it had something to do with a Dr. Dee. Do you know a Dr. Dee who might have lived at that time?"

Timothy Hodge was already peering in the well-filled bookcase lining one entire end of the room. He extracted a small volume, thumbed some pages, then said, "Here it is, Andrew: 'Dr. John Dee, English astrologer, born London, July 13, 1527, died, Mortlake, England, 1608.' That's a pretty good age for those days, Andrew—eighty-one the old boy was. So he was alive during the reign of Henry and all the subsequent Tudors, and he outlived Elizabeth herself. Here's what else it says: 'In early life, he devoted much time to mathematical, astronomical and chemical studies and in 1548 rumours began to prevail that he was addicted to the black arts. They were probably well founded.' " Hodge read on silently. "There's a lot more, but the gist of it is that he went abroad to still the rumors, came back later and ingratiated himself with William Cecil, Queen Elizabeth's great minister. Dee was greatly favored by her for the rest of his life. It says he cast a chart to find an auspicious day for her coronation, and he rose so much in her esteem that in 1594 she gave him the Chancellorship of St. Paul's and a year later the Wardenship of Manchester College, which he held for nine years. He continued his interest in the occult, however, and his work was published posthumously in 1659."

" 'Greatly favored.' That reminds me of what was written opposite Chloe Cuddington's name in the family's genealogy," said Andrew. "It said she was 'a great favorite of the Quene.' Perhaps Dee even knew the original Chloe? Certainly the rest of the Cuddingtons didn't care much for him and considered him a 'fakir' as Julian's Chloe wrote, saying he had 'hoodwinked the Quene.' "

"That was probably his reputation during his lifetime," Hodge agreed. "Undoubtedly he had his detractors. You may be sure, Andrew, that anyone with influence on royalty always provokes jealousy. I wonder *what* the Lure was?"

"Tim, I know you're going to think me crazy"—Andrew put the diary aside—"but will you come with me to Nonsuch tomorrow? We'll walk the route that Julian and Chloe took and see what happens." He was silent for a moment, as if reliving his previous experience. "I'm not exactly looking forward to it, but I won't feel so uneasy if you're there. Let's go early if you don't mind. Oh, damn it, I forgot that's a working day for you."

"Well, you're in luck, old buddy, because tomorrow just quite coincidentally happens to be my day off." Hodge settled back in his chair, sipping his drink. "But are you sure you want to go back there, Andrew? You've got me intrigued as hell with this whole thing, I must admit, but there might be some risk. . . ." His voice trailed off.

"I wouldn't go on my own, Tim. Not for money. But if we go very early and if you're with me—well, I'm prepared to face whatever demon is there . . . and that god-awful nausea and terror, too. I just want somebody to verify that it isn't just *me*. It gave me quite a turn to find that Julian had experienced the same thing. But I want *you* to see it; then we'll take it from there."

"Surely, if I can help. I certainly don't want you to go back by yourself."

Andrew gathered the books and papers together and said in a relieved voice, "Well, for now let's go out and talk about everything and anything *except* Julian Cushing and Nonsuch. I'd really like to catch up on the last year or so with you, my friend."

Hodge was on his feet, draining the last of his drink. "And I'll be around to pick you up in my car at eight o'clock sharp."

They were at the Nonsuch site by eight forty-five. As Timothy drove by the red-brick wall, Andrew pointed out the backyard of Sparrow Field, where he could see Mrs. Williams hanging out an early wash. A few moments later they left the automobile at the parking lot inside Nonsuch Park and walked the few hundred yards to the site. It was a beautifully cool morning, and in the shady spots along the path the dew still lingered. The air was fresh with the earthy smell of new-cut grass; it was so still the early-morning activity of flocks of birds nesting in the trees overnight continued. They swooped in great numbers from tree to tree, greeting the visitors with raucous cries. Andrew pointed out the tower bases and the crumbling foundation still showing traces of a tiled floor.

"This was once the Privy Garden," he told Timothy, who appeared impressed with the vast expanse of palatial remains spread before him. "Here's where the 'Falcon Perches' and the obelisk were." They walked on toward the inner court, where a few workmen were preparing to dig. "Now," he continued, "it's my own private theory that when the builders got to here—the inner court part—they found the basements, the vaults and the crypt of the old Cuddington church that had been previously leveled. Rather than excavate and clean up the mess, which included several graves, *they simply built on top of it*, which accounts for the inner court being higher than the outer. Here, in the middle, was a white marble fountain supported by brass dragons. It was built directly over the old church's chancel."

"And that's where our demon lives?"

Andrew grimaced. "Well, Tim, let's get the damn thing over with. . . . Come on." They walked past mounds of excavated dirt and rubble. No one disturbed them.

About fifty feet from the chancel site he began to feel uncomfortable. As the sensation intensified, he touched Timothy, who put a supporting hand at his elbow. Slowly and deliberately, taking a few steps at a time, they reached within five feet of the chancel. Andrew felt engulfed by a sticky warmth. Perspiration beaded his forehead. He hadn't taken off his coat, and underneath, his shirt was beginning to feel wet. His mouth was parched, while his tongue seemed to thicken. There was a noticeable weakness he hadn't experienced before. ***It was almost as if a force stronger than he were intent on taking over not only just his body, but his mind too.*** He stumbled and would have fallen but for Hodge's restraining hand. "Careful, old man, do you want to go on?"

"Yes, damn it." Andrew could barely mutter the words. He was sweating profusely now, and nausea churned in his throat. He had purposely remained breakfastless and was now glad of it. Upchucking on old Henry's inner court would be a fine thing—he hoped the humor might divert him from his discomfort. Yet the nausea gnawed at him, and his head felt as if it were being bludgeoned. Suddenly, his mouth constricted and tightened. He felt he couldn't go on—his tongue seemed to fill his mouth. He felt something dragging at him.

•

"Jesus, Andrew, that was a near thing!" Timothy was fanning him with a newspaper he'd pulled from his pocket, and Andrew could see through a murky blue that he was now safely away from the chancel area. He had no memory of having walked the last few steps, and he lay now, propped against a tree, while Hodge loosened his tie, removed his coat and sat on the ground beside him. "Andrew, that's the goddamnedest thing I've ever seen in my life. I'd never have believed it! I still don't know whether I *do* believe it. But, Jesus, look at you!'' He rattled on in what Andrew wished he had the breath to say was a typical hodgepodge way. But he didn't have the strength. He supposed Timothy must have pulled him, half-conscious, from the site to the base of the tree. He'd never have made it alone. He knew, as well as he'd ever known anything in his life, that if Hodge hadn't been with him, he'd have died—quickly and terribly—by strangulation on the old chancel site.

Chapter Six

Despite a quick recovery and Andrew's desire to rummage in Sparrow Field's attic, Timothy insisted on their immediate return to London. They arrived at Hans Place shortly before eleven o'clock to the chagrin of Mrs. Hall, the charwoman. She had just arrived from an apartment on the upper floor and told her employer she was "about ready to have a good go at the place, sir." Instead, she was dispatched to the nearest market to choose whatever she might cook for luncheon. Mr. Moffatt had had a bit of a turn at Ewell, Timothy explained. Privately, Mrs. Hall—who knew Andrew of old—thought he looked a bit done in. She bustled out as Timothy suggested Andrew remove his shoes and stretch out on the sofa.

They'd both remained silent on the short ride back to London, preoccupied with their own thoughts on the near-disastrous occurrence at Nonsuch. It clearly had to be discussed, but neither knew where to begin. As Timothy handed Andrew a generously filled brandy snifter, he said, "I don't often prescribe such strong medicine so early in the day, old man, but you need this. Down the hatch—it'll warm your stomach for whatever Madame Hall brings back. . . ."

They sipped their drinks for a moment, and it was Timothy who broke the silence. "Do you want to talk about it?"

"You bet I do"—Andrew sighed—"but there are so many missing pieces! That's why I wanted to go to Sparrow Field. There's supposed to be a lot of family memorabilia in the attic."

"Another day," Timothy advised. "I don't think you realize just how close a call you had." When there was no reply, he continued. "Andrew, yesterday you said—if I remember your words—'I think I know what's there. . . .' Well, after your experience today, I wish you'd tell *me* what it is. It's not just personal curiosity. I'd like to know—for medical reasons—what you exposed yourself to."

"Okay." Andrew shifted upright, glass in hand. "The nearest I can come to it is that in several letters I found in the Cuddington House attic, a reference is made to a 'legend.' It somehow seems to have been started by or connected with Dr. Dee. It's about something called 'the Lure' that's supposed to be buried at Nonsuch. It was buried, presumably, *before the palace was even built*. Which would place it in the late 1530s—when the Cuddington manor house, the church and the priory all were leveled. Something—God knows what—was placed somewhere on the site. What I don't know, and where I don't know. Is it in the chancel area, and was it perhaps cursed? Anyway, the Cuddington family 'legend' has it that the Lure was connected with Chloe Cuddington—my gorgeous lady of the portrait—and with Dr. Dee. The palace was built over the hiding place, and the legend evolved afterward. I feel even more strongly after what happened today that it's something hidden in the chancel area and that the curse—if there is one—still has the power to torment."

"Damned near killed you."

"Well, I wouldn't be the first." Hodge's eyes widened in astonishment as Andrew hurried to explain. "In a letter written in 1730 from one Cuddington to another—an otherwise innocuous letter actually—the death years ago of someone prowling in the ruins is mentioned. Seems he was found dead from strangulation near, as the letter describes it, 'the site of the great fountain.' Of course, that's all they knew was there in those days—it wasn't an excavated area, you remember."

"My God! Incredible!" Timothy was aghast. "So you think at the site of the old chancel there lives or exists an evil force capable of murder?"

"Sure seems that way." Andrew sipped his brandy reflectively. There was the sound of Mrs. Hall's return, and she called out cheerily that she'd found "a nice pair of plaice, sir, and a few veg—it won't be long." Timothy went to his desk, took out a long yellow legal pad and began to make a few notes.

Andrew walked to the window to look at the charming old circle of Hans Place. Quiet and remote, a small London enclave only a few minutes' walk from busy Knightsbridge, Sloane Street and the back door of Harrods, the red-brick terraced buildings retained a faded Victorian elegance. The leaves at the top of the great cluster of trees in the center were touched with an early turning of color. A fine mist had begun to fall; Andrew could visualize the workers at Nonsuch packing it in for the day. It was never any good digging in the rain, though he'd done it plenty of times, sloshing around in water well over his ankles. He wondered if the chancel site was clear enough to hold water. "Drown the goddamned thing that's there, I hope," he muttered to himself, as Mrs. Hall summoned them to lunch.

" 'Tis all set, gentlemen, do come while it's hot." She'd set a little table between the windows overlooking the small parklike circle outside. Andrew was hungry; he remembered now he'd had no breakfast. He was doing full justice to Mrs. Hall's excellent cooking when Timothy broke the silence.

"Andrew, I've got an idea,. I've just made some notes. I'll read them to you if you want, but I don't think I have to. It's all so simple; just let me itemize. Julian Cushing sees portrait of girl and falls in love. James Cuddington asks him to return the picture to family in England, as he knows he's too old ever to get home. He tells Julian of family tradition—of names. of resemblance—and perhaps hints or tells him outright that a young lady resembling the one in the portrait now lives near Nonsuch. He pays Julian's passage and sends him to the family at Number 18, where he meets Rosa Cuddington. She sends him to Sparwefeld, where, as she says, 'he will find things little changed. . . .' "

Timothy consulted his notes, then continued. "Then he goes to Sparwefeld. He meets Chloe. Probably he was told on arriving that she was out painting at the Nonsuch site, and he goes there to find her. How anxious and excited he must have been! Apparently, they got on very well indeed, and while walking around, they hit on the same spot as you. Although it wasn't excavated at the time, Julian had a similarly distressing experience. They must have then returned to Sparwefeld. But we know from Julian's *Journal* that they went back a fourth time, for Chloe insisted the Lure still had to be there. They were looking for it, no doubt of that. But, my God, what a task! They'd have had to *dig*—the ruins were aboveground then."

Andrew shook his head slightly. "Remember they were both very young. It was probably as good an excuse as any other for them to be alone together. The early 1700s was a romantic era. Can't you just see him in some foppish coat and trousers and a tall topper and Chloe in a flowing dress with a large hat with ribbons? Probably he was carrying her easel, and they were planning to spend a day among the ruins . . . maybe they even brought a picnic. They might not have done as much looking as they did lovemaking—or whatever they called it in those days."

"I've been meaning to ask you about that," said Timothy. "Did she finally accept Julian since he was so unhinged by her? And did they live happily ever after?"

"That's one of those frustraing *lacunae*, Tim. The family genealogy lists her birth as 1682—so she'd have been about seventeen when she met Julian. She died, still Miss Chloe Cuddington, as far as I can make out, in 1708. Age, twenty six. God, that's too young to die. . . ."

"And Julian?"

"Who knows? His *Journal* ends about three weeks after he arrived. There are a few notes at the back, and I have a feeling he just stopped writing in it. That in itself is unusual—he'd been so faithful before. *Something* happened to their romance. Maybe she wouldn't have him or didn't want to live in Williamsburg. And Julian *had* to return, remember—there was nothing for him in England. Or maybe she didn't have a dowry. Maybe Julian even recognized that while it had all been exciting and pleasurable, they really weren't meant for each other. Although, somehow, they seem so *right* together, don't they? Anyway, I sssume he went back to the Colonies—probably married a girl he'd left behind and lived to a ripe old age. Believe me, when I get back to Williamsburg, I'm going to look him up. There must be something—a death certificate, a marriage license."

While Mrs. Hall cleared away the lunch plates, Timothy went to the kitchen. He emerged a few minutes later with a tray containing a coffeepot and cups. He motioned them back to the sofa and poured a cup for Andrew. Stirring his own, he said thoughtfully, "Andrew, I have an idea. You'll think me bonkers, no doubt. But damn it all, I'm not going to apologize! I *am* a doctor, and I *am* a psychiatrist. If you'd come to me as a stranger with this experience, I probably would have subjected you to half a dozen or more medical tests to determine if there was any physical reason for your reaction at Nonsuch. I'd also want to know about your background, your work, your childhood and how well you got along with your parents, how you relate to your friends and colleagues. I'd try to determine from observation and tests how sound your mental and emotional processes were. In short, you'd have had a damned thorough going-over both psychologically and physically before I'd even begin to suggest any diagnosis or treatment at all."

Andrew remained silent, sipping his coffee. Yet it was obvious to Hodge he was paying close attention. He leaned back on the sofa and continued. "But the hell of it is, old man, I *know* practically everything I need to know about you. And you seem to be in sound shape—even though you were badly shaken this morning."

"I had a complete physical about a month ago, Tim. It was my annual checkup—I usually arrange to have it before I leave the States. It's hell to be sick while you're digging in the Caucasus Mountains, for instance. And the results were fine. There's *nothing* wrong with me."

"Well, that makes it simpler then to suggest what I'm going to suggest."

"Which is?"

"Hypnosis."

"Hypnosis?" Andrew broke into a wide grin. "Tim, you're joking. Hypnosis! Oh, I know it's not the cheap theatrics it was a couple of decades ago. As a matter of fact,

I've heard it's become virtually respectable. But—hypnosis!"

"You've heard right, Andrew," Timothy replied, "but you haven't heard it all. Hypnosis is a terrific medical tool, provided it's handled by people who know what they're doing. Under the right circumstances, it can be a formidable adjunct to a doctor's professional knowledge, especially in tracing deep psychiatric disorders. Would you believe I've seen surgery, deep surgery—amputations, Caesarian sections, that sort of thing—performed while a patient was under hypnosis? It was used in the late nineteenth century when general anesthetics were unknown. Some people are allergic to certain modern anesthetics, particularly in the dental field, and many dentists have learned to lightly hypnotize a patient in order not to have to use a drug. When it's done correctly, there's little or no risk, and there can be a great, great benefit."

"But what good would hypnotizing me do? What do you want to find out? Hell, Tim, I'm holding nothing back. I'll *tell* you anything you want to know." Andrew looked mildly irritated.

"It's not what you know—but what you *don't know* you know," Timothy replied, "that's what I want to find out." Seeing Andrew's honest bewilderment, he hurried on, leaning forward and ticking his words off on his fingers. "First, there's got to be *something* in you—it's the something that responds to that brutalizing force at Nonsuch—that I think hypnosis could reveal. Second, you obviously don't know what it is, and you're hoping to find the answer to this and several other questions by going through books and papers at Cuddington House and Sparrow Field. And that's going to take weeks, if not months. Third, in the meantime, you're quite frankly wearing yourself out, you're becoming unhealthily preoccupied with Julian Cushing, with Nonsuch Palace and with your lady of the portrait. I don't think even *you* yourself know how much you've changed in the week or so since you've been here—even since I've seen you."

"I'll buy all that, Tim," Andrew replied soberly. "Every once in a while I'm amazed myself. Hell, I've got a *dozen* irons in the fire at home: letters I haven't answered requesting lecture dates, article deadlines, questions about university conferences. Even a lovely, lonesome woman writing me sad letters from Williamsburg. Sure, there are plenty of reasons for me to cool everything and return home. But I have to be honest, Tim, I don't give a damn about anything else, and I won't—until I have this mystery solved. In a way, I almost feel *committed* to it, as though it's a debt I have to honor. I can imagine your concern—and, Tim, I appreciate it. Especially what you did this morning. . . ." The memory of his anguish caused Andrew's face to darken, and he put down his cup. "Now tell me what's involved in this hypnosis business. Certainly I'm not going to shoot down any viable idea of yours, Tim. But I'd like to know a little more about it."

Timothy glanced at his watch. "Wait a moment." He left the room, and Andrew could hear him talking pleasantly with Mrs. Hall in the kitchen. He went into the bedroom and emerged a few moments later, carrying a check for her and a large box. He set the box down near Andrew, disappeared into the kitchen again and returned carrying a tray with several glasses and a pitcher of water. Mrs. Hall trailed him, promising to return "Tuesday week, sir, and I'll give it all a good going-over then." Nodding to Andrew, she let herself out.

"Good old soul, that," Timothy said as he set the tray on the table. "I'm afraid we interrupted her plans for a 'good go,' but she's going to treat herself to the cinema at Islington, she says, so not to worry." He took a tape recorder from the box and set it up on the table between the chair and sofa.

"Now, Andrew, I want to explain this as simply as possible. There's nothing new about hypnotism. It's been practiced in some form or another for thousands of years. It's no more than the induction of a trance that can vary in depth from light, medium to deep or, technically, from lethargic, somnabulistic to cataleptic. I don't want this to sound too complicated, so I'm going to simplify. What the hypnotist does is simply guide *you* yourself to put aside your conscious mind—that everyday mind which runs your life and makes your decisions—so your subconscious mind, or unconscious mind, that storehouse of all memories and impressions, can take over. It doesn't weaken the body and there'll be no lingering aftereffects. As a matter of fact, hypnosis is a relaxing process. Some of my patients tell me a half hour of it makes them feel extraordinarily refreshed, as if they've had a full night's sleep."

He waited for a question. When there was none, he continued.

"Therefore, hypnotism by itself isn't dangerous. Like any instrument, medicine or force, though, it can be misused. There's no danger of addiction—that's one question I'm often asked in this drug-conscious age. Another is the effect on your *mind*. If it has any effect at all, you might find your perception and sensibilities a little sharpened. Then again, you might not. It certainly will have no detrimental effect."

"I wonder, if I *can* be hypnotized," Andrew said, "and if it's so great, why isn't it used more frequently?"

"I think you'd be the perfect subject, old man." Timothy busied himself with the recording equipment. He didn't wish to hurry Andrew, who must come to it in his own way. "The more intelligent, sharp and normal a person is, the better a subject. Mentally deficient, lethargic, stupid or seriously ill patients don't make good subjects. I don't know the answer medically—no one does—except there just doesn't seem to be anything *there* for the hypnotist to work with. I've always thought myself that many of these people live their lives very much on the surface. Their own subconscious minds are relatively barren. On the other hand, extremely nervous, anxious or the arrogant know-everything types are also difficult, but not impossible to work with. Often they're the ones who benefit most, for hypnotism can help separate a patient from all his preconceived hang-ups. It permits the 'real you,' the inner essence of the you-personality, to scan the depths the conscious mind often ignores. And whatever you, as Andrew Moffatt, have put into that subconscious reservoir—by thought, impression or remembrance—it's still there, waiting to be retrieved, although, consciously, you may have forgotten most of it. Your subconscious always observes, deduces, appraises and remembers, though most of what it retains, you yourself have long since put aside.

"As to why hypnosis isn't used more frequently? It *is* used more often than the average person realizes. It took a long time for the medical profession to accept it. After all, what doctor wants to admit certain ailments may be cured by speaking directly to the subconscious mind when all his hard-learned skills are of no avail? It was beginning to be acepted when anesthesia was discovered. Again, it was making headway medically when Freud—who used it, incidentally—hit on the idea of psychoanalysis. And once again, hypnosis was sidelined. But now, I think, its time has come."

"And how do you do it, Tim? Swinging a bright metal object, lighting a candle and muttering incantations? Sorry, friend, I'm not making fun of you, but I still can't quite equate hypnosis with the brilliant Dr. Timothy Hodge."

Hodge laughed. "Andrew, your reactions are so utterly normal I *know* you're feeling better! No, I don't swing objects, I don't light candles. They're used merely to induce a receptive attitude, which *is* necessary, to hold a person's concentration or tire his eyes, frankly. There's no incense, no yoga positioning, no background music. I just talk to you as I'm talking now. I could probably hypnotize you without your being aware it was happening. But a good pro doesn't do that. I want your consent and your cooperation."

"How long will it take?" Andrew finished off the coffee and, not waiting for an answer, refused Timothy's offer of another cup. "If I'm going to sleep, my friend, I can't have any more coffee! Well, let's get going. You can explain more about it later; certainly I'll have more questions when I wake up."

"Andrew, this isn't exactly like sleep—you'll be aware of me, of my questioning and of your answering. Whether you remember any of it or not is up to me. I can, as the hypnotist, tell you to remember what you reveal—or I can tell you to forget it. I'm sorry, old man, but you'll have to leave that part up to me. That's the good hypnotist's prerogative. Still want to try it?"

"Right. Shall I lie down?"

Timothy rose and rearranged the sofa pillows to give Andrew's large frame more space. "Put your head on this one, take off your tie, your shoes are already off—just lie back, Andrew, and relax. Close your eyes if you feel like it; put your hands across your chest—anything you wish that makes you comfortable and relaxed." There was no reluctance. Andrew was obviously cooperating because he wanted to—he didn't feel compelled. "Are you all right now?"

"Fine, Tim. . . . Go ahead." Andrew raised a hand and jauntily saluted. "Wish me happy landings." He laughed at Hodge's grimace.

"Andrew, stretch out. All right now, stretch all the way out. Rest and relax. Take a deep breath, hold it and exhale; try it again. Rest and relax. Inhale again. Take a good breath, that's it. You're doing fine. Try again, and after you exhale, relax. Relax deeply and comfortably. Now, after the next breath, you're going to feel sleepy. That relaxation is becoming sleep. You'll become more sleepy as I continue to talk. And I'm going to start to count. Rest and relax, Andrew—no more deep breathing now. All you're doing is resting and relaxing. And falling deeper and deeper into sleep. Your eyelids are heavy; your whole body is relaxed and rested; you've never felt more at ease. Now I'm going to start to count, Andrew, but it won't interrupt your rest, your relaxation or your sleep. One, two, three . . . rest and relax and sleep deeply, and by the time I come to five you'll be . . . asleep. Four . . . five. . . ."

There was complete silence in the apartment. Hodge could hear Andrew's steady breathing and the faint spatter of rain on the outside windows. The mist they'd watched at luncheon had turned into a gentle rainfall. He rose and pulled down the shades. He switched on a lamp behind the prone figure on the sofa, turned on the tape recorder and said in a low voice, "This is August fifteenth. The time is two o'clock at my apartment in Hans Place. Dr. Timothy Hodge speaking. The patient is Andrew Moffatt." He clicked off the recorder and watched the figure on the couch for a moment. "Now, Andrew, are you all right—are you relaxed and at ease?" He then clicked the recorder back on.

"I am, yes, thank you. . . ."Andrew's voice was firm, despite his trancelike state. He lay with his hands clasped across his chest, his head turned in the direction of Timothy's voice, his hair slightly rumpled. His eyes were closed.

After watching him for a moment, Timothy looked at the notes on the pad. He ticked off an item, saying, "Andrew, I want you to go back in time a bit. Quite a way back. You are now in a much earlier time, Andrew, when you were—oh, let's say—when you were eight years old. Your mother and father were visiting here in England, and they brought you with them. You're going back to that time, to how happy you were to be here, and you'll recall a day when you were visiting in Ewell—do you remember?"

"It was at Lord Sidney Breed's." The answer came more quickly than Hodge had anticipated. He watched Andrew. He lay as he had before, but there was a subtle difference in the way the lips were pursed, and the voice was a young boy's. "At Lord Breed's house, Morehaven. He's a great friend of Mother's and Father's."

"Do you like it at Lord Breed's, Andrew?"

"Oh, well, it's okay, I guess." The voice was a bit petulant. "Yes, it's okay. He doesn't have any other kids to play with, but I get to spend a lot of time in the stables with the grooms, and they take me riding sometimes."

"Where do you ride, Andrew?"

"In Nonsuch Park . . . with the grooms." Timothy put the tape recorder nearer Andrew's mouth. As a child he spoke with less emphasis and timbre than he did ordinarily.

"And what are the grooms' names?" Timothy waited with pencil poised.

"Their names are Speed and Robert. . . . They're *old*, about twenty, I guess, but they're nice to me. We ride in Nonsuch Park."

"You have a pony, Andrew?"

"Well, I *had* a pony until the accident. I cried about that, and Speed and Robert were very scared. So was I."

"Tell me about the accident, Andrew. You weren't hurt, were you? Or was it someone else?" Timothy was watchful. Had Andrew been hurt, he'd relive the pain and distress, and after the shock of the morning episode, the doctor wanted no additional stress on his friend.

"No, I wasn't hurt, but Father says it's a miracle. He

didn't get mad at Speed and Robert, either, though Lord Breed was mean to them."

"Well, if you didn't get hurt, then tell me about it. If you want to, that is. Tell me what happened that day in Nonsuch Park."

"It was Mother's idea. She knew I didn't like it that there were no kids there. She asked Lord Breed if we could take the pony and cart and if Speed and Robert would take me to the park. They had their own horses, of course. Well, we got to the park, and the serving girl, Maud, was going to bring a picnic for all of us—"

"A picnic! That must have been fun."

"It *would* have been except for the accident." Andrew's features screwed up in a perfect imitation of an outraged little boy deprived of a looked-for treat. "We were coming into the park, you see, and Speed was ahead, and Robert was behind, and I had the reins."

"Was this the first time you'd driven a pony cart?" Timothy quickly made a note before he glanced to see that the tape recorder was performing correctly.

"Oh, no, but it was the first time I'd ever had such a *nice* cart and such a *beautiful* pony. Her name was Merrylegs." His face clouded. "She had to be put to sleep." His chin quivered, and he brushed at something on his face. Quickly, Timothy interrupted.

"Well, that was too bad, Andrew. Tell me, instead, about how you came to Nonsuch Park. Let's forget about everything else. How did you come to Nonsuch Park?" He was relieved to see the figure relax and the features return to normal.

"Speed and Robert were taking me to the park—the part that was very level, you know—so we could ride the pony cart around. I really don't know how it happened because it was all so quick. All I did was hold onto the reins, but I wasn't making Merrylegs go fast. I *wasn't* trying to show off." Again his voice trailed off as he remembered, but he forced himself on. "And all of a sudden the pony was rearing up in front like something had exploded in front of her. I was thrown out on the ground, and when I fell, I got very hot all over, and my head seemed about to split. The cart was on top of me." He waited a moment, plainly expecting a question, but when none came, he finished. "Then Robert and Speed came back. They were scared, and so was I."

"Did you just lie there?"

"Well, what did you expect me to do?" Timothy almost laughed aloud at the sudden thrusting of a belligerently boyish chin. "Of *course*, I didn't just lie there, dummy! I was so sick I could hardly move. I was hot, and my head was aching, and I was throwing up all over the place. The cart was heavy on me, and I had to move as best I could so the poor pony didn't kick me. She was all mixed up in the gear." The voice quivered, and the tears started. "They had to shoot her, poor Merrylegs."

Quickly, Timothy soothed. "Now, Andrew, relax and forget. I'm sure the horse didn't suffer long. It was an accident, and it certainly wasn't your fault. She probably stepped into a hole or something; or maybe one of the cartwheels was defective. But it wasn't your fault. Remember that—it was *not* your fault. Now rest and relax and don't dwell on it. Just relax for a moment."

Hodge scribbled furiously—here was something he hadn't anticipated. He'd hoped to hit on the day Andrew had picnicked with the serving girl, but apparently, there'd been an earlier visit to Nonsuch Park. And what a visit! Nothing less than a childish recurrence of the distressing episode Andrew had suffered that morning. Without any doubt, the horse, Merrylegs, had run toward the very site of the fountain with the chancel—and what else?—buried beneath it. Had the horse felt whatever force was there and reared up in protest—or fright? It certainly seemed so. And after being tipped out, the boy had experienced the exact symptoms that recurred a quarter of a century later. It was extraordinary.

He asked Andrew, "And your picnic? Did you have your picnic?"

"We got back to the house before the girl left, and I was promised it another time. I felt very bad about Merrylegs and what happened, and Mother put me to bed for the day. We didn't go back to Nonsuch for a couple of days. It was nice then; we just sat near the trees, had our picnic, and I flew a terrific kite Lord Breed bought me."

"And nothing happened?"

"What else could happen? What do you mean what happened? I just told you—we had a picnic, and I flew a kite!"

Hodge could see that shortly after the accident Andrew had put the painful episode out of his mind. He was now reliving a few days later, and the accident, which had tossed him around amid the tangled gear of a cart and the frantic thrashings of an anguished and terrified pony, had been relegated to the limbo of the repressed.

Guilt? He doubted it. He knew Andrew well and had never seen his friend avoid any moral responsibility. It was simply that Andrew couldn't face the fact that although he'd done nothing to cause the pony's death he'd been the one in the cart. And equally important, Hodge realized, it was in keeping with Andrew's character that he chose to erase from his mind an incident in which, even as a child, he'd been in a position where he'd lost control. Throwing up, screaming, sobbing, probably frightened to death—these were things his childish pride could and would not accept. The picnic was remembered; the pony and cart had been completely obliterated from his conscious.

So far, so good. Hodge pondered his next move. He'd used hypnotic regression to a time long past on several occasions and had been very successful. He hadn't discussed the possibility with Andrew because he'd thought regressing Andrew to the eight-year-old state would give him all the information he needed. He was no longer so sure. Something urged him to go farther back. Andrew had agreed to be hypnotized and had left how deeply—or how far back in time—to his friend's discretion. Timothy checked the time left on the tape and, reassured, settled back and spoke to Andrew once more.

"All right, Andrew, let's move a little back in time. You will continue to feel rested and relaxed, but we are going farther back. You are no longer eight years old, but even younger. Take a day, a happy day, and relive it for a moment if you want. Let's say you're five—how about your fifth birthday party? Did you have one?" Andrew nodded vigorously and smiled broadly. Hodge continued. "That's good. I'm sure it was a happy day. Now try to remember when you were even younger, Andrew. You were only a baby—

perhaps learning to walk. I know you can't talk about it, but do you remember learning to walk, Andrew? Do you remember how it felt to take that first step?" Again Andrew shook his head and seemed to smile to himself, and he gestured quickly with his hand, as if brushing away help.

Encouraged, Hodge said, "That's very good, Andrew. And I think now we'll go farther back. Yet, let's go back—farther and farther. Back *before* you were born. You'll continue to be relaxed and comfortable. Can we pick a time, Andrew? A time long ago? How about the eighteenth century? No, let's make it just a few months before the beginning of the eighteenth century. That would be about 1699. I wonder—were you alive then, Andrew? Have you gone back as I've asked? Stay rested and relaxed and take your time. When you feel you want to, look around and tell me. Were you there then? If you were, what was it like—in 1699?"

Timothy Hodge watched the figure on the sofa closely. Andrew's color was good, and he was relaxed; a quick touch of his pulse showed it normal. But a subtle change was occurring, reflecting what was going on in Andrew's mind. Timothy had seen this change in other regressed patients before, and it was encouraging. So often there was—nothing. The very *quietness* of the room seemed to indicate that, for the moment at least, the person on the sofa had left. His body was there, but that was all. The mind of Andrew Moffatt was obviously on a long journey. He had also changed his position slightly. His hands were no longer clasped across his chest. One was along his right side; his left hand lay above his head, encircling it on the pillow. He shifted his hips a bit as he opened his mouth to speak. He seemed to be searching for the right words and his mouth became more compressed. Timothy had the impression that had his eyes been open, they'd have been narrowed in scornful suspicion.

"What do you mean, sir? What is it *like* in 1699? That's a frivolous question, if you will pardon my saying so, sir. Aren't you here, too? Can't you *see* what it is *like*?"

The voice issuing from Andrew's mouth was so different Timothy almost dropped his pencil in astonishment. It was crisp, young, with a slight touch of a burr or graveled accent.

Damned imperious, too. Again he brought the tape recorder closer.

"Well, yes, I suppose you're right," he answered. "Of course, it *was* a foolish question. I guess I just wondered if I had the year right." Timothy was aware he sounded like the complete idiot. But whoever he was talking to now—and it certainly was not Andrew Moffatt—had the power to make him feel thoroughly inadequate.

"Well, sir, that often happens at the change of the year. I guess that must be your problem! Only one more year, and we'll be celebrating a new century—1700!" A sunny smile enveloped Andrew's features, touching them with boyish enthusiasm that reminded Hodge of their own younger years together. That decided the next question.

"If you don't think me impertinent, young man, would you mind telling me how old you are? You seem very mature for your years." Timothy wasn't particularly proud of the ploy, but he didn't want to provoke the young gallant again.

"I'm just twenty, sir, and I do not mind your asking." The boy seemed about to say something, then thought better of it. "I do not mind your asking at all." He sighed and burrowed deeper into the sofa. "I just seem a bit tired, that's all."

Timothy wondered if he should awaken Andrew. He hadn't been under very long. All his vital signs appeared good, and his tiredness could very well be a combination of the unusual experience at Nonsuch that morning and the recollection of that disastrous pony ride. Or was it a tiredness of the day he was talking about—sometime in 1699? Apparently very soon after the year had turned 1699?

"And what has tired you, young man? Have you been working too hard?"

"Study does tire one, you know," Andrew answered, "and the hours are long. I think there will be a change for the better, sir, when the college is more organized. We are still without the requisite complement of teachers."

"You're a teacher then?"

There was a suppressed sound of indignation from the figure on the sofa. "Well, I thought you knew *that*." The boy was clearly disgusted. "Everyone seems to know what I do."

"Well, perhaps I would know if I were more familiar with everything. But you see, sir, I'm a bit of a stranger here." The words seemed to mollify Andrew, who acknowledged them with a curt nod. Timothy went on. "Perhaps you'd be good enough, sir, to tell me your name? Then I wouldn't feel so strange, and I would know *which* teacher I'm talking to." He tried to sound lighthearted and laughed, but the reclining figure didn't respond. He seemed to be considering whether to divulge the information or not. He turned slightly in Timothy's direction, waited and then, surprisingly, held out his hand. Somewhat stunned, Timothy rose, put down his pad and pencil and leaned across the tape recorder to grasp Andrew's outstretched hand. It felt surprisingly young, with a firm, yet gentle clasp.

"I am delighted to introduce myself to you, sir. And gratified to make your acquaintance." He withdrew his hand and settled back. A smile—as unlike Andrew's as possible—spread across his face. "I am very pleased to meet you indeed. My name?" He smiled again.

"My name, sir, is Julian Cushing."

Julian

Chapter Seven

Julian Cushing II, the son of a successful seventeenth-century Virginia tobacco planter, had been sheltered and cosseted as a child. There were no other white children on the plantation, and he'd been tutored privately, which perhaps accounted in some measure for his sensitivity and introspective nature.

The elder Cushing had refused to send his only son to England to be educated. "He is a Virginian," he said, as if that explained everything. "I do not wish him returned to me with poor health, corrupt morals and bad manners." But strict attention was paid to Julian's curriculum. English, Latin, Greek, writing, arithmetic, geography, astronomy, sketching, together with music, dancing and fencing lessons—all ensured that Julian Cushing would be a credit to his name, background and New World heritage. When he was thirteen, a college in honor of the reigning English sovereigns, William and Mary, was commenced at Middle Plantation, which would later be called Williamsburg. There, said his father, Julian might one day enter to complete whatever in his education his tutor had missed.

Julian's one great talent was drawing, and that, in turn, had revealed an undiscovered longing. He was proficient, imaginative and very assured when confronted with pencil and paper. As a young child he often sketched the ships and figures at his father's wharf at Fairhaven, the Cushing home on the James River. Later he drew handsome buildings and homes, small cabins that looked like toys and the "follies" several wealthy planters had erected on their estates. It was while drawing these and other buildings that his attraction to the religious life was most vivid. His father's library contained drawings of the famous English abbeys and cathedrals as they'd appeared before the devastation of the Reformation, and the boy spent long hours examining them. Later pamphlets and booklets shipped to the Colony illustrated the havoc wrought by Cromwellian forces on the noble structures—the destruction made Julian's heart ache.

He would pore over the prints, tracing the cloistered walks and paths, minutely examining the tiny figures of monks and priests as they walked together or alone, some with a book in their hands. In his mind's eye, Julian could see the shadows between the pillared buildings and almost feel the soft wind that swept along the ground during the brief walk from his cell-like cubicle to Evensong services. Once, as he worked in his mother's garden—a garden similar to those in the sketches showing monks at labor—an elusive memory evoked the sound of a mighty *Te Deum* echoing from a distant church, followed by the voice of a prior raised in benediction.

Julian attended the little church at Jamestown. It bore no resemblance to the mighty English structures that had so impressed him. There, in the crude wooden building, he often found himself similarly uplifted and transported by the music and by the godly sermon—if one were lucky—which might be delivered that Sabbath. He entered with full heart into prayer, certain he'd made contact with his Saviour, with whom he considered himself on good terms. But always something was missing. Was it the splendor lacking in the building? Was it the undependability of the priest's exhortations or the appeal of the sermon so often the result of the man's mood—or even the weather? Was it the simple music that lacked everything his imagination told him it was possible for music in a house of God to be?

Julian was too young to ponder very long, and inevitably, with the demands on his time and his growing responsibility on his father's plantation, he gave it up. The attraction remained, but the longing was diluted and set in proper perspective. Ultimately, much to his parents' relief, his deep emotional attachment to the religious life vanished altogether.

However, one sketch in a book of England's great buildings continued to intrigue. It was, so the inscription read, "*Palatium Regium in Anglae Regno Appelatum Nonciutz*" and was an engraving of an earlier drawing by the Flemish artist Joris Hoefnagel in 1582. The scene was to the southeast where a plumed carriage was approaching across the green fields toward a palace apparently named Nonsuch. The occupant, "Gloriana" herself, Elizabeth I, was talking and gesturing to a man who rode a richly caparisoned horse beside her. Other attendants, their emblems of office in hand, walked or rode in front, while at the rear another vehicle carrying the queen's companions was being bedeviled by barking dogs. In the distance the Surrey plain, dotted with trees and meadows, rolled away as far as the eye could see.

Up a slight rise reared the proud palace of Nonsuch, its two mighty eight-sided towers girdled by the high brick Privy Garden wall. How Julian had yearned to peek over that wall! He showed the sketch to his father, and the elder Cushing had in turn invited one of the Percy family then visiting in the Colony to dinner. Percy told Julian that in his youth, he'd often stayed at Nonsuch, which had been built by a Tudor king who'd vowed to build a palace "as there would be none such in the land." He described the endless corridors, bursting with ornaments and tapestries and told of the priceless statuary, the beauty of the maze and the wonder of the Privy Garden. He recalled the great fountain, supported by brass dragons, spouting water many feet high into the air. A carillon played daily, and there was a certain place in the archway to the royal apartments where, when the trumpeter blew, the sound was so magnified it echoed as if an army were on hand to welcome the monarch.

All such reminiscences were fuel to the fire of Julian's youthful imagination, and his parents were enlightened enough to allow it free reign. And by the time Julian was sixteen he was firmly committed to the profession of architecture. The Cushings were pleased and proud—it was a "gentlemen's" profession and one he might carry on from Fairhaven or in Jamestown. Money from imported tobacco was flowing into the Colony, and the planters were beginning to build the gracious houses that would symbolize their prosperity. Julian would have a rewarding and a lucrative career.

It was just at the completion of his formal education that, in a devastating night of terror, disaster struck the Cushing family. And in the aftermath of desolation and despair the young boy's destiny was changed forever.

By 1697 tobacco—that golden crop on which so many fortunes depended—had been overproduced. Prices had been driven down, and everyone connected with the trade wished to prohibit its planting for at least one year or until prices stabilized. When the royal governor—at the behest of the wealthier planters, who could afford a few years' loss—refused to stop planting, community zealots banded together at night and stealthily spread out across the tobacco fields to "cut out" the young shoots. Everyone was apprehensive for the future of the Colony's only money crop, and in such an atmosphere, violence was inevitable. It erupted on the night of May 11, 1698, at Fairhaven, where at two o'clock in the morning the entire crop was "cut out" to the ground. Not being satisfied with the destruction of planter Cushing's income for a year, a departing malcontent fired a pile of lumber at the rear of the house used for repairing the adjacent slave cabins.

It had been a dry spring, and sparks from the burning wood drifted onto the house. Within moments the roof was aflame, and the culprits had sped away. When the elder Cushing awoke, smoke in his room was dense. He pulled his sleeping wife from the bed, and together they shouted a warning to Julian and the nurse, Tabby. It was, apparently, their last act. They had run as far as the bedroom doorway, where flames confronted them. No one could hear them at the window, where they ran for help while the smoke rolled in from the flaming roof and stairwell. Their bodies—the man's arms around his wife—were found the following morning in the charred ruins of the once proud and beautiful mansion.

Julian Cushing II—now the only Cushing left in the Colony his grandfather had helped found—was stunned and sickened at his parents' loss. He'd been awakened by Tabby, who'd heard the shouted warning. Still groggy with sleep, she'd pulled the boy from his bed and down the stairs where flames were already beginning to gnaw at the handsomely turned balustrade. When he asked after his parents, she assured him they'd certainly left; neither she nor the boy questioned that they would already have abandoned the burning wing where the flames were so much more intense. When neither could be found, it had taken all available hands to hold both Julian and Tab from returning to the flaming interior to find them.

Shocked and grief-stricken, feeling ill and shamed that he'd taken old Tab's word without assuring himself of his parents' safety, young Julian was further bewildered to find that most of his heritage had gone up in smoke. His father had borrowed heavily to maintain his fields in a declining market. The crop had been "cut out," the house was in ruins, and everything that had belonged to Julian's family—the furniture, paintings, the good china, even his mother's jewelry—had all been lost. In one terrifying night of hell Julian Cushing's world had vanished. From being the scion of a proud family with a secure and gracious future, he was now just another penniless boy advised by his family lawyer to sell the acreage to settle the estate's debts.

He did as he was told. There was little else he could do. Friends were kind, but he could accept hospitality and help for just so long. There were, providentially, several fields apart from the Fairhaven boundaries that were unmortgaged and these were not sacrificed. He let them on a long lease to a young planter and left Jamestown forever. His books, clothes, his cherished artbooks and the portfolios of his sketches—all had gone up in the holocaust. When a friend of his father's said he was certain he could obtain a post for him at the new college in Williamsburg, Julian was not too proud to accept. He told his friend with grim amusement his father had always promised he'd attend the College of William and Mary. He'd let his father down once; he would not again.

He'd gone to the little college town, still raw and new, and settled into one room, spending a little of his hoarded coins and bills on new clothes, a few books and sketching materials. There he met a young cousin, who, aware of the boy's tragedy, gave him a *Journal* belongong to his great-grandfather, Amos Cushing, one of the original founders of the Jamestown colony. Perhaps, the cousin hoped, Julian might take inspiration from the challenges his ancestor had spent a lifetime overcoming. Julian was grateful for his kin's thoughtfulness.

Another student, aware of the boy's slim financial resources, told him of old James Cuddington, living now in his new house on Francis Street, who was looking for someone to read to him each day. Perhaps Julian would like the opportunity?

The following day Julian set out, his mind on the pile of papers he must correct by the following morning rather than on his appointment. As he approached the house, he recalled the name. Cuddington. It seemed familiar, yet he knew he'd never met anyone of that name. Shaking his head at his own fantasy, he rang the bell and waited to see what James Cuddington would be like and how he, a nineteen-year-old boy, might fit his requests into his own overworked and cheerless days.

A servant opened the door at Julian's ring. Behind him, one hand braced against the stair's balustrade, stood a small, hawklike figure of a man, his shoulders permanently rounded, burdened with the weight of his years. He held out his other hand in welcome to his visitor, and Julian quickly stepped forward, introducing himself, murmuring his gratitude for his reception.

"My pleasure, young man." Old Cuddington's voice was high and weak. A new and maddening unsteadiness had lately gripped him now that he could no longer see clearly. He'd ordered that nothing in the rooms of his home be changed, so he made his way about easily—his hands touching here and there for the comforting reassurance of the familiar furnishings. He pointed out to Julian certain handsome family pieces or delicate ornaments that had accompanied him to the New World so long ago. Julian was properly appreciative; there had been many pieces like them at Fairhaven.

He gripped James Cuddington's bony arm and guided him toward the front parlor, where the servants were to bring refreshments. He settled the old man in a chair facing the fireplace and looked around him. The handsome room was resplendent in a fresh coat of yellow paint. He savored its spaciousness, the fading light from the garden bordering on two sides, the handsome arrangement of the furniture and objects of which his host was so proud. And then, as if impelled by a magnet, he turned to look at the portrait over the fireplace. Its impact on him was almost physical.

Julian was beset by dozens of conflicting emotions. The yellow room and everything in it faded. The sound of James' voice as he talked to the servant and the man's soft replies—all faded as Julian's eyes met the gray gaze of the most beautiful woman he'd ever seen. She was magical. The soft skin on her face, arms and the shoulders bared beneath the golden chain with its huge hanging pearl, took on the rosy duskiness of a peach at the height of ripeness. Julian had often seen fruit of just that hue in his father's orchards. The deep cleft in the chin and the winged black brows were distinguishing; the candid gaze seemed almost questioning. *What are you trying to tell me?* He almost blurted the words aloud. His eyes were drawn to that silvery nimbus of hair; he'd never seen hair that color. Surely the artist must have taken liberties? Immediately, he felt himself seemingly reproved and wrenched his gaze away from hers to look at her magnificent setting. It was unlike anything he'd ever seen; even the rooms of the beautiful James River plantations didn't resemble the room in the portrait.

Old James wanted to talk, and Julian tried hard to listen; he could sense the old gentleman's loneliness. Though his eyes continued to wander to the portrait, he answered James' questions soberly and seriously. He accepted the wine and biscuits the servant brought before laying a fire against the chill that always came when the sun went down. At one point his eyes strayed to the portrait again, and once more the sound of his host's voice seemed to vanish. When the old man reached out to touch him questioningly, Julian said, truthfully, "It's the portrait, sir. I've never seen anything like it. The young lady is enchanting . . . quite beautiful."

"Enchantress—that's it!" James Cuddington chuckled. "You've hit it right on the head, young Cushing! She was an enchantress, although I think 'witch' would have been more appropriate during her time. But I've always loved her." He chuckled again as he bit into a biscuit and raised his glass in salute to the portrait. Julian smiled and did the same.

The old man told him the portrait came from London—from Cuddington House in the Strand. How, as a second son, he'd taken his inheritance and some fine family antiques to make his fortune in the New World. There he had hoped to grasp at an elusive independence and power denied him in England, where the laws of primogeniture decreed that everything go to his older brother, Richard. James recalled his earlier years in the Colony. He'd worked hard, he said, setting up a small iron foundry in the hinterlands northeast of Jamestown which had prospered beyond his wildest expectations. He'd made a good life for himself and his family. Now his sons supervised the business; his daughters had married and gone off into the wilderness to rear their own families.

As he spoke, James noticed how Julian's eyes kept returning to the portrait. All his life he'd cherished it despite the "taint"—something concerning witchcraft—that had clung to the sitter. Chloe Cuddington was her name, he told his entranced visitor. The portrait had been a great favorite of his wife's, whose own red-haired beauty had been the equal of the stunning creature in the gilded frame. How well he remembered the room where it had been painted! The fireplace had been there during his youth. The little portrait within a portrait showed the house's exterior. It had mellowed with the years, of course, but the black iron railing was still strong, and his father had had the paint on the coat of arms renewed regularly. It was all as intact in his memory as the day he'd left it forever in 1649—nearly fifty years before—when the house was almost one hundred and thirty years old.

James then explained that he liked to keep abreast of the papers and broadsheets sent to him from his Jamestown office and his London agent. Julian tore his eyes from the portrait and obligingly spent the next hour reading. When he saw weariness descend on his host, he suggested he come the following day at the same time. James smiled and waved his visitor away.

He hoped young Cushing had not been bored, for he'd enjoyed his visit. He sipped his wine while gazing at the portrait with much the same earnestness as Julian had. The room was warm, lit only by the firelight. Chloe gazed at him with those incredible gray eyes; it seemed almost as if she were trying to tell him something. As an old black servant padded in to refill his glass and put another log on the fire, James Cuddington wondered at the portrait's fate. He'd taken extremely good care of it during the years of his stewardship. He didn't want it moldering in the damp of a son's riverfront mansion or at the mercy of careless indifference in a daughter's rustic home far inland. He was still looking at the portrait when the wine and warmth overtook him and he fell asleep. He awakened a half hour later to a deepened dusk within the room and the knowledge that Chloe Cuddington was going home. He was convinced that somehow—in some way he couldn't explain—the decision had been made for him while he napped.

For Julian, the Cuddington house on Francis Street soon became the focal point of his day. Within a week of their first meeting the young boy and the older man were great friends, and it seemed natural to both for Julian to appear in the late afternoon for wine and biscuits. Always they sat in the parlor before a fire, and he'd read James his mail and whatever he thought might interest him in the packet of books and papers. Then they'd talk. Old Cuddington had a remarkable memory and a wide-ranging mind—the result of a lifetime interest in history, art, his English home, thc bcauties of the Continent, which he'd visited in his youth, as well as his earlier years in Virginia. More than once it occurred to Julian that he was getting a far greater education at old Cuddington's elbow than he'd ever acquired in the schoolroom at Fairhaven.

There was another reason for his eagerness to visit the Francis Street house each day. Several times, on his arrival, he'd seen James Cuddington, well wrapped against the chilly weather, dozing in his garden. Putting fingers to lips to warn the servant who opened the door, Julian would go to the parlor, seat himself in old Cuddington's chair and had often as much as half an hour to sit in solitary adoration at Chloe Cuddington's feet.

He never tired of the portrati: at times it seemed he'd stepped into the frame and was there in those beautifully spacious surroundings. He could hear the busy river traffic and, inside, the soft scratching of the palette knife or the whisk of the artist's brush as he committed that remarkable beauty to canvas. What had she been like? Julian's eyes lingered on the folded hands, serene and graceful against the peach velvet of the gown. Had she been complacent? Smug? Dull? Immediately, he felt guilty at his own thoughts. He would then seek her gaze, finding amusement and sympathy there as if she, too, enjoyed the game. He wondered how tall she'd been and how she'd moved. Quickly and impatiently, yet graceful? Or awkwardly—all in a hurry—perhaps even shyly? The straight little shoulders indicated a good carriage, and Julian decided she'd moved . . . *proudly*. Odd he should use that word, for the girl gave no indication of arrogance. Confidence, perhaps, but not arrogance.

Inevitably, after a few moments, he gave it up. The beautiful enigmatic creature had become an obsession. He often dreamed of Chloe at night—dreams he wouldn't have divulged to a living soul. In one, they rode together over green fields which he knew he'd never seen, but which were somehow familiar. Once they'd come upon an old abbey that Julian was certain he'd seen in the books lost in the Fairhaven fire. At other times they were in a large comfortable boat skimming a great river.

The most significant dream was one in which he stood in the midst of a ruin attempting to dispose of something without Chloe Cuddington—whom he sensed was nearby—learning of it. All too soon he would awaken whenever the dream's significance seemed about to be disclosed. Often, it took several moments for the impressions to fade completely, and as he dressed and breakfasted, his mind was leaping ahead to that hour when he would present himself at Francis Street and once more be with his beloved. As ridiculous as it seemed, he'd fallen in love with an improbable beauty in a hundred-and-fifty-year-old painting, and there seemed little he could do about it. Except wait for that session each afternoon so he might gaze on her loveliness again.

James Cuddington recognized the young man's infatuation with the subject of the portrait; he'd suffered a similar malady all his life. He told Julian how, when his inheritance had been parceled out, he'd been prepared to sacrifice it all if only he might have the portrait. Miraculously, it had come his way with little family protest. He well remembered the room where it had been painted—that was old Durham House outside the window. There, during the years before Cuddington House had been built, young Catherine of Aragon, Henry VIII's first queen, had lived as a penniless and often hungry princess. Later, when Chloe had been much at court with her husband, who was a well-known painter, it had been occupied by Sir Walter Raleigh. Cuddington House had looked the same the day he'd left for the New World. He was sure it was still the same now that another Cuddington owned it, although the family spent a great deal of their time at Sparwefeld, a medieval house in Surrey that had been in the family for nearly two hundred years.

Julian was curious to learn of old Cuddington's history. James told him the major family lands had been taken by Henry VIII so that he might build a palace in an area convenient for his hunting. "Seems he didn't have enough palaces already"—the old man sniffed—"and he had to take our holdings, and we'd had them nearly five hundred years!" Cuddington said he could remember his grandfather telling him what distress the king's confiscation had caused, for he'd heard it from *his* father, who'd been a famous painter and had been alive when it happened. Henry had given the Cuddingtons adequate lands elsewhere, of course, but things had never been the same. The king had torn down their ancestral home, swept away Cuddington village, destroyed the church and nearby priory—all to build Nonsuch Palace. James Cuddington's bony hands shook with anger as he retold the story he'd not thought of for years.

Julian was intensely interested at the mention of Nonsuch. He remembered his childhood fancy with the sketch of the palace. How often he'd pored over that print! How familiar he was with the towers, trees, paths and gardens to the front—and how he'd let his imagination roam to whatever might be in the rear! He'd peopled the buildings with kings and queens, dukes and duchesses. Julian wondered—had Chloe Cuddington ever been to Nonsuch? Had she sat with the Virgin Queen in the inner court, being entertained by minstrels and mummers on a soft spring eve? Had she seen it in all its glory, with pennants flying, that echoing trumpet chamber sending rolling silvery notes to every corner of the garden, meadow and fields? If she'd been a favorite of Elizabeth's, she must have. Soon Chloe and Nonsuch were one: enchanting, timeless—and unattainable. Both had one thing in common; they inspired, even as they frustrated.

James Cuddington fanned Julian's interest in his faraway family at Sparwefeld and Cuddington House in the Strand. There were few who wished to listen to an old man's reminiscences, and the boy was obviously enthralled. In talking with Julian, he himself could recapture happy moments he'd thought lost forever. He was amused at the depth of Julian's fascination with the portrait, and soon the idea of using that interest in a way advantageous to them both came to him. He bided his time with the patience of age. Caution was now important; he mustn't scare the young man away.

As for Julian, he tried in every way he knew to reciprocate and please James Cuddington. Not only was the position financially rewarding, but he had an affectionate regard for his employer. Old Cuddington insisted that Julian come to him for the feast of Christmas, and what might have been an intolerably lonely day was spent at Francis Street, where, after an inspiring service at the new Bruton Parish Church, they all shared a great repast. After the meal everyone sang hymns and carols. James' daughter played the pianoforte, and there was dancing to the music of a fiddler from the backcountry whom she'd brought along for the festivities.

Walking home, full of good food and the warmth of his acceptance within the family, Julian wondered how he could repay his employer. Often, as he corrected the students' papers in the cold, bare little room at the back of the college, he'd wonder what he could discuss the following day that would interest James. It was then he remembered Amos Cushing's *Journal* which his cousin had given him, and he carried it on his next visit to Francis Street. James not only had recognized the Cushing name, but had spoken fervently of his admiration for men like old Amos and those faceless others who'd endured the hardships of the founding years. It was all there in the *Journal*—how Amos Cushing, late of the

Isle of Wight, had, in 1606, sailed in the *Susan Constant* for a long, hazardous eighteen-week voyage. He described movingly the trials that beset the settlement established in the spring of 1607 on a flat peninsula on the north side of a river they'd called the James. Amos complained of the boggy soil and the deadly mosquito but praised it for its defensible position—important in the days of the Spanish plunderers. The settlers worked hard, copying the Indian methods of planting corn, beans and squash and building plaited reed dams to trap fish. They'd cut trees, pitched tents, made clapboards, dug gardens and mended nets. Soon a triangular fort, built of rough-hewn timber from the adjacent forest, faced the river. Inside, crude houses and storage bins were erected, and two months after landing the first communion rites of the Church of England were celebrated in the small church that stood at one end of the fort area. Amos had survived the "Starving Time" during the winter of 1609-10 that winnowed out the weak, and those who remained, their faith in God still strong, worked harder than ever. By 1622 Amos had brought his wife and sons from England and erected a little clapboard house, Fairhaven, on his one hundred acres along the James River. He'd died in 1657, only eight years before James Cuddington arrived in the Colony.

Julian remembered those years at Fairhaven before the dreadful fire—his father had added to the house, making it more comfortable and gracious than in old Amos' day. He told James Cuddington his favorite place had been the Cushing wharf, where his black nurse, Tabby, would take him so he might mingle with the blacks who boarded ships for England and the Continent. The sight, sound and smell of the foreign fired Julian's imagination, and he dreamed that one day he, too, might board a great vessel with its brightly colored pennants and discover the water route to the wonders of Cathay and Muscovy.

So while they sipped claret and munched biscuits, Julian read the *Journal*, which he hadn't seen since he was a child. As he turned the pages of strong, slashing handwriting and as the words rolled from his tongue, he felt himself moved with a new respect for his family's founder.

James Cuddington sensed his young companion's feelings. As Julian gathered up the yellowing sheets and stuffed them between two linen boards which made a press, he asked curiously, "Have you ever thought of visiting England, Julian?"

Julian answered truthfully that such a trip might have been possible at the end of his college years had his father remained alive, but it was now out of the question. "But of course, I would like to go, sir," he said. "I think there are a good many Cushings on the Isle of Wight, and since I have no one left here . . ." His face darkened, and he remained silent.

"Well, we won't discuss it anymore, young Cushing." The elder man understood Julian's sadness. He stood up, holding out an arm for his companion's firm grip. "Come again tomorrow, my friend. You've paid me a great honor to read to me from your family's *Journal*. My respect to the Honorable Amos!" He laughed his high, weak laugh and then, changing his mind, indicated his chair. "I think I'll just stay here, Julian, until it's time for my supper. I might even doze a bit."

Moments later when he heard the front door close and the sound of footsteps going past the window toward the picket fence gate, he relaxed in the chair and gazed upward in the direction where he knew the portrait of Chloe Cuddington to be. Though all he could see was a blur, the memory of the incandescent beauty was vivid in his mind. He raised a thin, trembling hand to her and said, "Now patience, m'dear. Patience. You've done your part, and I think you're going to have your way. Just as you always have." He chuckled at his words.

He shifted in the chair, remaining silent for a moment, and then addressed the portrait once more. "Yes, I think it will work, m'dear. If we play our cards right—and if God wills it—I think it will work. I think, m'dear, you're going home." He paused a moment, the old sightless eyes glistening and said sadly, "But oh, Chloe, my darling, how I'm going to miss you. . . ."

Chapter Eight

In the spring of 1700, the twenty-year-old Julian Cushing arrived in England. Sunlit spray made the green coastline luminous as the *Sovereign of the Seas* plowed steadily forward. Julian regarded the ship's unerring approach to the land he'd expected to be bathed in fog as a good augury. He was profoundly relieved the hazardous several-week crossing had ended and had neither the courage nor the stomach to contemplate the return voyage.

He'd been fortunate to have a tiny cabin to himself. Before sailing, he'd insisted that he must, at any cost, have the large wrapped bundle he was taking to England in his own quarters; it could not be consigned to the hold. Space had been found at the aft end, but the cabin had been barely large enough for both man and parcel, and once Julian had taken his necessities from his trunk, it was removed for lack of space.

It hadn't disturbed him, however, for he now had Miss Chloe Cuddington as his solitary traveling companion. How he'd longed to remove the coverings and feast his eyes on her loveliness! Yet he hadn't dared. The portrait had been professionally wrapped by a Jamestown shipper, and Julian knew he could never replace the covering properly. So he amused himself instead with thoughts of Chloe and the England she had known—of visits he'd make to the very house in the Strand where she'd once lived. Perhaps, if he were lucky, he might find other portraits or mementos of this beloved creature who so suddenly and completely had come to dominate his life.

Julian had needed all the amusement—and solace—available. He'd lived most of his life within sight of the James

River and the Atlantic. He couldn't consciously remember learning to sail any more than he could consciously remember learning to swim. The storms and gales that ravaged the Virginia coastline and the killing savagery of the hurricanes that cast ships on the Carolina banks were legendary; they'd been an integral part of his youth. More than once in an emergency, he'd helped workers at the Cushing warehouse load precious bundles of golden tobacco into a ship's hold before inclement weather could reduce it to sodden pulp.

But nothing had prepared him for the cruel ferocity of the mid-Atlantic. Ten days after departure a storm of gigantic proportions had clutched at the *Sovereign* and tossed it from a watery trough to topmost wave tip, plunging its prow sharply into boiling white water. Outside, the wind shrieked along the shuddering timber decks. Julian had sought to quench his fear and allay his heaving stomach by listening intently to the murderous howl and thrust of the wind. In the past he'd heard the Indians' war cry and yell of ugly triumph as they stooped to scalp a screaming victim. He'd heard the pitiful shriek of animals being slaughtered on his father's plantation during the killing season in the autumn. But nothing had prepared him for the brutal noise of the sea wind; it terrified even as it awed. And finally he'd succumbed. After burying his head for hours in the cot's bolster, he had emerged only to sit hunched over a chamber pot and give way to nausea.

Though there were two more storms after the first tempest, Julian had retained a firm grip on his stomach, but fear had not disappeared. He recalled the numerous ships he'd watched sail proudly out of Virginia harbors. Months later their mysterious loss at sea and the disastrous consequences to the merchants who'd underwritten their voyage would be discussed at the noonday meal. No one believed in sea dragons anymore—or those monsters of the deep that might surround a vessel and smash it to bits or breathe fire on its hull, consigning it to a watery grave. Yet everyone had a genuine respect for the havoc Atlantic storms could wreak. At the end of his crossing Julian considered that if he hadn't emerged a victor in his contest with the sea, he had at least held his own.

And the precious parcel had remained unscathed. In his misery Julian had seen it lean and fall precariously from one wall to another; the cabin area was too small for it to smash to the floor. But the Jamestown shipper had done his job well. The thick linen folds that gave the parcel the appearance of a mummy had held strong, and he knew the contents were unharmed.

Once on land, with predictably unsteady legs, he'd wisely made for the nearest inn which the ship's captain had recommended as comfortable, safe and "wi' fine victuals." Refreshed by a good night's sleep and an ample breakfast, he'd arranged for the hire of a litter to carry his boxes and the portrait, as well as a guide to direct him to London. And now, as he emerged from the steamily pungent stables where horses pawed and stamped in the cool morning air, the parcel and boxes were stowed in the litter, and by seven o'clock he was London-bound.

The little group turned northwest, the horses settled down to a rhythmically steady plodding, and Julian had his first opportunity to absorb the beauty of the English countryside so much more green and lush than Virginia. The roads were deeply rutted, muddy and unusually wide. There were tidy fields on each side, some enclosed by hedges and dotted with sheep. Old gnarled trees of elm and oak stood in green parks, and in the distance a forest range stretched for miles. Julian was unaccustomed to such vistas; cleared land in Virginia did not extend for miles! He marveled also at the age of the byres and red-tiled cart sheds—an ancient mill, crumbling and decaying, still turned its wheel and millstones as it had, he was sure, for hundreds of years.

At one point, astonished, he stopped to ask the guide the name of a vast building silhouetted against the horizon. Canterbury Cathedral, the guide replied, the home of old Thomas à Becket, he who'd been done in by the king's men hundreds of years before. Julian recalled the story from his childhood books; Thomas' murder had always brought tears to his eyes. He felt that old sadness now as he shaded his eyes, straining to see more of the tremendous pile before it disappeared from view. A little farther on, he remembered his

Chaucer when, remarking on the many travelers walking in the opposite direction, the guide replied they were now on the "Pilgrim's Way."

Privately, Julian marveled at his own good fortune. Who would have thought, eighteen months ago, that he'd be in this beautiful land? Who would have believed after his appalling family tragedy that fate would send him to the home of that kindly man in Francis Street? Who would have guessed that the same man would tell him of a magical place—could it be very far from where they were?—where he had grown to manhood near a palace, the very name of which seemed as familiar as his own?

And who would have believed that the chance encounter with James Cuddington could result in his discovering the only person who seemed to have a direct and special appeal to him alone? That it was all so implausible did not, for one moment, lessen its importance. Every feature of Chloe Cuddington's face and every line and curve of her body were dear to him. He could imagine how that silvery nimbus of hair would feel under his fingers, how the line of that strong clefted chin might touch his heart if it were lifted to his own, how the curve of breast or hip might feel under his hand. Chloe Cuddington might be, as he repeatedly told himself, only a face and form on canvas, but she was endearingly real and more richly his than he suspected any contemporary ever would be.

Straight ahead, Julian could see a small village. Herons and kingfishers fed in a willow-bordered stream; even the clattering of the horses' hooves on the rough bridge did not disturb them. An ancient church with a square Norman tower brooded protectively over the village center. As the little group rode past, a monk—book in hand—came out the side door and Julian felt the familiar stirring he'd not experienced for years. He remembered his fascination with the tiny figures walking cloistered paths in his childhood books. The monk did not notice them. Quickly he turned a corner of the church, his coarse brown woolen habit swelling out as the breeze caught it, and disappeared.

The horses picked up speed on the wide dry road out of the village, and Julian continued his reverie. How, he thought, would he have appealed to the bewitching Chloe? He had no lofty illusions of his own appearance. He was a slight young man with sandy hair and a normally fair skin tanned and toughened by the sea wind and sun. He had his mother's eyes: startingly blue, clear and alert, and heavily rimmed with dark lashes that had guaranteed many a childhood teasing. The straight, proud nose of all the Cushings—a direct gift from old Amos himself—was above lips that smiled easily or could, just as quickly, compress into a thin, angry or contemptuous line. This mercurial change of expression—sober one moment and humorous the next—often puzzled those meeting the Cushing men for the first time. "He's a changeling, that'un, a blessed changeling," his old nurse, Tabby, had said fondly when he was less than a year old. In all the years of his growing up, she'd never changed her mind.

Julian smiled to himself, recalling old Tab on the morning he'd last seen her. All the Cushing servants, house and field, had been taken by neighbors after the fire. Even in the midst of his sorrow, Julian had argued and finally persuaded a tearful Tab she'd be better off in the home of his mother's dearest friend than accompanying him to Williamsburg. Especially since he didn't know how he was to provide for himself, much less an old black woman who was as dear to him as any family member. When, before his departure, his lawyer had sent a steward with the rent payments from his Jamestown fields, old Tab had bullied the man into letting her ride a mule behind him so she might see her former charge before he departed for the other side of the world and out of her life. They'd had a mutually tearful farewell while Julian had sought to console the thin, shabby old woman. Hoping to cheer her, he'd promised to be back in six months and to bring her a shawl—a shawl such as she'd never seen. He'd been gratified by her wide disarming smile. A flash of old Tab's spirit was clear in her glistening eyes as she said, "And, Master Julie, you make it a bright green taffety one!" Julian had laughed, hugged her skinny frame and promised she'd have the brightest green taffety shawl he could find.

So engrossed had he become in his reminiscences. Julian hadn't noticed the large and impressive homes coming into view. The country had been left behind, and the road had become a broad avenue. They were approaching Southwark, the guide shouted, and Julian knew London Bridge must be straight ahead. Shifting excitedly in his saddle, he joined his companion, who explained they would cross at the horse ferry landing near Lambeth Palace because the bridge would be crowded at that hour. Hoping to hide his disappointment, Julian returned to his place behind the litter horses.

Directly they were out of the mainstream of traffic, riding through the busy little village of Walworth, past Newington Butts and toward Lambeth's marshy fields. Following the guide's pointing finger, Julian could see Lambeth Palace, home of the Archbishops of Canterbury, straight ahead. It was the largest building he'd ever seen. On his journey to London, Julian had realized more than once that life in the New World had not prepared him for his first vision of the Old. Why, the palace gardens that stretched as far as he could see were almost the length of Williamsburg's main street! Acre upon acre of fruit orchards bordered a vast shrubbery maze, while trees of incredible height flung their branches together making a sun-dappled vault below. Shrubs, flowers and herbs bordered neat paths or, in some instances, rioted along walkways. And, over all, the great palace's bells pealed across the marsh, flowing over the small cemetery where crosses and carved statuary reared in eternal remembrance atop turf so vividly green it challenged the senses.

Lambeth Palace had hidden any view of what was beyond, and it wasn't until the guide passed the end of the courtyard wall that Julian could see the Thames. And there, suddenly, spread as far as the eye could see, was the London of the Plantagenets, the Tudors and the Stuarts. Although, he was quick to remember, Mr. Pepys had written that much of it had been destroyed in that ghastly fire some thirty-four years ago. The great red structure of Lambeth he'd thought so grand was now seen in perspective; it was dwarfed by the glorious Abbey almost directly opposite. Nearer the shore was the crumbling splendor of what had once been Westminster Palace; grass more than a foot high grew in the ruins. Churches, many rebuilt since the Great Fire, thrust their spires heavenward, and farther to the northwest, Julian could see scaffolding around the immense building he recognized as St. Paul's.

Once aboard the tiny ferry, Julian kept a careful eye on the litter. Safely on the other side, he followed in the steward's wake and was pleased to see they would pass near the great Abbey. He gazed at the awesome structure now nearly six hundred years old. The afternoon sun touched each brilliant window with pink and rose and lingered in the intricate tracery carvings. Nearby were lush fruit orchards; many of the apple trees were a riot of pink, white and rose, and in an adjacent garden the Abbey monks toiled with barrow and hoe.

Ahead was Palace Yard, once the entry to proud Westminster Palace. How magnificent it must have been! And what personages had lived there! Henry VIII, Henry VII and Edward IV. Wasn't it right here in this vicinity that Edward's queen, the lovely Elizabeth Woodville, had taken sanctuary when she felt her life and family imperiled? Immediately his thoughts of the past were swept away by the swarms of people and animals who thronged in the Yard. Merchants who'd traded in the Abbey's shadow and among the palace ruins now packed their produce away by the fading light, while pie sellers and orange girls cried their wares, hoping not to have to carry them home. The Antelope, a grayish-green building tucked against the side of vast Westminster Hall, made Julian realize how hungry and thirsty he was. Yet the guide gave no indication of stopping but picked his way expertly through the teeming crowd, glancing back often to see that Julian and the litter horses were following.

"Not far now, young sir!" he called back. " 'Tis Cuddington House in the Strand you be wanting? 'Tis straight ahead. We'll go through the gates and past Charing, and you'll be there. That's the palace to the right and the pennants up. That means the king is in his parlorhouse, counting all his money." He grinned at Julian, who laughed and nodded his head. He was too busy trying to see everything to reply. The Whitehall gardens were resplendent in spring dress—green circles, squares, oblongs and the "knots" he recognized from his mother's gardens. The King's Beasts—large painted statues of animals—reared like multicolored chess pieces on striking green cloth. A fountain suddenly spouted water, giving a group of unwary strollers an unexpected shower, and Julian was amused at the shrieking as they fled the spot, shaking their damp clothing.

People were everywhere—in the gardens, the roadway and emerging from the buildings which lined the thoroughfare. A whole procession of horsemen in half armor were riding swiftly toward the Tiltyard straight ahead. They were clad in clothes the like of which he'd never seen before—the men as colorful as the ladies. Brilliant satins and delicate laces were adorned with ribbons and jewels. The ladies carried ornate fans or parasols; the men, gleaming, tapering swords. One dress, the exact shade of peach in which Miss Chloe Cuddington had posed, made Julian wonder: had she, too, walked these paths as a favored companion of old Elizabeth? Had she stood at that wall where espaliered blossoms dotted the gnarled old bark and watched the swift barges on the Thames? Had she passed, as they were now, under the sturdily beautiful black and white gate he knew to have been designed by the renowned Holbein? Certainly she must have, and not only that, she also must have *known* Holbein. . . .

At the end of the broad thoroughfare the guide pointed ahead. They were curving eastward again, following that bend in the river where St. Paul's could be seen in the distance; Julian could even make out the tiny figures moving on the dome scaffolding.

" 'Tis Durham House, there by the river edge," the guide called back, "and opposite is Cuddington House."

It was Durham House all right. Julian recognized the stone and the uniquely shaped red-tile roof from Chloe's portrait. And opposite Durham House was the exact representation of the little picture within the portrait which had so intrigued his fancy. Julian was so excited at seeing Cuddington House at last that he rode ahead, past his guide, oblivious to those in the roadway who darted from his path and called after him, shaking their heads at his impetuousness. Here, too, the sun had touched the faded old stone with pale pink, and it gleamed along the windows through which he could see the familiar green hangings. Here it was, the home of Miss Chloe

Cuddington, its handsome balustraded steps with the family crest in black, gold and red all fresh and new, just as James Cuddington had told him. Old Durham House looked older and badly in need of repair. Farther along the Strand, Julian was shocked at the condition of the great river houses. Old Cuddington had told him of their splendor—of the vast lawns, terraces, galleries, pools, orchards and stairs of houses that had sheltered Essex, Raleigh, Cecil and Richard III. Now many lacked roofs, others were being torn down, and people rummaged in the foundations for stone.

"Be you expected?" The guide's question broke into Julian's musings, and then, not waiting for an answer, he pointed to the front door. "You go in there, young sir. I'll take the horses around to the courtyard in the back."

"Be you expected?" The words lingered in Julian's mind as he crossed the Strand to mount the handsome stone steps. His legs were stiff, his back ached from the unaccustomed long ride, and he was tired, thirsty and hungry. Yet he'd never been happier in his life. Was he expected? He didn't know, nor did he care. He carried letters from James Cuddington, who also, he remembered, had sent word to his London agent of Julian's departure long before he'd actually boarded the *Sovereign*. Yes, he was expected. Quickly, he bounded up the steps and rang the bell beside the massive double doorway. For the first time in months—ever since the devastating loss of his home and parents—Julian felt anticipation, joy and a strange, yet comforting feeling that he had come home.

The bedroom into which the old servant ushered him was larger than any he'd ever seen in a private home. "This is where Mr. James lived when he was at Cuddington House, sir. I remember him well as a boy. My great-grandfather was stableman to old Mr. Richard, Mr. James' great-grandfather—he was the Tudor painter, sir. Mr. James and I were of an age, and we had many happy times in the stable when we were young ones."

"I will tell Mr. Cuddington when I return," Julian replied. "May I have your name so he will remember?"

"Evans, sir . . . just Evans. He'll remember." The old

man chuckled to himself as he removed a cloak from Julian's portmanteau and set to brushing it vigorously. "Many's the time we had out there in back, sir. My grandfather was a bit of a Tatar, sir, if you know what I mean. Very strict and firm, he was,but young Mr. James . . . Well, now, he was a bit of a mischief, and my grandfather excused all sorts of nonsense in him that I'd have been tanned for."

It was difficult to think of James Cuddington as a "bit of a mischief," probably the bane of an old stableman's existence. But it was not difficult to place him in this house. Julian gazed appreciatively at the splendor of the room and the richness of its furnishings. A huge canopied bed occupied one wall, its mulberry hangings festooned with silver trim, and a chair of similar color and decoration was near the mullioned window. Julian sank into it to watch the deepening dusk on the Strand. Wagons, carts, horsemen and solitary men and women hurried in each direction; on the river every boat was occupied. To his left he could see London Bridge, its stately span bordered in lights from the buildings lining the great arch; several pedestrians had also lit torches as they crossed in the twilight.

". . . and no one ever knew it but me, but the reason young Mr. James always insisted on this room was because of Miss Chloe. It was where she used to stay."

The words brought Julian to his feet. "Chloe Cuddington stayed in this room, Evans?" The old man nodded, absorbed in his unpacking. "What else did your young friend James know about her?"

"Oh, now, he—he didn't know anything about her, sir, except what we all did. But he was much smitten, if you'll pardon my saying so, with her looks. That's when her portrait was hanging downstairs in the Hall, sir, over the fireplace it was. I can remember seeing it there as a boy. I understand he has sent it back to us"—the old man allowed himself a moment's reflection—"and it'll be nice to see it again, sir. It was there in the Hall for as long as I can remember. My grandfather could remember the time it was painted, and he said Miss Chloe was even prettier than young Penn made her."

"Your grandfather *knew* the girl in the portrait—actually

knew her?" Julian could barely contain his excitement. Here was something he hadn't expected—a living link with Chloe Cuddington!

"Oh, my, yes, my grandfather knew all the Cuddingtons, sir. Our family has been in their service for generations. Some of the Evanses were living at the family seat in Surrey when the land was taken away."

"And what else did your grandfather tell you about Chloe Cuddington—forgive me, Evans, but I've heard about her from your friend James, and I'm curious about the young lady myself!"

Evans laughed. "I think everyone used to be curious about her, sir. The portrait was quite famous in its time, and she was also a great favorite of Queen Elizabeth. My grandfather knew *her*, too—she used to live in the house across the Strand before she was queen, and he said she rode a horse like a man. Always had an eye for a great horse, he said." Evans joined Julian at the window, adjusting the hanging, and they both gazed a moment at old Durham House, whose stables, even now, abutted on the Strand. "My grandfather always said he thought that nonsense about Miss Chloe being a witch was poppycock—pure poppycock—that the little girl just had a gift of seeing into the future, and there was nothing bewitched about it, that she was just using the senses the good God gave her." He twitched angrily at a hanging. "Don't you believe anyone ever says she was a witch, sir. My grandfather—and my father, too, who heard even more stories than I can remember—said it was Dr. Dee who was more to blame than Miss Chloe. Old Dee was a fair rascal, he was—even hoodwinked the old queen, if you could believe all you heard, sir."

Julian was bewildered. Old Evans' mind seemed to dart from the past to the present. It all seemed like one time to him. "I look forward to seeing the picture again, sir," he told Julian, "and now if you'll excuse me, I'll tell Miss Rosa you're here." Giving the hanging a final twitch, he shuffled from the room, leaving Julian gazing thoughtfully at the river below.

* * *

Half an hour later Evans ushered a freshly shaved and attired Julian into the large room off the Hall. "Miss Rosa will be with you in a moment, Mr. Cushing. Pray be seated there by the fire, sir." The old man bowed his way from the room. Julian thanked him, hoping his hostess would not be too prompt. He was now in the very room where Chloe Cuddington had posed, and it looked as if she had only stepped out for a moment.

Originally, he suspected, the ground floor of Cuddington House had been one Great Hall. Now there were two or three rooms, each of good size, but this particular area had been left as it was in the portrait. The fireplace, faced with Sienese marble, was the same, and so was the vivid Oriental carpet. The window hangings, if not the original, had been duplicated in the same color. Somewhere—somewhere—there had to be a chair. He looked around, and there, in a corner near the window that showed the edge of Durham House, he found it. It was larger than he'd expected—the artist undoubtedly had painted it smaller so as not to overwhelm the sitter. It was deeply carved, and its gilt paint had recently been renewed. Julian took up a stance about where the artist would have placed his easel and felt a shiver go through him. It was uncanny. It was the room of the portrait—all that was missing was the glowing beauty sitting in the chair and the portrait of the outside of Cuddington House over the fireplace. That, old James Cuddington had told him, had been a figment of the artist's imagination. The space above the fireplace was empty, for it was where the completed portrait of Chloe had been hung until James had taken it across the sea more than fifty years before.

"Mr. Cushing, forgive me for keeping you waiting! You are most welcome, sir! My uncle has written about you!"

Julian turned, bowing deeply and was impressed by the graceful curtsy performed by Rosa Cuddington. "Madam, you are most kind to receive me," he murmured as he helped her to her feet.

Rosa Cuddington bore no resemblance to her uncle James. She was a tiny woman, past the first flush of youth, yet still nicely rounded and curved. The low, square neckline of her dress thrust her breasts upward in a fashion which had not as yet reached Virginia. There was paint on her lips, Julian was certain, and the small black mark on her chin was surely not real. The light-brown hair, curled and piled high, was her own and adorned with ribbons the same blue as the dress that billowed out in front like a small ship under sail. Her smile was quick and bright, and her eyes—gray as his Chloe's, but smaller and differently shaped—were kind. Instantly Julian was at ease and found he liked this Cuddington woman. She was not a descendant of his Chloe, but she fitted into the family history somewhere, and it would be rewarding in the days ahead to find out where.

The door opened, and another servant, younger and stronger than Evans, entered with the wrapped portrait. Julian felt a warm excitement and anticipation; soon he'd see that beloved face again. His voice trembled when he spoke. "Ah, this is it, madam. This is the gift your uncle has honored me by asking that I return it to the family. It is a portrait of an ancestress of yours, I believe. It is very lovely."

The servant carefully cut the wrappings. "Save them, Temple," Rosa Cuddington advised. She turned, smiling, to Julian. "That is fine quality for the Colonies, Mr. Cushing. Uncle James had written he was having his treasure properly prepared for its journey. I've never seen the fabled Chloe Cuddington, for the portrait was gone before I was born. Pray be seated, sir. I expect you're anxious to see if it has survived the voyage well."

The question remained unanswered, for the wrappings had fallen, and the servant turned it in the direction of his mistress. Julian heard her quick intake of breath. "Ah! How beautiful—how beautiful!"

He himself was gratified. If anything, it looked even more remarkable here in its home surroundings than it had in Virginia. The color seemed brighter and fresher—he suspected it was because of the similar light in which it had been painted. As the servant turned the frame slightly one way and another, Chloe gazed with eternal grace on the scene she had known so well. "Ah, yes, it is very beautiful." Rosa went to examine it more closely. "It is everything I had expected and—something more." She smiled with secret amusement. "Hang it over the fireplace, Temple; that's where it belongs."

Climbing onto a small stool, the servant hoisted the heavy frame easily and hung it in its original setting. He stepped back, to judge if it hung properly, and his expression, deferential and aloof, changed to one of astonishment. His mistress joined him, and the two continued to gaze at the portrait. "Beautiful," she murmured again. "An amazing likeness, eh, Temple? Amazing." Seemingly, the two had forgotten Julian.

"Likeness, madam?" He joined them at the fireplace. "It *is* beautiful, is it not? You mention likeness—a likeness of whom, pray?"

Instantly, his hostess' face, under its delicate paint, was suffused with pink. She hesitated a moment and then, laughing lightly, whipped a fan from her billowing skirt and fanned herself rapidly. "Why, it's a likeness of—of—of Miss Chloe Cuddington, sir!" She laughed again, and Temple joined her. They seemingly shared a secret, and Julian felt annoyed. Obviously, it was a likeness of Miss Chloe Cuddington. Did they think their visitor from the Colonies was daft?

During the next half hour, as Julian talked of his journey, old Evans brought a tray of refreshments. After placing it in front of his mistress, he stopped at the fireplace and gazed for several moments at the portrait. Julian noticed the old man's eyes were glistening. Then, with a heavy sigh, he silently left the room.

Rosa Cuddington served tea—a new drink, she told Julian, that was enjoying a great vogue. He liked the hot brew and ate several of the tiny seedcakes she pressed on him. He remembered the many hours he'd spent with James Cuddington, drinking wine and munching biscuits, gazing at the glorious portrait which at last hung in its rightful place. As he murmured polite replies to Rosa's gracious inquiries, his gaze often met Chloe's and for the first time he felt sadness. *She has come home*, he thought. *I've done as I was asked, but now I've lost her.* The more he dwelled on it, the more depressed he felt. Once he returned to Virginia, she would be gone from his life forever.

Rosa was watching him closely. "And you, sir," she said, "you seem much taken with the infamous Chloe, as I have heard her called. She was quite a charmer in her day, y'know, and, some say, something of a witch." She stared at the picture. "Although I must say, I don't think she looks like a witch, d'you?"

"No, I don't think she was a witch. But pray, madam, tell me about her. I've heard bits and pieces of her story, but not the whole." Julian didn't want to appear too eager. Rosa Cuddington was, he could see, a very perceptive woman; he didn't want his feelings to be apparent. How silly she'd think him to have fallen in love with a girl in a picture!

"Well, she was the daughter, you know, of Sir Richard Cuddington, who was lord of the manor of Cuddington village in Surrey. There was a great deal of land—thousands of acres. Pity we don't have some of it today! There was a manor house and proper village and several tenant farms, of course. But the king took it all."

"Henry the Eighth," Julian volunteered. "James Cuddington told me about that."

"Of course, it was nearer his time than mine," Rosa replied, setting down her teacup. "I may not have all the facts properly, Mr. Cushing, but as I understand it, the king took all the Cuddington land, including a church and priory, which he later destroyed in order to build Nonsuch Palace—have you heard of Nonsuch, sir?"

"Oh yes!" Julian's enthusiasm mounted. "I've seen pictures and sketches of it, Miss Cuddington. It was very beautiful."

"It may have been beautiful, but obviously the Cuddingtons of that time had little enthusiasm for it—which I am sure you can understand. Oh, they were polite enough about it—what else *could* they do? The king gave them land and a manor house of equal importance and value in Suffolk, and materially, they suffered no hardship—but that, of course, did not compensate for their emotional distress, particularly Chloe Cuddington's."

"Why 'particularly Chloe Cuddington's'?"

"Chloe was Sir Richard's only child—his heiress—and since his holdings were vast, she would have been very rich.

But aside from the value of the lands for which, supposedly, the property in Suffolk was compensation, she had a great pride in her Surrey heritage. Cuddingtons had been on that land for more than five hundred years. Chloe loved the outdoors. She could ride like the wind, took a great interest in the running of the farms and was a proper scholar at a time when most women in her position stuck to their needlework and childbearing."

Rosa Cuddington poured Julian another cup of tea and continued. "The family story goes that when the king announced he'd take the land, Chloe Cuddington was outraged. She wanted no part of Suffolk—Surrey was her home. She was so angry and hurt she wrangled the king's commissioners into letting one house, Sparwefeld, an old gardener's cottage, be saved. She was to have life tenancy, after which it would revert to the crown. And it was at Sparwefeld that she seems to have fallen into all that trouble."

"What kind of trouble?" Julian's heart was racing. He realized once more just how little he really knew of his beloved. Rosa Cuddington's words only stimulated his interest.

"I'm afraid it all gets rather murky, here, Mr. Cushing." Rosa laughed—a pleasant, tinkling sound. "One never knows how much is rumor or fact. I don't know myself what to believe. However, there is a family legend that Chloe Cuddington was connected with something called the Lure—no, don't ask me what it was because I don't know. Neither does anyone else. The only other people who knew were Dr. Dee, who was a famous astrologer during the time of Elizabeth, and a monk whose name was Thomas. He lived at Merton Priory near the village of Cuddington."

"A monk named Thomas," Julian pondered, repeating the words and then looking at the portrait. "What on earth would Chloe Cuddington have had to do with a monk?"

"That's one of the mysteries I wish I could explain." Rosa sighed, taking Julian's cup and pushing the tea tray toward Temple, who had come into the room. "I dearly wish I knew. As a child, we used to play games—to try to figure it all out."

"What else is known of the Lure?"

"The Lure was something that was buried at Nonsuch

Palace—it would have had to been buried *before* the palace was completely built, because the tragedy took place just before Chloe Cuddington was twenty-one."

"Tragedy? What tragedy? Was this when she was accused of being a witch?"

"I believe so. The girl seems to have had some unusual knowledge of things that were going to happen. Somehow she knew the Lure was buried in the foundations of Nonsuch Palace. The knowledge was shared by a minor servant at the Cuddington manor house who had, on several occasions, accosted the girl and put her in what I think was a most compromising situation, if you know what I mean. . . ." Her voice trailed off, and Julian was amused to see the pink flood her features again. He said nothing, not wishing to heighten her embarrassment. At the same time he wondered how his Chloe had dealt with the "compromising situation."

"Well, sir, eventually, the monk Thomas and this servant had quite a falling-out. Probably over the girl. She and Thomas had an odd relationship, never one properly explained to me, because there was no explanation for it. The two were close—too close for a young girl and a monk to be, if you'll pardon my saying so, Mr. Cushing. And that didn't help her reputation either, I'm afraid. The family moved soon after to Suffolk, and it was about that time that various things came out about her—Chloe, I mean. Witnesses spoke of things she'd predicted coming true and of things she'd described as of the future. Again and again she was asked about the Lure and always refused to answer. And of course, people figured the Lure was a curse of some sort that only a witch would know about. Shortly afterwards she married Bartholomew Penn and came here to stay with James Cuddington—your friend James' great-grandfather. They seemed to have been very happy. They moved in court circles, and she was a great favorite of Queen Elizabeth. Penn was almost as famous as Holbein. When city and court life palled, they went to the little house she got from the king's commissioners—the little place called Sparwefeld."

"Your uncle James in Williamsburg has told me about Sparwefeld, Miss Cuddington, and that's a fascinating story about your ancestress. After hearing it, I can only say that

Chloe Cuddington must have been a most unusual young lady."

"Just as she has those unusual looks—that's a family tradition too, y'know. That whitish hair and the large dark eyes, that clefted chin—it's a resemblance that surfaces every once in a while. Usually with a first daughter, one who's inevitably named Chloe."

Julian had gone to gaze more closely at the portrait. The sitter's eyes seemed to bore into his; he could amost feel their warmth and the soft sound of breathing. "Such beauty and grace," he murmured.

"You are greatly taken with my ancestress!" His hostess smiled and joined him at the fireplace. "Well, I don't blame you. Her reputation has survived for so long, she must have been unusually clever as well as beautiful." Julian noticed Rosa Cuddington regarding him shrewdly. He must not make a fool of himself over the portrait in her presence. What would that kindly soul who had received him so graciously think if she realized he'd fallen in love with a creature dead for over one hundred and fifty years?

He was thankful when the door opened and Evans announced supper was ready. Proffering his arm to his hostess in what he hoped was the proper manner, he accompanied her from the room, noting that the eyes of the girl in the portrait—back in her home after fifty years—seemed to follow their departure.

Chapter Nine

The following morning before the sun was at its highest, a small cavalcade turned off the London Road into the little medieval town of Ewell. It reminded Julian of the English villages seen in his childhood books. Here was the Market House and Cross, the same black and white timbered houses, with a butcher's stall next to an ironmonger's shop. The King's Head, the village inn, was colorful with window boxes of heartsease and herbs. Ahead the square teemed with animals and people. It was Market Day, and even at a distance the sound of the livestock and the farmers' cries could be heard.

Rosa Cuddington urged her stableman toward the nearest road away from the village center. Following a small, clear stream shaded by elm trees, the group soon reached a wide bridle road lined with hedges over which Julian could see cherry trees in full blossom. All during the journey south, as each turn in the road revealed England's sylvan splendor, Julian had longed for his sketch pad. Never had he seen anything like the soft rolling hillocks and copses, the sweeping meadows, filled now with buttercups, or the raw beauty of freshly plowed land. The flat country, the tidal marshes and great black forests of Virginia were so different. Time and again Rosa pointed out an especially magnificent view toward the Banstead Downs where the earth's beauty was rivaled by the delicate fleeciness of startling white clouds in an almost azure sky.

As they left Ewell behind, she pointed out certain features of the land. Arriving at four crossroads, she said, "We think this is about where Cuddington village once stood, Mr. Cushing. We know the church was leveled and Nonsuch

Palace built on its site, but the manor house and village were some distance away. Local history has placed the village here—we know it was near the crossroads, and several wells belonging to the manor house and its outbuildings have been discovered nearby."

"Then we're near Nonsuch!" Julian felt an intense twinge of excitement and anticipation.

"Indeed we are," his companion replied, swiveling around in her saddle and pointing to a hollow to their left. "Over there is a site even older than Nonsuch. A Ewell man who worked at the palace came this way one evening to visit a sick cow on his farm. It was well past midnight, and he was tired. Coming to just over the hedge there, he sat on a stile to rest. Down in the hollow, he saw a funeral taking place. The people were dressed strangely, at least to the cowman's eyes. As he watched, he remembered the legend that there had once been a church in the dell. He was too frightened to go the rest of the way and returned to the palace. Later someone who heard the story looked up Ewell's history in a book and found there'd been a church in that dell in the time of the Romans."

Julian was about to remark on the curious tale when Rosa pointed to a large circular grove, heavily wooded and dominated by a great elm—the largest he'd ever seen. Its limbs were broken, and its girth was riddled with a sickness that had left it hollow in spots. Yet its top branches were in full leaf. "That's Queen Elizabeth's Elm," his companion explained. Seeing Julian's skeptical look, she smiled and said, "It really is, Mr. Cushing. There's where the queen used to stand and shoot deer, for this was once open land with forests on all sides. Once Nonsuch was built, much of the land was made into deer parks. Just beyond that is a canal called Diana's Dike—the mythological Diana was a huntress, you know, and there were statues of Diana and Actaeon around here somewhere. Diana's Dike was once a fishpond for the old manor house at Cuddington which was incorporated into Nonsuch. Local legend has it that the queen had a marble bathhouse built there." She laughed. "I don't know about the bathhouse, but there's no doubt that's where she used to hunt. Fifty years ago there were local men alive who remembered—when they were very young—seeing her ride through

Ewell from Nonsuch to take up her position there. That's why the tree has never been cut down."

As they rode on, Julian blessed the good fortune that would enable him to see Nonsuch with such a knowledgeable guide. The previous evening he'd told Rosa of his deep interest in the palace and how he'd once talked with a Mr. Percy, who'd spent a night at Nonsuch.

"Well, there's still a great deal left, Mr. Cushing," Rosa had replied, "and coming this far, you should see it." His hostess, he'd found, was not only perceptive, but very decisive. No sooner had he mentioned the ruins than she'd made plans for an early departure. During the pleasant ride south she'd told Julian further bits of the palace's history.

Henry VIII apparently had died shortly after Nonsuch was completed. Edward VI, his young son, had visited there often during the short years of his reign. But when his sister, Mary Tudor, came to the throne, she had no use for it. Mary disliked hunting and considered the palace an extravagant waste. Rosa, however, felt Mary hated Nonsuch because the king had decided to build it when he was married to Anne Boleyn, who'd usurped Mary's mother, Catherine of Aragon, as queen. Mary sold Nonsuch to Henry Fitzalan, the Earl of Arundel, for more than four hundred pounds and the exchange of properties more to her liking.

Arundel and his heir, John, Lord Lumley, had further embellished the palace, and after Mary's death Queen Elizabeth repurchased it from the aging Lumley. The years of "Gloriana's" reign, said Rosa, were Nonsuch's golden age, for Elizabeth loved the place. She enjoyed hunting and entertaining foreign dignitaries, and the palace and grounds were ideal for both. At her death, in 1603, Nonsuch lost its greatest protector. Her successor, James I, used it occasionally for hunting and hawking, and later his son, the martyred Charles I, and his queen—"that monkey-faced Henrietta," Rosa called her—often stayed at Nonsuch. When Charles was beheaded, it was, in effect, the end of Royal Nonsuch, and kings and queens no longer walked its halls and rode in its vast parks. The martyred king's successor, Charles II, had little use for the place. He preferred the London scene, where the court and mistresses who provided for his dissipations were more conveniently at hand. It was one of Charles' mistresses who had provided literally for Nonsuch's downfall. In 1670 the king gave the palace to Barbara Villiers, the notorious Countess Castlemaine and Duchess of Cleveland, by whom he'd had several illegitimate children. Lady Castlemaine needed ready cash to pay her gambling debts, and she proceeded to lease or sell hunting, grazing and park rights. As she rarely visited Nonsuch, those who lived or were employed there zealously plundered it during the next few years. Several small buildings were destroyed, and the materials sold; even the soil in the park was for sale. In 1682 demolition started in earnest. Everything—the magnificent carvings, the lead, stone, wooden timbers—was sold. Barbara Villiers was an old woman now, said Rosa, still living somewhere on the Continent. She had never, as far as anyone knew, seen the wanton destruction of the proud towers and turrets for which she was responsible.

"A sad tale . . ." Julian sighed, depressed at the ease with which a noble palace might vanish forever.

They rode on in silence until Rosa pointed straight ahead. "And now, Mr. Cushing, we're almost there. Sparwefeld is just at the end of this wall. You can always tell when you're near because of the birds. I think the little house must have got its name from the sparrows!"

It was then Julian noticed the great grove of lime trees across the road—trees alive with birds. The flat field had once been farmland, but now sheep nibbled at the grass as birds swooped down, singly and in pairs, to peck in the earth and then disappear into the trees. They sat in great numbers along the red-brick wall which enclosed a courtyard. Gesturing toward them, Rosa laughed. "They've been here forever. They can be a nuisance, too, Ah, here we are!"

A pleasant scene greeted the travelers as they rounded the wall's corners. What Rosa had called "the little house" was larger than Julian had expected. Already more than two hundred years old, it had obviously been rebuilt, expanded and maintained with loving care. The center portion, probably the original, was square with a steep thatched roof, and at each end, side wings extended at right angles. At the end of one was an old well almost obscured by a clump of white lilacs, while a dovecote, large and populous, stood at the other end. Mature shrubs girdled the building, softening its outline; their flowers were striking against the pale washed stone. The sun, high now, gave each sparkling window a delicate radiance, emphasizing the solid square substance of what had once been a humble cottage.

Lawns of the vivid green that Julian still felt were unreal were on each side of the long, straight cobbled path where thyme grew between the stones. Huge leafy trees dotted the far border and, to the right, hung over another path which led to an arbor; it held something that looked oddly like a sign in the shape of a domino. He was still musing on the unlikely sign when the horses stopped at the entrance. The front door—one massive piece of heavily carved wood studded with nails—swung open, and a servant emerged. Rosa turned to Julian as she removed her riding gloves. "And now, Mr. Cushing . . . welcome to Sparwefeld! It's not grand, as you can see! Not as grand as Sir Richard's old manor house. That was around to the rear. I'll show you the site later on. But we all cherish this little place. It's all we have left in Surrey. Do come inside, sir. You will want some rest and refreshment."

During the next hour Julian wandered, bemused, through Sparwefeld's rooms. They were plain, unadorned by the tapestries, mirrors and lush carpets so evident at Cuddington House. There was one large "receiving room," as Rosa called it, and here were heavy Tudor pieces, probably left from the manor house and given to Chloe for her "little house" before her family went to their new home in Suffolk. There was a large table, black with age, similar to one Julian had seen in the governor's house in Jamestown. At one end, shelves carved out of the thick stone walls held books, pottery figures and rows of candlesticks, probably for use at bedtime. Bowls of spring flowers were placed around the room—bright accents against the stark white walls.

At the opposite end was a magnificent fieldstone fireplace; on each side its walls were almost covered with handsome portraits. Rosa led him to them.

"These are the portraits by Bartholomew Penn," she said. "We are very proud of them. He was a master himself, as you can see."

Julian felt a twinge of jealousy as he was confronted by the almost profligate display of talent of the man who'd won Chloe's love and become her husband. Several were outdoor scenes, reminiscent of the rolling meadows they'd passed that morning. Another was of a river, shadowed by stands of giant elm, with sunlight filtering through the leafy branches. "We think Bartholomew painted these so his wife would always have a visual remembrance of her childhood home," explained Rosa. "These were parts of the land upon which Nonsuch was built."

The remaining portraits were of Elizabethan courtiers or, possibly, friends and neighbors. Rosa didn't know, for the artist hadn't labeled them. "Many were bought by my family over the years as they came on the market," she said. "They belonged to families who later sold them for one reason or another. There are still many others we haven't been able to acquire."

These were the people who'd undoubtedly known Bartholomew and Chloe well. Their faces—wary, friendly, arrogant or merely studious—were supremely executed. And each fold of satin, lace, each sparkle of jewel, ribbon or crest was minutely rendered. Penn had been supremely gifted.

One portrait, of a boy of twelve or thirteen, was especially interesting; Julian felt himself drawn to it immediately. The child sat in front of the same Sienese marble fireplace in Cuddington House that appeared in Chloe's portrait. A paint-box was on the floor, and the small canvas was stretched tautly on his knee. The artist had portrayed the child with an almost startled expression; he appeared to have looked up for a moment from his work. It was innocent and charming; the boy's face was especially appealing with its fair coloring, the long hair sweeping across his brow and resting on the lace collar of his red jacket. Watching him, Rosa explained, "Richard Cuddington, sir. That was your James Cuddington's great-grandfather. He became a very famous Tudor painter. He was an especial favorite of your Chloe's."

A servant came to show Julian to his room. After bowing to his hostess, he followed the man up a short flight of stairs, hoping the view from his window might show the famous Nonsuch ruins. As he walked along the short corridor, he was conscious once more of the feeling he'd experienced at Cuddington House—a feeling of joy and anticipation and the unusual certainty that once more he'd come home.

There were no ruins to be seen from his window—only that lovely arbor. Beyond the walls, myriad birds swooped in great curving arcs toward open fields. To his left was a large flat area and in its middle the outline of what had been a circular path. At one side of the path was a magnificently gnarled old beech and, beneath it, the rotting remains of a bench upon which several birds alighted before returning to their leafy perches. Clumps of lilacs and rhododendrons bordered on an area that seemed to contain a small maze. Julian realized the cleared site was where the old Cuddington manor house had probably stood. Then he was not far from Nonsuch.

The thought made him hurry through his toilette. Quickly, he changed from his riding clothes, donning the comfortable hose, shirt and doublet the servant laid out. He was about to leave when suddenly the high, tinkling laughter of his hostess could be heard down the hall. Others joined her, and in the general rush of conversation which followed, he clearly heard the name "Chloe" several times. Were they discussing the portrait? Seemingly, there were others in the house whom he hadn't met. Somewhere a door slammed, and he heard soft footsteps running down the stairs as someone urged, "Hurry!"—and again the high gust of laughter as another door closed. Julian felt uncomfortable. Somehow the laughter seemed directed at him. Soon came a discreet knock on the door, and the servant announced that his hostess and a simple meal were awaiting him below.

It was a pleasant affair, with Rosa exerting every effort to make Julian feel at home. "Mr. Cushing, sir, you have been so kind to take such an interest in our family. My Uncle James has written of you with great affection. I hope you'll stay at Sparwefeld—and at Cuddington House, too—as long as you like, and you must feel perfectly free to do whatever you wish. The servants and I will be happy to help whenever we can."

Julian was touched. As Rosa spoke, his apprehension disappeared. She wore a simple gown of cream-colored muslin; a white fichu demurely hid her décolletage. She had disdained any paint, as well as the black mark on her chin. Her hair, curly but loose, was pulled back from her face with a plain black velvet ribbon. The Rosa at Sparwefeld was very different from the Rosa of Cuddington House in the Strand. Again, Julian was reminded of the simplicity of his colonial heritage. His mother might have changed her dress in the late afternoon from the one she'd worn earlier in the day, but essentially her appearance remained the same. The Old World apparently did things differently. Yet he had to admit its unpredictability added a tone and sparkle that was new and exciting.

"Madam, you are very kind and I thank you for your thoughtfulness. I am very eager to see everything at Sparwefeld—especially the Nonsuch ruins. Perhaps you would join me?"

"Ah, Mr. Cushing, I am afraid I must disappoint you. There's much for me to attend to here with the servants, and then I shall have a short rest. But you, sir, pray take a horse if you please and ask any stableman to point you in the right direction. But my advice would be for you to walk. It isn't far, and a horse can be a nuisance at the ruins; sometimes they wander off and stumble in the loose foundations. Yes, I think you should walk." She pointed to the window looking out on the circular path. "That's where the old Cuddington manor house was. Walk past the tree with the bench and around the corner of the wall. Keep straight to the path, and you come to the ruins. Now, sir, there you are—pray be off and have a good visit! I think you will find many things little changed." She smiled again and waved him away.

Filled with anticipation and feeling foolishly happy and free, Julian did as she suggested. He passed through the pleasant grounds, around the wall and found the circular path. This must be the very route his Chloe had taken dozens of times. She'd been born in a handsome house very near those lilacs and rhododendrons. Had she sat on that rotting bench under the tree where the birds fluttered in protest as he walked beneath? Had she run along this path as a child to greet her parents returning from Market Day in Ewell? Had she ridden that long green field, fearlessly jumping those hedges and leaping across that stream?

He was at Nonsuch almost before he knew it. A few low-lying heaps of rubble in which a man was loading stone into a cart indicated he must be near. A courtyard with grass growing between the cobbles signified the heap was all that remained of what had once been the stables. A large hedge, thick and unkempt, separated it from the palace. And as Julian stepped through an opening in the dense shrubbery, he had his first view of what remained of Royal Nonsuch after Barbara Villers had finished with it.

He had approached it from the southwest, and the remains of one of the great octagonal structures thrust about three feet aboveground; there was still some indication of its magnificent frescoes. The enclosing wall had been dismantled except in spots; inside was a ruinous assortment of broken stone and glass, heaps of rubble, cobblestone and broken brick, some overgrown with grass and mold. Other piles seemed newly disturbed—probably taken by villagers to repair their cottages and farms. In the center of what he knew to be the inner court was a large plinth, and around it the broken remains of cobblestones lay in small dusty fragments. Ahead, several steps down—the site of the archway to the royal apartments where the trumpets' sound was so magnified—was the outer court. The wall to the east abutted on the kitchen gardens, and Julian was touched to see clumps of herbs and wild flowers growing amid the overwhelming rubble.

The sun had climbed much higher—it was becoming increasingly warm. He turned toward where he thought Diana's Dike and the statue of the goddess had stood. There he'd plan a systematic, yet leisurely exploration. He'd see a little each day, examining everything thoroughly so that once he was back in Virginia, his memory would still be fresh and true. As he walked along, powdery swirls of dust, disturbed by his steps, rose about him and he felt a momentary sadness. Pausing to glance around, he thought, what beauty and elegance had once graced this spot! What magnificence now lay in ruins. . . .

As he approached what remained of the old wall that bordered on the "wilderness" where kings had kept aviaries and wild animals among the great overhanging trees, he heard an odd scraping sound. It came from just beyond the wall, and curious, Julian walked in that direction. The sound grew louder as he approached. Someone must be dragging an especially large stone toward a barrow. Quickly he rounded the wall and then stopped—thunderstruck—by what he saw.

Only a few yards away a young girl with her back to him was pulling an easel over a rubble-strewn path. Julian's first inclination was to rush and offer help. Yet he was powerless to do so. There was something familiar about the girl. She was slight, dressed in a simple pale-yellow gown, and a large-brimmed hat sat lightly on her hair. *That hair.* That was it. Of whitish silver, it curled just along the nape of her slim neck. The girl seemed in no hurry; she dragged the easel carefully and with such assurance Julian knew she'd done it many times before. Finally in place, she wiped her sweating hands on her dress, turned and faced him head-on.

He felt as if someone had given him a sharp blow directly in the pit of the stomach. The girl was identical to the girl in the portrait; her features were a living duplicate. Only her hair was shorter. She gazed at him with large gray eyes over which the winged black brows were raised in curious questioning. Julian was speechless. He raised a hand in disbelief, feeling he should rub his eyes to be certain he was not seeing a mirage, yet knowing he'd look foolish if he did. As he waited, immobile, she advanced a few steps. The strong clefted chin was raised almost as if in challenge.

"Sir?" Her voice was low and soft, yet firm and with great self-confidence. Julian wanted to laugh aloud. It fitted the girl of the portrait so completely. The odd thought ran through his head: it almost seems as though she owns this place and resents my intrusion! She'd been about to paint; now he'd appeared on the scene, and she was probably wondering how to get rid of him.

Recovering his poise, though still shaken inside, Julian bowed deeply. "My apologies, mistress. I'm sorry if I startled you. My name is Julian Cushing, and I come from Virginia. I'm staying with friends quite nearby." He waved in the direction of Sparwefeld. Then, lamely: "This is my first visit to Nonsuch. I'm very desirous of seeing the ruins, for I've seen a picture of the palace as it once was."

The girl's expression softened, and the challenging look left her face. *She seems almost protective of this place*, Julian thought. Suddenly, she smiled, and all misgiving left him. So familiar was he with Chloe Cuddington's features in repose—with that deep, sweet gaze—that he was completely unprepared for *this* girl's sunny and carefree smile. Her strong white teeth gleamed in the shadow cast by the brimmed hat. There was humor and sparkle in the gray eyes; even the strong chin lost its belligerency. Suddenly, she swept him a deep curtsy and said, "You are most welcome to Nonsuch, Mr. Cushing." Rising, she clasped her hands in front and said, "I am Chloe Cuddington, sir, and I think you must be staying with my Aunt Rosa at Sparwefeld. She was naughty not to let me know. I think it must have been meant as a surprise! She said nothing when I saw her this morning after her arrival, and I left shortly to paint my tree at Nonsuch—she was in such a hurry to get me out of the house!" She smiled again and, with mock exasperation, said, "Yes, it was very naughty of Aunt Rosa, and I shall tell her so when I return!"

Julian now understood the sounds he'd heard. Chloe had probably come home after their arrival; likely she'd been out for an early ride, and Rosa—his perceptive, decisive Rosa—had decided to surprise them both! She'd urged him to visit Nonsuch when she knew her niece would be there. "You will find things little changed," she'd laughed. Now he more than ever appreciated her wit. He also understood the astonishment she and the servant, Temple, had shown when they'd seen the portrait of the original Chloe at Cuddington House. "An amazing likeness," he remembered her words. But she hadn't lied. When asked, "A likeness to whom?" she had instantly replied, "Why a likeness to—to—to Miss Chloe Cuddington, sir!"

Julian agreed their meeting was surely meant to be a surprise. Certainly old James Cuddington had had a part in it too. Doubtless he'd written his great-niece Rosa that his young friend, Julian, was showing all the youthful love pangs that had consumed numerous others on seeing the portrait of the infamous Chloe Cuddington. Possibly Rosa had written him of the peculiar physiological identity that had surfaced once more, and since Julian had agreed to return the portrait, James had kept secret the knowledge that there was another Chloe waiting at the end of his journey.

Chloe continued speaking, rescuing Julian from the immediate necessity of making any sense in his reply. He was grateful. He needed time to absorb the fact that here were the face and form of the girl who'd haunted his dreams for months. Now she was walking beside him, lovely and wholly unaffected. Each turn of her head, each glance and smile were pure joy; he almost felt as if a spell had been cast on him. She was taller than he'd envisioned Chloe Cuddington, with an agile and slim figure, undoubtedly the product of hours in the saddle. Yet she moved gracefully, and her bearing was—he sought the word—*proud*. Her fingers were long and supple; they gave him a clue and the courage to question her.

"You paint, mistress? That easel is heavy, but you handle it with great assurance."

"Ah, well, Mr. Cushing"—she sighed—"I try. Yes, I paint, but it is very frustrating at times, sir. I am—or was—going to paint that tree over there." She pointed to a graceful twisted old oak that hung partly over the crumbling wall, while its lower branches swept the ground. "I'm afraid the sun is too high now."

Julian apologized. "Mistress, I feel I have kept you from your work. Pray do forgive me. It is because I've been so spellbound by this magical place." He indicated the ruins. "I have longed to see it since I was a child. I hadn't expected so much to be left, yet I confess to great sadness in seeing such devastation."

"I agree, sir. . . ." Chloe paused reflectively, following his gaze. "I have often felt the same. There are men in the village who remember Nonsuch when it was all standing, and I can tell you, Mr. Cushing, it must have been a proud sight! Some of them who know Aunt Rosa well have escorted me about, telling me what everything was—sometimes it's easy to tell, sometimes not so easy. But in just a few years, much of it has disappeared. The poor of Ewell come here and take what they need for their houses. I can't say I blame them, but it does make for further destruction."

Suddenly, she brightened. "Sir, would you like to have what I call my Grand Tour? May I escort you on your first visit to Royal Nonsuch?" She laughed joyously, a high, tinkling laugh like her Aunt Rosa's, clasping her hands excitedly. "Now, Julian Cushing from Virginia, will you walk where kings and queens have walked? Are you ready to see Nonsuch as it was? Will you be able to visualize the proud towers with pennants flying and the fountain with water spouting high towards the sky? Will you be able to feel its magic and see how splendid it was with all the fine people in their court dress? Tell me, Mr. Cushing—can you see in your mind as well as with your eyes?"

Julian was dazzled by Chloe's exuberance; he'd never met anyone quite like her. His confidence had returned, and with it an unusual feeling that this girl, tugging at his sleeve with infectious good humor, was not only a youthful beauty who intrigued his senses, but a friend and companion as well. And since friends and companions were of the spirit, there was little reason to dissemble. Julian did not.

"Mistress . . . Mistress Chloe . . . if I may." He swept her a mock bow, amused at the startled look in her eyes at his easy use of her first name. "Mistress Chloe, in the New World we do not stand long on formality. And since I have won your trust and that of your family—pray, mistress, my name is Julian." And then, another bow: "I hope you will not think me overfamiliar, Mistress Chloe."

Relishing the moment, she sank to the ground in a deep curtsy. "All right, Master Julian, even though we may shock Madam Rosa!" She laughed aloud. "Now, sir. I am Chloe and you are Julian, and we will forget all about masters and mistresses and talk instead of kings and queens! You haven't answered my question, Julian—are you ready to see Royal Nonsuch?'' She held out her hand.

Julian took the small hand in his. It was warm and pulsing—the very identical hand he'd admired so often in the portrait. He clasped the long fingers, gazing into the smiling gray eyes beneath the strands of loose, silvery hair. "Chloe," he replied, "I am ready to see Royal Nonsuch." His voice was so sober and his gaze so intent her amused expression changed to a questioning one. "In fact," he finished, "I have never been more ready for anything in my life."

"We will start near the old Banqueting House," Chloe decided as she directed him away from the "wilderness." They plunged into a green area where grass grew between sunken paving stones along the path and the shrubbery was thick and rough. "This is where royalty had their refreshment before or after the hunt, where they had their masques and mummeries," she explained. The clearing was circled by tall chestnut trees whose very height prevented sunlight from entering. In the center was the remains of a polygonal brick retaining wall with bastions at four of its angles. "That's all that's left of the Banqueting House," Chloe said. "It was built of timber and approached by a ramp. An old man in the village said he remembered *horses* being led up the ramp to take part in the festivities inside! The house was several stories high, and there were little balconies in each of its four corners where people could look out at the beautiful view. He said at night lanterns or beacons were placed in the windows to guide people out of the 'wilderness.' " She sighed. "It must have been lovely to see. Something like the little summerhouse in the garden at Cuddington House—although, of course, much larger!"

Julian tried to picture the building. Part of the ramp was still in place, though any loose brick, tile or wood had long been carted away. There was thick grass in what had been the first floor, yet the irregular shape of the house was perfectly visible. "What revelry this place must have seen," he said almost to himself, "and now so quiet and still." He followed Chloe as she circled the foundation.

"It's not always so quiet," she replied thoughtfully. "There was a time when I brought my easel here, hoping to paint these ruins, but the place somehow seemed almost *alive*. I tried it only once—it's a long way to bring the easel. It's dark because of the trees, and the light is so poor. When I finally settled down to painting, I was so distracted I gave it up. I've not been back since."

"Distracted by what? What could distract you here?"

"I don't know. I never really *saw* anything—not even a bird, which is unusual because birds are all over Nonsuch. But it seemed as if there were people rushing about, riding and calling to each other. There used to be a statue of Diana somewhere close by, near a stream that fed into a fishpond that belonged to the manor house at Cuddington. In the old days the queen used to hunt there. The times when I've been in here alone, it almost seems as if I can hear them shouting at the chase." She shivered. "I've always thought it's the only place at Nonsuch that's haunted." She glanced at him impishly and said, "Now, Master Julian, you'll think me properly addled."

They left the clearing behind and approached a long treelined avenue ending in the palace ruins. The sun was high, and it cast shadows between the precisely straight row of old elms, which had grown to such a great size that in many places their branches met overhead. "That was the entrance to Nonsuch Palace," Chloe explained. And then, with mock imperiousness, she drew herself up straightly and, with a stiff bow, said, "This is the way it would have been for *you*, sir, if you'd come riding to Royal Nonsuch with the queen! You'd have come from London and ridden down the path to the gatehouse just there." She pointed to the right. "Of course, it would have been open and waiting for you because you were with the queen! Once inside, you'd have dismounted in the outer court, and servants would have been everywhere. . . ."

Suddenly she grasped Julian's hand, and together they ran down the long drive between the trees, vaulting with youthful ease over the rubble marking the gatehouse's position.

"Over there"—Chloe stopped to catch her breath—"there were the kitchens, and you may be sure they were busy! But *you*, sir, you've come with the queen—and would not pay any attention to kitchens!" Julian smiled and vigorously shook his head, joining in the fantasy. "Instead, more likely, you'd have been spellbound by the splendor of the middle gatehouse straight ahead. Shall we go, sir?" She held out her hand, he took her fingertips, and in silence they walked sedately, restraining their mirth until they reached a slight rise in the ground.

"Now up, sir, up eight steps, and here we are—at the middle gatehouse. Here we must . . . look up." Obediently, Julian looked at the bright sky. "There, sir," said Chloe, "is the finest astronomical clock in the land, grander even than the one at Hampton Court. It is painted light blue, but the hands and figures are gilded. It has six golden horoscopes and chimes on the half hour. Can you see the clock, Julian?"

Julian's heart was racing. He *could* almost see the clock. He wouldn't have been surprised to hear silvery chimes echo among the rubble and earthy debris. Chloe continued. "There was an oriel window beneath it and a cupola above with a great bell. And statues everywhere. In the front near the Privy Garden were a great white Pegasus and an enormous marble obelisk from Romany. This gatehouse was the entrance to the royal apartments. The king's side was guarded by a statue of Scipio, clothed in bronze garments, and the queen's side by Penthesilea." Her brow clouded. "I don't know very much about Penthesilea—we'll have to ask Aunt Rosa."

"And did you know," asked Julian, "that here in the middle archway was an echo chamber that magnified the sound of trumpets every time the king or queen appeared?"

"Oh, Julian, that's wonderful! How do you know that?" They were through the archway debris, and Julian told Chloe about Mr. Percy's story. "There were probably lots of secret entrances and exits we'll never know about."

Chloe started ahead, eager to get to the towers, when Julian stopped her. To the left was a long rectangular section filled with an immense amount of debris. At his questioning look Chloe said, "That was the wine cellar. I guess with all the royal celebration, lots of wine was needed." As they walked on, Julian looked back at the mound. He felt an unaccountable urge to scrabble in the debris, to see what was underneath. Surely he'd find only broken bottles, flasks—perhaps some warped casks. Anything of value would have been taken by Barbara Villiers' workmen.

Almost at once they were at the site of the famous towers. Several feet of broken and jagged wooden frames with bits of slate and plaster were still visible, and Chloe explained about the famous panels. "There were figures of Caesar, the Greek gods, unicorns and dragons, soldiers and emperors—all bigger than life, and so beautiful even Mr. Pepys said it was a shame a museum could not have been found for them. He often visited here."

They had come almost full circle and were nearing the place where Chloe had left her easel. Walking across the inner court, Julian thought: how beautiful it must have been. Throughout the courtyard, grass grew where cobblestones had been ripped out; in a few years, it would probably be covered with weeds. How long would it take to obliterate it entirely? The thought so depressed him he turned to Chloe, knowing her bright beauty, the very miracle of her being there, would raise his spirits. It had been an incredible morning—one of the best of his life. He could hardly wait to thank Rosa, and, later, to write James Cuddington, who was really responsible for it all.

James Cuddington was almost his last conscious thought. Suddenly, it seemed as though the earth were rocking beneath his feet, and while he knew he remained on the ground, his body seemed lifted and tossed. He felt as if he were being consumed by flames. From somewhere he heard a loud, agonized groan as he reached for what he knew to be the solid stone plinth. If only he could lie down on it. . . . Instead, the stone was red-hot, and he turned away, feeling buffeted and pummeled. The groans became louder, and something seemed to close about his throat. He groped for the buttons of his doublet; it was getting so tight. . . .

"Mr. Cushing! Julian! What is it?" From a long way off

he heard the words. His eyes were closed—closed on a scene of purple and black and slashing yellow fragments. He felt his consciousness slipping away. A dragging sensation seemed to enclose his lower body.

"Julian—dear God—tell me what it is. Oh, help me . . . don't . . . oh, don't, sir." Those were the last words he remembered before a merciful darkness descended.

Gradually, his sight and senses returned. The dragging sensation had subsided, and he realized he was leaning against the tree where Chloe had propped her easel. A firm shoulder beneath his armpit seemed his only support. Dizzily, he attempted to stand upright, and the support gave way as Chloe solicitously turned him around and helped him to the ground. He felt a great urge to be sick in the grass and prayed, in the midst of his discomfort, not to disgrace himself in her presence. She was kneeling and helping him take off his doublet, and for the first time he realized he was sweating profusely.

"Oh, Chloe, I can't imagine. . . ." The words were weak.

She interrupted. "Don't talk, Julian. Lie flat and rest your head on your clothing. In a few moments I am sure you'll feel better. Perhaps it was an attack of vertigo."

In moments he felt his energy return. He knew from his shipboard experience that despite his slight body, he had a strong constitution. Chloe had had the good sense to steer him into the shade. She also had the tact now to remain silent as she sat close by, looking out over the ruins, giving him every chance to regain his composure. What a blessed creature she was. . . .

He sat up, testing his balance. "I think I'm all right now. I've never felt that way before—there was some sickness on the ship coming to England, but nothing like this. God, nothing like this."

Chloe was thoughtful. She had either removed her hat or dropped it in the attempt to help him, and the silvery hair lay in soft waves against her brow. She was in profile, and he caught his breath at the clear, sweet beauty of the straight little nose, the strong chin, the almost bold mark of that dark winged brow. Cautiously, he put out a hand and touched the strands of silvery hair that lay along her neck. They were soft and springy, just as he knew they'd be and, somehow, comfortably familiar. That was the word he'd been seeking —*familiar*. What was it about this girl that was so natural and right it was almost intimate?

She was not uncomfortable at his touch; there was no coy evasion. "You're feeling better, Julian?" And then, not waiting for his answer: "It happened right at the site of the old fountain—I wonder why the fountain?"

He hoisted himself to a sitting position and followed her glance. The solid plinth in the middle of the inner court was what had felt scalding to his touch. He told Chloe of his reaction. "*Hmmmmm*," was all she replied. "The old fountain—it had brass dragons on the base—one of the villagers told me. He'd seen it, he said."

"Then maybe the dragons tried to catch me." Julian rose and donned his doublet. His strength had returned, and with it a feeling of shame at his weakness. He must make light of it. "Yes, I'm sure the Nonsuch dragons were after me."

Chloe rose, too, brushing the grass from her skirt. She put on her hat and tied the ribbons under her chin carefully, smiling at him almost maternally. "No, Julian, it wasn't the dragons. It's part of the same sort of thing I feel at the Banqueting House and at the fishpond, although *your* feeling was far more intense. I don't like to be there, and certainly not alone. Sometimes, I think it's the Lure."

"Your Aunt Rosa told me about the Lure—that it's supposed to be buried somewhere here at Nonsuch."

"Yes, it's been a family legend since the time of the first Chloe Cuddington. Then lots of other people knew about it because there was such a scandal. Some thought she was a witch."

Julian told her about Evans' remarks about the original Chloe. She smiled. "Yes, I know—he's told me the same thing. Perhaps it's true. Perhaps she had second sight. But whatever it was, no one ever knew about it until the scandal of the Lure."

"What do you think the Lure is—or was?"

"I don't know, and sometimes I don't want to find out. Other times I come here and almost *will* myself to find it—so the mystery of the first Chloe will be solved. I'm supposed to look like her, but I don't want to be like her. She had a great taint to her name."

Julian felt almost compelled to protect the image of the long-dead enchantress whose likeness he'd worshiped for months. Yet he could understand Chloe's dilemma. It couldn't be pleasant knowing you were the duplicate of someone who might have been a witch. Especially if you were as sensitive as he knew Chloe to be.

"Has anyone ever tried to find the Lure?" Julian thought of the days ahead—he and Chloe could look for it themselves! "Certainly if those who destroyed Nonsuch never found it, then it must still be here?"

"Oh, yes, the Lure is still here, Julian." Chloe was very positive. "I *know* it's still here. There's never been any record of its discovery. Supposedly it was buried *before* the palace was built, and as you see, there are no excavations. There were some cellars near the kitchens, of course, and the old wine cellar, and they were merely filled in with rubble. Other than that, nothing beneath the ground was disturbed when the palace was pulled down."

They were nearing the wine cellar, and Julian, with Chloe's easel under his arm, stopped before it. "I'd like to dig in there sometime," he said. "I don't know why, but it's as good a place as any to begin. Why don't we come here tomorrow and look underneath that rubble? We might be lucky enough to find the Lure right away."

"Julian, people have scrabbled in that debris for years!" Chloe laughed. "I doubt if it could be that easy." Seeing his disappointment, she said quickly, "But if you want to—of course—*you* can dig and *I* will paint!" Then, more soberly: "But there is something you must promise me, Julian. Promise me you'll never go near that old fountain again. Just as the Banqueting House is wrong for me, that ground near the fountain is wrong for you. Others walk there and never seem to feel anything. But I know one thing—*you* must stay away. It may have been pure accident, but it's a feeling I understand. Promise me you won't go there again, Julian." The bright face was questioning, her tone urgent. Julian was touched by her concern.

"I promise, Chloe. I won't go there again. But you

mustn't worry. Royal Nonsuch may have a few secret dragons, but we know where they are—and we'll stay away."
As they started up the treelined avenue toward Sparwefeld, he looked back at the long rectangular mound of the wine cellar. "But there's where I'd like to look someday—someday soon. . . ."

Chapter Ten

Chloe and Julian returned to Nonsuch twice. Chloe painted while Julian attempted to remove several barrows of rubble from the wine cellar. He soon realized how futile it was. The task seemed endless. A great deal of time and effort would be needed merely to clear the area, and then there would be the foundations themselves to be broken into. Nevertheless, as he worked, the more convinced he became that the Lure was underfoot. Rosa and Chloe, however, believed it had been buried in the church foundations where the possibility of discovery would be remote. And these were under the fountain site where he'd suffered that incredible reaction.

It was all very frustrating. Ever since hearing of the Lure, he'd been convinced that finding it might clear the original Chloe's reputation as a witch. And he felt committed—almost impelled—to help redeem her name, though so many years had passed. Even Rosa's dry comment that the Lure might establish once and for all that Chloe *had* been a witch didn't deter him. He'd fallen in love with her portrait and crossed a sea to bring it home. But until the mystery of the Lure was resolved, Julian did not feel his mission would be complete.

Finding the Lure would also ease the mind and heart of Chloe's namesake, for Julian sensed her doubt about whether her ancestress possessed a "taint" or not. As he dug, he marveled at the kind fate which had given him a replica of his beloved to adore, even though he hadn't dared speak of his feelings. What had he to offer Chloe Cuddington? A loving heart, but no permanent home. A timeless adoration, but no concrete means of support. He was willing to work, and he knew there were many opportunities in the New World that were lacking in the Old. But had he the right to ask this sheltered girl of such noble heritage to gamble her future with him? Julian remembered the heartbreaking reversals in his own family's fortunes, as well as the very real physical danger of life in Virginia. How could he ask someone as sensitive and lovely as Chloe to share such a life?

It was a relief to communicate something of his feelings to James Cuddington. The old gentleman had written Julian his appreciation at seeing the portrait safely home and, with gentle humor, said how much he envied him seeing "our enchantress in the flesh." Months before, he wrote, Rosa had written that older family members who remembered the portrait said that her niece greatly resembled the original Chloe. He hoped his friend, young Cushing, would enjoy the family and remember him while exploring the scenes he'd known so well as a youth.

Julian could sense the old man's loneliness and felt a momentary sadness that James could not be with them. He took great pains in his replies to describe the ruins and the places in Ewell that James might remember. He wrote of Chloe, Rosa and Evans, the rooms at Cuddington House and Sparwefeld and his delight in the glory of an English spring. It was one way he could repay the old gentleman whose friendship had so changed his life.

It was obvious to Rosa Cuddington that Julian had fallen in love with her niece. He scarcely took his eyes from her, as though he still couldn't believe his good fortune; he seemed restless when she was absent. Which wasn't often, for Chloe was also clearly taken with Julian. She was seventeen and of an age to be married—as her aunt had pointedly mentioned more than once. Chloe hadn't lacked for beaux. Cuddington House had long been a magnet for the young London gallants. They came in their satins, laces and scents, with their affected manners and extravagant speech, to run the gauntlet of Rosa's cool appraisal. Chloe was not only beautiful but also her aunt's heiress, and Rosa had no use for fortune hunters, no matter how distinguished. Being unwed at seventeen might have alarmed another less assured. But Chloe vowed she'd have no marriage of convenience. She had guarded her emotions skillfully. She was adept at handling an overenthusiastic admirer with politeness—and disdain—and was rigid in her determination to maintain her individuality and freedom. Which, to Rosa's eyes, made her interest in Julian and her eagerness to be with him remarkable. For all the bluebloods she'd known since birth, none had touched her heart or roused her senses. Until Julian.

It was all very frustrating for Rosa. A matchmaker at heart, she optimistically regarded Julian's adoration and Chloe's shy, awakening interest, hoping for the spark to ignite the relationship. She gave them more opportunity to be alone than propriety allowed—and still their diffidence with each other continued. She guessed Julian's difficulty. He was penniless. She knew that while this was important to him, it mattered little to her niece. Couldn't the girl see he was afire with love for her? And couldn't he see how Chloe's eyes followed him as they cantered in the leafy lanes of Sparwefeld, or how they sparkled with delight when he commended one of her paintings? As his visit wore on, Rosa despaired that Chloe would ever encourage him to declare himself and he'd return to Virginia with his love unspoken.

The thought of Julian's leaving so depressed Rosa that when, two weeks after his arrival, he and Chloe returned tired and thirsty from a day at Nonsuch, she decided to leave for London the following morning. Perhaps away from the ruins and comparative simplicity of Sparwefeld, something might happen to make them realize how right they were for each other. It was worth a gamble.

Slowly, luxuriating in the soft thick pallet of the great canopied bed, Chloe awoke. She relished the warmth of the room where an early-morning darkness would soon be dispelled by the daylight outlining the edges of the thick draperies. They were closed against the river's damp. The occupants of Cuddington House must be still asleep, for there were no sounds except the muffled calls of the stableman in the rear courtyard and the clatter of a few early horsemen in the Strand below.

Chloe arose, pulling on her robe and thrusting her feet into small velvet sandals. She padded to the window and pushed the draperies aside. It was grayish dark; the lightening rays of the still-hidden sun cast a pinkish glow in the horizon over Southwark and Lambeth Palace upstream. Someone had built a fire in the Durham House courtyard for warmth during the night. It was being doused now, and she could hear the hissing steam and the shout of the stableman as he called for more water. A few wherries were abroad on the river, while an occasional light could be seen in the houses lining London Bridge. Aside from that, London slept, as did Cuddington House. It could be no later than half after four. Within an hour, Chloe knew, the city would come to life, and her maid would be knocking softly at her door with a can of hot water for her toilette.

She returned to bed, picking up a small book on her way. Her writing box was on the night table, and sinking once more into the warmth of the covers, she lit a candle and opened the book with its delicately embroidered cover. Dipping her quill into the ink, she wrote:

"*May 4, 1700*: It is not nearly three weeks since Julian arrived and I think I love him more each Day. Surely God has been good to send him to me who is so Undeserving of such Grace. I think I knew the first day at Nonsuch that I would love him, for I felt so at Ease—almost as if he were a very Old and dear Friend. Sometimes, I think he feels the same Way, but something keeps him from speaking.

Often I feel his eyes upon me, as if he is trying to Remember something. At times, I feel he's Willing me to remember also! It is most Unusual, but not Frightening, nor does it spoil our time together.

I feel a good deal of his Reserve is because of his great Modesty and because he is very uncertain of his Future."

Putting pen aside, Chloe sank back among the pillows. She knew she'd been a great strain to her beloved Aunt Rosa for discouraging several suitors who might have given her a life of luxury and unquestioned devotion. Even she herself had begun to doubt her motives and wondered if she'd ever be capable of giving her love to anyone. And then Julian Cushing had come into her life, and she realized immediately why she'd been reluctant to form any other connection. The mere sight of him in the distance—or the sound of his voice with that peculiar intonation one heard only in a colonial—could make her pulses race and her knees tremble. Often she felt that intense blue-eyed gaze upon her, and she sensed a yearning that matched her own. Yet he remained silent.

And, Chloe recognized, she'd also hidden her true feelings. Not only was it immodest to parade one's naked hope and desire, but there was another reason. She couldn't name it, for she hadn't thought of it in years. Now, watching the daylight brighten, she fought the niggling specter of doubt and fear forming in her mind. It was not Julian she doubted, but herself. Surely she loved him as she'd never loved anyone—and she was sure he felt the same. But was she worthy? How could she explain that "queerness" that made her so unlike others? How was she to interpret the senses or faculties she seemingly possessed—which others did not?

It was strange. Strange. That was the word for it. It made her different, and at first, it had been frightening. For years she had thrust the knowledge to the back of her mind. But now—now that she'd met someone she could love—how could she tell him? She had not even told her Aunt Rosa. Long ago she'd accepted that if no one was hurt by her "queerness," it needed no explanation. But if one were in love, surely one would need to divulge everything?

She remembered the first time the odd faculty had appeared. As a child she was scampering about the Cuddington House attic with a maid her aunt had sent to find some old lace stored in a box. The maid had been bad-tempered; the mistress hadn't told her which box, and there were so many! She was muttering to herself when Chloe pointed to a flat dusty box on a low shelf and said, "It's in there, Annie." The maid continued her search; clearly she considered Chloe impudent. Finally, outraged that her help was being so casually dismissed, the determined little girl had gone to the box, opened it, handed it to the maid and said, "There—just as I told you!" stamping a small foot for emphasis.

"Well, and you've bin up here a-lookin' before . . . and

the mistress doesn't know of your peekin'. I'll not be tellin' on ye!'' Annie had taken the lace and gone, leaving Chloe to wonder at the strange assurance that made her know just which box it was in.

And then there had been the incident of the cap.

That had happened months later at Sparwefeld. She'd been embroidering a small hanging for her aunt's birthday, and her chubby fingers were awkward. She'd never be as adept at needlework as her Aunt Rosa! But she struggled on, pricking her fingers and leaving tiny dots of blood on the muslin pattern. Her aunt, aware of her niece's disdain for the work, finally pulled it away. ''My dear, you'll never be a 'broiderer. But never mind, each has his own talent, and you paint quite nicely. Stop now and get your paint box.'' She gestured toward the box lying near a glass-topped cabinet. Chloe knew all the treasures it contained. An old missal, its delicate parchment pages filled with spidery handwriting in a language she couldn't read. But oh, the glorious colors! Glowing angels and archangels, twining leaves and vines around a delicate border, tiny blobs of gold accenting a robe or a tiara. ''It was Elizabeth Cuddington's ***Book of Hours***,'' her aunt explained, ''made for her by the monks of Merton Priory.'' Then Chloe would ask again for the story of Richard and Elizabeth Cuddington, her ancestors and parents of that infamous Chloe for whom she'd been named. Aunt Rosa would patiently repeat how they'd owned everything for miles and miles around. Then an old king had come down from London and taken it all away and had all the buildings, including nearby Merton Priory, destroyed.

Chloe was always incensed at the story, her youthful sense of justice outraged. Her aunt would mollify her by taking the missal from underneath the glass and letting her stroke the pages. Then she would take out a small faded violet cap, made of stiff brocade and trimmed with a darkening silver thread, into which tiny seed pearls had been sewn. The violet was of a deeper hue in the folds, revealing the luminosity of the original color. ''And this cap—you remember, I told you—this is the cap which your ancestress, the first Chloe Cuddington, embroidered when she was about your age.'' Rosa placed the delicate little cap in her hands.

Chloe had looked as it lay there, and she could visualize—oh, so easily!—how it had appeared the day it was new. A beautiful lavender-violet, with the silver trim bright and shining. And then, without thinking, she'd said, "Chloe Cuddington didn't make it, Aunt. It was made *for* her. It was a birthday present." She handed it back to her aunt, and feeling strange and reluctant to discuss the cap further, she'd run from the room and gone to the old bench outside near the garden where the birds came for food. There she sat and wondered why the vision of the violet cap *as it had been* was stronger than the sight of it now, nearly two hundred years later?

Inevitably, such childish concern faded, and as the years passed, they'd have been forgotten except for the odd incidents that occasionally happened to remind her of them. Never, *never* had she told anyone of running with her dog outside the red-brick wall enclosing the backyard of Sparwefeld. Quickly rounding the corner, she'd stopped, speechless at what she saw. There, under the great beech tree which was considerably smaller than it actually was—and where she knew an old rotting bench to be—sat an old man. He was dressed in strange clothes and was throwing seed to the birds with the great sweeping motions she'd seen the village farmers use when they sowed their fields. Behind the man—*who was he?*—was a beautiful old farmhouse. Farmhouse? It was too handsome for a farmhouse.

As she watched, more than a little frightened, an old dog padded out from the farmhouse and lay at the base of the tree, heaving a contented sigh. Neither the dog, the birds, nor the man paid any attention to her or her dog. It was the sound of his whining that caused her to turn around, for the little dog was slinking away, his hair taut on his back and a terrified look in his great brown eyes. She tried to console him for a moment and then, gazing back, found the vision had disappeared. There was the bench, the flowers and the tree. But the man and birds, the house and dog were gone.

She'd been uneasy over it for weeks. Not only for the vague dread with which the incident filled her—but it brought to mind all the other little experiences that had puzzled her so. She knew of the ancestress who was supposed to be a witch.

She'd had the same name and been involved in a frightful scandal. She'd been beautiful, of course, yet that beauty might have hidden a black heart as well as eyes that could look into the future. Just as she herself seemed to be able to look into the past.

Chloe had never told a soul of her experiences. And now, she wondered, how she could ever tell Julian? Tell him that the sounds she heard in the Banqueting House were sounds out of the past? And that she felt it was somehow linked to his frightful experience at the fountain? She couldn't explain the old man feeding the birds, but years later her Aunt Rosa had told her that the Cuddington manor house had been on that very site. And that the black and white board above the arbor was a domino, named for an old gardener who'd worked for the Cuddingtons and remained at Sparwefeld when they'd gone to Suffolk.

There had been no recent episodes of her "queerness." Perhaps it had all been childish imagination. Perhaps over the years it would disappear, especially if she were involved and happy with someone she dearly loved. The thought—and the brightening rays of the early sun now flooding the room—brought Chloe from her reverie. She picked up the diary once more:

> "I am going to write no more until I have resolved this matter with Julian. I shall try to show him how I feel, though he will Doubtless think me a shameless hussy. I shall wait until we return to Nonsuch where we are to look for the Lure again. How I wish we could find it! Somehow, I feel that my Uneasiness at the Banqueting House and Julian's dreadful Experience at the fountain, are all connected to events of the Past. And I feel all such Events are linked with the original Chloe. I may look like her, but *I will not be like her*. . . . I thank God I do not have her taint."

Her words recalled the scene that had occurred on their arrival at Cuddington House. Though Aunt Rosa usually served tea in the privacy of her own rooms, that day she'd insisted they all gather in her "receiving room" downstairs.

Julian and Rosa were waiting as she entered. Immediately, her attention had been caught by the portrait on the wall. Seeing it, she felt almost faint, raising fingers to her mouth to stifle a gasp. Here was the Chloe whose namesake she was, *and it might have been a portrait of herself*. She was aware of Julian's keen gaze and her aunt's amused expression. She walked, as one in a dream, close to the fireplace. There she gazed at her own mirror image, clothed in a beautiful peach gown, hands so like her own folded demurely in her lap. The room now was exactly as it had been then. For a moment, Chloe felt she was caught in a time vacuum—she was *here*, but she was also *there*. She knew something was expected of her and welcomed her aunt's cheery words, "And amazingly like you, my dear, aren't you pleased?"

Chloe had wanted to cry out, "No, I'm *not* pleased—and I will *not* be like her!" and run from the room. Instead, she'd regained her composure and smilingly agreed the resemblance was remarkable. Julian had sensed her strain and immediately changed the subject. It was most unusual—this rapport between them. As her aunt chattered on and served the tea, she'd smiled gratefully at Julian, loving him all the more for his perceptiveness.

A knock on the door—her maid had arrived with the hot water. Chloe hurriedly put the book away. This was going to be a happy day. She'd forget about Lures and scandals, witches and taints. All London was waiting to be explored, and courtesy demanded their New World visitor see its wonders. Today was as good a day to start as any.

Rosa was pleased to yield her place as guide to Chloe, and after an early breakfast she waved them off to the stables. There they chose their mounts and, with one servant to accompany them, were soon abroad in the Strand. It was beginning to be crowded with coaches, carriages and sedan chairs. Inside them, tipsy occupants returning from late-night revels snored loudly. Ahead the dome of St. Paul's was pearly-pink in the weak sunlight cutting through the river's fog. On the Southwark side, in the low-lying pockets of marsh and reeds, the haze was still dense, yet the air was brisk enough to turn the windmills in Lambeth's marshy fields. As the mail coach clattered by, destined for the Belle Sauvage Inn in Ludgate, Chloe called, "And now, Master Cushing from Virginia, where to? What is your pleasure? Ludgate, Aldgate, Whitehall? Smithfield? The Tower?"

Downriver, almost obscured by the jutting low land of Southwark, Julian could see the great span of London Bridge. He pointed to it. "Not the Tower! Not today—*that's* where I want to go, Chloe! We crossed before at Lambeth, and I didn't get to see the bridge."

"Then London Bridge it shall be! When you were little, Julian, did you sing the rhyme about it falling down?" The servant started ahead, and Chloe's mount fell into place beside his. He glanced at her admiringly. She was wearing a pale-green velvet jacket with an oyster-colored fichu at her throat and tiny rows of lace at her wrists. The green skirt spread gracefully over the burnished chestnut of the mare, for she rode sidesaddle as his mother and other Jamestown ladies had done. "Oh, yes, we sang of London Bridge falling down and"—eyeing her costume—"also about 'My Lady Greensleeves.' " Together they hummed a few bars and followed the servant's lead down the Strand, past the rotting remains of ancient Savoy Palace. Approaching Ludgate, they crossed a small bridge over the Fleet Ditch, and Chloe pointed to the vast pile of the Blackfriars where the Fleet waters lapped at its walls. "Last winter the Thames froze over," she said, "and we all went on the river—walking, Julian!—for it was frozen to a depth of over twenty feet. There were booths and tents for trade and bonfires—and we could eat and skate! It was lovely in the moonlight, too. We came home by the Blackfriar water stairs."

Through Ludgate, they climbed the hill toward St. Paul's, and Julian could see the workmen on the scaffold around the great dome. "They're still abuilding after the fire," she said. "On the return we'll see the great windows and Paul's Cross."

At St. Paul's the servant led them into Cheapside, bustling with early-morning traffic. Merchants opening their stalls doffed their caps as Julian and Chloe passed, their breaths frosty on the cool air. Julian was amazed at the sight of the great thoroughfare—the largest he'd ever seen. Cheapside was filled with gabled and turreted houses, some of timber, others of brick. Opposite the famed Goldsmiths' Row was the Great Conduit, where, Chloe explained, everyone came for the water piped in from the countryside. Housewives were already busily filling mugs and flasks. Passing beautiful old Bow Church, Chloe told him how all London had marveled that the Norman crypt had escaped the Great Fire, although old Mr. Wren had had to rebuild the church itself, along with so many others.

They rode into the Poultry, up the Corn Hill, turning south into Gracechurch Street. Ahead was the bridge. "There it is, Julian," Chloe cried, "one of the wonders of the world! Better see it for the first time from this end—the other end may have criminals' heads on pikes! Not a very nice welcome to London, I'm afraid."

At the newly rebuilt Church of St. Magnus, the Martyr, a line was waiting for admittance. Nearby, filthy beggars were making themselves comfortable for the day, spreading their rags on the ground to display the festering sores covering arms and legs. One called beseechingly, and Julian was pleased to see the servant toss him a coin. It was the first beggar he'd ever seen; he thought how odd the man would have looked in Williamsburg.

While the horse pawed impatiently to be on its way, Julian's attention was caught by the little church across the river near Winchester House, the former mansion of the Bishop of Winchester. He remembered how Mr. Shakespeare had referred to the inhabitants of the nearby brothels (which stood on land owned by the bishopric) as "Winchester Geese." And how shocked a visiting Frenchman, hearing the Thames boatmen cry, "Oars! Oars!" when they were for hire, thought they were promoting the harlots' charms. He must remember to tell Rosa and Chloe the story. On the other hand, perhaps he'd better not. Amusing in Virginia, it might possibly be of questionable taste at Cuddington House.

The crowd thinned as they approached the bridge, where, after the servant paid a toll, they clattered onto the cobbled roadway. "Julian, I've a surprise!" Chloe cried as she rode beside him. "It's just ahead." She called to the servant, and they all pulled to one side to escape the traffic. Julian savored the quiet moment on the ancient bridge lined on both sides with houses and shops. Some of the occupants were already at the windows, gazing at the river scene, some with breakfast in their hands. "There it is, Julian!" she cried.

Ahead was a magnificent building, four stories high, with two great turrets. It spanned the entire width of the bridge with archways below through which traffic passed. The four stories were covered with carved stucco panels of various designs: soldiers, Roman emperors in flowing togas, carved griffins, flowers or heraldic emblems. It all looked somehow familiar.

"It's Nonsuch House, Julian." Chloe answered his unspoken question, "Nonsuch House—named after our Nonsuch in Surrey! But as you can see, the towers here are a little different." She sounded so knowledgeable Julian had to suppress a smile, even as he gazed in awe at the great structure so lightly striding the bridge. There was little doubt it had been modeled after Nonsuch. Chloe said it was now the home of the Lord Mayor.

As they approached the bridge's center, the rotting foundations of a long-vanished building were still visible. "That was the Chapel of Thomas à Becket," Chloe said. "It was destroyed, probably about the time Nonsuch House was being built. There were many religious troubles then, I guess. But it must have been very beautiful." Julian was reminded of the vast cathedral he'd seen silhouetted against the Kentish horizon. Thomas had been its archbishop and murdered within its very walls.

There were no rotting heads atop Traitors' Gate, much to Chloe's relief. Emerging at the Southwark end, Julian saw boats for hire and felt a sudden longing to be on the river. Quickly, he said, "Chloe, send the servant back with the horses, and let's go on the water! I remember once reading that the only way to see London is from the river."

Chloe's heart thudded with excitement; she blushed as she dismissed the servant. Julian was busy choosing a boat; he finally settled on a bright yellow skiff. "Not as grand as the queen's barge, Mistress Cuddington, but it'll have to do." He smiled as he handed her in.

She sat quietly opposite as the boatman poled out from the water stairs, trailing her fingers in the water as it rushed toward the marshy shore. Though it was barely midmorning, the sun was already warm, and her face was flushed with pleasure. Julian gazed at the slim figure reclining so gracefully among the cushions, the sunlight making a silvery nimbus of the hair escaping from the little green cap. The jacket was tight across her young breasts and accented the tiny waist he was sure his hands could span. The mere thought made his pulses race. Her skirt was disarrayed among the cushions and revealed two slim ankles encased in white hose and square-toed shoes of soft leather with lustrous gold buckles. She was so desirable, so completely the embodiment of everything he'd dreamed since he'd first seen Chloe Cuddington's portrait! His eyes lingered on the curve of her cheek; he could see the tiny golden hairs near the full lips, so odd in contrast with the deep black brows and incredibly smoky gray eyes.

As she turned to face him, her features seemed to enlarge and brighten. She was the same, yet so different. She was speaking to him, but it seemed from a distance. He must have replied, for she smiled and spoke to the boatman, who appeared amused at her comment. For just a moment it was almost like a mirage or illusion—some trick of his fancy. It was all so familiar; he seemed to be reliving a youthful memory. Then, suddenly, he recalled his dreams of skimming a broad river. *This was it*, just as he'd seen in his dreams. And he was sure, it was not the first time. *We have done this before*, he thought.

Chloe felt the intensity of his gaze. She knew he was thinking of her, for his eyes were alight with an intimacy—almost a *knowledge*—she'd not seen previously. She remembered the words she'd written that morning—perhaps she wouldn't have to be a "shameless hussy" after all. Perhaps he'd give her some chance to show how she felt. The thought made her heart pound. What could she say? Feeling a little light-headed, she said, "Now the view, Julian. It won't be really spectacular until we're near the Temple. There you can see back where you've been and also where you're going."

"An admirable situation under any circumstances," he replied, breaking the spell. "I know where I've been. Yet

I'm not so sure where I'm going. . . ." He frowned, and they both were silent for a moment. Then, taking her hand, he said, "But we're not going to let my uncertainties spoil our day! Chloe, you'll never know how I've dreamed of seeing London like this. Actually, I *have* dreamed of seeing London—and with someone very like you. It's all so beautiful. And *you*—you are making it very special. I never expected to meet *you*." Her hand lay unprotestingly in his; he longed to raise it to his lips.

"Nor I you, Julian. I never expected really to meet *anyone*." Her voice was almost a whisper. His grasp tightened. It really would not do to kiss a young lady's hand under the boatman's amused stare while midstream on the Thames. At least not *this* young lady. "Chloe," he said, "let's make this a day to remember. I want you to show me *your* London—just as you showed me *your* Nonsuch. We'll pretend that this is the queen's barge and I'm your suitor with sword and cap and you, of course, are a great lady in a farthingale with satin and lace all encrusted with jewels."

She caught his mood instantly. "If we're in the queen's barge, Julian, we shouldn't be holding hands. Royalty doesn't always approve of such goings-on"—she giggled—"at least not in the open." Promptly he released her hand, and laughing, they relaxed back in their seats and watched the panorama of London unfold before them.

By late afternoon they were back at Cuddington House. It had been a joyous time, and Chloe was eager to set it down in her diary. She sat at her desk near the window facing on the river from which they had just come and wrote:

"*May 4, 1700*. This has been the most wonderful day of my life. And all because it has been spent with Julian. We were Abroad very early, for he wished to see the city. After the bridge where we both saw Nonsuch House—such a Surprise to him!—we took a skiff. On the River, Julian said we must pretend to be in the Queen's barge. I answered him that if we were Royal, then we must go to the Court. The boatman left us at Whitehall Stairs and we strolled in the Privy Garden where Julian led me Unaware to the fountain and I was immediately sprayed and wet!

There was much amusement as we walked down the street towards the Hall and the Abbey. We bought some hot pies and fruit and ate them in the Westminster Palace ruins. I had not known they were so Extensive. The Jewel Tower is almost all that is left, and we tossed the Remains of our meal to the fish in the little moat.

We went into the Abbey—Julian approaching it almost with reverence and he was clearly awed by the Nobleness of the building. As we knelt in prayer, his face was almost Transfigured with joy. Walking home along the riverbank, he told me that for the first Time, worship had been as Glorious as he knew it could be. His soul had seemed consumed, and he said that when he was Young, he had thought of entering the church. He described the little church at Jamestown and how Dissatisfied he'd been with the Musick and Sermons. He said now he Felt he was not good enough to offer his Soul to God, that perhaps the best Way to serve Him was by teaching the young of the country that is a-building across the Sea. But in our time in the Abbey, I could see he had found great Joy and Release, and he intimated as much to me as we walked Homeward.

Tonight Aunt Rosa is taking us to Vauxhall Gardens. She says Julian must see a proper Publick garden and Vauxhall is the best. Tomorrow we shall visit the *Golden Hind*, which is moored near the Temple. Julian wishes also to see Greenwich Palace—he says he doesn't expect it to compare with Nonsuch. He is eager to return for one last visit before he leaves for Virginia.

I do not think I can stand the thought of his leaving here for ever."

Shortly after dusk that afternoon, three costumed and masked figures left Cuddington House for the renowned public gardens at Vauxhall on the Surrey side of the Thames. One was a shepherdess with a mask as silvery as her hair; the other a handsome juggler who wore his particolored tights and belled cap with easy elegance. The third, more plumply rounded, was easily recognizable as Nell Gwynn, the orange girl. Chloe blushed at the depth of her Aunt Rosa'd décolletage. She'd also adorned her cheeks—a tribute to the cosmetician's art—with *two* black beauty marks. Her hair, unpowdered, lay disheveled about her shoulders. There were no oranges in her basket, only a fan and a small velvet bag swollen with coins. Clearly, Rosa was not going to Vauxhall merely to see its wonders.

In the coach as it rumbled toward the horse ferry that would take them across the river, she said, "Vauxhall is famous throughout Europe, Julian, and you mustn't leave our city without seeing it. I am certain there's nothing to compare with it in the Colony."

"Of that I am sure, madam," the juggler replied. "Truly, you have so much here that we do not have at home." His eyes behind the mask were on Chloe as he spoke, and Rosa was gratified to see her niece's pleasure. Something had surely happened on their river excursion. They'd seemed very close on their return, with eyes only for each other. Julian appeared confident, and Chloe radiantly happy. Rosa sighed. If Vauxhall didn't provoke something more than confidence and radiance, Julian would surely return to Virginia unspoken, and her niece might well become a spinster, being as particular as she was.

Once across the river, they boarded another coach bound for Vauxhall. They could hear the merriment and music before the gardens came into view. As the coach left them at the entrance, Rosa explained that Vauxhall covered twelve acres, and it seemed they were all ablaze with light. Lamps were everywhere: on lawns, graveled walks, along gooseberry hedges, in an acre of rose garden and along treelined avenues. They shone on tiny summerhouses with espaliered cherry trees on their sides, on triumphal arches decked with bunting and greens, on "follies" and several large rotundas or temples, where musicians vied with the noisy crowd to be heard. One large lacy structure—fashioned after a maharaja's temple—was filled with exotic birds and tropical plants Julian had never before seen. Stands draped in gauze and muslin and hung with bright banners sold scraped beef and fragrant ham slices, while tea booths provided tea, wines and syllabub. Some had brought their own picnics and chosen vine-laden arbors or booths where they might eat in privacy. Others sat idly on the lawns, listening to the music or watching a pantomime while the *beau monde* rubbed shoulders with the *demi monde*.

And everywhere there were statues: of Apollo, Minerva and Athena and of Mr. Purcell, whose music was often performed in one particularly large temple which, their hostess explained, was used when the royal family came to Vauxhall.

At the gaming pavilion Rosa looped the velvet purse over her wrist, snapped open her fan and waved Julian and Chloe away. She intended to try her luck at the tables and encouraged them to enjoy the revels as she hoped to do.

A loud crackle and a shower of sparks in the sky announced the beginning of the fireworks. Julian took Chloe's hand, and together they ran to the site just as the colorful display began. Each salvo and its resulting explosion colored the horizon before its sparks fell in the fields of Lambeth. Between explosions they could hear the smothered laughter and conversation of amorous couples all around them in the darkness. Occasionally, a satyr or an overendowed nymph would approach them, wriggling suggestively, but it was clear the juggler and the shepherdess had little interest, and soon they were left alone.

Chloe thought Rosa's absence might be awkward, but her experience with Julian in the Abbey that afternoon—*was it only that afternoon?*—had given her a deeper glimpse into his nature. He was not one for idle flirtation; neither was she. Often she'd wondered if she'd ever meet someone to whom she could give herself. Now she knew Julian to be that person, and she knew, intuitively, that he felt the same.

"And what do you think of Aunt Rosa's Vauxhall, Julian?" A great sparkling explosion in the sky lit her features. They had both taken off their masks. "Will you remember this when you return to Virginia?"

"It's a fairyland, Chloe, and when I tell people in Jamestown and Williamsburg what it was like here, they won't believe me." He laughed. "Especially when I tell them all this wanton gaiety is right in sight of the homes of the Bishop of Winchester and the Archbishop of Canterbury!" He gestured toward Lambeth Palace in the distance. "They don't understand things like that in Williamsburg. We're a simple people."

"Tell me about Williamsburg, Julian."

"There's no way to describe it to make you understand. Perhaps the best way is to say that everything is *new*. Here in London, at Cuddington House or at Sparwefeld, you measure time in *centuries*. Everything is ancient and justified by tradition. At home we measure in *decades*, and we're still making our tradition. It's a great responsibility, but also a great opportunity."

"You'll do well, Julian." Chloe laid a small hand on his as it lay on the bench. "You'll do well. But oh, I wish. . . ."

"What do you wish, Chloe?" Julian tipped her chin with his fingers, that strong chin with its deep cleft. He was stirred at the inviting look in the gray eyes so confidently raised to his. She did not answer. Instead, she put both arms around his neck and laid her lips against his. He could feel the thrust of her strong young breasts against the thin costume. The perfume of her hair, the softness of her kiss aroused his senses as never before. Everything—the music, the murmuring voices nearby, the thump and explosion of the fireworks—faded. There was nothing but this warm sensation slowly engulfing him, making him one with the girl in his arms.

She finally spoke. "And now, dear Julian, are you still so anxious to return home?" She was smiling, though a little pale, and her voice was trembling. Julian understood. His Chloe was obviously a little taken aback at her own impetuousness.

"Never. I never want to go home, darling Chloe." He tipped her chin again and lightly brushed her cheek with his lips. "You know I love you. How could you not know? From the moment I saw you there at Nonsuch I've been living a dream. I think I fell in love with the portrait first, but that was a distant love, obviously. The lady had been dead a long while." Suddenly they both laughed, and the last of the tension disappeared. "But *you* are here—alive and lovely—and oh, Chloe, I do love you and I want you so. . . ." At this he gathered her again in his arms, kissing her fervently, yet with great tenderness.

No longer was there any pretense. They walked away from the fireworks to a small arbor where the flowers appeared ghostlike in the moonlight. With arms about each other's waists, they spoke of their feelings. Chloe wanted to fling her arms around Julian's neck, to dance and to skip for joy. Pure happiness flooded her as she tightened her hand in his. How would they tell Aunt Rosa? she asked. And when? Her eagerness was contagious, and Julian, responsive to her mood, caught at her waist; his fingers almost *did* span its curve. He kissed her cheeks and lips, her throat, and she returned his caresses with a passion that surprised and shook him.

And with the release of their love, they talked and talked. As they sat on a bench, eating ices purchased from a passing vendor, it seemed to Julian they were part of a scene he knew well. Slowly, just as it had on the river, everything in the background appeared to fade. Chloe had donned a cloak against the river's damp, and its hood covered her hair, while her features were shadowy in its curve. She was speaking and smiling, eating the delicate ice gracefully, yet Julian didn't hear a word. Again, as on the river, she appeared larger than life, strong and brighter. An illusion? A fantasy? She seemed to notice nothing amiss, so he must be making the appropriate replies. Yet another part of his mind was carrying on a conversation with *another* Chloe—a very *different* Chloe. It was about love, sensual and pure; about marriage, elusive and impossible. And about themselves—two young people caught in a situation for which they weren't responsible and for which there appeared to be no resolution. It was so similar to the river experience that Julian realized—indeed *knew*—that again, *this was something they'd done before*. Even as his heart accepted the fact, his mind rebelled. How foolish! How could they have done such things before when they'd only just met?

". . . and you must remember, Julian, I won't mind waiting. Oh, I have such faith in you, my dear! And when you're ready, you'll send for me, and I'll come to you in Williamsburg. Oh, Julian, how I'll miss you! And how I'll long to be with you every day." Chloe rested her head on his shoulder, and Julian, not daydreaming now, caught her close. It had all come true. Even as months before and miles away, he'd gazed at a portrait and fallen in love, so now the embodiment of all that was beautiful and graceful was here in his arms. And Chloe loved him. As his senses were stirred by her passion, his soul was now humble at her understanding and generosity. Chloe said she'd wait for him, and Julian knew it was true. He would wait, too. He'd been waiting not merely since he'd seen a portrait in Williamsburg, but much longer, and so had Chloe. The feelings he'd experienced on the river and just moments before convinced him it was not only years they'd waited. It had been centuries.

Chapter Eleven

On their return from Vauxhall, they told Rosa what had happened. She threw up her fan, flung her basket to the ground and embraced them both. As if she needed to be told, she said, tearful but happy, for two more starry-eyed creatures she'd never seen! No one slept much that night, and they rose early, for Julian wished to pay one last visit to Sparwefeld and Nonsuch. He hoped to sketch the house, the ruins and some scenes in Ewell to take back to James Cuddington in Williamsburg. Everyone agreed it would be one way to repay the old gentleman—Julian could imagine his pleasure in looking upon the scenes he'd left so long ago.

Rosa vowed that she, too, must find a present for James, and, after some time in the attic, emerged dusty but triumphant, with a small framed picture. "You take this to Uncle James, Julian, with my love," she said, "and tell him this is for sending the original Chloe back to us. I think he'll recognize it, for it hung in this house when he was a child."

"What is it, Aunt?" Chloe leaned over Julian's arm to look at the picture. "I haven't seen it before . . ." Her voice trailed off. She appeared shaken and pale.

"My dear, what is it?" Rosa patted her shoulder. "Are you unwell? Too much merrymaking last night?"

Chloe struggled to regain her composure. Catching her breath, she laughed lightly. "Oh, it's nothing, Aunt—I only thought I'd seen the place before. But, of course, I haven't."

It was a lie, and while she might fool her aunt, she knew she wasn't fooling Julian. Again she looked at the picture. It was of a large manor house, sumptuous and fine, with rhododendrons and lilacs in front, and sunlight gleaming on its many-paned casement windows. Steeply gabled and ornamented, it had a timelessness the artist had captured as distinctly as he had the noble old beech tree in the center of a lawn curving to the front entrance. Under the tree was a sturdy bench. It was the very building of her long-ago vision, and seeing it brought back that special moment when the old man had sat, throwing seed to the birds.

"That's Richard Cuddington's manor house—it used to be out to the rear," Rosa explained. "You remember, Julian, I pointed the place out to you. This picture was painted by Chloe Cuddington herself in the year the king took the land. It was intended as a gift for her cousin, little Richard Cuddington, who later became a very famous painter himself. Chloe herself was never a great artist, but I do think this little picture is charming." She handed it to Julian.

He took it with hands that suddenly trembled. Here was something tenable and physical, something Chloe herself had once held. He could almost sense her touch, almost visualize the scene with *her* eyes, as she worked to record a beloved home. He could almost feel her sadness.

"So this was her house—this is what the king tore down. How they must have hated to leave!" He agreed James would indeed treasure the little picture. "You are generous, madam, and will give him much pleasure with your gift. I'll deliver it with all the care I took to deliver Chloe Cuddington herself."

Rosa excused herself, and picture in hand, Julian followed Chloe, who was tugging excitedly at his arm. Out to the rear they raced, past the stables, toward the great arching beech tree. Using the tree as a pivotal point, they finally stood about where Chloe had brought her paint box to record the scene so soon to be destroyed. "It's so much the same," Chloe whispered. "Oh, Julian, I've seen it like this. Just like this! Except there was an old man feeding the birds." She pointed to the board with the white dots hanging near the arbor. "It was Domino. My aunt told me about the Cuddington's gardener, old Domino. That was his garden. He was a great friend of Elizabeth Cuddington, Chloe's mother, and the little girl was devoted to him, too. She made the king keep a house for him because he was too old to go to Suffolk with the others. That's how we have Sparwefeld, for at one time it was his cottage. But, Julian, I *saw* him!" She explained how the vision had occurred, how she felt when her dog began whining in terror.

Julian was silent, remembering the day he'd first walked toward Nonsuch. He'd come this way and had placed the house near the lilacs and rhododendrons and pictured young Chloe waiting for her parents' return. He gazed again at the little portrait—it was a beautiful home, mellow and welcoming. He almost expected to see its owners walk out the front entrance.

"My darling Chloe," he said, "I don't think you have to be afraid. This is not an evil place. What you saw was really a very peaceful scene. You are sensitive and gifted, just as your ancestress was."

Immediately, he was sorry he'd uttered the words, for Chloe gasped, her fingers to her face, which had gone very white. "I'm not a witch, Julian Cushing!" she cried. "Don't compare me to *her*!"

She turned to run, but Julian caught her. "Oh, darling, I didn't mean anything like that." He held her close, still clutching at the picture. "Chloe, stop it. I didn't mean anything wrong. You tell me you've seen—actually *seen* this before. You tell me about other incidents like the violet cap. My dear, this is nothing to be ashamed of! I think you should consider yourself fortunate! How many other people can claim to see something that existed centuries ago?" She seemed mollified, and he continued, "Of course, the original Chloe was no witch! I've never believed she was. Your own experiences are the *real* explanation—she had a similar gift. And it is a true gift. But people of her time looked at it otherwise—it was a very superstitious era." He was uncomfortably reminded of his own two previous instances while speaking with her when seemingly she'd been replaced by another creature who was Chloe and yet not *his* Chloe. How would such experiences be viewed today? Not as natural happenings, he knew. He'd thought a great deal about it all and an explanation—farfetched and impossible—was forming in his mind. Dare he tell his beloved what he thought?

"Chloe, darling, now listen to me. I've an idea what all

this might be. And it's all connected with the original Chloe, with Nonsuch and with the Lure, whatever that was. I think maybe that's one reason why I was brought across the sea. Maybe it's fate or some sort of lure or something magnetic. Remember old Dr. Dee was involved in that scandal with Chloe, and he was an alchemist. Perhaps he perfected a magnet of some kind. Maybe, even, that *was* the Lure?"

Chloe was soothed by Julian's words—anything to rid herself of association with her ancestress, with lures and Dr. Dee. There was still much she didn't understand, and she felt that Julian—dear, protective Julian—had some knowledge he'd not shared with her. However, she wasn't going to let that spoil their remaining time together. They must make the most of every moment she'd have to treasure and remember after he'd returned to Virginia.

"Julian, darling, I've a wonderful idea." She took both his hands. "Oh, Julian, let's go back to Nonsuch—tonight! I've never been there at night—my aunt would never hear of it. So we must keep it a secret. It'll be perfectly safe, for we'll be together. Oh, Julian, it's going to be a wonderful night—to see Nonsuch in the moonlight!"

Julian's face lit up. It *was* a wonderful idea. "Marvelous! We'll sit near the wine cellar and *will* ourselves to find the Lure! How I'd like to find it before I go! If we have to, we'll call upon all the spirits of heaven—and hell, if necessary—to tell us where it is. Chloe, darling, I'm more sure than ever that Nonsuch has the answer for us. Tonight maybe we'll find out what it is."

After supper they sat with Rosa as she worked her embroidery near the warmth of the great stone fireplace. Julian had rummaged in the bookshelves and found some manuscripts Rosa described as accounts of visits travelers had made to Nonsuch in the years of its glory. She'd read them to Chloe as a child and was sure Julian would be interested.

"Read them again, Julian—it's been a long time since I've heard them," Chloe urged.

Julian picked up the first manuscript. "This is by a Paul Hentzner—from his *Travels*."

> "The Palace itself is Encompassed with parks full of deer, delicious gardens, and groves Ornamented with trees. In the pleasure and artificial gardens are many Columns and pyramids of marble, two fountains that spout water, one Round, the other like a pyramid, upon which are perched small birds that stream water out of their bills. In the Grove of Diana is a very agreeable fountain. . . ."

"And further in the other manuscript, Julian—find it, do!—there's a firsthand account of a man who saw Queen Elizabeth at Nonsuch. Do you remember, Chloe, my reading these to you years ago?" Rosa put aside her needlework, listening intently as Julian read.

"Here it is—a visit by a Mr. Thomas Platter." He smoothed the page. "Oh, this is beautiful—listen!"

> "On Sunday, Sept. 23, 1599, we drove from London by coach to see Nonsuch. It is a fine Royal residence; it takes its name from its magnificence, for None Such is equivalent to *non-pareille*—without equal, for there is not its equal in England. It is built entirely of great blocks of white stone. Above the doors of the Inner Court, stone statues of three Roman emperors are erected and I Noticed a very handsome and elaborate snow-white stone fountain upheld by dragons."

Chloe and Julian exchanged glances; that had been the site of the extraordinary experience which had made him so ill. Julian continued reading:

> "I was shown over the Palace but unable to go into many Apartments as they were occupied. I was taken to the Presence Chamber to await the arrival of the Queen. Between Noon and One o'clock, men with white Staffs came in from one of the Inner Chambers; these were followed by a great number of Lords of high standing and then, alone, the Queen.
>
> She was most Lavishly attired, in a gown of pure white satin, gold-embroidered, with a whole Bird of

Paradise for panache, set Forward on her Head studded with Costly jewels; she wore a string of huge Pearls about her neck and elegant gloves over which were drawn Costly rings. In short, she was most gorgeously apparelled, and although she was already sixty-six, she was very youthful still in her appearance."

Julian's voice was mellow as he set the manuscript aside and they all savored the moment in Nonsuch's history his words had evoked. Rosa was the first to break the spell. "It's much better when you read it, Julian, dear." She rose, taking her needlework. "And I'm for my rest, my dears. I shall leave you now." She embraced her niece, who rose to kiss her good-night and then, hesitating only a moment, kissed Julian too, her eyes misty. "It would be lovely if you were here to stay for good," she said. And then she was gone.

Julian returned the manuscripts to the bookshelves and joined Chloe, who was waiting at the door. Silently, they crept out the back, past Domino's garden and the dilapidated bench. The great beech tree spread a protective shadow over their path; they would be unobserved from the house. Looking back at the point where Chloe had painted her picture, they could see the tree silhouetted against the sky. Moonlight cascading through its branches dappled the path, and there was a muted soughing as the thick limbs rustled in the warm night air. Chloe shivered and would have stopped, but Julian pulled her on, around the gate and on the path to Nonsuch.

The palace was very different in the moonlight. The treelined drive, so majestic during the day, was now a long tunnel of inky blackness. Chloe clung to Julian, and he put a protective arm around her. Both were relieved when they emerged into the outer courtyard with the rubble-strewn wine cellar to their left and the "wilderness" to their right. Ahead was the rise in the ground—the site of the gatehouse leading to the inner chamber. The jagged humps of the towers at the opposite end were sharply distinct in the moonlight. It was difficult to envision their former splendor in the play of black and white on such starkly defined destruction. The devastation was, oddly, more heart-rending in the soft moonlight than in the brightness of day. Julian spoke of this to Chloe.

"That's because in the day you can *see* what it once was and your imagination can rebuild it," she said softly. "Now—now all you can see is the ruin and desolation."

They sat "under the clock" as Chloe remarked on the rounded hump under which the eight gatehouse steps were buried. Facing them were the wine cellar and, up the slight rise, the fountain's stone plinth. Julian pulled Chloe close, and though the night was warm, she shivered slightly. "Remember what happened there, Julian."

"My darling, I'm not likely to forget," he whispered. "There's something evil there, but it's the only place in Nonsuch that is so. It was wonderful to read as we did tonight the memories of men who'd actually *seen* the palace. Think of all that's happened here, Chloe! Think of all the thousands of people who've roamed these courtyards and lived in those rooms." He gestured toward the Privy Gallery. "Chloe, you're going to think me the complete fool when I say—"

"That you think you've seen Nonsuch before?" She finished the sentence, gratified that he didn't laugh, only pulled her closer.

"I'm sure," Julian replied. With her head on his shoulder, he recounted his experiences on the river and at the gardens when it seemed he was speaking with a Chloe, but not the one he held in his arms. "And what made me so obsessed with the portrait? What led me to James Cuddington's house? What made him decide to send me—when he could just as easily have hired a courier—to be the one to bring the portrait home? And why is it that you and I—that you and I. . . ."

"That we've fallen in love? Oh, Julian, I, too, have wondered! Why could I never feel anything for anyone else? Some of my friends have been content to marry men they barely knew—they never actually expected to fall in love! But that was not for me. It was very important to me, Julian, not to wed. Sometimes, I almost felt as though I were waiting for someone."

"I hope"—he kissed her cheek—"I was the one."

"You *know* you were the one. I think I knew it the day we met and went to the Banqueting House. That used to be the only part at Nonsuch I thought haunted, but now I'm not so sure. I think maybe it's *all* haunted. . . . Sometimes I *know*

I've been here before. When the old men in the village tell me how they remember the palace when they were young, sometimes I've wanted to say to them, 'No! No! That's not true—you have it all mixed up!' For instance"—she sat up—"I've always thought that wine cellar was meant for something other than just wine. It's too big for one thing. And I've often wondered why the workmen left that plinth under the fountain. It's a solid marble block—why didn't they take it away? Do you suppose, Julian, they felt what *you* felt there?"

"We'll never know, darling, we'll never know"—he gathered her close, and they lay back on the ground—"but I know what I feel now."

Chloe's arms tightened around his neck, and she returned his kiss with ingenuous ardor. Her body pressed close to his as he kissed her throat and breast. As her eyes closed, she drew her hands slowly along the nape of his neck and across his shoulders; her warm breath came in little passionate gasps. He felt her breasts beneath his hand, and her whole body arched toward his. She was as consumed with her love as he, and there in the darkness he thought—who would see? His limbs were fluid and warm and yearned to have her softness even more close. Surely their love for each other made it all right? Her kisses were becoming more abandoned, and she whispered, "Ah, Julian—my love."

In his desire, as he pressed her hips tightly to him, something stirred in his memory. It gnawed at the back of his mind. He remembered a night on his father's Virginia plantation when he, a shy eleven-year-old child, had lain in bed, listening to the drums beating softly from the slave quarters. They kept him from sleep and stirred a latent excitement that only grew as he tossed and turned on his bed in the stifling air. After what seemed hours, exhausted with the effort to sleep, he rose and crept into the hall, past Tabby's room, out the front door and sped quickly across the lawn toward the slave quarters. He knew he was breaking a very important plantation rule, for his father was adamant that no whites visit the slaves' cabins after dusk. The black people had their ways, said Mr. Cushing, just as the whites had theirs. Julian now realized why his father had been so firm. While there were many half-white babies on other river plantations, there were none at Fairhaven. Mr. Cushing also insisted all merriment cease at midnight so the slaves would be fit to work the following day.

Julian knew it must be nearly that hour as he ran down the little lane which divided the slave quarters from the big house, following the sound of the drums. He kept out of the moonlight, near the trees and bushes where he planned to hide as soon as he saw the men beating the drums. He was small and very likely would go unnoticed.

He never got that far. The drums sounded louder, and as he paused for a moment to get his bearings, someone sped across his path, while others shouted in the rear. He huddled down in the bushes and, only a few feet away, saw Sarah, one of his mother's housemaids. She was a dusky black girl with flashing eyes and teeth and a long, sinuous body with high, full breasts. She was calling to three husky young blacks who had followed her; Julian presumed they were field hands since he didn't recognize them. Sarah seemed to be taunting them in a dialect he didn't understand. One of them caught her and, in two quick motions, ripped the thin calico dress from her body. Julian caught his breath, for Sarah wore nothing underneath. He had never seen a naked woman before and thought the girl would protest. But instead, she only threw back her head and laughed loudly. The men clapped their hands and roared with delight as she whirled around, showing herself with great pride.

In a moment the scene changed, and the first man threw her to the ground where she lay—supple and eager—her legs thrust apart, her arms held upward. Immediately, the man was on top of her. The other two, shedding their ragged pants, were urging the two on the ground to hurry; someone might find them! But the man and the girl were heedless, she moaning softly, her eyes closed while the man did things to her that caused Julian to feel hot shame running through his small body. He felt revolted, yet curiously stirred; he'd not known such things existed. No sooner had the first man risen than the second man flung himself on the girl and her legs intertwined with him. Suddenly, it was too much for Julian, and he'd turned, sweaty and fearful, and fled to his room to lie awake long after the drums had ceased.

Now it almost seemed he could hear the drums again—but they were in his pulse and in the throb of Chloe's heart beneath his hand. This girl was his, and he loved her, but the memory of the wanton Sarah on that hot summer night overcame him. Was this the way to repay Rosa's trust? Was this the way to dishonor the ardor and violate the passion he'd aroused in this innocent girl? Their whole lives were before them. They were in love, and ultimately, they would marry. This was not the way it should be.

With one last lingering kiss, Julian put Chloe to one side, saying lightly, "And that, my girl, is enough! What would the spirits of Henry the Eighth and all those queens who might still roam these ruins think of us treating their palace in such a wayward manner?"

Chloe's face was flushed, and her clothing disarrayed, but Julian was gratified to see a smile as she ran her fingers through her hair and adjusted her bodice. "I'm sure Henry would approve"—she almost giggled—"but as for the queens, well, it depends on which one you're thinking of. Some of them. . . ."

Julian laid a finger on her lips and kissed her forehead. "Let's leave the royal shades to their own pleasure, darling. Remember why we came here? We have work to do." He stood up, pulling her toward the wine cellar. "We came here to look for the famous—or infamous—Nonsuch Lure, remember? Well, let's try! Shall we be very still and *will* ourselves to find it?"

They stood on the edge of the long stone-laden rectangle, both very quiet. Chloe wanted to ask what they were supposed to do but could not find the words. Perhaps this was best left to Julian. He was gazing at the cellar stones, as if willing them to release their secret—if, indeed, they held one. He began to speak softly. . . .

"The Nonsuch Lure . . . you must be here. Somewhere in all these ruins, you are waiting, a portent for good—or evil? I think for good. We come in peace, not to disturb you, only to find you, for whatever good you may bring to us—and to others." He was quiet for a moment, as if seeking the right words. "It will not be the first time we've met, you know. Wherever you are, we have seen you before. Perhaps you've been waiting for us as we have waited for you. We need only a sign—only a sign."

There was utter quiet. Chloe found the silence almost overwhelming—and frightening. It seemed the very air had lost any semblance of life, as if she and Julian were suspended in a vacuum. She could see the moonlight, Julian and the jagged, sharp stones of the cellar, yet it seemed as if her mind was empty and her will gone. "Julian, do you think . . ." she whispered, breaking the silence.

"Hush, oh, hush!" Julian appeared almost angry. "Listen, listen, Chloe, and *feel*." He clasped her hand and urged her along. "Let's walk around the cellar. Perhaps the feeling will be stronger on the other side." Chloe wanted to ask, "What feeling?" but Julian's tone silenced her.

Together they walked the outline of the wine cellar—along one edge, around the end, back along the other side, until they reached their starting point. Then they did the same thing again; it took only a moment. On the third time around, Chloe said, "Julian, we're going in circles—in an ever-widening circle." She sounded frightened.

"Will you hush!" Julian's voice was sharp, and Chloe bit her lip. She was afraid to keep going, and suddenly she was afraid of Julian. But that was foolish! Why be afraid of Julian! Julian, whom she loved and to whom she'd almost given herself a moment ago, until he'd proved the stronger of the two. How could she be afraid of Julian?

She watched him as he stood at the cellar end, his strong features clearly etched in the moonlight. His head was thrown back, and his expression was quizzical—almost searching—as if he were desperately trying to remember something. He looked older, somehow different, and less her Julian. . . .

Suddenly, he grasped her arm, and his tone was firm. "Chloe, darling, it's getting late, and the longer you delay, the darker it is going to be. Please, do this for me—go back to Sparwefeld."

"And leave you here alone? Julian, I'll do no such thing!"

He put his arms around her, smiling, yet somehow still

distant. "You foolish child! What can happen to me here? In a field of ruins with moonlight as bright as day? Nothing! Nothing will happen to you either, but somehow I feel I may be able to find the Lure if I can concentrate on it *alone*. You're a very distracting influence, my darling." He kissed her lightly. "And if I find anything, I promise I'll come to you immediately—we won't even wait until morning. . . ." Seeing the doubt and concern in the great gray eyes, he became firm. "Now, you little goose—go! I've come all this way to find you, and ever since, I've heard of nothing but the Lure. Now I want to find *it*, too. Think of it, Chloe, if I find it, it might change our lives! I've written your uncle James that I feel you and I had met before—and that the Lure is somehow connected with us. I'm sure it will explain many things. Just trust me, my darling, and remember—we're for all time and we'll always be together."

Chloe, near tears, but powerless to combat the will which was so much stronger than her own, remained in the circle of his arms. They were warm and reassuring. Suddenly, she almost laughed at her own fears. What a fool she was. Of course, he'd concentrate better if he were by himself!

"All right, Julian, good luck, my darling," she whispered, "do take care. Remember, we've waited a long time." She kissed him, and his arms encircled her, but the hunger was gone. Clearly, Julian's mind was on other things. "Oh, darling, find the Lure and come back and tell me! Find it, please, Julian." Quickly she turned and stumbled toward the gatehouse rubble. "Under the clock" she turned to wave good-bye. Julian was standing with his arm raised in farewell—eager to begin his exploration, yet kind enough to remain so until she'd left. Suddenly, her eyes filled with tears, and she felt an intense sadness. But she must not let him know. She stood on tiptoe, blew a kiss, waved back and then disappeared into the dark tunnel of the drive.

Interim

Chapter Twelve

"And then what happened?" Timothy Hodge, clearly impatient, spoke as the tape spun to its end.

"Nothing! I told you—nothing." It was Andrew's voice speaking as Julian Cushing.

"But *something* must have happened—what did you find after Chloe left? Did you find the Lure?"

"I found nothing! Damn you, sir, can't you understand? Leave me alone." The voice broke off with a stifled sob. "Oh, God . . ."

Timothy decided then the interview must end. No harm must come to Andrew, who was obviously distraught. Gently, he reminded his friend that he was all right, that he'd forget any discomfort and awaken refreshed and clearheaded. Repeating each suggestion several times, he was pleased to see Andrew taking his time awakening, for each moment would diminish any stress. Ultimately, yawning and stretching, Andrew opened his eyes and smiled. "Well, that wasn't so bad, Tim. I feel like I've had a good sleep—just a little stiff. How long did it take?" He looked at his watch. "My God, Tim, *three hours*!" Then, noting the pile of tapes, "Well, I hope it was worth it!"

"It was . . . very much so." Often, during Julian's long recital, as he'd changed a tape, Timothy had wondered what to do when Andrew woke up. Should he tell the truth? Or merely say he'd received a lot of garbled nonsense? At the end, when Julian refused to go further, he determined it was only fair to ask Andrew outright if he wanted to hear the tapes. At least he owed him that.

Andrew, still skeptical, wanted to hear the recordings. Silently, Timothy inserted the first cartridge into the machine and settled back, noting the amusement in Andrew's eyes at the words, "This is August fifteenth. The time is two o'clock. . . ." Clearly, he considered it all something of a lark. But as the childish voice of eight-year-old Andrew said, "It was at Lord Sidney Breed's," his expression changed to one of astonishment. As the boy recited the story of Merrylegs and his experience at the fountain, Andrew appeared more guarded. Now, obviously, he recalled the story he'd repressed for years. As Timothy regressed him, suggesting a time "a few months before the beginning of the eighteenth century," Andrew seemed about to comment, then apparently thought better of it. Yet he remained attentive. He was startled at the sound of a voice so unlike his own admitting to the name "Julian Cushing." Again, with a hint of amusement in his expression, he settled back on the couch, his stockinged feet on the coffee table, and closed his eyes as Julian commenced his story.

He remained silent all through the first tape. As Julian recalled his deep grief at his parents' death, Andrew's face darkened. On meeting Chloe at Nonsuch, his eyes mirrored the wonder and astonishment so apparent in Julian's voice as he recalled the marvel of meeting his adored in the flesh. Elbows on knees, his head bent forward and shadowed in the dimly lit room, he listened to Julian's distress as Chloe dragged him from the fountain, sighing with relief that the boy was unharmed. His eyes glistened unashamedly as Julian, naïve and enthralled, described, with the soft voice of a poet, the wonder of his experience in the Abbey. And they closed, almost with hurt, upon the ecstasy in the boy's voice as he described his love for the silver-haired Chloe Cuddington.

At last, three hours later, the words ended on a sob. Andrew, smoking a cigarette soon destined for the overflowing ashtray, gulped at the scotch he'd made as Timothy had changed the second tape. With disheveled hair and tired eyes, he looked battered and oddly defenseless. He stamped out the cigarette, ran his fingers through his hair and said, "Tim, this is unbelievable. If it were anyone but you, I'd hoot. God, what to make of it all! What can I say? Do you think it's true?"

"Absolutely, every word—at least as Julian Cushing saw it." Timothy removed the last tape. "Frankly, Andrew, I've never had such a success. You may not think so, but this is quite remarkable. Often people founder—they forget dates they didn't remember even long ago! Their recall of events is sketchy; they mix up names and places. But *you*—sweet God, you remembered everything! You gave the name of the ship *your ancestor* wrote in his *Journal*! You gave the name of the ship Julian took to England and recalled what London Bridge looked like in 1700! You remembered the Indian methods of catching fish and hunting! All these things can be checked. There certainly must be a record of the Cushing family—they were evidently prominent. There are so many, many instances we can prove—or disprove."

"What do you think happened to the boy at the wine cellar?" Andrew rose and made himself and Timothy a drink. "Why in hell wouldn't he say?"

"Julian Cushing was an obstinate young man, and he didn't *want* to talk, obviously," Timothy replied. Then, with a hint of humor: "Any more than one can get *you* to talk today if you don't wish to."

"Well, I'm sure I had me reasons." Andrew's voice was an excellent imitation of Julian's colonial speech. Suddenly, the bizarre aspect of their conversation struck them both, and tension disappearing, they roared with laughter.

"And now, Julian-Andrew—now that we've got all that information, what in the name of God do we do with it?"

Andrew drew on his cigarette reflectively. "First, Tim, let's be serious a minute. I'd like to clear up a few things. You, obviously, have been through this before, and you must have some idea of what happened at the moment when I told the story of Merrylegs. But what happened to *me* then? What happened when you suggested going back to the beginning of the eighteenth century and I told you my name was Julian Cushing? Where was *I*—the real *me*? Where was Andrew Moffatt?"

"That's only a name just as Julian Cushing is only a name," Tim replied. "Essentially you're one and the same person in a new body at a different period of time."

"That's reincarnation, isn't it?"

"That's what it's called, for want of a better word. Unfortunately, there's an element of the sensational about it, but we've never come up with a better term. Forget the terminology, Andrew. In essence what happened when I put you under was this: your conscious mind was completely put aside. Remember, I told you that was the everyday mind you live with that makes your decisions, that plans and strives and so on. Once you put that aside, your subconscious mind can emerge. That—you remember I told you—is the mind that retains all impressions, suggestions, thoughts and experiences, that have ever been put into it, not only now, but *forever*. It is, I'm convinced, eternal. Everything that has ever gone through it is remembered—no matter what the century—or who you happened to be then. It does not die, but please don't ask me where it goes when the physical body dies. I don't know! Heaven? Hell? Perhaps. It could be what some people call a 'soul,' but I don't think that's so. I think it's *part of the soul*—the thinking, intelligent, independent part that retains an identity. Such identity is subordinate to the time in which you lived. And if you can be regressed to that time, your subconscious has total recall—if there was anything to recall."

"In other words, it's like a computer printout—all stored and retrievable, but someone has to tap it."

"Exactly—a good comparison, Andrew! Perhaps the subconscious mind is all that remains of us that *is* immortal. The body dies, but that part of you—the subconscious—seems to remain alive, in some other state, and can, supposedly, be reborn again. And I'm convinced in each incarnation we reap what we have sown in former lives. And what we do in the *present* incarnation will most assuredly determine what we reap in a *future* life. Maybe not here, maybe on another planet." As Andrew's eyebrows shot up in amazement, Timothy laughed. "Who the hell knows, Andrew? A generation ago people would have thought it impossible for men to walk on the moon! Is it so incredible to believe that a *mind* couldn't incarnate on another planet in a different guise from the body it wore *here*? If a mind can travel through thousands of years in a medium where time doesn't exist, why can't it travel through thousands of miles in a medium where perhaps *space* doesn't exist. Who knows?"

"Unbelievable, absolutely fantastic and unbelievable," was all Andrew could say. "How many others have you regressed, as you call it?"

"Quite a few," Timothy replied, "but none—none whatsoever—like this. Some of them are quite dull, with vast periods of blankness and lives bordering on idiocy. Some people, as I've said, live very much on the surface; there isn't much that *ever* goes into their subconscious. Now Julian, God rest his soul, had something to say. He was alive, compassionate, loving, with a fantastic memory, talented and artistic. Actually, Andrew"—Timothy jabbed a forefinger in his friend's direction—"you haven't changed, old boy. You've all the things you were then—you've got everything Julian had—even including that attraction and love for England. But you've taken it several steps further. Your career, for instance, is certainly the result of Julian's interest in art, travel and history."

"Tim, there's more here than that, and you know it." Andrew stubbed out his cigarette. "I've not only reincarnated—and I feel fool enough in saying that!—but I've followed Julian's footsteps almost completely from the time I was young. I had wonderful parents, perhaps a gift from whoever runs this road show called life for losing my Cushing parents so early. I've never had to worry about money as Julian did, and I've pursued the interests he was forced to give up because of his economic circumstances. I love architecture and art, traveling and design, sketching and writing. He'd have been good at *that*, too—think how well he recalled everything for you: not a dull moment! We both have had a minor catastrophe at Nonsuch. My God, I even ended up in Williamsburg! I wish I knew the Francis Street house that belonged to old Cuddington. I know them all well. Cuddington probably didn't live in it long enough to have his name cling. Actually, Williamsburg's real prominence didn't occur for another fifty to sixty years after Julian left. He was there at the very beginning, when it was being built."

"And remember, something led you to his *Journal*."

"That's what I mean when I say there's something more to all this. But what *is* this *Something*? It led me to the *Journal*. It led me—via a travel folder—to Cuddington House and to Rosa Caudle, who 'just happened' to have all that stuff in the attic to which I was given easy and immediate access."

"I admit, it's uncanny"—Timothy rubbed a chin and drained his glass—"even to having Sparwefeld—or Sparrow Field Farm—virtually intact for you to visit. And here's a puzzler: *you* as Andrew had the 'vision' of Domino outside the manor house that Julian actually never saw himself, for it was Chloe who saw it and described it to Julian. It tallies, though, with the description and sketch you gave Rosa Caudle. I agree, Andrew, it *is* remarkable. And more—much more—than mere coincidence. I wish I could describe what's taking place here, but frankly, there's nothing in my experience to give it a proper tag. Fate? Destiny? Fortune? I don't know."

"Or Karma?" Seeing Timothy's look of surprise, Andrew laughed. "Listen, Tim, I've worked in India and know the Indian belief in reincarnation. Karma is something you build up—for good or bad—during all the soul's reincarnations on earth. I know the Indian who is born to a comfortably wealthy life as one of the higher castes—or one of the lower castes who has fantastic 'luck'—is supposed to have earned a good Karma. By contrast, the poor old sot who grubs for food in the alleys and trash piles—and there are millions of them!—has inherited or earned a bad Karma. I'm simplifying, obviously."

"You're right, however," Timothy replied. "Reincarnation and Karma have been a Hindu belief for thousands of years. But the belief's not limited to them. As a matter of fact, reincarnation as a doctrine is accepted by much of mankind. Only we in the West are a bit stubborn about it. I guess we don't like to admit we're not always efficient masters of our own fate. Yet even philosophers and statesmen like Cicero, Virgil, Plato, Caesar, literary geniuses like Donne, Goethe, and Milton believed in reincarnation. Your own countrymen, Ben Franklin, Oliver Wendell Holmes and Longfellow and Whitman—even General Patton!—were believers. Why, even a recent Prime-Minister of Canada admitted his belief! Like hypnosis, it's attracted some kooks and frauds, but always, throughout recorded time, there've been a score of sincere believers, and it's growing. Even world-renowned professors are interested, and some colleges in your country, Andrew, have endowed chairs to study it! Would you believe it?" He didn't wait for an answer. "Yes, I think yours is a classic case of something similar to Karma, with a single difference: it's not a superficial reaping and sowing from a previous existence. Here it's more a *reliving* and a *reenacting* the scenes, *with the same principals*. And I don't know what the end is. It would have been helpful if Julian had gone further."

Andrew glanced at his watch. "Tim, Madam Hall's luncheon is now only a fond memory. I've been on quite a journey since then, and—if I may borrow your bathroom for a shave—I suggest we take this conversation to that good little restaurant over on Sloane Street." As Timothy rose to clear away the glasses, Andrew thumped him on the back. "And while we're enjoying one of their overpriced vintages, I want to talk seriously about going back to Nonsuch—particularly, to the wine cellar."

Andrew spent the following two days at Hatchards Book Store in Piccadilly, the London Library, the British Museum and the bookstore at Westminster Abbey. Timothy had lent him the tapes, and in the privacy of his room, lying on his bed in the semidarkness, he'd replayed them. All the while, as he listened to Julian Cushing recount his love for Chloe Cuddington, the enigmatic dark-eyed original gazed at him from the wall. As Julian discussed his love, she seemed almost to come to life. It was a moving experience, and Andrew, more emotionally involved than he'd anticipated, found it difficult to stop the tape and jot down the names, places and dates—anything traceable—that Julian mentioned.

Armed with his list, he spent the next day researching the time needed to cross the ocean in 1699, the names of seventeenth-century ships, the road one might have taken to Ewell, the villages in Southwark and the buildings in existence on London Bridge. One book in particular, *Old London* found in the Abbey bookstore, was a treasure trove. Destined for the tourist trade, it was, nevertheless, a remarkable compendium of sketches, drawn from contemporary sources, of every part of London considered important during the Tudor era. One section, entitled "Ludgate from the West," clearly depicted the way Chloe and Julian had ridden to London Bridge. There were the Fleet Ditch waters lapping at Blackfriars exactly as Chloe had pointed out. And the next sketch showed a *frost fair* on the Thames in the year 1699 with people skating, roasting their meals on bonfires or buying refreshments from stalls set up on the twenty-foot-thick ice.

Lloyds of London supplied a list of all seventeenth-century ships owned by the London Company, and in the British Museum, Andrew found that the *Susan Constant* sailing from Blackwall in 1606 carried the name "Amos Cushing, yeoman" among its passengers. He also discovered John White's sketches of the Virginia Indians which were considered most valuable. And in 1649 the passenger list of the *Duke of York* carried the name of "James Cuddington, gentleman." On a hunch he checked the passenger lists at Lloyds for all ships docking *from* the New World, and in the spring of 1700 the name of "Julian Cushing" was listed aboard the *Sovereign of the Seas*.

He also did some firsthand research. He crossed the new London Bridge and, hiring a taxi at Southwark Cathedral, directed the driver through Walworth and Newington. Sure enough, as they neared the river, Lambeth Palace was clearly visible. Hedged in now by developments and St. Thomas's Hospital, it was no longer girdled by the vast trees, gardens and orchards that had so impressed young Julian. Andrew paid the driver at Lambeth Bridge and walked across, emerging about where Julian would have landed from the horse ferry. The street was named, appropriately enough, Horseferry Road. He walked up Millbank, toward the Abbey, imagining the boy's wonder could he now see the vast Houses of Parliament where before he'd seen only the rotting remains of Westminster Palace.

It all checked out. However much he might, with his twentieth-century skepticism, disdain the thought that he'd lived before, the fast-growing pile of notes he'd made for

Timothy proved otherwise. One thing surprised Andrew. As the notes confirmed the tapes, much of his reluctance to accept disappeared. He'd been brought up and educated to respect things that could be proved and that—above all—were irrefutable. But it did surprise—and intrigue—him that the fact that so many of his previous beliefs and values were in danger of being destroyed or at least altered seemed really to matter very little. What *was* important was that he discover the *truth*.

And then there was the matter of Chloe Cuddington herself. She was as much a mystery as the Lure. And what had brought him to England and Cuddington House? And what was the seemingly malign force at Nonsuch that could kill?

At the end of two days of visiting all over London, he went to Timothy Hodge's apartment and, over an excellent meal which Mrs. Hall remained to cook, laid his notes out for his friend's inspection. Timothy was gratified at Andrew's findings. "Not that I expected anything else," he said, pouring an after-dinner coffee. "Our friend Julian was *not* a liar."

"Well, our friend Julian left several things unsolved, however," Andrew replied, "and here's what they are. First, what happened to him? He couldn't just disappear. I checked the ships' passenger lists until 1702—no great task, for there weren't that many—but no Julian Cushing is listed as returning to America. I don't really think he ever went home. Second, was the Lure ever discovered? The legend hasn't persisted to this day. Does that mean it was found? And that whatever was found was hushed up? Or was the legend allowed to die a natural death? That probably would have happened in a generation or so, especially as the ruins deteriorated even further. One thing I'm absolutely certain of, Tim, is *they are all connected with each other and with Chloe Cuddington*."

Several books on the coffee table with paper slips in various places testified that Timothy had also done research. "And right in my own bookshelves, too. Here, Andrew, you won't believe this! It's such a small coincidence—but this is the sort of thing researchers consider *much* more valid than a name, a date or a place. Listen to this—it's from a *Short History of Ewell and Nonsuch* by an estimable gentleman named Cloudesley S. Willis, whom, believe it or not, my father knew. Old Willis died just a few years ago. Here's what he writes: 'A cowman named Pilgrim who worked at Nonsuch Park and lived in Ewell one night left his home and walked across the fields to visit a sick cow. It was two o'clock in the morning. When he got to this field, there was a high stile on which he sat. There in the hollow, he saw a funeral. He gazed at it and remembered that people said that a church once stood in the dell. He was too frightened to go on and turned back, leaving the cow to take her chances. He told the story to Mr. Gadedsan, who looked in a book and said there had been a church in that dell *in the time of the Romans*.' "

"Just as Rosa Cuddington told Julian," said Andrew.

"Right. And in this book, which is most explicit, Queen Elizabeth's Elm, the Banqueting House, each and every description of Nonsuch that Julian Cushing gave tallies completely. He might have taken it from this book—except, of course, he didn't. It wasn't written until 1931."

Andrew was silent, mulling over Timothy's words. They didn't surprise him; he'd developed a compelling respect for Julian Cushing's veracity. And there was a strong conviction growing in him that the story had to have an end—and that he'd been brought to England to end it.

"Tim, I'm sure the answer is not here in London. I think it's at Nonsuch."

"You're not to go back there, Andrew! I warn you, there's nothing there for you except something rotten and evil. I thought so before the tapes, and now I'm convinced. I won't be responsible!"

"I won't go to Nonsuch without you, Tim. Jesus, we'll take a policeman if we have to." The thought—so incongruous—struck them both, and they laughed heartily. Andrew poured them a brandy. "Now don't worry, old chum. I have no desire to meet up with the Nonsuch demon, but oh, God, I *do* want to find the Lure! It will somehow justify Julian and *his* Chloe. That's what *they* wanted, too—to find the Lure. We've left it all hanging midair." He set his brandy down. "Tell you what. I know your patients can't do without you, but I'm going to ask my Artless Charmer if I may have the hospitality of Sparrow Field Farm." He could see

Timothy's protests forming. "I promise not to go to Nonsuch unless you're there with me. Also, I'm anxious to have a chance at that attic! Think what I found upstairs at Cuddington House. Now Julian didn't stay *there* very long, but he was at Sparrow Field off and on for three weeks. There must be *something* of his visit there that we could trace. How about those manuscripts he read? How about the *Book of Hours* the child Chloe so loved? People don't throw those things away. Granted they won't tell us anything we don't already know, but *if* they exist, then something *else* might still remain. Something else that will tell us what happened to Julian—and if he ever discovered the Lure"—and then, almost as an afterthought—"and what happened to Chloe, too."

"Well, if you insist, I see I can't stop you. I can't join you till the weekend, for unlike a few lucky people I know, I *do* have to slave for a living." Timothy grinned at Andrew. "Promise me you'll leave the demon and Lure until I get there. Just stay in Madame Caudle's attic—I can't imagine any harm can come to you there!"

Andrew left the next day for Sparrow Field Farm. "Mrs. Williams will be glad to have you, sir," Rosa Caudle said, "and you should be comfortable. They have two rooms, a bedroom and one for the telly on the first floor. Harry and me are at the back, but there are three large rooms at the front where we used to take in paying guests. Are you looking for anything in particular, sir?"

Andrew hesitated. He didn't want to deceive Rosa Caudle, but the story he'd have to tell her now would be so farfetched and with so many loose ends he'd only stretch his credibility—or her credulity. When everything was solved, he'd tell his hostess the whole tale. "I want to see everything that's up there, Mrs. Caudle, particularly any diaries, letters, journals—I've pretty well combed through everything you have upstairs here." She nodded and wished him a good journey.

An hour later he was in a large room overlooking Domino's garden. Was it the one Julian had stayed in? Or had it been occupied by Chloe or Rosa Cuddington? He remembered the tapes and Julian's hearing the name "Chloe" and his annoyance at the laughter that followed. And then he'd gone on to Nonsuch and met his charmer. Would that I had *that* luck, Andrew thought grimly—all I find there is a demon that's out to kill. After Mrs. Williams' comfortable lunch and her "good hunting, sir," she left him at the attic stairs. He climbed to the garretlike room, smaller than he'd expected. The pitch of the roof didn't leave much floor space, and he made a mental note to move carefully or he'd surely hit his head on the beams.

He switched on the one overhead light, and his heart sank. There wasn't nearly as much as he thought. Several old trunks, some dilapidated chairs and lamps of no particular period. A venerable sewing machine and several handmade radio sets. A rusted and chipped filing cabinet disclosed scrapbooks, newspapers and magazines of fifty years ago that some Cuddington had thought important. There were boxes of bank statements, checks, bill stubs and tax forms—all obviously brought from Cuddington House to Sparrow Field, where the family had more time to work on them. Ancient Christmas tree ornaments and a box of old frayed and tarnished costumes. But *how* old? Carefully, he sat on a trunk and sorted out the eight or nine pieces. Simple country clothing—anything ornate would be in London. The dress, he guessed, was early Victorian. A shawl—probably vintage Empire. A handsome riding habit belonging to a Georgian Cuddington was moldy and torn in spots. A fan and a pair of ivory satin slippers, small and trimmed with pearls and a darkened silver buckle. Well, we're getting there, thought Andrew; they're about 1750. Most of the clothing, he realized, had been kept for costuming. Undoubtedly instead of discarding these items, they'd found their way to the trunk, and with no children at Sparrow Field in years, the garments had lain untouched for over a generation.

At the bottom Andrew found a small linen bundle. An accessory, he decided, that needed wrapping against the ravages of time. Carefully, he picked it up and, turning toward the light, uncovered a small coffer—the kind that might once have held jewelry, potpourri or hairpins. A handsome piece and very old. With hands that suddenly shook, he opened the lid, and there, on the bottom, lay the faded remains of what had once been a very elegant cap—the kind one might give a child. It was of violet brocade, creased and worn. In places, the cloth had given way, revealing the stitches holding tiny seed pearls. They appeared pristine and fresh. An empty circle near the top was certainly where a jewel—long lifted out—had originally been placed.

Andrew felt a tightening in his throat. Here it was—just as Julian's Chloe had described it—the cap she'd visualized in all its fresh beauty that had been the original Chloe's birthday present. He could imagine the delight of that little girl at receiving such an elegant gift. As he stroked the little cap, he felt an unwonted tenderness for that long-dead child. He was playing the complete fool, and he knew it. Yet here was a tangible reminder of the two Chloes that had meant a lot to them both. So he'd play the fool and be content.

After a few minutes he carefully replaced the clothing, laying the bundle at the bottom as he'd found it. One down and several to go, he thought. What next? Well, just for starters, how about the Lure, Madam Fate? If it's not out there in that pile of ruins—and I really think it is—how about up here? He rummaged in trunks of blankets and sheets, others with table linens and piles of napkins—remnants of a time before the paper doily. And a small portmanteau filled with books. Andrew began to comprehend the system inaugurated by a long-dead Cuddington. Trunks and boxes for "costumes," some for "household goods," one for outmoded and out-of-season "clothing," another for "business items." And here one for books.

The contents seemed, as in the others, to be in time layers. Books on top won as a school prize by some intellectual Cuddington in 1915. Music books, art books, histories—all old and probably worth something in the rare book market. He must tell Rosa Caudle. They'd be better off restored and in a proper collection. Gardening books and produce records of Domino's garden dated 1783. Then several thicknesses of newsprint. He picked one up and read, "Barrons' Broadsheet, printed in Ewell at the Sign of the Quill, May 7, 1700."

May 7, 1700? The date was familiar. Then he remembered. That was the year Julian had arrived in England, and—surely he had it correct, for he'd been meticulous in jotting down the tape dates—it had been May 4 when Julian, Rosa and Chloe had gone to Vauxhall. The next day they'd returned to Sparwefeld, and that night Chloe and Julian had stolen out of the house to visit Nonsuch in the moonlight. Andrew felt the hackles on his neck rise. There had to be a reason this forerunner of the newspaper had been saved. Gingerly, he replaced the books, took the several sheets in hand and returned to his room.

"All right, Andrew! All right! I understand—yes, I'll leave directly after my last appointment, which is"—Timothy Hodge consulted his calendar—"at five o'clock. I'll be in Ewell by six thirty. Steady, old boy, you're about to come through the phone! Calm down, I have to ring off now—it'll all keep for another few hours!"

By six Timothy was en route to Ewell. He'd been surprised by the agitation in his friend's voice and wondered at the hornet's nest Andrew's hypnotic regression had stirred up. He didn't know whether to be pleased or troubled—so much depended on whether Andrew discovered what he was looking for. If he didn't—and unless he could put it behind him as an unsolved and tantalizing mystery and get on with the business of twentieth-century living—Timothy could visualize some emotional difficulty ahead. Already Andrew had been in London for more than a month, spending most of his time in the elusive search for a palace, a woman and now a Lure. And it was consuming him. The physician in Timothy was concerned, even as the companion of Andrew's search was intrigued and excited at his apparent find. Clearly, the attic had yielded *something*.

Andrew was pacing the drive when he arrived at Sparrow Field. Timothy admired the building previously seen only at a distance—Julian had described it very accurately. The site of the "vision" and the old manor house were in the back, he remembered. Andrew came bounding toward him and nearly pushed him through the front door. Timothy commented on his eagerness, even as he stopped to admire the glowing

Elizabethan portraits on the wall. By Bartholomew Penn, Rosa Cuddington had said. He hoped he'd have time later for a more careful scrutiny. Right now, Andrew could hardly wait.

"Tim, I've got something to show you—God, what a find! If they hadn't saved the newspaper, we'd never have known. Sit down, Tim. Can I get you anything? You were great to come—you'll never believe. . . ."

"Steady, old boy, steady, you're sounding like quite a hodgepodge! No, I don't need anything—it's early for liquor and too late for tea! Now what have you found? And sit down, Andrew, for God's sake, and stop pacing! Tell me."

Already Andrew was lifting what appeared to be an old newspaper from the table and, smoothing it carefully, said, "Now listen, Tim. The date, incidentally, is May 7, 1700. Does that mean anything to you?" Before Timothy could answer, Andrew said, "It was just a few days after Julian, Chloe and Rosa returned here after visiting Vauxhall Gardens. Now here—the headline, if you can call it that—is 'Tragedy at Nonsuch.'

> "The body of a young man in his early twenties was discovered at Nonsuch Palace on the morning of May 6. He was found lying semidistant between the site of the wine cellar and plinth of the fountain which is in the middle of the Inner Court. Although his clothing was not disarranged and there was no evidence of a struggle, he had obviously been strangled."

"Oh, Jesus, Andrew, that's what happened!" Timothy remembered Julian's voice near the end of the moonlight visit to Nonsuch as he'd urged Chloe to leave. Eager and expectant—certainly he thought he'd found something. Timothy felt suddenly drained. What a waste!—a bright young life snuffed out by that hellish energy force which even he now, with all his twentieth-century knowledge, could not explain. "It was that demon force, of course—it got to the boy and killed him. Andrew, what do *you* think?"

"I know what I think and feel—and it's sadness, anger,

pity and, yes, a little fear! Hell, Tim, I almost went the same way—not once but *twice*! And it took two times for whatever it is to get Julian! What a pity . . . and all so needless." He struck the table with his hand. "And if we only knew what it was! God, Tim, I know what that boy felt when he died." Andrew's face was pale, and his voice shook as he continued reading:

"The corpse was identified as Mr. Julian Cushing of Williamsburg in the colony of Virginia. Mr. Cushing had been visiting Sparwefeld as the guest of its owner, Mistress Rosa Cuddington, and her niece, Mistress Chloe Cuddington. When questioned by the Ewell sheriff, I. L. Hinton, both Cuddington ladies said Mr. Cushing had been in good humour and health at supper. Miss Chloe Cuddington stated she had left him at the ruins at about nine o'clock, had returned home and retired. She had endeavoured to listen for his return, but sleep overtook her. In the morning, she assumed he was still a-bed, having, perchance, spent a long time at the palace site. It was well known that Mr. Cushing was immensely interested in sketching antiquities, and she said they had gone to see the ruins by moonlight.

It was not until late afternoon that authorities informed the occupants at Sparwefeld of the discovery of Mr. Cushing's body. It was brought to the house where Miss Chloe Cuddington, who swooned at the sight, said she and her aunt would take responsibility and prepare it for burial. There was some rumour among the Sparwefeld servants that Miss Cuddington and Mr. Cushing were affianced. It is not known whether the young man had any survivors.

The sheriff and his staff have been plagued with complaints of highwaymen and thieves who inhabit Nonsuch Park at night, and it is believed one of them accosted Mr. Cushing, strangling him when, as Miss Cuddington verified, they found he had nothing of value to give. The sheriff has pledged more supervision of the park and its environs in the immediate future."

"Andrew, what that must have meant to both Chloe and Rosa!"

"A supreme tragedy—for them as well as Julian. Everything had been going so well." Andrew's distress was apparent. "I still can't get it out of my mind that that force could get to him so overwhelmingly, and he was a fair distance from the fountain, too." He referred back to the newspaper. " 'Between the site of the wine cellar and the plinth of the fountain in the middle of the Inner Court'—I know exactly where. . . ." He broke off. "Tim, let's go! It's still daylight, but the workers will have gone." He rose, waving away the objections he could see forming on Timothy's lips. "Listen, Tim, we can be there in ten minutes. What can happen? I won't go near the goddamned fountain—not even midway between it and the wine cellar. I just feel I *have* to go back at least once more. I feel I owe it to that poor boy."

Timothy rose. He knew Andrew in this mood, and he'd go alone unless someone went with him. In moments they were out beyond the wall, walking quickly to the site. The traffic was heavy with homebound workers from the excavations, as well as from Ewell village. But once inside the treelined drive, they were alone. A light burned in a caretaker's mobile home at the far end, and excusing himself, Andrew sprinted toward it, emerging a few moment's later and pointing to the ruins themselves as a meeting place. He jogged up to meet Timothy. "It's over there . . . and we have official permission. I introduced myself to the caretaker the first day here. I told him we'd only be a few minutes, that I had a friend who wanted to see where old Henry kept his firewater." He was pulling Timothy in his eagerness.

Almost at once they faced the long, deep expanse of the wine cellar. "Now what do you suppose Julian was thinking when he stood here and sent Chloe away?" Andrew's voice was quiet, almost as if he were talking to himself. "I'm convinced he sent her home because he'd figured something out or realized something—but what?"

Timothy didn't answer. He watched as Andrew descended the broken stone steps and walked around the cellar. The cobbled floor slanted with a gully in the center running to a soakway. How many bottles of royal bubbly had gone down that drain? Timothy wondered. The walls, at least seven feet high, had probably been covered by casks or storage vaults with shelves for jugs and bottles. They were faced with oddly shaped stones interspersed with blocks of chalk and brick. Some were smooth; others, exceedingly crude and rough. An interesting mix; apparently odds and ends of several types of building material had been used in the foundations. One piece, a rounded, deeply carved stone, caught his attention.

"Norman," said Andrew, following his gaze, "pure Norman. A wonderful piece, called a roundel. It must have come from some building here, perhaps the church or priory. I think a good part of the foundation here is rubble from other buildings old Henry had pulled down."

Andrew had begun to walk along one rectangular side; Timothy followed along behind him. The sun had set, but it was not yet dark—that special moment of mellow twilight before true darkness falls. The air was still, and the sound of traffic outside the park seemed muted. Andrew, shoulders hunched, hands in his pockets, appeared lost in thought. At the far end, about sixty feet, Timothy judged, he turned around the shorter end and retraced his steps, but in an ever-widening arc.

It was Timothy who first realized what was happening. Andrew was walking exactly as Julian had walked. Along one side, around the end and back, going farther from the wine cellar each time. "We're going in circles, Andrew," he spoke quietly.

"Will you hush!" Andrew's tone was sharp. His expression was quizzical, almost searching. He looks as if he's trying to remember something, Timothy thought. He looked like Andrew, yet somehow different. He seemed younger, more vulnerable—and apart. Angered at the remark, Timothy wanted to protest further. They *were* going in circles—couldn't he *see* that? Julian had been walking in an ever-widening arc when he'd sent Chloe home. And later, apparently, he'd walked such a wide arc he'd been drawn toward that fountain site just as Andrew was now drawn. . . .

"Andrew, I insist, this is foolish, it's getting dark." Timothy got no further. Ahead, his friend had stopped in his tracks and was staring at the fountain as if he were seeing a ghost. His face was dead white and contorted with rage. As he took a step in the fountain's direction, Timothy ran and pulled at his sleeve. Andrew jerked it away. "Let go, oh, let go! I can handle this." His tone was authoritative and unafraid. Suddenly, leaning down, he picked up two sticks from the ground. Advancing a few steps, he stopped, as if bracing himself for an onslaught or to ward off a blow. He seemed to be entangled with something Timothy couldn't see, but he could *feel* its power and presence. There was a deadness in the air, almost as if they were suspended in a vacuum, and an icy chill seeped deeply into his bones. This wasn't the same as before when Andrew had been engulfed by heat. Yet it had to be the same force. . . .

Only a few feet from the fountain. Andrew stopped, a queer smile on his face. "All right, Hurst, you devil, you've killed me before, you won't do it again." He spoke quietly, coldly, "Come at me, you pig, and fight fair this time. I'm not afraid of you!" Suddenly, Andrew threw back his head and laughed; he seemed almost exultant. "No, I'm not afraid of you because God is on my side, and you are of the very devil. You belong in Hades—go back to Hades, Hurst! And don't come near me again!"

Rooted to the spot, Timothy could only listen amazed. The voice was not Andrew Moffatt's. The tone was reasonant and low-pitched, yet even his body appeared different. The stance, the slant of one shoulder, his hands with those ridiculous sticks clenched tightly appeared almost *alien*. They were raised out in front of him now. In benediction or in defense? Timothy could not tell. But Andrew's feet were firmly planted, and his whole attitude suggested strength. He obviously meant to stand his ground. Timothy knew intuitively there was little he could do now, for it was not Andrew Moffatt shouting at—whom? *Who was Hurst?*

". . . and you are an obscene spirit, Hurst, obscene and impure! Jesus has given the power to drive out demons and to speak in tongues and has ordained one may even take up serpents with their hands! *You* are a serpent, Hurst, but you cannot hide from the Hosts of Heaven or the Lord. You will fall like the most spent star, Hurst. See, I make the sign of the cross that held our Lord! Begone, you hostile soul!" Andrew had straightened up. He appeared full of confidence and authority, and Timothy felt his own concern subside, even though his heart was pumping and he felt ice cold. He kept his eyes on Andrew, who showed no sign of relenting. Instead, raising the two sticks high in front of him so they formed a crude cross, he took another step in the direction of the fountain and shouted at whatever it was he saw.

"I call upon St. Michael, the Archangel, the noble and magnificent lieutenant of the heavenly army, to protect us in the battle against the powers of evil, of darkness and against those would rule a world of sins. Come to the rescue, St. Michael!" Andrew struck the sticks together; they seemed almost to emit sparks. "I cast you out, you obscene and impure spirit, cast out your satanic powers, every hellish demon that may have befriended you! In the name of our Lord Jesus Christ, I make the sign of the cross and command and order you to depart in the name of the Father, of the Son and of the Holy Spirit. . . ."

There was silence for a moment as if a deadly battle for possession were taking place. Possession of place or possession of body? Timothy wondered. Or was Andrew fighting for his life? If so, he was certainly unafraid and deadly self-confident. A few more steps, and again he raised the sticks high in the sign of a cross and shouted, "I pray to our Sovereign in heaven, creator and defender of all humanity. Who made man in His own image, to look down and take pity on you—*you*, Hurst—caught now in the labyrinth of the obscene spirit who dulls and terrorizes the human mind and spirit, overwhelms it with fear and alarm and slays without shame! I command, you ancient unclean spirit, in the name of God, by the Judge of the Living and the Dead, by your God, by Him who hath the power to send you to Hades, to depart forthwith in fear. It is the power of Christ that compels you, Who brought you low by His cross. Tremble before Him—and go, depart, leave then! Depart and give way—I insist you submit—to Christ in Whom you found none of your wicked works! For He has already stripped you, Hurst, of your powers and bound you prisoner and taken away your weapons. . . . You have nothing!"

As Andrew shouted into the empty, dead air, Timothy felt a tingling excitement along his spine. *Something* was taking place—something he could *feel* but could not see. His own mind felt black, and he was drained of emotions. It was almost as if his own spiritual and emotional power were there, helping Andrew, helping him—do what?

". . . and the longer you take, the greater the punishment will be meted out to you. You have stayed too long, Hurst! It is not mortals you are treating with such contempt, but rather your Sovereign Lord in heaven, the very Creator of your soul. Begone! Go, leave, depart, sinful, murderous one! Take your sins with you, for God has ordained that man as He created him should be His temple, the dwelling place of the immortal soul. Why do you still linger, Hurst? Give honor to God, the Father of us all, before Whom all must bend. Give place to the Holy Spirit! Begone now, begone to wherever the Holy Father will receive you—or go to everlasting hellfire—the choice is yours. But . . . *go*!"

Andrew sank to the ground. He laid the sticks to one side and, hands pressed together, bent his head, his lips murmuring silently. Timothy felt a strange compunction to do the same. His mind, so empty a moment before, surged now with the implications of what he'd just witnessed. Though his insides were churning with excitement, he felt completely himself again, as though his own spiritual forces had returned to his body. But it was obvious his companion was not yet himself. He was still—*who?*—praying for what Timothy was beginning to realize had been an exorcism of what they had—and how truly!—called the Nonsuch "demon." The air, so lifeless just a short time before, was now fresh and brisk, and traffic outside the park sounded normal. It was, however, getting darker every moment, and soon they'd be unable to see anything in the wine cellar. On an impulse, Timothy went to the still-kneeling Andrew. He laid a hand on one shoulder. "Well, that's that," Andrew said. Taking Timothy's hand, he pulled himself to his feet. His face looked ravaged, his mouth was working, and he said, "I feel sick, Tim, just sick. . . . Let's get out of here."

Timothy took Andrew's arm. He appeared unsteady and, as they walked toward the gate, grateful for support. Timothy sensed his friend did not wish to talk of what had taken place. He didn't know yet what to make of the incident. To his untutored mind, it had very much resembled a religious rite. But how could a layman like Andrew Moffatt perform a ritual known only to a man of God and his church?

As they turned in at Sparrow Field's gate—the place where Andrew had described his vision of Domino and the birds—the answer hit Timothy with the force of the rhetorical thunderbolts Andrew had unloosed against the unseen demon. Andrew had performed that ritual because he'd once been trained to do so—and he'd *remembered*. Across hundreds of years, faced with the necessity—death if he failed—he'd used the faith and power inherent in a Catholic priest to exorcise a murderous earthbound force and had sent it into some limbo of heaven or hell.

Clearly, Timothy decided, there was more than one personality other than Julian Cushing, alive and with memories intact, in the person of Andrew Moffatt. And if the Lure was to be found and the mystery of why Andrew had been brought across the sea understood, then that person had to be set free.

Chapter Thirteen

At Sparrow Field they found a note from Mrs. Williams. She and her husband had gone to the cinema at Ewell. There was a cold supper on the kitchen table, she wrote. But neither Timothy nor Andrew was hungry, and they decided to return to London. Within an hour they were at Cuddington House. Andrew was thankful Rosa Caudle wasn't at the desk, for he'd have felt obliged to explain his early return. Timothy would see him safely to his room, could pack the tapes and recorder, and he, Andrew, would then sink gratefully into bed. He wanted to be alone, to lie in the darkness and mull over that incredible experience. He'd been shaken to the depths of his soul, and at the moment his emotions, intellect, and spirit could not accept or rationally explain what had happened. He needed peace, quiet and time for reflection.

He switched on the light. "*Ahhh-hh-h* . . ." Timothy walked to the wall where Chloe Cuddington's portrait hung. He looked closely, returning to the doorway to see it in perspective. The soft yellow light lent a pinkish luster to the peach velvet of the gown—a luster repeated in the bare arms, neck and breast. Chloe's face was more shadowed than in the daylight, but the luminosity of her gaze was still piercing. She seemed about to rise and greet them. Andrew wondered —for the hundredth time—at the extraordinary talent of the man who'd captured not only that superb loveliness, but her heart as well.

"I—I—hadn't seen the lady . . . before." Timothy appeared almost dumbstruck. "Well, no wonder you and Julian. . . ." He was silent for a moment. "She's quite the most exquisite creature I've ever seen."

"And one of the most mystifying." Andrew stuffed the

tape recorder into its case. "I still think the solution of our mystery—of the Lure—rests with her. We cleared up one part tonight, out there, though God knows what it was. Hello, what have we here?"

Andrew had picked up the little velvet-bound book with a clasp which he remembered seeing the day he'd explored the Cuddington House attic. It had been wedged in between gardening and art books and children's histories. He'd thought it merely a child's diary and passed it by in his eagerness to get to the trunks and boxes. A note slipped from the inside cover. "It's from Rosa Caudle," he explained. " 'Mr. Moffatt—you remember the girl Jennifer at the desk. She helps us out here on the weekend. She's a history major at London University and asked if she might look in the attic for any souvenirs, books or papers for a paper she's writing on Napoleon. Harry gave her permission. Before she left, she dropped this off at the desk. I told her—I didn't think you'd care, sir—of your interest in Cuddington House, it being so old and all. I told her how you'd found Julian Cushing's *Journal* in Williamsburg and the portrait of Chloe Cuddington. She says you must have missed this and you'd certainly want to read it. We are going to visit Harry's cousin in Brighton for a few days. Jennifer will be on duty on the weekend if you want to talk to her about it. I'll be glad to know what you find and I hope everything worked out well at Sparrow Field.' "

"The good Rosa will never believe *how* well things worked out at Sparrow Field!" Timothy laughed and lit a cigarette, wishing he had a drink. "Listen, old man, I'll take the machine and tapes and run back home. I think you need a good night's sleep."

But Andrew was lost in the book. He motioned to Timothy to sit down. "This is *her* diary—Chloe Cuddington's diary, Julian's Chloe—the diary he told us she wrote in. Do you suppose?" He ruffled through the pages quickly. "It's here, Tim. My God, sit down and listen."

"*May 9, 1700*. The past two days have been the saddest and most horrible of my Life. I do not know if I can put down the tragic and melancholy Accident which has befallen my dear Julian. And I know that I am to Blame! I should never have left him at the Dreadful spot. I should never have thought so much of the Lure and so Little of my Darling.

When I awoke that morning, I almost had a Premonition that something was Wrong and even Aunt commented on my Depression. I kept waiting for Julian to arise, and when a servant was bidden to go to his room and returned to say his bed had not been Slept in, I knew he was gone. I did not know whether he had left Sparwefeld, but I knew he was gone. All during the Day I avoided Aunt's company, for she was Concerned and Mystified.

In the afternoon, finally, Sheriff Hinton came and, with many Apologies and with due kindness for our Feelings, said Julian's body had been found on the Inner Court. This so confirmed my own dreary Thoughts I was immediately faint, and when they brought his poor limp dear Body in, the face contorted and blue, I swooned. Even now I cannot bear to think of it.

When I awoke, Aunt was bathing my forehead and wrists, and we Wept together for a long time. How I wish I had not left him at Nonsuch! How I wish I had never returned from whatever vale of Soft comfort one's spirit goes to when one swoons. Life will be too Terrible to contemplate now without my darling Julian.

Aunt said the servants will prepare his body for Burial and the Vicar would have the service in Ewell Church. We know not yet where to bury him or who to inform, he having no family.

She has refused to have me look upon him Again; she says he would not wish to Distress me and it will do no good."

Andrew's voice was trembling as he finished, and Timothy, stricken, gazed at the wall, attempting to visualize the radiant young woman so similar to the one in the portrait broken and despairing. Andrew resumed reading.

"*May 11, 1700*. It is all Over. We laid my poor Darling Julian to rest here today. Of course, many Curious came, for Barrons has put the Accident on the front page. Accident—it was no Accident! It was murder—outright murder for whatever devil it is that is there almost killed Julian once before. And it is still there. I think it to be the Lure—cursed Lure and at times I want to run there and Scream and send the devil that Lives there to the fiery Hell that awaits him.

Aunt and I wept again this afternoon when the post brought a letter to Julian—in answer to one of his—from James Cuddington. We thought it proper to open it. In it, Mr. Cuddington informed Julian he was leaving him the little house in Williamsburg in his Will. He said he had made his daughters and sons very comfortable with money and given them many of his belongings and they had great Opportunity in the colony. They did not need the little House too and Mr. Cuddington said he would have great Joy in giving it to Julian if he would bring his bride back with him to live in the little House. It would really be Julian's Home, and Mr. Cuddington said he would only desire a room, until he died—which he does not think will be very long now.

I weep as I write this. How Lovely and Sweet it would have been. To have been with Julian Always. Now all is Lost. Aunt says she will write to Mr. Cuddington immediately and will Remind me to do so when I am again Myself. I did not say to her that I will never again be Myself. I do not wish to remain in any World in which my Darling is not with me. I shall eagerly await the day when I Join him."

Andrew laid the book aside. "God, the poor girl. She blamed herself, of course. And it could all have been so different! For them, as well as old Cuddington. They would have been so happy. Such a waste, such a waste." He looked at her last words. "I shall eagerly await the day when I join him."

"Does one die of a broken heart, Tim? Does the medical profession have a name for it? She lasted only six more years, you know; she died at twenty-six. I wonder what of?" Then, placing the book on the bedside table, he said, "I can't read any more tonight, Tim. I've had it for the day. I can't say you didn't warn me! But whatever it was out there, it's knocked the wind out of me, and I can't wait to hit the sack. What in hell do you think happened out there, Tim?"

"You really don't know, Andrew? You have no idea?"

"None whatsoever! One moment I was speculating on the rocks and describing the roundel to you. The next, I felt an inner certainty that *something* was approaching. It wasn't hot and didn't make me sick. But there was an aura—*something* in the atmosphere—I guess you didn't feel it?" Not waiting for an answer, he went on. "I never *saw* anything, Tim, not a thing. But I *felt* this presence. I could even tell when it was very near me, and yet it had no shape; it was like a replay of an old event like the ones I told you about under hypnosis. Only this time I *wasn't* hypnotized—I knew what I was doing and saying all the time. Something said to me, 'Don't let it get you, get it first!' The next thing I realized—absolutely knew for certain—was that I needed a cross and didn't have one. But the sticks were okay. It was the power I put into the sticks that counted, not the fact that they weren't a real cross. That's what's so mystifying. That power! Where did it come from? Suddenly, out of nowhere, I felt *flooded*, almost overcome, by an inrush of power that would have made several demons insignificant. I *knew*—I had complete assurance—that I wasn't going to be hurt. But that's all. I didn't know what was going to happen to that *thing*. All I know is that as I got stronger and more powerful, it got weaker. Whatever it was that was threatening me got smaller and smaller, and finally, it just disappeared! Then I felt drained, exhausted, weak, sick to my stomach. But *it* . . . was gone."

"Andrew, I think I have the answer. Not in its entirety, but some kind of answer. You must know that what you performed out there tonight was some sort of exorcism?"

"Exorcism? Well, I hadn't thought. . . . I suppose it was. If that's what it was, however, God spare me another experience. Do you suppose whatever I . . . exorcised . . . was the Lure?"

"I don't know—all I know is that walking around the wine

cellar as you did acted as a sort of magnet. And whatever was near the fountain site was able to move away from it. With the pony Merrylegs and later as Andrew, you had to be *on* the site. Here you were sixty to seventy-five feet away. Didn't we read somewhere that old Dr. Dee was interested in magnets? Yes, I imagine the Lure is some kind of magnet. But I don't think what you did away with tonight was the Lure. I think it was a force, an *entity*. Something evil. But it's gone—for the moment at least.'' Timothy packed the last of the tapes. ''Get a good night's sleep, Andrew. Try not to think of what happened. Read through the rest of the diary for any information that might be helpful if you feel like it. And then relax. Come to my office tomorrow. I'll have my girl phone you the hour. I've an idea I know what we need to do. And how we need to do it.''

The following afternoon Andrew left Cuddington House for Timothy Hodge's office. At the desk he returned Chloe's diary to Jennifer.

''I thought it most interesting, sir,'' she said. ''Especially seeing as how you'd found the young man's *Journal*.'' Clearly, Jennifer would have liked to discuss it further, but Andrew excused himself. Chloe Cuddington's impassioned words, the agonizingly sad years of her life, combined with his experience at Nonsuch, had left him drained. He seemed to have difficulty in ''getting back to himself.'' As he stepped through the revolving door, automatically raising his hand for a cab, even the noise and jumble of the Strand traffic came as a shock.

He waited only a few moments before Timothy's last patient left, and after the nurse had wished them both a pleasant good afternoon, they had the office to themselves. Andrew admired the handsome reception room with its paintings and the dying fire in the grate. The office itself was furnished as a comfortable living room with other paintings, bowls of flowers and books. Only the couch with its well-worn easy chair beside it, the table and note pads looked clinical.

''The girl left us some tea on the hot plate over there,

Andrew." Timothy was clearing his desk as he spoke. "Did you have a good rest?"

"Yes and no. I read through to the diary's end. It stayed with me for a bit of tossing and turning, and then I guess I slept. No dreams—none that I remember anyway. I feel okay. Not a hell of a lot of energy, though."

"I'm not surprised after what you went through yesterday afternoon." Timothy accepted a teacup and sat down. "What did you find in the diary?"

"The story of a broken young lady who, to the end of her days, which were only six years away, blamed herself incessantly for Julian's death. *She* had suggested going to Nonsuch by moonlight; *she* had left him there alone. It gnawed at her constantly. That and the vision of 'what might have been' at the little house in Williamsburg. But she felt that somehow—sometime—she and Julian would be together again. As for James Cuddington—he died about a year later; he was distraught at Julian's end and said he was sure the Lure was responsible. Blamed himself also that he'd sent young Cushing to England. Seems everyone blamed themselves for something which, of course, they hadn't one iota of power to stop. Not if it was a Karmic working out, that is."

"What did she die of?"

"I think a form of tuberculosis." Andrew sipped his tea. "A wasting disease the local doctor called consumption. That term has covered a multitude of medical sins for centuries, you know. I would imagine TB, however—there was coughing, losing weight, spitting blood and melancholy. Every day she hoped she'd get worse. She'd completely lost the will to live. Rosa Cuddington buried her next to Julian in the Ewell churchyard." Andrew shaded his forehead with his hand and was silent a moment. Clearly, the diary had touched him deeply.

Timothy put the teacup aside. "Andrew, I want to talk to you now as your doctor—and as your friend. You are, or were, one of the most normal people I know. You had a childhood experience, much of which was repressed for years, which we can hardly call traumatic. It took a newspaper clipping to revive a dormant interest in a fairly mundane subject—excavation. Nothing new there in your life.

But this *particular* excavation suddenly became of primary importance to you. Then you discovered a journal, and it became an obsession. Since then you've disregarded almost every pursuit of normal life: your friends, your profession, your responsibilities back in America. You've been on this witch-hunt—and I use the word advisedly—for a long time now, and it is consuming you. I've seen the difference in your personality—and now I see the toll it's taking of you physically. Either you have to accept what you know so far and leave it at that—or decide to go further *and then accept whatever transpires*. If you don't find what you're looking for—and at the moment, it seems to be the Lure, for we know what happened to Julian and Chloe—then you must put it aside and start living in the twentieth century again. You've got to make a decision one way or the other. Last night you were protected by what you call a power. It *could* have gone another way—it almost did twice before—just the same as it did for Julian."

Andrew looked out the window. "You're right, of course, Tim. I accept everything you're saying. But you seem to think I have a choice—to accept what we know now or go further. What do you mean by going further?"

"That's why I asked you here this afternoon. I want to explain carefully to you, as a medical man and also as one who's shared this adventure with you. The world won't come to an end, Andrew, if you don't find the Lure. Whatever it is, and if it's at Nonsuch, it's been there for several hundred years, and outside of killing once, it's hurt no one else. That letter you found at Cuddington House, written in the 1730s, about someone being killed—"

"That, I'm positive, was a reference to Julian's death, written years after it happened."

"All right, so it's killed once, but it won't kill anymore. You got rid of it last night. Now you can close the subject."

"Well, I don't want to, God damn it!" Andrew rose and began to pace around the room. "I've come this far, and I want to finish this whole thing. But we still don't know where the Lure is—and we still don't know whether Chloe Cuddington was a devil or an angel. I'm opting for angel, of course.

but who knows? I want to clear up her part in this whole mysterious little saga. Just as we did with Chloe and Julian. There's *got* to be a way. The answer's got to be somewhere."

"Well, that's the other part of my little speech, Andrew," Timothy replied. "You have an alternative. I said you could decide to go further—but"—he raised his hand—"now don't interrupt! We can go further, but if we do, *you must accept whatever we find*. And it may not be to your liking, remember! It might change your life, just as your experience so far has certainly changed a good many of your values. Are you willing to take that chance, Andrew?"

"Hell, Tim, I'll take *any* chance. I think I know what you're driving at. You mean another dose of hypnosis?"

"Exactly—there's no other way. I'm sure by combing the attics of Cuddington House and Sparrow Field you might conceivably come up with a few more clues, but if the *true answer* hasn't been known for four hundred years, I doubt if it's in either of those places in its entirety. Do you feel equal to another dose of hypnosis, as you so respectfully put it?"

"Oh, sure, but tell me why?"

"I'm not going to tell you anything, Andrew. If I told you, it'd be there in your subconscious when I want to question it. I want to find out what already *is* there, not give it any suggestions. Another cup of tea before we start?"

But Andrew was already on his way to the couch. "I presume this is the throne?" He turned and laughed. "Tim, you *are* a good friend to go through this with me, and I'm damn grateful. But tell me, did you ever expect to see me *here*?" He lay down, settling his long frame into position. "Mighty comfortable, old boy."

"We aim to please—*and* comfort." Timothy was busy setting up the tape recorder. "No, Andrew, I never thought to see you there. We've come a long way—both of us. Remember, this experience so far has shaken a few of my own medical certainties. You might become something of a *cause célèbre* if this experience were ever published." Aware of Andrew's disdainful look, he concluded, "Which it isn't going to be, I know."

"You'd better believe it," Andrew muttered. "Let's get going, Tim. I'm liable to fall asleep if you don't do something fast."

Timothy rose and pulled the curtains shut, for the late-afternoon sun was distracting. Returning, he spoke to the recumbent form. "Still with us?"

"Just waiting for you, Tim."

"All right, Andrew, take a deep breath and relax. That's good. Now another. That's just fine. Another deep breath—and relax. You should be beginning to feel drowsy by now. Let that feeling go all through your body. Just relax. And let your eyelids feel heavy. Can you feel them becoming heavier? You're getting sleepier and sleepier, and your eyelids are heavier. Your whole body is relaxed and comfortable. It's harder and harder for you to stay awake. Now you know you must sleep. Sleep long and deeply. Stay very relaxed. Be sure you are relaxed and sleepy. Think of nothing else. I'm going to count to five now, and when I'm finished, you'll be asleep. Here we go. One . . . two . . . three . . . four . . . relax deeply now . . . you are asleep . . . four . . . five."

As before, there was complete silence. Andrew's breathing was deep and normal, his color good, though his expression was still tired. He was completely asleep. Timothy spoke into the recorder, giving the time, place and date, and then stopped the machine. He made several notes on his yellow legal pad, rubbed his forehead as if to stimulate his thought and then, with the air of one knowing he's reached a point of no return, clicked on the recorder and spoke to the sleeping figure.

"Now, Andrew, we're going back in time . . . back quite a long way. This will be a long journey for you. You needn't answer if you don't want to. You don't need to go either. Do you understand?" He was gratified by the slight nod from the inert figure.

"All right, then, Andrew, come with me, back to a time long, long ago." Patiently, with great care, Timothy regressed Andrew again to his youth—to a happy time with his parents on safari in Africa, to a birthday party when he was ten, to a tiny toddler learning to walk. It was possible to regress a consciousness to a time within a womb, a feat popular with many doctors at the moment, but Timothy bypassed the opportunity. Instead, he said, "Andrew, this is now the time for our long journey. You'll pass many milestones as you go, yet I want you to take it slowly. Don't stop to examine any experiences along the way. Visualize them if you wish, but don't relive them. They're only memories, remember. Do you understand?" Again, the slight nod.

"Then, Andrew, this is now the year—about—let's say—1536. Yes, I'm sure that's the year, and that's all I know. Perhaps you weren't alive then; perhaps you'll see nothing. But can you go back and tell me if you were there and if you saw anything? It's a long way back, Andrew, so take your time. . . . I'll wait."

Timothy clicked off the recorder, settled back in the chair and watched his friend closely. This was always one of the most interesting parts of hypnosis, as the mind in the sleeping body took off on its journey into time—perhaps even into space. Somewhere—wherever the mind was going—there had to be a spatial unit. But what was it? Infinity? Timothy wondered.

As he watched, Andrew stirred several times. Shifting his position slightly, he unclasped his hands. A muscle in his jaw throbbed for a moment, then quieted. Clearly, he'd started on his journey, and his body was reacting to whatever he was visualizing. But he was not participating. No expression or change in position lasted for more than a moment. Eventually, he seemed more settled and more—Timothy sought the word—in *repose*. His hands were clasped, as if holding something. A book? He seemed quite comfortable, very relaxed and . . . waiting. . . .

Timothy spoke. "Are you there? In 1536?" He avoided using Andrew's name. If there was to be an answer, any name would be unfamiliar at the moment. "Do you wish to tell me, my friend, what you see?"

"Yes, I can tell you. . . ." Again Timothy experienced that little shock when a regressed patient spoke for the first time. The voice was always different. As it was now. Andrew's words were pleasant, even-timbered, not unlike his own, except his speech was dissimilar. "Yes, I can tell you," Andrew repeated, "it's most pleasant. I am in a garden reading my book." It was pronounced "ga-a-a-r-den." Was it Scottish? Irish?

"And where is the garden, my friend?" Timothy waited, pencil poised.

"Why, right here, in this beautiful Surrey!" The man's enthusiasm was noticeable. "And only in England in May do we have so many flowers in bloom! It's a sight to see. You cannot see it, my man?"

"No, I can't see it . . . perhaps you'll tell me where it is so that if I get the chance, I could always—"

"Oh, but of course—you *must* come! The Priory does not admit visitors, which I'm sure you know, but you can see the garden from the road. Even the king has seen the garden from the road—but, of course, he took no notice of us."

"The king?" Timothy was busily writing. "What king?"

"Our good King Henry the Eighth—the only king in England! I think you must really be a stranger here if you have not heard of King Henry. Why, he hunts hereabouts very often! Many times, I'm afraid"—here the voice became conspiratorial—"even on the Sabbath." Andrew's lips were pursed in disapproval.

"You do not hunt on the Sabbath then?"

"Of course not! I think you must be blind, my man! Do you not see this habit I wear? Do you think monks hunt? We labor—oh, yes, we labor for God and for man. But we do not hunt."

"You are a monk, then, my friend?" Timothy sighed with relief. It *was* as he had thought. "A monk—and would your name by any chance be Thomas? And the Priory you speak of—would it be Merton Priory?"

There was a moment's silence, and then a beatific smile spread across Andrew's face, which had somehow become rounder and fuller as he spoke. His eyes were closed, but Timothy knew, had they been open, they'd have been alight with pleasure and welcome.

"You *did* know! Yes, Thomas is my name. How kind you are to come and see our beautiful garden. We work very hard here. But tell me, my man, how *did* you know my name? I am no one important."

"Oh, you are important, Thomas. Does not our Lord say all souls are important? I will tell you how I knew, Thomas. But first, I want you to tell me *your* story. It's such a beautiful day and such a lovely place to talk . . . here in this garden. Would you mind telling me your story, Thomas?"

There was a moment's pause. Timothy could almost picture the monk looking around, wondering whether they'd be overheard. He waited several moments, and then Andrew spoke again.

"I have told Father Felix I am going to meditate in the orchard for some time." Andrew bit his lip. "It was a bit of a fib, you understand, my man, but you seemed so eager." Then, as an afterthought: "I like to be helpful."

"That was kind of you, Thomas, and kind of Father Felix. Now let's sit down, you and I, and make ourselves comfortable. I'm just going to listen, and I won't interrupt. Will you begin?"

With that, Timothy checked the recorder, put his pencil and paper aside and sat back to hear what Brother Thomas of Merton Priory in Surrey had to say on that May morning in the year 1536.

Thomas

Chapter Fourteen

Later Thomas often wondered what his life might have been like had the king not ridden through Cuddington village to hunt on that fine May morning.

Thomas lived—in what he hoped was a state of God's grace—in the holy house of Merton Priory. He watched now with his brother monks as dust, disturbed by the royal party, wafted over the roadside hedge and settled on the herbs they'd later distill for medicines. The king rode at the head of the group—still a fine-looking man despite the rumors of dissipation and excesses from which they all prayed daily he might be delivered. Several of the party shouted greetings, and the monks bowed their heads; the king did not favor them with a glance. Most *religieux* were in bad repute with royalty. Rome had not been understanding about a divorce from his good wife, Catherine, of unhappy memory.

It was 1536, the twenty-fifth year of the eighth Henry's reign. It would have been difficult, indeed almost impossible, for even the monks of Merton Priory not to know of the drastic events occurring at the Tudor court. Cloistered they might be, with much time spent in good works, manual labor, prayer and meditation. Yet Thomas and his brethren were still worldly enough to listen to the gossip that arrived at the Priory gates with the delivery of those materials they didn't provide for themselves. Thomas worked with the monks in baking bread, brewing ale, growing vegetables and herbs, but they did not weave, tan hides, keep a piggery or chicken house or slaughter animals. Thus, almost daily, someone from the outside world clanged the great bell and, in a few moments' conversation at the back gates, brought the world to the cloister.

So they'd learned that the king's first wife, Catherine of Aragon, had finally been exiled after a quarter century of marriage. They were shocked and saddened at the death of Sir Thomas More, her great friend and supporter, who went to the scaffold rather than swear that the king, and not the pope, was the head of the English church. And they were fearful of the Machiavellian Cromwell—by his own admission a "ruffian"—who had successfully dissolved many monasteries and abbeys. While Thomas Cromwell and Henry insisted such measures were only to limit papal jurisdiction in England, still they hadn't hesitated to confiscate the churches' revenues and keep its considerable treasure. Schism, they'd found, was quite rewarding.

As the royal party passed by, Thomas laid aside his hoe and went to the cloister to dip in the cool rain barrel hidden in the shade of an old wisteria bush. Watching as the dust settled on the dry road, he remembered the three Carthusian friars dragged to Tyburn to suffer the monstrous death of hanging, drawing and quartering, whose mutilated sections were later exhibited at London Bridge and over the gate of their own Charterhouse. *A stern and stubborn man, the king*, thought Thomas. No sooner had Catherine been exiled than he'd married Anne Boleyn—just in time to make the birth of their daughter, Elizabeth, legitimate (if one didn't count too closely). Thomas crossed himself at the disrespectful thought of his sovereign Lord on earth.

And yet since that time it seemed even his sovereign Lord in heaven had taken matters into His own hands. The union of Henry and Anne hadn't been fruitful where a son was concerned, and the highly volatile and basically selfish personalities of the two made for discord in the royal bed. Now the queen was in the Tower, accused of things no right-thinking monk should even *know* about. It was ironic, too, for she'd encouraged the king in his heresy. Indeed, Thomas knew, could the church blame anyone for the religious "troubles," they'd blame the Boleyn. Yet Christian principle demanded they pray she be dealt with according to God's will. God, so far, had seen fit to leave her in the Tower, and Thomas was relieved to let it go at that.

As he walked to his cell, Thomas saw Father Felix, the

Prior of Merton, hurrying toward him along the cloistered walk. A tall, frail man, with luxuriant white hair and a long, white, forked beard, the prior had the darkly burning eyes of the ascetic; their piercing gaze seemed to emphasize the waxy transparency of his skin. He smiled and acknowledged Thomas' deferential bow.

"Thomas, I was just coming to find you! A good excuse to exercise these old bones and find a moment in the fresh air." He, too, dipped into the rain barrel and watched the royal party now almost out of sight. "Who goes to Cuddington?"

"It was the king, Father."

Father Felix's face darkened. "The king—I'm sorry to hear that. Perhaps what I've heard is true. He's going to look at the land, his messenger said. Come into my chamber, Thomas."

The young monk followed dutifully, the soles of his sandals making a comfortable shuffling sound on the stone walk. He was untidy from working in the garden; there was dust and dirt on his gown and feet. But he knew Father Felix wouldn't notice. The prior was a man wise with the span of his many years—years that had only increased his faith and dedication to a life of service. Thomas knew how fortunate they were at Merton, for Father Felix's sanctity, godliness and devotion permeated every crevice. Their house lacked much of the dissension, pride and corruption—and certainly the outright sexual abuses—of which the king and Cromwell had complained. Unfortunately, such conditions existed in only a few holy houses, but it had been enough to condemn many. No one with any real understanding, however, doubted that the tranquility and merit of Merton was due to anyone other than its prior. Thomas found the thought comforting as he closed the great carved door and waited for Father Felix to speak.

"It has come," was all the prior said. And he held out a parchment from which dangled an official seal.

Quickly, Thomas crossed himself. He felt stunned—almost ill—and wondered what to say. "For Merton? I can't believe they would. . . ." The prior's one great dread was that their beloved house would suffer the fate of those other religious houses closed by the king's orders. Their one consolation was that Merton was small and insignificant. They possessed no great treasure, no holy relics like a bone of St. Andrew's arm. Their holdings were respectable, but not impressive, a few hundred acres. Merton's real value lay elsewhere—in succoring those unfortunates in Cuddington who were poor and ill. Bread and ale were doled out daily at the gate, and much of the garden's produce went to the poor. Those who showed promise were taught to read and write; a few had even entered the Priory to serve God and man. What could Cromwell and the king want with so modest a holy house? Even the food sent to the Priory by such as Sir Richard Cuddington—fat capons, molds of sweet butter and baskets of fruit from his orchards—were always shared with the villagers. Whatever was consumed by the brothers provided the energy they used for one another's welfare. There were no fat monks at Merton.

"This was left here this morning." Father Felix's tone was sad. "We are commanded to vacate Merton within six weeks, for the Priory will be dissolved."

"So soon!" Thomas gasped. "So soon—but where will we go, Father? What will happen to you? To the others? To the novices!" He felt an unholylike anger rising within him. "What do we have that the king wants?"

Father Felix read from the parchment in a voice that suddenly trembled. " 'The inhabitants of Merton Priory are free to choose their place of abode and the King's grace and largess will see to their expense and subsistence in their move.' Of course, His Majesty doesn't seem to recall that there are fewer houses now than ever for the brothers to find refuge." He read further. " 'All religious property, gold and silver plate, tapestries, copes, altar cloths, holy vessels and statues are to remain. All records must remain and will revert to His Majesty, King Henry VIII.' " Father Felix laid the parchment aside. "They even want the lead from the roof and the stone. . . ." Suddenly the prior looked old and ill.

Alarmed, the monk asked, "Father, are you all right?"

"This is only a reaction to anxiety, Thomas. We've waited a long time to know what the king would do. In a way, it's best to know . . . for sure. . . . But *you*, Thomas. This is why I wanted to talk with you. We must discuss *your* future."

Thomas was puzzled. There were more than a score of monks at Merton. Why single him out? Noting his dilemma, Father Felix rose and crossed the room. He was not normally demonstrative; his affection and efforts were for God, not man. Despite the lewd charges made by Cromwell's commissioners, there was little physical contact or favoritism on the prior's part toward his flock—or even with the monks toward each other. Therefore, Thomas was astonished when Father Felix stopped directly in front of him and put two strong hands on his shoulders. He was impressed by their strength, for Father Felix had that look of frailty often seen in the *religieux*—the result of cold nights spent in prayer with tired knees and hands blue with cold.

"Thomas, our worst fears are now here. But no matter what the result—no matter where you go—you must promise me you'll remember your vows and you'll continue in the great devotion you've shown to your work."

Startled, Thomas nodded, though he was amazed at the prior's words. He had no record of great achievement at Merton. Father Felix had, at times, consulted with him on Priory matters and favored him with companionship occasionally here in his chamber. Yet he never thought he'd made any great impression.

As if sensing the monk's surprise, Father Felix said, "You are young, Thomas, and I have no doubt whatsoever that, given the true and normal course of events that might have passed, you would one day sit in *my* chair. You have great faith and ability—and the two don't often go together." He sighed and walked to the window. "You'll stay in the Order, Thomas?"

"Of course." Thomas was fervent. "Father, I know nothing else. I cannot—could not—live any other way." His face darkened for a moment. "I once gave it a . . . great deal of thought. Before I took my vows. Oh, yes, Father, I'll stay in the Order!"

"Good! I thought I'd chosen right." Father Felix smiled. "Thomas, I have two tasks for you. One for now. One for later. I must inform the others. A sad task—I don't relish it. But for now, would you go, please, to the manor house. Sir Richard and I must talk. Ask him to come here or ask if he'll see me—whatever he wishes." He waved his frail hands, attempting a false lightness. "And pray, Thomas. Your prayers are important. We're all going to need them."

Thomas left for Cuddington village immediately. He spoke with no one as he let himself out the back gate, knowing his voice would betray him. Anger, disappointment, frustration—all churned inside him as he set out on the dusty road over which the king had just passed. For four hundred years Merton Priory had educated, housed and trained many who'd gone on to distinguished careers or callings, including Thomas, the saintly Becket, who'd once tilted with another King Henry. *We need another Becket*, Thomas thought sadly. *We're all giving in to Cromwell too easily.*

Soon, with the sun warm on the bare spot of his tonsured head and the air fragrant with the sweetbriar, whitethorn and privet that grew wild along the roadside, Thomas gave himself up to the pleasure of his surroundings. Ahead the road ran through a dense stand of oak and elm which sheltered the great coveys of partridge and pheasant and provided shelter for the deer and hare the king and his companions sought. Shading his eyes, Thomas watched the fleecy clouds sailing like great white galleons across an azure sky and, heady with the solitude, listened to the soughing of the huge cypress trees where the gentle rise of the land gave the wind free play. He'd always enjoyed the walk to the village. Never more so than today with the bitter knowledge such simple pleasure would soon be a thing of the past.

Cuddington lay at the foot of the North Downs, a few hours' ride from London. Thomas remembered how absorbed he'd been when, as a novice, he'd first read its history. The village had been inhabited since ancient times, and the Merton monks often exhibited—with unmonklike pride—a document almost 900 years old, a copy of a deed dated A.D. 675 in which a sub-king of Surrey, Frithwald, and the then Bishop of Erkwald, gave some dwellings, "apuud Euuelle cum Cotintone" to the nearby Abbey of Chertsey. Cuddington was mentioned in the Domesday Survey of 1086 as "the manor of Cudyton or Codington," and for centuries, the descendants of that family—the Cuddingtons—had existed side by side with the Merton brethren. Often the monks helped the lord of the manor, Sir Richard Cuddington, at harvesttime when labor was short; as often, Sir Richard sent his laborers to repair a Priory wall or barn. Father Felix frequently mentioned how fortunate they were that Sir Richard lacked the very real arrogance of many of his class. He was genuinely interested in his tenants' welfare, possessing an abiding love for the land of his ancestors and regarding his inheritance as a moral means for dispensing his many responsibilities.

Thomas slowed his pace, for the village lay just ahead. Beyond its center, he knew, was the manor house of Sir Richard and Lady Elizabeth, enclosed by its great brick wall. He felt his anxiety and frustration lessen and turn to joyous anticipation. Immediately a little prayer formed on his lips. Still that feeling! Would he never quench it? How many years had it been now—three, four? Stubbornly, he sought to quiet his mind and deal rationally, in true holy fashion, with this tingle of excitement. It was, he knew, no more than a lust of the flesh—and a thorn in the fabric of his faith. And he'd thought it subdued! In the quiet of the cloister, in the glorious chapel, listening to the monks' mellow chant, the feeling never assaulted him. There he was complete and whole and one with his God. But here, on the road to Cuddington, with the fresh fragrant breeze whipping his coarse brown woolen habit around his bare sandal-shod feet, he felt young, free and almost light-headed. The temptations of the flesh and the world still found him a willing vessel, it seemed. He sighed. Father Felix should know . . .

Just before the village, the Church of St. Mary the Virgin came into view, and Thomas was reassured. Here was stability and strength. It, too, had a history as long as the village, for its records, kept at the Priory, went back to the twelfth century. It was a larger building than the small village required, but of handsome flint with stone dressings, still retaining its Norman tower. Richard Cuddington had recently made a gift of a new floor of ornamental tile, more than an inch thick, that reached to the ancient font overlooking the chancel. Thomas thought longingly of the cool interior, of the spacious nave, crossed by aisles that entered from wide arcades on each side. The soft breeze would be whispering through the open windows, the gilded statues gazing timelessly from their niches. He might, perchance, stop and pray to the Virgin that all temptations be removed from his flesh.

Then, looking at the sun's height, Thomas realized there was no time for prayerful intercession. If he must deal with earthly allurements, then he must deal with them himself. He'd taken longer than usual on this walk, absorbing the beauty of the fragrant green countryside and reveling in his solitude. He passed through the church courtyard, where trees, identical kin to those of the great forest, cast long shadows over the tombstones and crosses of the little graveyard. There he felt a measure of returning peace and invoked a silent thankful prayer that he might be strong in the difficult time ahead.

The home of Sir Richard Cuddington lay at the western end of the village, separated from the church by the long, flat graveyard where Cuddingtons and villagers alike had been buried for centuries. The early fourteenth-century house had been enlarged until it had grown to a substantial home about a small courtyard. It was approached by a long circular drive along a green area dominated by a handsome young beech tree. It now consisted of three parlors, lavishly wainscoted, and other living chambers for gentry and servants alike, a pastry house, three larders, a kitchen garden, dovecote and well. Richard Cuddington had recently erected a timber tithe barn on the eastern slope near the stables; the handsome tiled roof had caused the villagers to comment for days. In the distance were four working farms, stables, barns and a fishpond, separated from the house by spacious gardens and orchards.

Brother Thomas was very familiar with his surroundings. They had once been his home. He'd been born into one of those very farms to a simple yeoman family whose forebears had served the Cuddingtons for generations. After his parents had been carried off in the plague of 1524, when Thomas was ten, another farmer had taken him into his home to bring up with his ample brood. He remembered how astonished his benefactors had been when he'd asked to attend the Priory school so he might learn to read and write. The Cuddingtons, however, impressed with the boy's ambition, had given their blessing, and a year later Thomas had gone—a raw, gangling youth, his hair hanging about his ears, in homespun jerkin and pants, thick boots and one long heavy cloak—to Father Felix. He carried with him his hornbook and quill pen, some books, gifts of the Cuddingtons, and his parents' Bible. Sir Richard, noting the boy's nervousness, had clapped him on the back and whispered that if he found the Priory routine other than he'd thought, he was to let him know; the cottage would still be there. Sir Richard had no son and had always treated Thomas with affectionate regard and concern. It had made his going easier.

As if in answer to his thoughts, the door opened, and Sir Richard emerged. He was an extremely handsome man. He wore rough work clothes that hardly suited his station, but his predilection for helping in the barns and around the vats and hogsheads in the dairy and brewery was tolerated indulgently by villager and farmer alike. Even in the simple clothes, his long, sinewy body moved with a lithe, easy grace. His face was very square, with the prominent cleft chin of all the Cuddingtons. His blond hair—almost silver and striking in one just turning forty—was hidden under a battered hat considerably older than his clothes. As the door slammed behind him, he glimpsed the approaching monk and smiled.

"Thomas! Good day to you! Have you come to help? We can use every hand." Then, noticing the monk's expression, he said, "Is something wrong?"

Thomas explained what had happened at the Priory. Richard Cuddington tensed, and his face took on a taut, almost concerned look. "Dissolution for Merton . . . I can't believe it." He gazed off in the distance and said quietly, "And confiscation of the land. Those acres the king is taking adjoin mine. The land belongs to my family. Some of it's owned by the church and some by village families. The common land belongs to the people. In God's name, what does the king want with the land? If he dissolves the Priory, what will he use the land for?''

They both turned at the sound of the door opening behind them, and a young girl stepped out into the sunlight. Again Thomas felt the tingle of joyous expectation that always accompanied his first glimpse of Chloe Cuddington. In other, less anxious moments, he'd often marveled at God's expertise in duplicating Richard Cuddington in this child-woman. The great dark eyes—alight now with pleasure at seeing him—were fringed with heavy lashes. The sun glinted on the whitish hair, making a silvery halo enveloping her beautifully shaped head. ''Thomas!'' She spoke in a low, caressing voice. ''I didn't know you were here.'' Her cheeks were flushed with pleasure and as deeply pink as the ripe lips parting in a welcoming smile. She held out a soft, ivory-tinged hand, its nails cut neatly across, giving a blunt look to long, shapely fingers. Then, noting her father's expression, she said, ''Father? Is something wrong?''

''Chloe, love, go to your mother. Tell her I'm off to Merton and ask that Domino assemble the workers to wait upon my return!'' With that he strode toward the stables, and seconds later, they heard the pounding of hooves as Sir Richard rounded the wall and set off for the Priory.

It was an awkward moment—one Thomas had hoped to avoid. He'd not been alone with Chloe since—his body recoiled from the memory. It was, he decided, nearly three years. Then she'd been an innocent seventeen-year-old, precocious beyond her years, sensitive, warm and intensely loving. And he, a few years older, thinking himself complete now that he'd followed the rigorous spiritual as well as physical exercises by which the Merton monks lived out their days. He'd learned his lessons well. He wrote a beautiful hand, and his exquisite lettering of the Priory's manuscripts would have been envied if that sin had been tolerated there. He was happily active working in all Priory functions—in the garden, the dairy, the stillroom—and whole-hearted in observing monastic routine. In the oratory or chapel where the monks gathered for psalmody and antiphon. Thomas participated vigorously in the Morning Office, in Prime, Terce,

Sext, None, Vespers and Compline. He had visited the sick and dying in the village and served the pilgrims en route to Canterbury. At Merton he was whole and complete. Yet now, here with the glowing figure of Chloe Cuddington before him, it almost seemed as though that satisfyingly rewarding life were a mere spiritual "overlay" that kept him from the side of this beautiful creature who'd once told him she loved him, would never love anyone else and had fiercely cried that she'd "wait until the end of time."

The memory of that unhappy occasion enveloped him, and Chloe, sensing his mood, said, "Thomas, do come in. Mother will want to see you. We still speak of you often—we all miss you. I must give her Father's message, but please wait for me!" She sped off toward the rear of the house, and Thomas, still ill at ease, went into the room that, he remembered, had been the scene of their unhappy farewell.

It was a large, comfortable chamber, its noble dimensions enhanced by elegant furnishings. There were family portraits on the wall—a new custom replacing the wall murals painted by itinerant artists. They were hung above the great fireplace, a new addition to the room as signified by the carved rose of the Tudors and the pomegranate, the device of the unfortunate Catherine of Aragon. Opposite was a glorious tapestry with biblical scenes hung over a heavy intricately carved chest, upon which lay a rich cushion of embroidered "Flemish work." The great Turkey carpet lit the room in an amber and red glow as the sun played among its patterns.

Thomas walked to the window and seated himself in its embrasure bench, savoring the stillness inside and the splendor of the magnificent trees in the park outside. He could see the king and his party off in the distance, emerging from a gully and riding up the promontory in the direction of the church. They'd ridden a good distance and were now obviously returning the way they'd come—undoubtedly, he'd meet them on his return to the Priory. Observing them, he felt a small presentiment of fear invade the quiet beauty of the surroundings. The king was on Cuddington land now, not Priory land. Obviously, he was hunting—but what was his quarry? The party did not appear interested in the area's ample game. Thomas remembered Father Felix's words:

"He's gone to look at the land." Again, the monk felt that anger, fear and resentment which had enveloped him that morning. He watched the royal party near the large forest of oak and elm. The king, erect and tall in his saddle, had stopped and, with a sweeping gesture, turned almost full circle as he pointed out various directions to his companions.

Thomas could see the royal party was impressed with the beauty of the manor house, its buildings and the park outside. He remembered his pleasant walk, and the fragrant scents. It was all Cuddington land, just as Sir Richard had said. Was the king merely admiring the rural splendor one of his subjects possessed? Or was there a deeper motive in his appraisal? Thomas remembered the words of a neighboring landowner that Father Felix had repeated when the man had been in danger of losing his farm. "The day that a man might have my lands or my goods, that day he would have my life also." Suddenly, the brilliance of the park and trees and sun smote Thomas' heart. In a way he couldn't explain, he knew as well as he knew that God was in His heaven and the devil below, that the land Richard Cuddington loved and served so well was in great danger.

Soft footsteps interrupted his thoughts, and Chloe Cuddington entered, followed by a maid carrying a tray with biscuits and a small carafe of wine. "Mother sends her excuses, Thomas. She's busy in the stillroom, but desires you to have some cheer before you go." As the maid left, she handed him a glass and said with that wisdom beyond her age, "Thomas, you're upset. I hope it's not because of me. You mustn't blame yourself for something you couldn't help. Please put it from you. I am happy, content with my parents, I have full days. I know you're in the right place for you, Thomas, at Merton."

Sipping his wine, Thomas explained why he'd come to Cuddington. And why her father had ridden so quickly to Merton. Chloe grew pale. One slim hand covered her breast, and tears formed in her eyes. "Thomas! The king wants Merton? Where will you all go? Oh, Thomas, where will *you* go?" The tears slipped from her eyes as the monk sought to console her. Yet there was so little he could say, for there was so little he actually *knew*. Her tears also recalled that unhappy time that would haunt his memory forever. He remembered the scalding wetness on his neck as Chloe had lain sobbing in his arms. Then he'd fought that sinful battle in which only the knowledge that Merton, Father Felix and his Saviour lay at the end of his dreams had prevented him from dishonoring the girl he loved and the parents' who'd trusted him as implicitly as one of their own.

Gently, Thomas set down his wineglass and prepared to leave. "My good wishes to your mother, Chloe," he said, hiding his hands in the ample folds of his habit. He didn't want her to take his hand again. "Please don't distress yourself further. There's nothing we can do about Merton—the king was explicit about that. I'm sure your father will be a great help to Father Felix. But now I must go. I'm needed there—we have much to do, and only a little time. . . ."

"Thomas! You'll not leave without saying good-bye?" Chloe's large gray eyes, still tear-filled, looked wounded. "You *will* come to say good-bye—and let us know where you're going?" Suddenly, her eyes were downcast. She, too, remembered that once before she'd said almost the same exact words. Suddenly she covered her eyes with her hands. "Oh, Thomas, I'm such a fool! You must hate me so! Begone with you now—Father Felix will be waiting." Quickly, she gathered up her flowing skirts and, without a backward glance, fled the room.

Heartsick, Thomas let himself out the front door. It would always be the same. They could not be together. Brother Thomas of Merton Priory and Chloe Cuddington had little to offer each other but pain. How often he'd hoped—since that day three years ago—that their lives and personalities would change. Change so that once outside his cloistered home, his mind did not automatically revert to the past—to the years of growing up when a silver-haired girl had been the dearest thing in the world to him. He'd hoped that she, too, would find someone worthy of her beauty, charm and lineage, that she'd have many sons to help administer her inheritance and daughters to enhance the family with their loveliness. Memories struck at Thomas as he walked, plodding now and ignorant of the beauty around him, toward the Priory. And soon even *that* would be no more! Bitterly, he thought: another home lost. At ten he'd lost his parents and the warmth of the comfortable cottage where he'd felt safe and loved. Now, thirteen years later, he was to lose the only other home in the world that mattered.

As he walked, further memories assailed him—of the many times he and Chloe had ridden over her father's vast lands. Even at twelve or thirteen, no one could touch her on a horse. She was as one with the wind. For years, they'd been together, climbing fences, stalking the barnyard animals, racing up hillocks and copses, paddling in the stream that filled the fishpond and looting the larder when the cook wasn't looking to feed the fat carp and trout that swam in its shimmery green depths. They'd been as close as brother and sister, and the Cuddingtons had taken pleasure in the relationship, realizing how intolerably lonely for both boy and girl it would be otherwise. Thomas had loved Chloe Cuddington with the simple, strong affection of a country boy, well aware she was above him in rank, and unattainable. She was his lodestar—gleaming and distant, yet fixed forever in his youthly firmament. He'd shared her intense thrust of joy and pride whenever they rode over her father's acres. She knew every stream and pond, especially those with flocks of geese. Every meadow, thicket, heath, copse, every small upland covered with furze and gorse were as familiar to her as the view from her window. She knew—even better than he did—where to find the patches of glorious honeysuckle and sweetbriar, where the vast clumps of beeches were breathtaking in silhouette against the sky. More than once she'd opened Thomas' boyish eyes to the beauty of nature that he accepted as mundanely as he accepted the sun would be there in the sky each day. Not so Chloe. She had an affinity with all nature that Thomas knew he lacked. Riding in the woods, she always knew where the animals were—the great herds of deer roaming at will, or the hare and pheasant, even the vixen and her cubs. Thomas remembered the day she'd tracked the shy, elusive fallow deer. He'd sat, taut and wondering, on a rock as she sighted the deer and noiselessly moved toward them. They let her come quite near. Several, braver than most, had stood—quivering and quiet—as she laid a hand on a furry back or stroked a velvet nose. Regularly, she brought home stricken animals who, if she ministered to them herself, seemed to recover overnight. She was known throughout the village for her "way with animals."

Thomas recalled the day Sir Richard and Lady Elizabeth had taken Chloe, then about thirteen, and himself, a manly sixteen, to Ewell Fair. Returning, they'd come upon a stranger savagely beating his horse. Too weak to ward off the blows, it had crumpled, inert and emaciated, to the ground, while the man hammered away, shouting a stream of obscenities. Chloe had flung herself from her horse, almost receiving a blow as she pounded on his back with her strong fists and screamed at him to stop. It had taken both Thomas and her father to pull her off before the drunken man struck her. They'd grappled with the stranger and angrily denounced his brutality, though Thomas noticed the unfortunate animal had closed its eyes and ceased to breathe. They'd taken the sobbing child home as Richard assured her he'd have the man chastised by the authorities and the horse removed from the road.

The scene was still vivid in his mind as Thomas emerged from the forest road and saw the outline of the Priory directly ahead, its bulk heartwarming and substantial against the sky. The afternoon sun glinted on the great golden cross, and almost as if in welcome, the bells pealed, their silvery sound rolling across the Surrey countryside to echo lingeringly in the distance. The sight and sound recalled for Thomas his earlier years at the Priory—joyous years when he'd learned his letters and knew instinctively that he'd chosen the right life. His love for and joy in his faith had nothing of the love he had for the Cuddingtons. Chloe was, by then, almost seventeen—a beauty already and showing signs of a sensitivity and a deep mystical love of nature that grew with each year. They'd complemented each other so well: if Chloe Cuddington was all that was beautiful, warm and gracious in his life, he was all that was eager, compassionate and trusting in hers. Yet she'd always be above him, and soon, he was sure, a marriage—arranged or otherwise—would separate them forever. His calling was to be the church. He remembered, smiling now at his naïveté, how he'd framed it all in his mind—the melodramatic posture in which he sacrificed an unattainable love for the greater love of Christ. At Merton, he was sure, the memory of those glowing childhood years with Chloe would fade and become only cherished memories.

He hadn't counted on the young woman herself.

Even as he remembered the day, his body was consumed by the same warmth and joyous tingle as he'd experienced that morning when Father Felix had asked him to walk to the manor house with his sad message. He'd put it from him all day, but now—before he took such carnal thoughts into the Priory—he'd recall it all once more, then put it from him forever. In a few weeks he'd be gone from Merton, he hoped to build another life in some other holy house. Chloe Cuddington, her love and her tears, would then have no further place in his mind and heart.

It had happened just before Chloe turned seventeen while he was still a novice at the Priory. They'd ridden past old Priest Hill—always a marker for them—for it was a good distance from the manor house. It had been a long day, one of the few he'd had away from his Priory duties. They'd taken a picnic and looked for plovers' nests in the upland area. After eating their food, they listened to the chatter of the woodpeckers, magpies and jays, while throwing out crumbs and laughing at the birds' antics. Skylarks swooped, dashing into hiding as the wild kestrel sought its prey. Off in the distance the manor house chimneys were barely visible, while the Priory was out of sight, beyond the great forest and Ewell Marsh. As the sun sank lower, Thomas rose, brushing crumbs from his woolen jerkin. "Come, my girl. It's late, and we have a ride yet."

Chloe refused to budge. Her blue velvet riding clothes were wrinkled and burr-stuck, her silvery hair in wild disarray; the upland wind was strong. "I don't want to leave, Thomas, not now—not ever," she said imperiously. "Oh, don't be such a clod! We've plenty of time, and Father will send a servant to the Priory and explain you're spending the night. They don't own you body and soul—not yet,

Thomas!'' She sighed. ''And all because they taught you to read and write!'' Her tone was scornful, even as she smiled up at him and motioned him to sit down beside her.

Thomas could never quite resist the appeal in those dark-gray eyes. They were close to him now; the long lashes made tiny black marks against the pink and white skin where the fair hair blew wild. Her mouth was invitingly close, and he could see her tiny white teeth and feel her warm breath against his cheek. ''Thomas, don't be such a clod.'' Before he knew what was happening, she laid that full pink mouth against his, and Thomas felt a sharp jolt of fire in his loins. Her lips parted, and her tongue sought his. The fire only increased, and suddenly, without knowing how it happened, they were lying, straining against each other on the hard ground that felt softer than any feather bed because of the miracle of having her in his arms.

''Oh, Thomas! I thought you'd never. . . . You *are* such a clod.'' She laughed up at him, beating his chest with small fists in simulated anger, and then, half closing her eyes, she put both hands behind his head and drew him to her once more. ''But such a beloved clod. Oh, God, I do love you, Thomas! Didn't you know—don't you care?'' And again he felt her soft lips against his. The fervor of her kiss and the warmth of the soft rounded body beneath his made Thomas forget everything except the hot, tearing, undreamed-of ecstasy. The girl was his for the taking, he knew, hating himself for the thought that kept recurring even as he rained kisses on her cheeks and throat. Unbuttoning the velvet jacket, he found one soft breast in its rough muslin shirt and, caressing it, was astounded at her reaction. It seemed to rouse her even more, and she moaned, ''Oh, Thomas! Thomas . . . let's never go back.''

Reliving that moment now, Thomas felt his body again consumed with the fire that Chloe's love had kindled. His eyes were on the Priory gates straight ahead. God, he was unfit to enter that holy door! His self-disgust bordered on loathing. He ought to strip naked and scourge himself in his cell, even though he knew Father Felix disapproved of flagellation. He'd almost taken the girl then and there, indeed might have, if there hadn't been an interruption. Would he have done so—dishonoring her and the trust her parents placed in him? He'd never know.

The interruption had been slight at first. A small rustling sound, not unlike the noise an animal might make, and in their ecstasy, the two figures, arms intertwined, hardly heard. It was the laugh that made them pull apart, Chloe hastily buttoning her jacket and Thomas running fingers through his rumpled hair. He sat up, his eyes sweeping the vicinity. Pulling Chloe to her feet, he'd said, "Someone's here, girl. We must leave. Take the cloth and leave the food." Suddenly the laugh came again, and they both turned.

Just above them, looking down in great amusement, was a tiny man, wiry, with sharp, pointed features twisted in a leer that showed broken teeth. His hair, straggling and greasy, blew in the wind. It was Hurst, the Cuddingtons' undergardener. He jerked a thumb toward them. "Your mother know you're here—with him?" He took a few steps toward them. "Your father—he wouldn't like what you're doing"—the lewd smile deepened—"wouldn't like who you're doing it with either." Hurst spat on the ground.

Thomas started forward, but Chloe pulled at his sleeve. "Leave well enough alone, Thomas!" Her tone was authoritative, and the boy obediently pulled back; he'd always taken her lead. Since no horse other than their own was in sight, she knew Hurst must have walked to the site—had he followed them? Their progress up the hill would have been visible from the manor house grounds. He'd struck out after them and had, undoubtedly, been watching her at one of the most intimate moments of her life. And laughing. Chloe felt her body burn with anger, shame and frustration.

"Keep going, Thomas!" she whispered as they mounted their horses, attempting all the while to muster as much dignity as she could, aware her burr-stuck clothing and tousled hair were highly compromising. Thomas rode close beside her and, at one point, reached out to clasp her small hand. They did not look back or speak until Hurst had disappeared from sight. They knew he was standing still, watching them make their way down the hillside. When they reached the bottom, he laughed again, loud and long, and the sound echoed evilly in their ears as they rode in the direction of the manor house.

Once out of sight, Thomas pulled close to Chloe, holding her hand as they stopped on the road. "Chloe, you're afraid of him? Has he bothered you?"

"He's done nothing. Nothing I can complain of, except I feel him watching me sometimes when I'm working outside in the garden or near the kitchen." Chloe's voice trembled. Hurst was Domino's helper, she said, and had been at the manor for more than ten years. The aging gardener considered him indispensable, for he took complete responsibility for the kitchen gardens and orchards. True, the man possessed a spiteful temper, and there'd been several scenes involving Hurst that had caused her father to rage and swear. For all his small frame he possessed an unusual strength, and those who'd made sport of his size usually found he could, in a few rapid moves, flatten them to the ground. Hurst was vicious to the young boys and girls from the village who came to help at harvesttime. Once Domino had pulled him from one of the farmers' lads who'd taunted him. Hurst had knocked the boy down and was angrily encircling his neck with strong fingers when Domino came upon them. A scene had followed, with Domino angrily cuffing Hurst about the head until he released the young lad. Both Richard Cuddington and Domino had chastised Hurst, telling him one more such display and he'd have to leave the manor. And they'd see to it that nobody else in the village hired him. Neither Chloe nor her mother could understand why Richard and Domino put up with the man; he was the single troublemaker about the place. Richard, however, said Hurst was Domino's responsibility and didn't wish to interfere; he was a good worker. But, said Chloe, he had an odd sense of power—an evil power. Her mother put it more simply, saying, "He's bad, bad, bad. . . ."

That had been nearly three years ago, Thomas recalled, his eyes still on the Priory buildings ahead. And only once since then had Hurst shadowed their day with his evil presence. It had been the day he and Chloe had said their last farewell, before he took his final vows. The remembrance was too much for Thomas. He'd recalled too much already. His duty lay ahead. Surely Father Felix was wondering what had happened to him? He'd been slothful on his walk to Cuddington and slack in his return. And there was so much to be done! Hurrying forward, thrusting the everyday world from his mind, Thomas remembered he was a man of God with God's work to do. As he let himself in the back gate, he said a small prayer of gratitude that the serenity and tranquillity of Merton was still there for him to share.

Chapter Fifteen

Several weeks later, as the fateful day for the departure from the Priory drew nearer, Thomas worked in the scriptorium, sorting and labeling precious folios and parchments, wrapping the valuable books and records to be given the king. As he finished the last of the work and prepared to return to his cell, he saw Sir Richard Cuddington ride in the back gate. Soon Father Felix came from his chamber, and the two settled on a cloister bench in deep conversation. Fondly, Thomas watched them both.

To the casual observer, the Prior of Merton and the lord of the manor seemed to have little in common. But Thomas was not a casual observer; he knew their many similarities. Both were dedicated men—Father Felix to his faith and its ensuing responsibilities, Richard Cuddington to his family and land and to the tenants and villagers who lived on its abundance.

Each might have advanced to more prominent positions in the church and at court. Thomas had often heard Father Felix abhor any yearning for a bishop's miter, and he knew Richard Cuddington well enough to know that life at court with its waste and hypocrisy would be stifling. Richard had lived too long in the open, delighting in the change of seasons, the almost profligate abundance of the land, in the great sweep of wind that came off the fine meadows surrounding his house. He often rode in the morning before the rising sun had lightened the horizon to the east. Heading homeward, a solitary figure, straight and tall atop his favorite mare, he might see the frail figure of Father Felix as he emerged from a cloistered hour of prayer. Richard would raise an arm in greeting to his friend, who bowed in return. Each recognized the other had been observing a form of worship: one on his knees at the altar, the other in the saddle, his eyes alert for the lightening rays of the sun that brightened and blessed the trees, meadows, the gullies and streams he'd known since childhood.

Richard Cuddington had been of invaluable assistance in the past difficult weeks as the Priory prepared for its dissolution. He'd written numerous letters attempting to find homes for the brethren and had been helpful in assessing the worth of the Priory's possessions. Father Felix's estimate was invariably one of spiritual—not commercial—worth. He'd also promised to provide food and other assistance to several of the indigent villagers who were unable to take care of themselves.

The sound of horses' hooves in the courtyard brought Richard and Father Felix to their feet and Thomas to the open window. He winced as Richard uttered a great oath and Father Felix cried, "It's your daughter, Sir Richard!"

Suddenly, Chloe, her face pale and stricken, came into view. "Father!" She raised her hand, beckoning. "Father! Come at once! Mother says you're to hurry—we have visitors at the house! They say they are from the king!"

"Begone with you, child!" Richard's voice was firm. "I'll be right behind you." He made no further farewell. Instead, as his daughter turned toward the arched gateway, he spurred his horse forward. Passing her, he raced down the road and disappeared in the clouds of dust that engulfed the frightened girl.

Quickly, Thomas ran to Father Felix. "I know what it is," said the prior, sadly. "I'm sure they'll take Sir Richard's land, too. The messenger spoke of the possibility the day he was here. I'd hoped the king had changed his mind." He ran a hand over his tired eyes. "Let us go in and pray for our friend, Thomas."

Dutifully, the monk went to the small altar at the end of Father Felix's chamber and, sinking to his knees, attempted a prayer for the ones who'd been as a family to him. It was not successful. He could not compose his mind. Even as he sought the words in his heart, his thoughts kept returning to that handsome house where even now Sir Richard must be facing the king's emissaries.

* * *

At the manor house, Richard Cuddington read the large roll, covered in a small, spidery hand that informed him that a "View and Survey of the Manor of Cuddington" had been undertaken by Crown representatives. The survey revealed that upon the site was a "fair place, well-builded and without decay" surrounded by "great timber trees." Besides the buildings that formed part of or enclosed the manor house, there was a "well for water which is very good and clear and which standeth at the kitchen door against the west with the gardens and woodyard for the cook." All this in addition to "a barn that is very large and great . . . the walls of timber and covered with tile, newly laid. . . ." It had impressed the king, who'd seen it all several weeks ago; it was just what he was looking for, the emissary said. What Majesty intended to do with it, neither the royal missive nor emissary said. Richard Cuddington was so distraught he did not think to ask.

The intent was clear. The king would like the manor of Cuddington—its church, village dwellings, the manor house and the Priory—to revert to him, and for this he was "Pleased of his Gracious goodness" to present to Richard and Elizabeth Cuddington the manor of Ixworth in Suffolk which those of his Council had deemed more than fair exchange. There was a house of similar size at Ixworth with buildings, barn, orchard and forests where Richard Cuddington might prosper as he had in Surrey. His Majesty wished no loss to the Cuddington family and was prepared to be not only generous, but tolerant as well, of the time expended in making the move. Though the Priory was to be dissolved at once, the Cuddingtons might remain through the winter, for no building could be commenced until the following spring. As there was no indication of what the building might be, there was also no appeal; the royal decision was final.

No mention was made of the villagers or farmers. Presumably, they would be compensated for their small holdings and left to decide their own fate. But the royal decree made it clear that Henry expected to gain six messuages, six hundred acres of arable land, fifty acres of meadow, six hundred acres of pasture, forty acres of wood, six hundred acres of heath and furze and twenty shillings in annual rent from the four farms surrounding the manor that were permitted to remain. The property—from Malden Manor, Ewell, Epsom, Banstead Downs, Cheam and Morden—would be enclosed by a fence or pale.

If Father Felix had been stunned by the king's demands, Richard Cuddington was aghast. He listened as the royal emissary read, his face white, a stricken look in his eyes. Bowing, the emissary departed, leaving the hateful document on the table, as Elizabeth Cuddington broke into tears. Chloe, recoiling from the import of the words, rushed to embrace her mother. The whole episode seemed like a bad dream. Her parents still appeared incredulous—only *she* seemed to recognize the agonizing reality of the moment. Never had she seen her father so helpless. Richard Cuddington had always been a bulwark of strength and protection. Now he was numb, his features anguished, completely demoralized by the royal fiat.

Late that afternoon, unable to work or tolerate the questioning look in his loved ones' eyes, Richard rode to Merton Priory. If nothing else, he must tell the prior he could no longer help, for he'd been similarly dispossessed.

Father Felix greeted Richard with compassion. He could see the man was shattered. After recounting the story, Richard said, "And we are to vacate by spring. . . ." His face flushed as he sought self-control; only his clenched fists gave evidence of his inner turmoil. "It's unbelievable!" he cried. "Everything will be gone! The house, the barn, the stables. We can remove our possessions, of course; the king isn't interested in our belongings." Bitterly, he said, "And we do have until spring. I think that almost makes it worse. This will be our last Christmas at Cuddington." He turned away, his frustration threatening to overwhelm him.

Immediately, Father Felix arose, his face concerned and gentle. "Sir Richard, I *am* sorry. I still cannot believe Merton is to go. But our loss is nothing compared to yours. I'm an old man; I'm sure some other house will take me in. Places may be found for the brethren, too. We are, I suppose, a rather insignificant Order. It is tragic enough for us, but for *you*. . . ." His voice shook as he put a frail hand on his friend's shoulder. "For you, I know this is devastating."

"But what does the king want it for? The whole village! The church! This, I can't understand." Richard's voice broke. "The decree didn't say—what would even a *monarch* want so much for?"

"I asked," replied the prior, "and was told that—while no decision is ever binding with the king should he wish to change his mind—that he plans a small palace here. It seems there's no suitable place for him to stay when he visits or hunts in this area. The whole manor will be annexed to his Honor of Hampton Court. I understand he doesn't like to visit Hampton since Queen Anne'e execution."

"A palace?" Wearily, Richard shook his head. "With Windsor, Enfield, Richmond, Greenwich and a few I'm sure I've forgotten—the king needs another residence?" Angrily he walked to the window. In the far distance the spire of the Cuddington church was stark against the sky; clouds lowered, and a cold wind forecast a coming storm. "Another palace, eh? Well, good luck to you, Henry, with your palace!" Richard's voice was laced with bitterness as he pounded the windowsill. "May you have little joy and no comfort in your blessed palace—may it be cursed for you and yours!" Then, oblivious to anything but his own misery, he hurried from the chamber.

The prior followed him into the courtyard. As Richard mounted his horse, he said, "The messenger told me the king and queen Jane will be visiting here soon. I doubt they'll pay us a visit, for we'll be gone within weeks." Mindful of his calling, he attempted to comfort his visitor. "If there's anything we can do for you, Sir Richard, I'll have the time." He attempted a smile as he concluded, "The messenger did tell me that both the king and queen are elated at coming here and have promised to erect a building as there'll be none such in the land."

But his attempt at consolation was fruitless. Richard Cuddington was already out of hearing, riding in the direction of the manor house which was no longer his.

* * *

That night Chloe lay in her bed, wrapped warmly in a cambric night rail. Though it was May, the nights were often chilly, and she disliked, once comfortably between the clean-smelling heavy linen sheets atop the thick feather mattress, to arise to put on another gown. She'd doused the wax candle and lay now, the covers drawn to the strong, square chin with the deep cleft so like her father's and gazed across the room to the window shut tightly against the cool night air. Though it was dark, she could see the branches of the huge plane tree outlined against the window. In the morning it would be full of magpies and chaffinches. Now it made a soft, sighing noise, yet it did not obliterate the sound of her parents' voices from their chamber across the hall. Chloe remembered the frequent occasions when as a little child she'd gone to the door to listen. She recalled the terrible hurt she'd felt on hearing them frankly discussing the lack of a son. She'd never mentioned the conversation—her parents would have been embarrassed, while her nurse might tartly have reflected that little good ever came of eavesdropping. Now, thought Chloe sadly, perhaps it was just as well there was no son since their ancestral lands were passing to the Crown.

Nor had Chloe ever told her parents about her feelings toward Hurst. Ever since that day he'd discovered Thomas and herself beyond Priest Hill, she'd been uncomfortable in his presence. Often, she felt his small pale eyes on her and, forcing herself to return his gaze, was disconcerted when he continued to stare audaciously. Yet one couldn't complain because a man looked at them. So she'd merely avoided him whenever possible—until today.

While her father was at Merton and her mother lay despairing in her chamber, Chloe had worked with the younger maids, helping cut up old clothing to be given to the poor. A large parcel of heavy serge, destined for servants' clothing, had arrived from London Town, and everyone crowded around to admire the cloth. Suddenly, the voices faded, and in the muted silence something compelled her to leave. The feeling was so new and different she felt weakened by its urgency and, at the same time, almost overcome by its power. She sat down, thinking to clear her mind, but the feeling persisted. Finally, it seemed the thing to do, and ignoring the puzzled look of her companions, she rose and left the room.

Once in the back courtyard, near the fishpond, the atmosphere seemed normal, and the muted silence disappeared. The barking of the family spaniels could be heard at Sparwefeld, Domino's little cottage, where they were probably bedeviling the old man as he worked in his garden. The soughing of the great trees whipped her skirts about her, and she was about to leave, to seek the fire's warmth, when she realized she was not alone. From behind a large hedge, a figure appeared. It was Hurst, carrying a tub of fish from the pond where they were kept for live food and for restocking the stream. He put the tub on the ground and advanced toward her. Uncomfortable in his presence, she nevertheless stood firm and said in a tone she'd heard her mother assume, "Yes, Hurst, did you want something?"

"Yes, I do," he replied, coming toward her smiling evilly. "I wanted to see you, and I wished it so hard you had to come out, didn't you?" Chloe fought the desire to run—anything to get away from the man with the pale eyes who gazed at her so intimately. Instead, she eyed the fish and said, "The cook will be looking for the fish, Hurst, and soon, too. I have work to do." She turned to leave. Suddenly the slight man was in front of her, and one hand, slimy from the fish, grasped hers so tightly she almost cried out.

"You don't have to leave right away, and fish'll keep well enow!" Chloe smelled his breath, he was so close. He'd been at the ale barrel again, not for the first time that day, she was sure. "I want to talk to you, Mistress Chloe. I never see you alone, yet you're friendly enough with others—I mind that day on the hill. . . . And the last time you said good-bye to Thomas." He thrust his face close to her. "He's a priest now, and not for you, miss. You could look elsewhere." His grip tightened on her hand.

Chloe knew she was in no actual danger—there were others too near. Yet never in her life had she been so overwhelmed; she felt the presence of evil in the slimy touch of Hurst's hand, in his foul breath, in the very smallness of his person. "What can you want with me?" was all she could gasp as she tried to pull her hand away. "Let me go!"

Her struggling only seemed to excite Hurst more. "You don't really want to leave, Mistress Chloe." He leered again, and his hand came up to fondle her breast. "You was hot enough for that young Thomas, you didn't mind when he—"

Suddenly, Chloe extricated herself and, giving Hurst a rude shove, cried, "Get out—get out! Don't you *ever* touch me again!" Then, near tears, she fled into the house and up to her room. She'd made excuses at mealtime and remained there ever since.

The scene with Hurst brought to mind the last farewell with Thomas which he'd recalled. Again Chloe burned with the embarrassing knowledge that the hateful undergardener had observed them in an intimate moment. Thomas was about to take his final vows. He'd renounced her love and the world of man for the love of Christ and the world of God. Her parents by now had guessed how she felt about the boy they regarded almost as a son. "You must let him go, dear," her mother had advised, her dark head bent over her needlework. "I'm sure the choice was not easy, but Thomas has always longed for the church. You mustn't make it difficult for him."

Chloe had tried her best, but each time Thomas appeared at the manor house she felt again that racing excitement in her blood, that yearning toward the boy with the nut-brown hair, the cool dark eyes and the manly bearing. She could feel again the crushing warmth of his lips, his body straining against hers. If he felt the same way as she did, why did he persist in a calling where they could never be together?

She put the question directly to him on the day he'd come to say good-bye. She knew it was unfair and only made it more difficult, but she couldn't help herself. She didn't feel joyous and thankful, as her mother said she should. Thomas, too, was pale and tense. And there was an odd diffidence she'd never noticed before. It was almost as though he'd already left her and was now here merely to observe the formalities. Her parents had greeted Thomas in the chamber where they all admired the new fireplace, and a servant had brought wine. Richard Cuddington had clasped Thomas' hand and told him how proud they were of him, how pleased they were he'd chosen a holy life. Elizabeth kissed him on the cheek and pressed his hand, and then they'd gone and left her alone with him.

"You'll wish me well, Chloe?" Thomas turned to her as they sat on the bench in front of the fire which cast its radiance over the spacious room. Yet Chloe did not feel the warmth. Her veins had turned to ice. All she knew was that soon Thomas would be wearing a plain brown wool robe and the thick luxuriant hair would be tonsured and covered by a cowl. He'd be a man of God. . . .

An intense inner anger almost consumed her. Pride and modesty were cast aside as she stood up and faced him, the firelight haloing her silvery hair and casting a pinkish glow on her pale skin.

"No! I don't wish you well, Thomas! I think you're a fool, throwing away your life, to cloister yourself behind four walls, never to give anything of yourself to anyone." Her voice was rising. She was miserable, and she knew her parents could probably hear every word. She didn't care.

"Chloe! That's not true. I'll *not* be throwing my life away—that's the whole meaning of what I'm doing! I'll be enlarging my life, filling it with care and love for those in need."

"*Anyone* can do that!" She flung at him scornfully. "*You* have more to offer." She noticed Thomas was even paler, though an understanding and compassionate look had come into his eyes. He took her hands in his and again she felt that familiar fire along her veins.

"No, Chloe, that's the whole point—anyone *cannot* do the work. Father Felix says—"

"I don't care *what* Father Felix says!" she half shouted at him. Then, as she realized she was fighting a losing battle, the knowledge that she was really saying good-bye to Thomas overwhelmed her, and she gave a racking sob. Her hands went to her face. She was behaving badly. It would only embarrass and disappoint Thomas more. But she knew she couldn't help herself.

Thomas looked at the shaking figure, the long, slim hands that covered a face dearer to him than anyone else on earth. No power could stop him from putting his arms around her, and they stood together, her head on his chest, his chin buried in the soft silver hair, while he caressed her shoulders and whispered, "Darling, do stop. You're tearing me apart. Oh, Chloe, dear God, do stop—I can't bear—"

She'd looked up at him then, and there, for a moment, Thomas the monk was gone and there was Thomas of her childhood, the boy she'd run and played and ridden with. There, more than anyone else, was Thomas the man to whom she'd offered herself on a faraway hillside, as the wind whipped about them. She could see that memory was warm in his mind, too, and before she knew it, he'd lowered his head and his lips met hers.

But the kiss was different. Thomas intended it to go no farther; he was in control now. There was love and warmth, but no fire, no passion in the kiss. And Chloe finally realized—as she hadn't before—that her battle was with a force larger than the love he felt for her. And at that moment she changed forever from a young girl—sure of her beauty and her ability to get anything she wanted—to a young woman who must now give way graciously and with an understanding and compassionate spirit.

Thomas thrust her from him, holding her at arm's length, and they looked deep into each other's eyes. Both knew it was the end. He was waiting for some word from her. Brushing the last of the tears from her face, Chloe whispered, "Good-bye, Thomas. This is, I know, *really* good-bye. It must be a proud and wonderful moment for you. I hadn't meant to spoil it."

Thomas smiled warmly, obviously relieved. "Oh, Chloe, thank you! I can go now with a freer heart. You know how important—"

"Yes, I know it's important that you follow your heart, Thomas. Just as I tried to follow mine. I know now the time is not yet. Not for us. But I know—oh, Thomas, I *do* know—we'll be together sometime! Perhaps not now, but someday! I don't care how long I have to wait. I'll wait until the end of time."

But Thomas wasn't listening. He was looking over her shoulder, out the window where Hurst stood watching them. Apparently, he'd been working nearby and stopped to peer into the room which the firelight made so bright. There was no leer on his face now, only a hard and bitter look, almost more frightening than his twisted smile. Quickly, Thomas pulled Chloe to the outside hall, and there, in the presence of her parents, they'd made a proper and courteous farewell.

Remembrance of Hurst made Chloe, now warm and safe in her bed, vastly uncomfortable. She burrowed under the covers, longing for sleep. She could still hear the heartening hum of her parents' voices. Perhaps I should have told Father about Hurst, she thought. But then he, cornered, might have blurted out the truth of her behavior with Thomas. She burned again with the remembrance of the man's lewd smile. Sleep seemed far away, and finally, she rose. Disdaining to light the candle, she went to the window and opened it, hoping the soft night air—for all its dangers of "coughs and rheums"—might sweep away her depression. She leaned on the rough stone sill, drinking in the play of moonlight through the trees and on the lawn that was Domino's pride and joy. Soon it would all be only a memory, and she'd be far away north in another house. Suddenly, the movement of a shadow caught her eye. It was only a quick motion, and she couldn't be sure it was not one of the servants pilfering a bird from the dovecote. Again the movement; only this time it seemed nearer. The sighing of the trees seemed to lessen and the silence grew oppressive. Again that strange, muted silence enveloped her. Then she knew. Quickly, she closed the casements and hurriedly drew the heavy hangings across the front.

Back in bed she burrowed even deeper, knowing sleep would be impossible. She wasn't frightened, only apprehensive. For the shadow was not one of the manor servants or a villager leaving a surreptitious rendezvous with a cullery maid. It wasn't one of the dogs. It had been Hurst. While she hadn't seen him clearly, he was there below, she was sure. How long had he stood there waiting? How long had it been before that muted silence told her he was willing her to come to him a second time? And how soon might it happen again?

* * *

For the next month the people of the manor house worked from dawn to dusk for it was harvesttime. Richard Cuddington had decided it was more sensible to move to Suffolk at once; to remain throughout the winter and then leave when spring was touching his park and meadows with glory would only increase their pain. So now the bakers, brewers, scullions, dairymaids and cooks within strove to match their labor to the unbelievable bounty from the outside. Elizabeth Cuddington's time in the dairy nearly doubled, and Chloe worked along with her mother and the dairymaids, helping mold the large wheels of butter and cheese and pouring the thickening cream into containers. In the orchards, apples, red and golden, were plucked and placed in baskets next to the pears and apricots. Root vegetables were dug from the kitchen garden and stored in the cool cellar. In the tithe barn, Richard supervised the packing of the wool, shorn in the spring from his sheep, which must now be bundled and sold to the visiting webster.

Underlying all the activity was the sad awareness that this was the last harvest from Cuddington land. When the move to Suffolk was made, all the bounty would be packed in wagons and carts to see the family through the first winter until their new acres could provide for their needs. Even now the trees in the park had lost their leaves, and beneath the bare branches the buck, hare and pheasant were being mercilessly hunted to provide meat against the cold weather.

Chloe worked in the garden with Domino as he selected the plants, trees and shrubs to be dug up and removed to Suffolk. Elizabeth Cuddington considered the garden her private domain. Her husband had left most of its planning and maintenance to her and the crusty, weather-beaten old soul who had carried him on his shoulders as a child and was proud of telling one and all that no one—including himself—knew how old he was. Domino was held in great respect by the undergardeners and laborers. Many had felt the clout of his roughened hand or the thrust of his boot in their backsides, for the kindly tyrant had no patience with idleness, extravagance or the waste of time or implements. He was indignant with those who took nature's largess for granted, knowing too well how much imagination, sweat and toil it took to wrest the great flaming dahlias, the tuberoses and carnations from the soil.

Chloe gazed at the old man fondly as he appraised the age and condition of each plant and consigned it for Suffolk or the king. As she tied a piece of soft twine on a graceful holly, she listened to his muttering. "An' nothin' will be left for the hoodlums—that's worth a ha'penny!" He spat on the ground. "Pullin' down and buildin' up again—and all to build a bloomin' *palace*!" Domino said the word disdainfully.

The sound of an approaching rider caused both to pause in their work, and Chloe was delighted to see Thomas, who usually walked, ride swiftly around the circular path and dismount at the front door. He hadn't noticed her, and she remained silent, drinking in the dear face with its tonsured hair. Thomas looked worried and—*drained*. Her father emerged and, after a few moments, disappeared toward the stables. Within seconds he'd joined Thomas and the two sped off—where? Chloe ran to the gate and watched them for a moment, then quickly went to the stables for her favorite mare. Within moments she was following the cloud of dust her father and Thomas had stirred up.

She could hear shouting and pitiful cries in the distance where a crowd had gathered. Intermittently, a great clap of noise not unlike thunder seemed to roll the earth beneath the horse's hooves. The noise came from the Church of St. Mary the Virgin, and as she rode into the midst, she stopped, appalled by what she saw.

Dozens of men, strangers all, were pulling down the church. An area had been set apart for the spectators so they wouldn't be in the way of falling debris; most of them were villagers. Only last Sunday the rector had sadly informed them that was their last day of worship within the structure that had been their spiritual home—and that of their forebears—for generations. They'd heard the rumor, of course, that the king had taken the land and church, but they hadn't believed it would happen so soon. They'd gazed at one another and then at the church—at the handsome new floor on which they'd knelt each Sunday and festival day. At the familiar saints in their niches, their features flooded with light from the glorious stained glass. While most couldn't read the Latin Bible chained in the priest's chambers—indeed couldn't read anything—they were familiar with the Bible stories, and they recognized the familiar gestures and actions of the priest during the Latin service. It solaced and comforted them. They'd listened to him as he proclaimed the church's doom, wondering what their response should be, knowing all the while they were powerless to do anything to save the beloved building.

They stood now, shaken to their simple cores, experiencing a burning sense of frustration and rebellion. For with little attempt to hide their pleasure in the job at hand, the king's hired minions were stripping the lead from the great roof, for it was, next to the stone, the most valuable item. Once that had crashed to the ground, no care was taken to preserve anything. The precious stained glass, the walls with their colorful frescoes, the intricately carved rood loft—all were the victim of man's eagerness to destroy, to smash, to mutilate with fist and tool. Great blocks of stone, some with gargoyles or massive carved beasts or flowers, came crashing to the ground in a heavy shower of dust that settled on trees and shrubs in the immediate area.

Chloe was bewildered and sickened. She saw her father and Thomas join Father Felix, who had also arrived on the scene to ask that several small statues of no particular worth be spared, noting that he and his companions would be responsible for their removal. The prior was greeted with loud hooting and obscenities as the workers struck only harder at the cherished objects. The statues were ripped from their niches and, as the villagers watched, removed some distance from the site. There, with obvious and gleefully mocking pleasure, the workers clubbed heads and hands from the life-sized figures, laughing obscenely as they battered other parts of the bodies into shapeless masses of marble and plaster. White with repressed rage, Father Felix accepted Thomas' suggestion that they return to the Priory, ignoring the cheering of the workers at his departure. Women in the crowd wept as the great carvings and wooden pews were thrown from the church door and stacked while workers, parodying the Mass, lit a large bonfire. Encouraged by frequent drafts from hidden bottles, they cheered in drunken frenzy as the ancient wood was consumed in the flames.

Heartsick, Chloe turned her mount homeward; she didn't want her father and Thomas to know she'd witnessed such desecration.

Passing Domino's little cottage, Sparwefeld, she noticed two handsomely dressed strangers talking to the gardener, who stood in the doorway. He seemed bewildered and ill at ease, twisting his greasy cap in his hands. His face lit up when he saw her.

"Mistress Chloe! These—uh, these gentlemen—they be from the king. They looked at Sparwefeld and know we be goin' soon. Sir Richard is not here . . ."

The men were gazing at her with that appreciative light Chloe had often seen in other men's eyes. She hated them and all they represented, but it would do little good to let them see it. She had to be as clever as they were brutal. Obviously, they'd been looking at Domino's cottage, which wasn't in the original survey except as "gardener's loft." It was much more than that—a comfortable dwelling which some ancestor had erected for his own lodging while the big manor house was being built. She loved the little place and had spent many happy moments with old Domino there in her growing-up years. The thought of its suffering the same fate as the church caused a deep pang, and when she thought of those obscene beings pulling down her home, she felt almost physically ill. But she mustered a smile—and it must have been a pleasant one, for Domino's eyes widened in disapproval—and said, "Sirs, you've come to take this poor man's lodging? You have the church, you are going to take my home"—she gestured toward the big house—"does your king need this simple dwelling, too? When he builds his palace, might he not need a small cottage such as this? Does it have to be destroyed?"

"Our orders, with all respect, mistress, are—"

"But *you*, gentlemen, *you* are obviously gentlemen of great quality—you *must* have some influence with the king?" Chloe gazed with what she hoped was appropriate wide-eyed wonder at the more important-looking of the visitors, a tall, burly man with a rich chestnut beard. "To whom am I speaking, good sirs?"

The tall man, clearly impressed with the dark-eyed creature, now pinning him with that piercing glance, swept a deep bow. "I am Charles Brandon, mistress."

Chloe finished for him. "Ah-h-h, the Duke of Suffolk. You are the king's brother-in-law."

"Such is mine honor, mistress."

"Well, as his brother-in-law and one of his foremost nobles of the land"—Chloe was pleased to see the man preen; he'd been a minor court figure until he'd wed the beautiful Mary Tudor, much to Henry's anger—"perhaps you'd be good enough to ask the king to allow this small cottage to remain in my family? It is a little request, sir, and would bring much credit to the king if he would honor it. I cannot think the king would deny it when he is taking so much." Aware she might sound critical, she stopped, giving them the benefit of her widest, most appealing smile.

The two men watched, struck almost dumb with the imperious beauty's assurance. Suddenly Chloe *knew*—knew as if it were being shouted aloud—that she'd won. They were really weak and pliant, but she'd impressed them. They'd find it demeaning now to refuse her. They might have a bit of explaining to do at court, but the king had more important things to worry about than an insignificant Surrey cottage. He might curse—even cuff them about a bit as was his wont—but he'd probably go along with the decision, maybe even chaff Brandon for letting a wench get the better of him.

Before they could speak, Chloe bowed low in the saddle, then, spurring her horse, shouted, "My Lord of Suffolk! Good day to you! My humble thanks to you—and to His Gracious Majesty!"

Supper was a sad affair, everyone silent remembering the monstrous events at the church, and Chloe went to her room early. She'd not told her father about Domino's cottage; Sparwefeld would be a secret until she was sure the king wouldn't change his mind. Yet she *knew* with absolute certainty that he would be agreeable to Brandon's decision. Or what Brandon *thought* was his decision. She laughed as she said good-night to her maid and brushed her long silvery hair before the shining glass on the wall, wondering where the strong certainty came from.

Lately, too, she'd had odd premonitions as she walked in the manor house vicinity or in the park outside. Brushing her hair, still flushed with a serene sense of accomplishment in wrangling Sparwefeld from a destructive fate, she recalled what she used to call—for want of a better word—her "taint." It had started years ago with the violet cap. She'd been no more than five or six, but she could remember it clearly. It was her birthday, and cleaned and dressed by her nurse, she was taken to her parents' chamber to be greeted with a profusion of hugs and kisses, after which her father solemnly gave her a small package wrapped in a clean linen cloth. Uncovering the linen, she found a small jeweled coffer, and without opening the lid, Chloe knew what was inside. She could describe it: a small jeweled cap to wear atop her silver-blond hair, such a cap as might befit the daughter of Sir Richard Cuddington. It was the first step in growing up, in having one's own jeweled cap and not just a plain unadorned one, made from a castoff of her mother's.

She'd opened the coffer and taken out a beautiful violet cap, trimmed in small pearls with a generous cluster of small diamonds and seed pearls and a larger table diamond in the center. While putting it on and basking in the smiles of her parents and nurse, she wondered if she should tell them of her foreknowledge. But something prompted her to remain quiet. Was it possible that her mother and father, her nurse and maybe even Domino also always knew what was in a birthday coffer before they opened it? She didn't think so, but she wasn't positive.

After that it had happened often. She'd know when she awoke that the priest of Cuddington church would choose to call in the morning, hoping to be asked to stay for the substantial noon meal that always graced the manor house table. And later he would arrive, and leave, at the exact moment she'd foreseen. When a villager or one of the farm tenants was ill, she always seemed to know which would eventually recover and which would die.

Chloe had never told her parents of her "taint." She didn't

feel it was bad or anything to be ashamed of, but she didn't know quite how to express it. It wasn't always pleasant, but mostly it seemed harmless enough—her ability to see just a bit more clearly, a little farther ahead than most.

There'd always been talk tinged with laughter, or terror, in the kitchen and stables about the local witches and their powers. Even she and Domino had discussed it, for Domino was a strong believer in wood sprites, tree fairies and witches. Some were supposedly good, he told her, but it seemed to Chloe that most were regarded with suspicion and alarm. If knowing what might occur before it actually happened made her a witch, then she supposed she was one. However, it seemed wise to remain silent about it.

She never told Thomas about her "taint"; it was a very private thing, and she wasn't sure Thomas—for all his talk of religion and the holy life—would understand. She hadn't wanted to endanger their relationship. And it seemed only now, since knowing she must soon leave Cuddington, that the taint was becoming—*stronger*? Walking outside, she would find the scene suddenly almost colorless and a strange silence pervading the atmosphere. Then she would know—with that same absolute certainty she'd known with Brandon that afternoon—that here, by a rickety old wooden bridge, flung across a small stream by her grandfather, the king's builders would erect a structure set apart from the palace, one designed mainly for banqueting. Another time, walking some distance from her home, as the spaniels romped at her heels, the familiar sensation occurred again. She could hear the thunder of horses' hooves, with spectators shouting in the distance, as they cheered or cried out. Were they hunting? Or cheering their favorites in a royal tournament? She didn't know, but she knew the scene would take place—perhaps in another time—or perhaps she'd even later see it herself.

Even the dogs had seemed disturbed. While scampering through thickets in search of a hare, they'd suddenly appear at her side, whimpering and frightened, licking her fingers and seemingly urging her to leave. Chloe was now very used to the sensation. For a moment, time appeared to stop; she and the dogs apparently existed in a timeless vacuum. She'd force herself to action, calm the dogs and quickly move on. In a moment the sensation would disappear and the dogs go off to burrow once more.

While in the woods, she sensed the wild animals' foreknowledge. They could hardly know their homes were threatened or their lives endangered. Yet they obviously had a presentiment that change was imminent. Many of them simply disappeared. When she went to look for the more familiar animals, deep in the forest or park, she usually found they'd moved on. Later, a good distance from their former habitat, she might come upon them, busily marking out their new territory. They acknowledged her presence but seemed more interested in satisfying themselves they'd found food, water and shelter from their enemies. Later, riding home, Chloe had thought their foreknowledge was not unlike her taint, so it couldn't be bad. She thought, too, how much simpler life was for nature's creatures: no household to disperse, no belongings to pack, no memories to store away.

Chapter Sixteen

At Merton Priory the sad task of dissolution was unde way. There was more haste than at the manor house, for, a Father Felix said in a moment of rare bitterness, the kin hadn't left them the time God had heretofore seen fit t bestow. Messengers sent to other religious houses had foun places for many of the brethren, while several novitiates los heart for theological life and returned home. Father Felix ha been invited to join the Benedictine Abbey at Westminster where he might end his days in peace; he hoped to persuad them to accept Brother Thomas as well.

Merton Priory's treasure was duly inventoried and sent t Thomas Cromwell, the king's Vicar-General. Blankets, mat tresses, coverlets and other everyday necessities were omit ted and given, instead, to the departing monks or the villag poor. The storehouse of food, wood, wine and other sundrie was doled out at the gate. The king might have the Priory' treasure, Father Felix thought grimly, but the product of thei own hard labor would be shared as it always had been.

They all hurried through the days, aware of the little tim left before they must leave the cherished house whose fate n one wished to witness. The destruction of the church had s sickened Father Felix and oppressed Thomas that neithe visited the site again.

The scene was fresh in the prior's mind as, during one o the last days while carts were loaded and farewells takin place hourly, he summoned Thomas to his chamber. Within very little time, unless the Abbey in London took the youn monk, they also would say farewell—never to see each othe again. While waiting for Thomas to appear, Father Feli went to a large chest near the altar and took from it a smal coffer of boxwood, inlaid with silver and pearls, its heavy clasp fashioned in the form of a Tudor rose.

At that moment Thomas arrived, obviously tired, yet solicitous and anxious to make the remaining few days as pleasant for the older man as possible. He was relieved to see Father Felix looking almost serene.

"Thomas, I have left this final task to the very end. It's one of which I'm very proud and to which I've been very faithful and one to which I'm sure you'll be equally obedient. This is what I want to show you and then I want to tell you its story."

Eagerly, with the quick enthusiasm of a child, he undid the rose clasp and took from the coffer a large ball of deep red velvet. He put the small bundle on the table so Thomas might see it. The monk's eyes widened, and he leaned forward. "But, Father, what is it?" He, too, was eager. The velvet glowed, its deeper hues reflected in the coffer's silver trim.

"First, I want to tell you the story, Thomas. I'll try to remember it just as it was told to me. This small chest was given to me by Abbot Ambrose of the Franciscan Friars of Richmond Palace. Many months ago, the Friary was dissolved, and when it was known that all the possessions would be confiscated by the king, the abbot rode here to visit with me for several days. You may even remember." Thomas nodded. He did indeed remember. Abbot Ambrose, a distinguished Franciscan, had been Queen Catherine of Aragon's personal confessor. Catherine had spent much time working with the Friars whenever she was at Richmond and had favored them in many ways during the quarter century she was England's queen. The day of his arrival at Merton had been one of great excitement, and even the holy brothers had jostled one another to catch a glimpse of the queen's renowned confessor. Yes, Thomas remembered.

"The abbot came here to deliver this to me," said Father Felix, gesturing at the coffer. "It was given to him by the queen when she was forced into exile. She felt her possessions might be taken from her—as I think a good many of them were. She wished to make certain this would be safe while she still had time to do so." With that the prior unfolded the velvet and smoothed it out so Thomas could see what it contained.

It was small, and at first he didn't recognize what it was. Then he smiled broadly. It was the device of Catherine of Aragon—a good-sized clump of gold, fashioned into the shape of a pomegranate. A fruit particularly Spanish, obviously the work of a sophisticated Spanish artisan, it was exquisitely made. As Father Felix placed it in the palm of his thin and shaking hand, Thomas was entranced to see the stem glitter as the light caught the facets of a multitude of tiny diamonds, emeralds and rubies. The stem's tip contained a large single diamond almost the size of his smallest fingernail.

The monk was enchanted and held out his hand for the ornament. Both men were silent, admiring the delicate, fragile workmanship.

"The queen must have been very sad to leave it." Thomas could almost sense her loss at parting with such a precious object.

"I'm sure she was," Father Felix replied, "but she was wise to do so. She was very attached to the treasure. Besides its priceless value, it had also belonged to her mother, the great Isabelle of Castile. She told Abbot Ambrose when she was very young, her mother had told her the pomegranate had helped her drive the Moors from Spain. During that time the tent in which her youngest child—who became our Queen Catherine—was staying caught on fire. Yet she was saved. Her mother believed it was because the pomegranate, along with the family's jewels, was in Catherine's tent. It had come down to her as a family treasure, and Isabelle was sure it possessed magical properties. Catherine said she didn't know of any magic—I'm sure if it had possessed any, she didn't feel it had helped *her* during all her troubles! But because it had belonged to her mother, she treasured it greatly. She told the abbot, 'It's a little part of Spain I've allowed myself to keep in a country I've come to love.' "

Thomas was very stirred. He'd grown up during the years when Catherine reigned and was one of thousands of Englishmen holding loving memories of the Spanish queen who'd been so ruthlessly tossed aside. And this glorious relic in his hand had belonged to her, had been loved and cherished by her. He suddenly felt very close to the dead queen, and his hand closed around the ornament. He almost hated to give it up.

"What are you going to do with it?" Thomas asked. "Surely we can't let this go to the king! Wouldn't someone at Westminster Abbey keep it safe and hidden until times are better?"

"I'm too old, Thomas, to take that risk." Father Felix shook his head. "I'm sure to be searched before I enter there, simply as a protection for those who are good enough to give me a home. I feel my responsibility in this regard heavily and cannot, with any conscience at all, turn this over to the king's representatives."

"Then what must you do with it?" Thomas' hand still held the lovely relic, and his sensitive features were concerned. "Is there no safe place for it?"

"I think it will be safe now." The prior smiled and waited until the import of his words sank in. "Yes, I think it's safe now."

"Father! You mean *I'm* to have it?" Thomas was excited, yet his voice was edged with doubt. "What will I do with it—my own future is so uncertain." The prior relaxed in his chair and said gently, "I hope to persuade the abbot at Westminster to have you accompany me there, Thomas. You are young and still untried, it is true. But I flatter myself—God forgive my sin!—that I have a bit of influence. I can't take the jewel there, but *you* could. No one will search a simple brother of the dissolved priory of Merton who happens to be calling at the Abbey on a visit. But once you're there, you can tell the abbot the story I've just told you and ask if there's a safe place in the Abbey for the queen's relic."

"Oh, I will!" Thomas gazed at the glittering pomegranate in his hand once more, and his features brightened. "Oh, indeed, I will ask, Father! The Abbey will be the safest place in the world! I am so honored—so honored." He smiled at the prior with affection. "Believe me, I'll take care of it."

"I know you will, Thomas." Father Felix rose, his relief clear in his face and voice. "It's decided then. You'll go to London tomorrow and ask the abbot. We'll return the relic to its hiding place until we have his answer. I'm glad we've found it a safe home."

Gently, Thomas wrapped the pomegranate in the red velvet, placed it in the coffer and set it in the chest. At the door, he turned and asked the prior, "Did the queen have a name for the bauble, Father? When something is that old . . ."

"Why, yes, Thomas, now that you mention it." The prior gazed out the window, as if attempting to remember. "She called it the Lure. I don't know why. I don't even think Abbot Ambrose knew the reason. But it seems a long time back in the family history it had been considered a 'lure' . . . one for good. Certainly Isabelle felt it had lured her to drive the Moors from Spain. Queen Catherine put it more simply. It was, for her, a lure that represented Spain, her former home and all that was good remembered from her childhood. She felt it would be safe with the Franciscans. Only when the abbot knew the Friary was to be dissolved did he make haste to leave it here with me." Father Felix smiled wanly. "I'm sure he thought we were so insignificant no one would bother us and the Lure would be safe."

Thomas' face was shining as the prior finished his story; he was tremendously moved. *The Queen would be happy to know what a safe abode her Lure has found*, thought Father Felix. *He's in love with the beauty of Queen Catherine's golden pomegranate, and he'll defend it with his life.* He himself felt relieved and gladdened. Out of the whole sorry mess of the dissolution, at least there was one priceless object that would not be destroyed.

On the following morning Thomas set out before daybreak, arriving in London before the sun was at its highest. Riding past the old Tabard Inn on the High Street of Southwark, he realized he hadn't been in London for more than a year. He was stimulated by the noise, the smells and sounds of the City. It would be very difficult living at the Abbey after the rural simplicity of Cuddington and Merton.

The procession of travelers, merchants, wagons and cattle, all waiting for admission to the bridge, jostled Thomas' horse, and he rode outside the crowd, noting the Abbey of Bermondsey set among the fields now stripped of their harvest. The sun glinted on the red-tiled roof of the venerable structure and cast its cloister into deep shade. Straight ahead was the handsome Church of St. Mary's Overy, somewhat overshadowed by the vast pile of Winchester House, the home of the Bishop of Winchester. Should the Westminster abbot have no place for him, Thomas reasoned, these other houses might receive him.

Suddenly, the gate opened, and there was much good-natured jostling as everyone surged onto the bridge. It was dark and cramped and, Thomas could see, no more than twenty feet at its widest, for houses and shops were built along its edges. Sun shone into the interiors, and he rode slowly so he might see inside.

The traffic thinned as he approached the magnificent Chapel of St. Thomas à Becket, square in the middle of the bridge. Since Becket was now unpopular with the king and reformers, it had been renamed the Chapel of Our Lady. Through the pointed arched windows, Thomas saw the elegant columns and even caught a glimpse of a vividly painted altar. He felt oddly touched—surely no city in Europe could rival London? What other metropolis would cause a chapel to be built in the middle of a busy bridge and wisely rename it when its patron saint became unpopular?

Passing Becket's chapel, he saw a break in the buildings and looked out to the river—the magnificent highway of London—with its hundreds of boats, barges and wherries plying the waters upstream, downstream and across to each bank. White swans dodged the swinging oars, and on the banks of a marshy area near the tower, children waded in the reeds. Along the river lay the decayed pile of the ancient Savoy Palace, and then, in jewellike procession, were the majestic mansions that had formerly belonged to the Church sees: Exeter, Worcester, Salisbury. All had been taken by the king and given to noblemen, who had further enhanced the grounds with statuary and handsome water stairs.

Thomas clattered off the bridge and made hurriedly for Cheapside, for he must see the abbot before the noon service. The street was at its busiest, and servants were abroad early for the best choice of produce. On past Old Jewry and the Eleanor Cross toward St. Paul's, its noble spire thrusting heavenward. Here the crowd was thickest, and Thomas was dismayed at the number of beggars, the maimed, diseased and poor who cried for alms. He'd barely ridden into the Strand when someone called his name. "Thomas! Thomas!"

The monk turned at the sound. Just ahead, opposite Durham House, was an imposing structure of cream-colored stone. It was a quadrangular building with a handsome double doorway banded by columns and pilasters on ornate pedestals. The walls were half covered with ivy that also grew around the large mullioned windows, fashionably wrought balustrade of strong black ironwork, and in its center was the crest of the Cuddington family. Thomas was amazed to see Sir Richard Cuddington standing on the steps. Quickly he rode forward.

"Thomas! What a grand surprise!" Sir Richard was dressed in rich town clothes such as Thomas had not seen before, not even at Sunday church services. "What brings you to London? Will you come inside and meet my brother?" As he spoke, he directed the monk toward a servant, who took his horse, and in a moment Thomas was ushered through the front door.

"It's fine to see you, Thomas—we've not set eyes on you since the day—" There was a moment's silence as both remembered the day of the church's destruction. "I came to London on business for several days. Thomas, you must stay too. You can return with us! You've not been here before? Well, what do you think of Cuddington House?"

Thomas murmured his appreciation. The room they entered was furnished as befitted one of James Cuddington's quality. It was spacious and bright, for an unusual number of windows let in light and air. Sideboards of silver, pewter and Venetian glass reflected their light and gleamed on the high polish of an ancient cupboard, on the long refectory table and straight-backed chairs. Sir Richard explained that his younger brother lived here with his twelve-year-old son since his wife had died some years before. He preferred the city to country life and had been happy with his legacy as he, Richard, had been with his. At the thought of the inheritance no longer his, his face darkened. Thinking to distract him, Thomas explained he'd come to ask if the Abbey might accept him as they'd offered refuge to Father Felix.

"I'm sure they'll take you, Thomas. Perhaps my brother can even help. James has many friends in London and at court." He poured a glass of wine and handed it to the monk. "You'll stay with us here? My brother will be delighted—there's plenty of room. Chloe will be so happy to see you!"

Thomas drank his wine slowly, realizing that surge of anticipation could not be attributed to its contents. He listened as Sir Richard explained that as evidence of their departure from Surrey became more noticeable—as tapestries were removed from walls and carpets aired and packed—Chloe had wandered from room to room, depressed and sad. Lady Elizabeth had insisted the girl accompany her father to London, where, happily, her spirits had picked up. Walking to the door, the monk told Sir Richard he must see the abbot before the noon services, but he'd be happy to accept the hospitality of Cuddington House later in the day. He left for the Abbey, feeling more lighthearted than he had in weeks.

James Cuddington sat in front of the fire in the gracious room looking out on the busy Strand. It was a luxury that fire—at midday—but it kept the river's damp from the furnishings. At nightfall, he insisted that myriad candles also be lit, and often he'd seen passersby on the outside stop and gaze into the comfortable mellow interior. He loved the house his father had built, against everyone's advice, on the unfashionable northern rim of the Strand. Opposite was Durham House which the king had taken from the Bishop of Durham and in which, at the moment, the three-year-old Princess Elizabeth, daughter of the executed Anne Boleyn, was temporarily lodged. Its large, untidy courtyard backed onto the Strand, as did most of the great houses along the river, and for this reason, building on the northern side had been largely neglected. But his father had done so, and now Cuddington House was something of a showplace with its fields and meadows running into open country in the rear. James remembered his father's quiet pride the day the house was complete. It must be nearly sixteen years now, for it was the year the king and Queen Catherine had gone to the Field of Cloth of Gold and they'd all gathered on the steps outside to watch their departure.

His reverie was interrupted by a soft footstep behind him. "Uncle James?"

"Come in, child, come in." He rose to meet his niece. "I still can't believe it's you, my girl. I wonder—can this be the young one who lived in the woods and was never off a horse?" He put an affectionate arm about Chloe and kissed her on the forehead. *She is a tremendous beauty*, he thought, at the same time wondering what made her so outstanding. No one feature was that extraordinary; he knew many court beauties with more perfect features. But the combination of that incredible silver-blond hair of her father's with the dark eyes and lashes of her mother was unusual, to say the least. She had the perfect complexion of one reared in good country air and had resorted to no artifice, he was sure. She was the image of his brother, whom he'd always considered one of the handsomest of men. But the same features and coloring in Chloe had produced a very different creature: wholly feminine in spite of the wide mouth and the deep cleft in her strong, square chin. Her figure was perfect. She was the type that would age beautifully, gracefully, with no hint of stoutness or thickening. All this beauty, combined with an air of fragile sensitivity, something he couldn't immediately understand, only piqued his curiosity to know her better.

"Uncle James, Richard has something to show you."

His son, Richard, named for Chloe's father, grinned impishly up at his father, who tousled his bright-red hair. "I hope this young man isn't making a nuisance of himself."

Quickly, Chloe sprang to her cousin's defense. "Not at all, Uncle James—he's really no trouble," she protested. "I enjoy his company—unless you think I'm spoiling him."

James laughed wryly. "My dear, I'm afraid the servants have already done that. They've mollycoddled him since the day he was born. They mean well, but it's been a problem, the lad having no mother . . . What's this, Richard? You're painting again?" Richard thrust a sketch at his father. "Very presentable, lad, very presentable indeed. What do you think of it, Chloe?'' Not waiting for an answer: ''This is only a pastime, lad, not an occupation.''

James Cuddington was immensely suspicious of anything artistic where his son was concerned. Manners, one's success with women and at the gaming tables, as well as one's skill in the tiltyard and during the hunt, were far more important at court and in London society. ''Your nose is in a book or a paint box too much, Richard,'' he said. Painting was hardly a gentleman's occupation, and his pained attitude said more bluntly than words that he'd like to wash his hands of all such activity. ''Eh, let's see what you have?''

It was a curious little painting. Richard had placed a chair square in the middle of Cuddington House's large formal Hall which fronted directly on the Strand. It showed Chloe, seated in the chair, her hands folded in her lap. She was gazing intently at the artist. Sunlight from the window cast an almost whitish aureole about her hair and played along the chair's back. There were vague outlines of other pieces of furniture; a section of the handsome Turkey carpet was evident. Through the front window, the boy had shown a small corner of Durham House, concentrating more fully on the beauty of the Thames beyond. Even with all the background detail, however, the main focus remained the quiet figure in the chair.

James had often conceded he was no judge of art, but even he could appreciate the composition and delicate coloring. He handed it back to his son. ''Excellent, lad, most worthy! But you must admit you have a beautiful subject. Here, now—here's your uncle, show him your work.''

As Richard Cuddington admired the little painting, an idea formed in his mind. This time in London presented a fine opportunity to have his daughter's portrait painted. It could be a gift to his wife to hang proudly in their new home, something entirely unconnected with their Surrey past and a lasting reminder of her youthful beauty. When Richard broached the possibility, everyone was enthusiastic.

The next day Bartholomew Penn was summoned to Cuddington House.

* * *

Everyone was crowded into the room when, two days later, the painter set up his materials for the first sitting. Penn, a student of Master Holbein, Sergeant-Painter to the king, was a young man of medium height with dark hair and eyes and the long, sensitive fingers of the artist. He was quiet-spoken, yet authoritative as he placed his materials near his easel and opened the pale-green velvet hangings to let in the early-morning light. Penn had painted several prominent London citizens and had assisted Master Holbein on larger group portraits, such as that of Sir Thomas More, commissioned during the latter years of the Lord Chancellor's life. But, he told Thomas in an awestruck whisper, he had never before seen—or painted—anyone as lovely as Chloe Cuddington. Clearly, he considered the task a challenge.

As Chloe entered the room, Thomas caught his breath. She was wearing a gown Penn had selected for its simplicity. "The background and carpet contain much color, Mistress; the gown must fit in," he advised. The gown, a gift from her Uncle James as a memento of her London visit, was of damask in the palest shade of peach. "Lady Blush" the dressmaker had called it. Its square neckline was unadorned. But James arrived after the first few moments with a flat oblong case from which he drew a small circlet of gold with a pendant of diamonds and pearls, in the center of which was the largest pearl Chloe had ever seen. It had been a particular favorite of his wife's, he said; it would give him much pleasure to have her wear it.

Richard tugged the carved and gilded chair into the room's center, and Chloe sat down. A hush fell over the room as Bartholomew arranged the long, flowing sleeves, faced with a deeper shade of damask, so they might drape gracefully over the full skirt. A tiny cap of blush-colored velvet, bordered with delicate golden scrollwork and pearls, covered a part of Chloe's fair hair which the sun obligingly caressed. She folded her hands in her lap and then raised her eyes to gaze directly at Bartholomew Penn.

Everyone went to opposite sides of the room to admire the effect, but in the different positions, no one saw exactly what the young artist perceived. The sun not only glinted on Chloe's hair, but touched the diamonds and pearls with sparkling facets of light, rivaling the luminous radiance of the young girl sitting composedly in the gilded chair, the soft color of her gown so incredibly right with her silvery hair and ivory skin. Penn appeared dazed by such splendor. Then, picking up his brush and palette, he confidently made the first stroke.

Quickly, everyone except young Richard tiptoed from the room. The boy sank into one corner, out of the artist's view, hoping to make himself insignificant in the drapery's shadow, so that even Chloe couldn't see him. His eyes never left Penn's hands.

The following morning Thomas returned from his second visit to the Abbey. He'd told the abbot the story of Queen Catherine's Lure, and the old priest had promised to give it sanctuary. "We have many hiding places, Brother Thomas, that the Vicar-General doesn't know about—nor will he ever!" The abbot had said grimly, "Tell Father Felix we're praying for him during these difficult times. Tell him we'll welcome him when he comes." As for Thomas, if no place could be found for him at the Abbey—for which he was quite young—they'd ask for him at York. "There the old ways still persist," the abbot explained. "There have been some closings, of course, but nothing like here. It's a mite too distant for even Cromwell. Do not worry, Brother Thomas, care will be taken. Father Felix says you have great faith and ability—do not lose it now."

At Cuddington House the family was just departing at the Ivy Lane water stairs between Durham House and the Savoy, where the handsome gilded barge with the Cuddington crest painted on its sides awaited them. Chloe had finished her sitting for the day and was in high spirits at the prospect of a ride on the river. "Do come, Thomas!" she cried. "Uncle James is taking us to Chelsea!" She pulled him to the rear of the barge, and the boatman obligingly poled out in the direction of Westminster.

She wore riding clothes of a deep-blue velvet, with delicate silver filigree trim, and a fashionable hat with a long plume was set rakishly atop the pale hair. She was very different, Thomas decided, from the hoydenish Chloe with whom he'd raced over the Surrey hills. Already a week in London had given her a mature and sophisticated sheen he'd never seen before. Settling herself back among the cushions, she smiled that wide and generous smile that lit the dark eyes and said mockingly, "Now, no long face, Brother Thomas! We're going to have an adventure!" She gazed at the panorama of Westminster unfolding before her. "Oh, this is all so lovely! How marvelous it would be if Master Penn could paint this scene." She gazed with almost impish glee at Thomas. "He says the portrait is going very well."

"Penn is a gifted artist, Chloe, I've no doubt the result will be pleasing." Thomas returned her smile. "*You* are pleasing—and lovely. How could he not paint a masterpiece?" They were passing Scotland Place where the Scottish kings resided during state visits. Opposite the deteriorating pile of Westminster Palace lay the splendid red-brick Palace of Lambeth, the home of the Archbishop of Canterbury. "Bartholomew comes from Canterbury," Chloe told Thomas. "He said as a child the colors in the cathedral windows were the most wonderful thing he ever saw. All he ever wanted to do was paint them."

"I vow I detect a note of great interest in the estimable person of Master Penn." Thomas laughed, hoping to sound jocular. "Could it be that the beauteous Mistress Cuddington is smitten?"

Chloe's delicate features were suffused with pink. She raised her great dark eyes, and suddenly all the impish glee, the joyous excitement was gone to be replaced by stark, naked hunger. There was no longer any pretense, no badinage. "Do not jest, Thomas. There is no one, there never will be anyone—but you. You know that." Her tone was almost harsh. "There's no need to mock me."

Distressed, Thomas whispered, "I do not scoff at you, Chloe, I asked honestly. I've made my choice. You know that. It would be so much more satisfying to me if I knew *you*, too, had also chosen. You yourself brought up young Penn's name," he reminded her softly.

"I did. You're right, Thomas, of course. You're always right, it seems." She sighed and brushed the silvery strands of hair the river's breeze had whipped about her cheeks. "One must think of oneself, I suppose. I have a whole lifetime to live yet—without you. I very much admire Master Penn. He is attractive. He seems kind and gentle and, as you say, very gifted." She was silent a moment. "Soon you may go to York, Thomas, and I doubt I'll ever see you again." For a moment there were tears in her eyes. Then, mindful of the others, she brought up her chin sharply, and again that wide smile flashed out and the bantering tone returned to her voice. "And in that case, one must have—plans. Am I not right, Thomas?"

Thomas understood. She was saying, in her own way, that she found Penn attractive, that she might encourage his interest. As if in answer to his thoughts, she finished, "Other than you, Thomas, he's the only one I could consider living with in the intimacy of marriage. I've found that London men are mostly fools."

"Penn is no fool, Chloe," Thomas replied, surprised at the urgency in his voice. "He would be kind and gentle. You would be well taken care of. He would, I'm sure, hold you in the highest regard. Marriage is no protection against the sensualist and the brute."

Chloe gibed at him. "And what would the simple Brother Thomas of Merton Priory know about the sensualist?" Her clear laugh floated across the water, yet Thomas kept silent, his thoughts on a distant hillside long ago. Always it was the same. They couldn't be together. It would be better when she was married—if indeed she was serious—and he was at York.

The barge glided on past small shore hamlets where people fished or bathed or washed their clothing at the river's edge. At the water stairs of Sir Thomas More's old home, they disembarked and, quiet and introspective, skirted the gardens of the executed Lord Chancellor whom many had considered the finest mind in Europe. Past the old church and the More manor house, they arrived at the King's Road, and there, hiring horses, their spirits picked up. It was a gay, chattering party that cantered up the leafy lane for home, for the bracing air of the river had given them good appetites.

At the Knight's Bridge, the fields stretched beyond. Up a slight hill, they could admire the scene: the newly built St. James's Palace and a few windmills were all that marred an otherwise perfect view of the Abbey and Lambeth Palace across the river. James pointed out spots of interest as they walked down "the Streete" toward Whitehall Palace. Passing under the magnificent Holbein Gate, they entered the royal gardens at Whitehall, and Chloe was entranced at the geometrical patterns and "knots" and the handsome topiary among which the gilded heads of the King's Beasts reared proudly. In the center a picturesque fountain spilled water amid the parterres and terraces. Ladies of the court—many carrying pet monkeys or accompanied by small dogs—walked the graveled paths toward the river or "the Streete."

Suddenly a rippling note filled the air. James quickly hurried them from the gardens a few paces to the court gate. "This might be interesting to see," he said.

At the gate they watched as a group of riders approached, obviously straight from the Tiltyard that bordered on St. James's Park a few hundred yards away. Pennons flying, lances aloft, they were still in armor. Some had removed their helmets, for they'd worked up a good sweat. All were laughing, in apparent good humor at their jousting efforts.

Suddenly, Thomas recognized the massive figure in the head. There could be no mistaking the regal way the man sat his horse. Even with his visor up, Thomas knew it was the king. Excitedly, Chloe whispered, "Could it be?"

She didn't wait for an answer, for James cried, "It's the king!"

As if the man had heard, he pushed down his visor and then, with one gesture, pulled the helmet roughly from his head. He was sweating profusely. The bright-red hair was matted to his forehead; his coloring was high. Even so, here—incarnate—was a picture of Majesty and all it could mean. He called to his companion, his brother-in-law, the Duke of Suffolk, and the two spurred their horses and rode faster for the gate. Everyone was jostled as the royal gentleman-usher rode up, shouting, "Make way for the king!"

Henry came abreast of the Cuddingtons. He was so close Chloe could see the perspiration on his brow and the incredible startling blueness of his eyes. His huge fist held a lance, which suddenly he tossed to Suffolk, who caught it deftly. Then, spying the group, Henry slowed his pace and, reigning in, raised his hand toward them. A loud cheer broke from everyone, and despite themselves, the Cuddingtons were moved. Richard was amazed at his own reaction. *This is the man who has taken my inheritance*, he thought, *who will break up my land, send families into exile, has dissolved a worthy holy house, and here I am admiring him!* Still he remained impressed. *He's our sovereign*, Richard reasoned. *We're born and bred to revere the king.* Yet he didn't join in the cheering, noting instead the expectant smiles on his brother's and daughter's faces.

The king approached the gate. Glancing at the assembled crowd, he noted nothing unusual except the slim figure of a young girl. A beauty in dark-blue velvet, her hands folded in front, her hair a most remarkable color. Even from the slight distance, Henry could see the magnificent dark eyes, smiling in anticipation. Good breeding and grace showed in every line of her person. The king rode nearer so he might observe her more closely. Richard leaned forward and, without consciously knowing he did so, put a protective arm on the girl's shoulder.

Henry observed the gesture, noticed the resemblance and smiled. He was in little doubt of his subjects' opinion of him where a good-looking wench was concerned. His companions had stopped and watched as, for a split second, the exquisite young girl, the man so like her and the king seemed to present a tableau in which all were waiting for something. . . .

It happened in the next moment. The throng had fallen silent and was waiting also. Henry eyed the others; they were the usual group to be found at every royal gate. But this girl and man were different. His companions were smiling at each other—never could the king resist a pretty face!

Then they, too, were nonplussed. For Henry had come to a complete stop. Gazing directly at Chloe and her father, he held out his hand and called, "Mistress! I give you a good day!" Then, turning slightly in his saddle, graceful in spite of his ample girth and heavy hot armor, he bowed deeply in homage. He was pleased to see the young beauty smile. Even the father relaxed his hold, and a certain wariness left his features.

Suffolk came abreast and whispered something to the king. Henry called again. "Mistress! My Lord of Suffolk tells me you've met before—that you're as clever as you are beautiful. A good combination, mistress! I pay tribute to your wit." And again he bowed low in Chloe's direction. Then, calling to the gentleman-usher, "Proceed!" he laughed aloud and—very aware of the effect he'd created—winked broadly and wickedly at her as he spurred his horse forward. His companions, mindful of Henry's behavior, copied him good-naturedly as they entered the gates that closed with a loud and dusty bang. Through the bars Chloe could see the king laughing and dismounting at a doorway, thumping several of his companions on their backs as they disappeared inside.

It had all taken but a few moments, yet each in the little group felt dazed by the royal accolade. James was relieved. It'd been an awkward moment, and he'd not have blamed his brother if he'd turned his back so as not to see the king.

"He is . . . magnificent." Chloe appeared bedazzled. Answering Richard's question, she explained her encounter with Suffolk and his promise to leave Sparwefeld for the Cuddingtons. Her father laughed appreciatively as she told the story. "That was most kind of His Majesty, most kind indeed," he said.

Thomas went for the mounts, and they all rode in silence to Cuddington House. It had been a wonderful afternoon, and as he rode along, it occurred to the monk that for the moment at least, the hate, bitterness and despair they'd brought to London had all but vanished in the magical moment when a king had bowed and smiled.

* * *

At Cuddington House a messenger awaited Sir Richard. There had been an accident, he explained, and Domino had been hurt while helping load the last of the wagons with plants and shrubs destined for the Suffolk garden. The wagon had been overloaded, had shifted as the old gardener had thrust the last shrub into place and had quickly spilled out, catching the man and pinning him to the ground. His leg was badly hurt, but even so, he told Richard, Domino had clouted those who picked him up, calling everyone lazy, stupid varlets. The Lady Elizabeth regretted bringing their London stay to an end, but she desired the family to return, for she would need all hands. Richard gave orders to leave at once; he felt an affectionate concern for the old gardener.

It was James who remembered first. "The portrait, Richard! It's not finished! It would be a shame to halt it now."

Richard agreed. Penn was working superbly; he would need little more than another few days. "You'll stay, child," he told Chloe, "finish the work and then perhaps I can come for you or James will bring you home."

And so it was decided. Early the next morning, while it was still dark, the family gathered for an early meal, and as the horses were being readied, Thomas disappeared into the chapel at the rear of Cuddington House. There at the altar he knelt, seeking to quiet his mind and heart. He gave thanks for his gracious reception at the Abbey, for the sanctuary provided Queen Catherine's Lure and for his pleasant days at Cuddington House. He asked that he be sent where he might be needed—either York or Westminster—it mattered little. All he cared about was to continue in the life to which he was so deeply committed.

Was that all that mattered? The picture of Chloe as she'd sat in the barge floated before him. "Do not jest, Thomas," she'd whispered. Already she'd wasted several years waiting for him until the very end, never relinquishing her hope of marrying him. Only his final vows had convinced her their love was hopeless. She needed love, the warmth and companionship of marriage. She deserved children who might one day inherit the vast Suffolk estates Sir Richard would leave her.

After their departure she'd undoubtedly in her peach damask gown return to the Hall where Barholomew Penn would be most vulnerable to her charm and sweetness. Thomas felt a catch in his throat. If Penn were right for her, let her receive him with an open heart. That was his prayer.

He rose from his knees, the peace that usually accompanied his prayer eluding him. Certainly he wished the creature dearest on earth to him to be loved and safely wed. But if that was what he wished, why did he feel sad? Why, he wondered as he closed the chapel door, did he suddenly feel almost engulfed by an overwhelming sense of loneliness and despair?

Chapter Seventeen

Three days later, as Bartholomew Penn was putting the finishing touches on the portrait, a letter from her mother was delivered to Chloe as she left the sitting. She took it to the Hall, where James was writing at the desk, and sat down to read it. Little gasps escaped her lips, and her uncle noticed her hands were shaking. "Chloe, dear! What is it?" He arose to comfort his niece, who handed him the letter.

"MY DARLING CHILD,

We were happy to receive your letter telling us news of London and that the sittings were going so well. We will be anxious to see the Portrait of our beloved girl, whom we miss very much.

All is going as well as could be expected here at Cuddington. We shall be departing this sad Place within the next few weeks, for most preparations are complete. There has been an unexpected Occurrence, however, of which I am sorry to have to write.

You'll remember that Father Felix was to go to Westminster Abbey. On the day he arrived home, Thomas went to say farewell to the Prior, for already the workers have begun to pull down some of the outer Walls. He was also to receive some Memento which Father Felix had promised to give him. When he entered the Prior's chamber—oh, Chloe, I am so saddened to write this—he found the old man had died. Father Felix was sitting in his chair, and according to Thomas (who was struck as Dumb by what he'd found), he had a most peaceful, almost serene expression on his face. There were no marks of any struggle or pain. Thomas said it looked as though the Prior had just sat down and "willed himself to die."

We were upset at this added Burden of sorrow, but perhaps it's best for Father Felix to go as he did, rather than have to start a new life at his age.

Thomas was saddened and Upset, of course. There are a few monks left at Merton, and so the funeral is to be held quickly with only tonight to visit the Bier. Then he will be buried in some Holy Ground in Ewell; your Father has promised to attend to it all for, in the general confusion at Merton, no one else is there to take the responsibility. Your Father is tired, and this was an added and distressing charge, but he would take on the dispensing of this debt, which he said he owed to an old and honorable Friend.

I am sorry to end on such an unhappy note. But you know, my dearest daughter, that these are sad Times at Cuddington. I pray that when we get to Ixworth, we may all be our happy Selves again."

Chloe went into the chapel to pray for Father Felix. She'd never known a day when he hadn't been at Merton Priory. The sad tone of her mother's letter remained in her mind throughout the day and was still there as she lay in bed at night, gazing at the window through which she could hear the busy noises of the Strand and the cry of the watermen at the bottom of the Durham House water stairs. At the thought of all the wearisome activities ahead before they journeyed to Suffolk, she buried her head in the pillow, realizing she was on the verge of sleep. And then, suddenly, she *was* asleep and had begun to dream.

In her dream—and, oddly, she knew it *was* a dream—she was standing in the ruins of a building which at first she didn't recognize. Everything seemed so real and even right for her to be there. As she walked among the ruins, she came upon a section of brightly tiled material which she recognized as the flooring her parents had given to the Cuddington church. Of course! She was in the ruins of the church. Part of the walls still stood, and one large beam near the chancel remained. Otherwise, it lay bare to the elements, and all around were piles of debris, as well as neatly stacked brick and stone which she assumed would be used for whatever edifice the king intended to build.

She wandered, seemingly at home, knowing just where she was going and what she was going to do. Here had been the crypt, and over there, under the nave, she knew were several burial vaults. The debris was interesting. Closer inspection revealed some roundels, corbels and fragments of statues—it was Merton Priory stone! She even recognized several gargoyle heads. The irony of priory stone filling in the foundation of the king's new building made her smile. For a brief moment the king's face floated before her in her dream. "I give you good day, mistress!" he called, his voice sounding far off before it disappeared altogether.

She walked along the edges of the ruins skirting the building materials until the sound of footsteps in the distance caused her to slip behind a huge pile of newly fired bricks. Yet she knew that even if she didn't hide, she couldn't be seen. It was—after all—only a *dream*, she reminded herself. But it seemed natural to hide. She made no attempt to still the gasp that came at first sight of her visitors. First came Thomas, carrying a heavy gold cross in his right hand, a small wooden coffer in the other. Following him was a tall blond man. Chloe almost cried out—it was her father!

Richard Cuddington was pulling a hurdle, a small sledlike conveyance, to which was fastened a long box resembling a coffin. He pulled it around the debris and piles of building materials which rimmed the foundations. Near the ruined church which she'd just seen, they stopped, and Chloe held her breath, knowing all the while they couldn't see or hear her, but feeling compelled to caution anyway. What were they doing? She crept farther out from her shelter and watched.

Obviously, the two men had visited the site previously and knew exactly where they were going. They stopped at what appeared to be the bricked-up portion of a doorway set into the wall, with its heavy lintel stone overhead. It was all part of a new foundation. Quickly, they removed the stone, and with one sweeping gesture, Richard Cuddington caused the piled-up bricks, which had no mortar between them, to topple to the ground. Peering through the dust as it settled, Chloe could see the large empty space. How had her father and Thomas discovered it?

Quickly, they worked, clearing the bricks so the hurdle might be drawn near. Then, swiftly, they lifted the coffin and placed it within the depths. There was just sufficient light for Chloe to see Thomas motion to her father to open the coffin lid. Quickly, he took the small coffer and placed it in what she assumed was the inside of the coffin. And then, in the strange way dreams always occurred, she could see *into* the coffin. She wasn't frightened. For there was Father Felix, dressed in a handsome cope of red and gold, a cap on his white hair, his waxen features serene. His hands had been arranged so that the small coffer just fit. How clever, thought Chloe in her dream, again reminding herself that it *was* only a dream.

Both men then stood up, barely clearing the still bricked-up portion of the wall, and she strained to hear their words. Thomas was intoning in Latin and making the sign of the cross. Her father stood by, his head bent. Then he closed the coffin lid, and the monk carefully and reverently placed the heavy golden cross on the cover. Both men moved back, crossed themselves and stood for a moment in silent prayer. Then, as one, they hurriedly began to brick up the wall, using mortar they'd carried in a heavy iron vat for that purpose. Swiftly they lined the bricks, placing the substance on them, then laying another line of bricks and doing it all so swiftly Chloe thought her dream was beginning to unravel. They didn't bother to line the bricks accurately, although they removed some of the excess mortar. Chloe heard her father say, "They'll never notice. Whoever left this task undone will think someone else finished it."

Thomas smiled and gesturing to the piles of Merton stone, replied, with what seemed like bitter humor, "We'll leave more than the body of Merton's prior here, Sir Richard. There's going to be a good bit of Merton itself, it seems." He smiled as he finished his work. "Yes, a good bit of Merton will always remain at Cuddington now, no matter what they do." He brightened as he finished off the last tier of bricks, and both men lifted the heavy lintel stone back into place.

As they did so, one of them tipped over the vat of mortar,

and it seeped onto the rough earthen floor. Quickly, Richard Cuddington righted the vat and, with one of the implements he'd worked with, scooped up the remainder of the mortar and replaced it in the vat. The space they were working in was restricted, and in their eagerness to be finished and gone, both men had stepped into the mortar. Now, laughing like two children once an unhappy task is completed, they moved back onto the ground, mortarlike bits clinging to boots and sandals. "No matter, Thomas," she heard her father say, "we must be gone, for it will be light very soon . . . come along!" And then, after one long backward glance, during which Thomas made the sign of the cross, they hurriedly disappeared into the shrubbery on the opposite side of the ruins.

As Chloe made ready to leave, she saw someone approaching in the opposite direction. Again she crouched below the bricks and watched as the figure continued in her direction. Stiffening, she recognized the man. It was Hurst. He was dressed in the familiar garb of an undergardener, but he looked very different. There was no deference in his manner; he seemed to possess complete authority and exuded a certainty, a knowledge she knew was foreign to the man as he actually was. Or was it?

She watched as he prowled along the rim of the new foundation. It was almost as if he *scented* an intrusion, she thought, but was relieved to see him pass by the burial place without stopping. Suddenly, he lifted his head and gazed about him, slowly . . . slowly . . . watching and waiting . . . in an eerie moment that seemed an eternity. She felt the cold trickle of fear in her stomach, and it crawled along the nape of her neck, down into her arms, weakening her hold on the pile of bricks. For he'd turned in her direction and was coming toward her. He was smiling—his brown teeth bared in a hateful smile—his hands stretching out to her. As he saw her, he broke into a run. Coming closer, he cried, "You're here! I *knew* you were here, and I had to come!" She gathered her strength to run, but her limbs felt heavy. She hoped she could run quickly to join her father and Thomas, who must still be nearby. Then she realized she mustn't divulge their presence, and as panic overcame her, she struggled to elude Hurst's grasp and, as he came closer, opened her mouth to scream.

Chloe awakened, trembling and in a cold sweat, at the edge of nausea. Weakly, she sat up in bed, pushing the silvery hair from her eyes with shaking hands and, at the same time, quickly glancing around the comfortably familiar room. She was alone. Her breath still came in heavy gasps, and her heart was pounding so fast she wondered if she should summon one of her uncle's maids. How to explain such a dream to anyone? How to explain it to herself? With shaking fingers, she lit the candle at her bedside and piled her pillows high, stretching up against them, hoping to still her quaking body and distraught mind. Gradually, as the candlelight glowed brighter, she became quieter and pondered what she'd seen. *She'd been there*—whatever had taken place—*she'd been there*. And so had Hurst. She was sure of it. Just as she was sure that for the remainder of the night, sleep was out of the question.

Early the next morning, Chloe, her Uncle James and young Richard set out for Cuddington. The portrait was complete, and Bartholomew Penn was instructed to find a suitable frame and deliver it at Cuddington within a few days.

The road they traveled into Surrey was worn with the passage of armies, hunting parties, peasants and farmers. The professional highwayman still made unexpected appearances, and her uncle had hired an armed escort. Their passage, however, was uneventful—much to young Richard's disappointment—and Chloe had time to speculate on her dream. Unlike other dreams, it hadn't faded with the arrival of morning or the bustle of their departure. She reviewed it all, deciding she possessed an overactive imagination that had been aroused by her mother's letter with its sad news of Father Felix's death.

Hours later all such thoughts were swept from her mind, for she recognized familiar landmarks. They were on Cuddington land. "I know the way from here!" she shouted to her uncle and, spurring her horse, waved for the group to follow. They pounded over the meadows, kicking up the barren earth that had not yet frozen, vaulting quickly over the sluggish streams that ran engorged with freshets in the spring. Quickly, through the deep forest that lay north of the manor house, and there, at the vaultlike opening at the end, just at the tip of the slope, lay her home. Still her home for a few more days. She pounded up the rise, shouting to whoever might be near and was relieved to see a crowd gathered in the courtyard. Calling and waving as she approached, she saw her father, expectant and happy, dismount and wait for her. Clattering into the courtyard, she flung herself into his arms and with tears of happy relief saw her mother and Thomas emerge from the kitchen wing.

"Darling! Chloe!" Her mother wrapped her in strong arms. "Darling, you are so welcome—we've missed you so." Choking back the tears, Chloe again embraced her father as Thomas clasped her hand. The rest of the group joined them, and amid the exchange of pleasantries, Chloe's eyes traveled to Thomas' sandals. Bits of mortar and dirt clung to them, but he seemed oblivious as he welcomed James Cuddington. She looked at her father's boots. He'd made an effort to clean them, but mortar still adhered to the heel and along one side. Again that feeling of nausea clutched at her as she remembered her dream. *It must be true*, she thought, *it must be true*. But how could it be?

It wasn't until she saw another figure emerge from behind her father that she knew it *was* true. For there was Hurst, wearing the same garments he'd worn in her dream and bearing that same indefinable air of evil authority. Her mother whispered that he no longer worked at the manor but was now employed by the king's surveyor as a laborer. He was smiling at her in just the same way he'd smiled in her dream. Suddenly, as he drew nearer, the dream and reality merged, and without knowing what was happening, her hold on her mother's arm loosened, and she slid to the ground unconscious.

The following day Bartholomew Penn arrived at the manor house with the portrait, and everyone crowded about to see it in its handsome new frame. "It's a great success, Master

Penn, and we must celebrate,'' Sir Richard said, ordering a servant to bring wine. ''You're to be congratulated—I am very pleased.''

The servant arrived with the wine, and Richard handed everyone a glass, even young Richard. ''After all, lad, it *was* your idea,'' he said, smiling at Penn. He'd been most impressed with the young artist's integrity, particularly his effect on his nephew, who spoke of nothing but Penn's work and how he himself wished to be such an artist when he grew up. Glasses in hand, they all moved away to view the portrait from a distance.

It was young Richard's sketch brought to luminous life. It compelled one's attention by the sheer virtuosity of the artist as much as the sitter's radiant beauty. Every color—the gown, Chloe's pale hair and dark winged brows and eyes—each complemented the whole. Penn had wrought each piece of furniture with superb craftsmanship; the lustrous colors of the Turkey carpet were warm and glowing. Sunlight lingered on the jewels and lay along a sleek border Penn had painted about the neckline. Young Richard had never recovered from the artist's dexterous rendering of the ermine which was nonexistent on the actual dress, telling everyone, ''He painted it just as if it were there!''

James approached the canvas, wineglass in hand, to look at the little portrait within a portrait which had been Penn's contribution to Richard's sketch. It was almost uncanny the way he'd caught the Cuddington House façade down to the last detail. From a distance, it was an impressive addition, but viewed more closely, remarkable. Even the animals on the family crest were clearly identifiable. Through the windows on each side of the doorway, the sunlit interiors were visible and rendered with minute skill. The perspective was striking.

''It's certainly a great success, Master Penn,'' he told the artist. ''It's very beautiful and you've given us much pleasure.''

Penn beamed at James' comment. The portrait had become very important to him; he knew it to be one of his finest works. He'd developed a warm camaraderie with young Richard and had shown the child many little tricks with brush, charcoal and pen which Richard had quickly assimilated. As for Chloe, he'd found her company very pleasant once he'd recovered from the awe which her beauty aroused in him. He knew her to be sensitive and understanding and felt, instinctively, that she liked him. Yet there was some part of her that was *unapproachable*, as if she were deliberately withholding any opportunity for an emotional response that might encourage him. Most girls her age would have flirted or played the coquette; she seemed virtually *sealed* against any advances he might make. Aware as he was of the difference in their rank and the trust her family had reposed in him in leaving them unattended for long periods each day, he'd said nothing to give her any hint of his feelings. Therefore, he knew that on this visit to Cuddington he must explain how he felt; otherwise, she'd soon be off to Suffolk and out of his life forever.

Bartholomew Penn was also much on Chloe's mind as she moved about the rooms on one of the last days at the manor house. Everywhere inside there was emptiness, and outside a ravaged wasteland: trees, shrubs and other growing things had been uprooted, and clumps of earth and sod tossed into random piles. She'd almost made up her mind to ask her father to have Penn paint portraits of himself and her mother; it would mean he'd go to Suffolk with them. It could mean the start of a new life for her. Probably she'd never see Thomas again, and that part of her which would always be his would go with him. What was left she must give to someone; Penn seemed a kind and gentle person. He was obviously attracted to her—it would take little effort to have that attraction ripen. Her parents might wish someone more grand for her. But theirs had been a love match, and they'd never force her. If she wanted Penn, she did not think her parents would object.

Walking near the fishpond, deep in thought, she saw Thomas coming along the road from Merton. He, too, would soon be leaving for London, and she knew they'd likely never see each other again. Ever since her return, she'd wanted to talk with him and tell him of her dream. Her parents had attributed her fainting to the long ride and the shock of Father Felix's death. She'd never questioned her father about the bits of mortar on his boots. But she knew she could talk to Thomas, and she sped quickly down the road, calling his name.

The monk waved and smiled at her approach, and Chloe's heart melted as it always did whenever Thomas was near. He'd donned a new robe and fresh sandals and carried a cloak against the chill he'd encounter on the walk home. His tonsured hair was neat, and he swept her a deep bow. "Has Master Penn arrived, Mistress Chloe? I've come to see the final result. Also to bring the Lady Elizabeth this *Book of Hours* which the monks made especially for her." He held up a little book with gold-edged parchment leaves. "I've also come to say good-bye."

There was a stab of burning pain beneath her heart. This was it. Thomas was going—forever. Chloe felt her throat tighten and a smarting sensation just behind her eyes. *Don't be a fool*, she told herself sternly, *you've cried enough over this man*! *He's not for you—he chose God.*

So she smiled brightly, thanking Thomas for her mother's book and then, curtsying: "Master Penn *and* the portrait are here. Father is pleased. *I* am pleased." She drew herself up with exaggerated hauteur, attempting a jocularity to match his. "He may come to Suffolk and paint Mother and Father's portraits."

"That's good." Thomas beamed. "I shall think of you often, Chloe, wherever I am. I'll send a message to Suffolk whether I'm to be at Westminster or York. I rather suspect it will be York."

They'd reached the fishpond, and even the hateful remembrance of her encounter there with Hurst couldn't diminish her happiness at being with Thomas. Always, her heart bounded at the pure pleasure of just walking with him. She longed to take his hand. And knew she wouldn't.

"Thomas, there's something I want to tell you. Please hear me out—it's very important to me! I only hope you won't think me mad! But you must be truthful with me. . . ." At the reproach in his eyes, she said quickly, "I know you *will* be,

Thomas. But this is a story that courts disbelief." Quickly, she described in detail what she'd seen in her dream.

Crossing himself, Thomas cried, "God save us! You *saw* it!" His features mirrored his own incredulity. "But this is fantasy! *How* could you know? You were in London! Yet it's exactly as you described it. Father Felix *was* buried in what is going to be the king's wine cellar. We chose that simply because it was the only new foundation ready. We buried him there because of the Lure." And then he told her the story he'd heard from the prior.

"Oh, Thomas, I wish I'd seen it!" Chloe was enchanted with the tale of the golden pomegranate.

"It's safe now—forever," the monk replied. He said upon returning from London and finding the prior dead, he'd gone to Chloe's father and told him the whole story. Thomas said he felt it a sacred trust that the Lure be safe. He might take it to Westminster, where the abbot had promised to give it sanctuary, but he felt it should stay with Father Felix now the old man had died. Luckily, Sir Richard had agreed but advised they could hardly have a proper burial and ceremony in Ewell with others in attendance if the Lure was to go in the coffin. Then her father had thought of the wine cellar—it was all raw stone and brick and would be complete in a day or two. *It was made entirely of Merton Priory stone.* That fact had convinced Thomas there'd be no desecration in laying the prior to his final rest in a wine cellar. "He'll be enclosed in consecrated stone," Thomas said, relieved. And so they'd buried him—and Queen Catherine's Lure—before dawn, just as she'd seen it in her dream. As Thomas retold the story, his features mirrored the wonder that she should have seen it all.

Chloe remembered the countless times in her childhood when she had seemingly possessed an odd foreknowledge of coming events. Already she'd tried Thomas' belief by recounting the dream, but she had to finish. So she told him how she'd encountered Hurst, how he'd come toward her, threatening. . . .

"And that's why you fainted—when you saw him," Thomas mused. "That man is evil. Pure evil. I've felt his power."

"Oh, Thomas, he *is*!" Chloe cried. "Once, very near here, he willed me—*willed* me, Thomas, to come to him from inside the house while he waited out here! What is this power? Is it of the devil?"

"I don't know"—Thomas was reflective—"but I do know, it's *not* from God."

"That's not all." Chloe spoke faintly, looking away to the ruined church on the horizon. "I've never told you, for I've been afraid. Or else I thought you might laugh. But sometimes, I feel I am . . . tainted."

"Tainted! *You!*" Thomas laughed aloud. "Mistress Chloe, my *dear* Mistress Chloe, of all the people I know, you have *no* taint."

"I'm not jesting, Thomas." Chloe turned her dark, serious gaze on him and recounted the many instances when, in her mind's eye, she'd foreseen an event. She told of the violet cap, of how she might know that a sick person—or animal—would live or die. "When I was little, I thought *everyone* was that way. But then I found out they weren't. . . ." Her voice trailed off. "Oh, Thomas, do you think I'm a witch?"

Thomas laughed—an indulgent laugh—and covered her hand with his. "My dear, if you are, you're a *blessed* witch. No, Chloe, I don't think you're a witch. I think you have a very sensitive soul, a great capacity for understanding, compassion and . . . love. You're a beautiful person, my dear, not only your face and body, but your spirit as well. You are—what would Father Felix have said?—*gifted* spiritually. Some people are endowed with a great talent, like your friend Master Penn. But *your* sensitivities and faculties are more deeply developed—that's all. The fact that you possess them is really an act of grace. They're not so very unusual either—some of the saints, for instance, have powers that—"

"Thomas, I'm *not* a saint." Chloe looked at the strong brown hand covering hers. The temptation was too great to resist. She lowered her head and laid her lips gently on the back.

Thomas felt his throat tighten. He yearned to bury his other hand in the silver hair—and knew that if he did, he'd be lost. He managed a grim chuckle. "No, my girl, you're no saint! But you mustn't let your power worry you either! It's never harmed or hurt anyone. It's a gift from God, Chloe. Cherish it and use it always for good."

There was a rude laugh from behind, and they sprang apart, startled, Thomas almost dropping the *Book of Hours*. Hurst had stepped from behind the hedge bordering the fishpond. "Caught you two again!" he cried, crossing his arms across his chest, his face contorted. "Don't think Sir Richard would be happy knowing his lass is taking up with the priest-boy again." He spat on the ground. "Can't leave each other alone, you two, can you? I mind the other times. . . ." Raising his eyebrows, he leered at Thomas. "And all this time you ain' bedded with her yet!"

"Thomas—don't!" Chloe grasped his arm, pulling him toward her as he lunged at Hurst. She remembered the man's incredible strength and was paralyzed with fright that he'd hurt Thomas. "Thomas, come along—we'll go inside. Mother will want to see your gift, and you have to say farewell. You'll want to see the portrait, and Bartholomew Penn is here." She knew she was babbling, yet she must keep them apart.

But Hurst would have none of it. "I listened, and I heard you tell of your dream. I was there! I knew you was there, too! I saw you in the dream—I saw you and Sir Richard and the priest-boy. What was you doin'? What happened? You buried somethin', didn't you? You must tell me. *I* was there, too, and I have a *right* to know—same as you. I'm just as good as you, Mistress Chloe, with your uppity way. No one's good enough for you except *him*." Hurst spat again. "I've heard rumors, Brother Thomas, of what goes on in holy houses—seems it goes on outside, too." And again that lewd smile she remembered from the day on the hill.

Thomas struggled to contain himself as Chloe pulled strongly at his sleeve. "Hurst, I want you to listen to me," he said, and Chloe marveled at his calm. "You don't belong here anymore. You're working for the King's Surveyor, I understand. That's good. Because you've *never* belonged here! You have a bitter mind and a twisted spirit. You have great strength, too, in your body and mind—but you're using both the wrong way. You *could* change. It's up to you. I'm sure you're a very unhappy man, Hurst. Surely, you're a very unhealthy—and unpleasant—spirit. But you have a soul, Hurst, just as we all have. It came from God. Yet you treat it as if it came from the devil."

"Maybe it did!" the small man shouted, waving a clenched fist threateningly. "Maybe it did! God and spirit and stuff like that never did nothin' for me. I got my mind and my strength my own way, priest-boy, and you needn't give me a lot of holy talk while you're always prowlin' around the girl here as if she was a bitch in heat."

Thomas was white-faced, his self-control almost disappearing. Suddenly, the blessed sound of horses' hooves came from down the road, and Chloe, weak with relief, saw her father and Bartholomew Penn reining up to join them. Hurst saw them, too, and moved away. "I'll find out about what you was doin' there that night if it's the last thing I do." His eyes narrowed, a vicious glint in their depths. "You buried somethin'. But you ain' seen the last o' me." He hurried away. Chloe sank weakly against Thomas, and he put an arm about her shoulders as they prepared to follow in the horses' wake toward the manor house.

Moments later the monk presented the *Book of Hours* to Lady Elizabeth, who exclaimed with delight at its beauty. "Thomas! That was so good of the brothers." Her eyes filled. "My dear boy, we're going to miss you and Father Felix so. I shall treasure this forever because it's from Merton." Thomas kissed the hand she extended, saying, "I'm going to the church. Just once more before I leave. I'll stop and say good-bye to Sir Richard when I return. Walk with me to the gate, Chloe?"

They started along the path near the red-brick wall toward the ruined church which stood stark against the sky. "Thomas, why do you go? It's so—grim."

"My happiest moments were spent there, Chloe. I remember sitting there with my parents. The music took me out of the building and sent something in me soaring up . . . up . . . to the highest part of the nave. I remember Father Felix celebrating the holy days there. I have to say good-bye."

They'd reached the gate in the wall, and a sound from inside made them stop. They saw Domino sitting on his bench under the young beech tree her father had planted. He was hunched over, crooning softly to birds diving from the wall and nearby trees. They flew about in great numbers, alighting on his shoulders and cap, and he swept them away impatiently. At the same time, muttering in that soft fashion, he plunged into a sack and, in a great sweeping motion, flung seed out to the birds. "He's to stay," Chloe whispered. "His leg hasn't healed. He's to have Sparwefeld. There'll be a little something of old Cuddington left as long as he lives here." The monk and the girl watched the scene, peaceful and quiet, with the rhythmic sweep of the man's hand and the soft cadence of his voice as he flung seed to the ground. Suddenly an old spaniel of Lady Elizabeth's padded out from behind the house, sniffed about and, finding a patch of weak sunlight, settled itself under the tree with a great sigh of contentment. "It's like a painting," Thomas whispered, "and a wonderful way to remember your old home, Chloe. Keep it in your mind like a treasure. I know I shall. I'll see you on my return." He patted her shoulder and walked in the easy, graceful way that even the shapeless brown gown couldn't hide toward the ruined church. Chloe watched him for a moment and then, remembering the tasks which still awaited her inside, walked down the circle toward the door in silence so she'd not disturb the old man, the dog and the birds.

Chapter Eighteen

"Well, now we know," was all Andrew said.

It was the afternoon of the following day, and he was returning the tapes of his last session to Timothy Hodge in his office. The final patient had departed and a fire was burning itself out in the grate, while Timothy busied himself with a teakettle. He'd been so moved by the story of Brother Thomas and his Chloe that once Andrew had finished, he'd insisted his friend take the tapes to Cuddington House and listen to them alone.

"Yes, now we know," Timothy agreed. "How do you feel about the story, Andrew?"

"I've never been so enthralled or excited"—Andrew accepted his tea—"and—quite touched, Tim. Listening to those tapes was a tremendous experience."

"Yes, and we now know what the Lure is. That it wasn't the evil force at the fountain where Julian became so ill. It was that force you exorcised, and you called it Hurst—we know now who Hurst was. And we even know where the Lure is buried! Do you think that accounts for your fascination—and Julian's too, for that matter—with the wine cellar?"

"I wish I knew." Andrew settled his long frame into an armchair. "Actually, you know, Tim, the tape still leaves a lot unanswered. What happened to Thomas? He'd go no further than when he said good-bye to Chloe. Did he go to York or Westminster? We know Chloe eventually married Bartholomew Penn, so he must have left her life completely. I found their, uh, love . . . very affecting. . . ." For a moment his features looked drawn. "I still find it all hard to believe."

"Especially Hurst. What an obscene little toad he was!" Timothy mused. "I wonder what happened to him? Why would he—or his spirit—wish to stay around for four hundred years. In one spot—the site of the old chancel?"

"That's what I mean, Tim, when I say that in some ways I'm still as confused as when we began this little drama"—Andrew smiled wryly—"and you said before we started the last session that I must be content with what I found. Well, we found that Chloe Cuddington wasn't a witch, that she was in love with a monk. We found out what the Lure is and where it's buried."

"We found much more than that, Andrew." Timothy leaned back in his chair as he studied his friend earnestly. "Can't you think of a little larger-than-life something that all this proves?"

"Like what?"

"Like, for instance, the fact that we are literally 'born again' as the Bible says. We *do* have a second—maybe more—chance on this old earth. Reincarnation. I've never seen more conclusive evidence of it—and its subsequent Karmic working out—than Brother Thomas, Julian and *you*. And, of course, Chloe. I've given this a lot of thought, Andrew. It's a most unusual case of two souls intertwined for centuries. You and the spirit—or girl—named Chloe. It's not all coincidence, you know. From the time of your birth this has been foreordained. First that you develop a love for England. Then you actually visit Nonsuch and have that accident in the park with the pony. Don't you remember after hearing the Julian tapes you were so impressed by the fact that you'd even been motivated to go to Williamsburg where you 'just happened' to find Julian's *Journal* . . . and the fact that Cuddington House still existed? And here in London, you 'just happened' to have a friend who could practice hypnosis, so we could discover a few facts no attic or journal could have revealed. There was even a nice cooperative Rosa Caudle, who 'just happened' to have a portrait of a girl named Chloe Cuddington. Don't you see a pattern to all this, Andrew?"

"Yes, I do. And it literally scares the bejesus out of me. I'm not a medical man like you, Tim. I find it difficult to accept. Also, that it was *I* who did all those things only makes it harder to rationalize. It also changes one's concept of time, for instance. As an archaeologist and architect I've worked with old buildings and civilizations long dead and gone. But if all we've been through is valid and acceptable, it's all still around in someone's memory—their idols, images and ideals are still intact. It's a mind-boggling concept. I just wish I weren't so tired."

"You've had a very emotional experience, Andrew," Timothy replied. "I'd be more worried about you if you *weren't* tired! But let's go back to your comment about accepting what we found. We've found that Chloe was a charmer—a sensitive woman and a gifted psychic in modern parlance. We know where the Lure is. Are you now going to put it all from your mind and let it go at that?"

"Seems I have no choice but to accept what we found. But one thing I want to do is find the Lure. Tim, I want to *see* it—again. Hold it in my hand."

Timothy looked nonplussed. He'd thought Andrew might find his sixteenth-century life as a monk difficult to accept, might dislike the fact that his association with Chloe had ended with her marriage to another. Might even—after all he'd been through—wonder what had been proved? He hadn't thought the Lure, buried for more than four hundred years in a Surrey wine cellar, would prove the main attraction! "What are you thinking, Andrew?" he asked.

"I'm thinking how terribly easy it would be to get it."

"Now, Andrew . . ."

"Oh, don't 'now, Andrew' me, man! I've got all the tools. We *know* where it is." Andrew's face shone with enthusiasm. "The Norman roundel has got to be the marking place. It's always intrigued me that such a prominent stone would be put in such an outlandish spot, not even centered, for instance. Oh, Tim, let's go and see if we can find it!"

"The authorities. . . ."

"The authorities be damned! Hang it all, man, don't you know what'll happen if the authorities are involved? We'll have to deal with this commission and that bureau and work with floodlights and a television camera zooming in on us. Hell, no. I won't do it! Don't you think after all this time I've earned the right to find the Lure *myself*?" His strong voice was insistent, and for a moment, Timothy could almost hear Thomas' vibrant promise to look after the Lure. He was still keeping that promise. . . .

He mentioned this to Andrew. "See what I mean? This same working out. You've got to see it again. You've got to satisfy yourself it's safe. What'll you do when you get it, Andrew? The British law has rather stiff regulations concerning this sort of thing."

"Well, I'm not going to steal it if that's what you mean! I'll worry about what to do with it when I have it in my hand. Oh, come with me, Tim! There's nothing at Nonsuch that can hurt us now! You've finished for the day. We can be there in a little over half an hour! Thank God it's getting darker a bit later now. Oh, come on. . . ."

They stopped only once en route to Nonsuch. At the Sparrow Field gate, Timothy slowed the car down, and for a brief moment they looked at the crumbling red-brick wall and the area where the beech tree and old bench had been. Where a girl and a monk had stopped to look at an old man feeding the birds. "There's what I call a real 'psychic overlay' here," Timothy said, pointing to the scene where the little cottage lights shone. "There was a lot of emotion involved on the day it happened. Domino was probably heartbroken because he couldn't go to Suffolk. His remedy was to stick to his usual routine and pretend nothing had happened. So he fed his birds . . . just as he'd always done. Thomas and Chloe stopped to watch, and since it was a final leave-taking for the monk and for the family, too, it imprinted itself on their minds forever. Just as Thomas suggested Chloe always remember what her old home looked like. That's why it can be seen by people with the proper receptivity."

"What do you mean by 'proper receptivity'?" Andrew, too, was gazing at the scene with something like wonder in his eyes. "When you actually see it, it looks as real as those lights."

"I've always thought that people are really walking 'electrical banks,' " Timothy responded, starting up the car again. "Some have more power than others—and often use it differently. That power, for instance, manifests as clairvoyance, ESP, telepathy. Why, even charm—plain, old *charm*—is really an electrical magnetism that some people possess in more abundance than others. I've always thought that most of us possess these faculties—some more so than others—but we're usually not aware of them, so some atrophy from disuse. You, for instance, didn't know you had any psychic power at all until you were told you'd seen Domino's ghost. It's no ghost at all, merely an etheric impression that's remained in this area and can be perceived by those who are psychic or on the same vibration or electrical wavelength. Come to think of it, Andrew, you've probably used this force more times than you'll ever know in your work. Haven't you often dug somewhere on a hunch? Or known what something you dug up was?''

"It happens all the time."

They both were silent until they reached Nonsuch Park and Andrew hastened off to the mobile home to inform the caretaker he was on the premises. He joined Timothy at the wine cellar a few moments later. "The man says to take our time." He laughed. He looked down into the excavated area with its prominent roundel. "I didn't tell him I'd already spent quite a bit of time here." He laughed again. "And to think that both the Lure and Father Felix have lain there undisturbed for over four hundred years with only a foot of wall between them and all the activity this old place has seen."

Timothy grinned. "It's a lot better than six feet under."

"I daresay Father Felix wouldn't have minded being in a wine cellar! He seemed a very forward-looking fellow for his time." Andrew continued to gaze into the interior. "Tim, why do you think my walking around the perimeter—and Julian's walking around, too, for that matter—seemed to have such an odd effect? We *sensed* something! We sensed a power—and we know now it was Hurst. But always before the reaction came at the fountain site. . . ."

"This is only guesswork," Timothy replied, "but I think possibly the very amount of concentration you and Julian put into your walking along this rectangle—you both were *willing* yourselves to remember and find the Lure—I'm sure that had something to do with it. Also, it was right under your feet! Queen Catherine's mother told her it possessed magical properties, you know. Perhaps those properties are nothing other than magnetic forces. There might have been some sort of power inherent in the Lure itself that brought that force over from the fountain. It's not far away. Perhaps the very power of your concentration—both yours and Julian's—gave the force enough power to leave. The power proved an attraction. That's only a theory, of course; we could never prove it. But it's a logical one. And I think, probably true."

"*Ummm . . . mmmm. . . .*" Andrew had dropped into the pit and, looking up, joked, "Now, you're my lookout man, Tim. Keep a sharp eye out for da cops." Quickly, he went to work, expertly chipping at the Norman roundel. Timothy watched carefully. After a few moments his long, sensitive fingers grasped the deep relief of the roundel's carving, and he attempted to dislodge it. But it was too firmly cemented in place. Again he picked up a little tool and chipped away for several moments. This time it gave a little. "They sure don't make them like this anymore," Andrew joked as a large cascade of dried mortar dropped to the ground with a thud, casting dust over Timothy's shoes. Plaster dust or Father Felix's dust, he thought grimly.

Andrew laid the roundel carefully on the ground, grunting in satisfaction that it didn't crumble. "A valuable piece that," he muttered. Timothy could see he appeared very introspective. He's done this before, he thought. How could he feel otherwise?

"Tim, come—look and see!"

Timothy cast a quick glance around the area. No one was in sight. He dropped into the pit beside Andrew, who'd taken a flashlight from his pocket and directed its beam into the interior.

It was a much larger space than either had imagined. "Almost the size of a large closet," Andrew said. "Incredible, the damned wall hasn't caved in all that time." He continued flashing the beam, then stopped suddenly. "Here it is."

Both men looked in—and there it was. Andrew felt that surge of intense excitement when the earth finally yielded its treasure. It was a long coffin, with no embellishment, covered now with plaster dust and bits of mortar and brick. On its top was a handsome golden cross, just as Brother Thomas had placed it more than four hundred years ago. "Oh, Tim, it's here." Andrew's voice was shaking. "Here, hold the light."

Timothy kept the beam steady, though he, too, was filled with wonder at seeing the physical representation of what Chloe Cuddington had so accurately described. Gently, Andrew removed the cross, shaking the dust from it and laying it carefully on the earthen floor. "Here goes," he said so quietly Timothy had to strain to hear him. He undid the two clasps and opened the lid of the coffin. Both men drew in their breaths in utter amazement.

For there was the body of the Prior of Merton, as uncorrupt and undefiled as the night Brother Thomas and Richard Cuddington had placed him in the coffin's depths. The bright red and gold cope glowed in the light that played along the thin waxen features with its prominent nose and long white beard. "I don't believe it—it's a miracle!" Andrew murmured. "Those monks must have been masters of embalming." He thrust his hand into the interior and quickly withdrew it, saying, "But let's not trust to luck too much. There's been no air or dampness in there for four hundred years. We must close it up very soon. Here"—his voice shook with excitement—"I've got it." He held up a small wooden coffer. Quickly, he replaced the lid, returned the cross to the coffin's top and, picking up the roundel, inserted it back into the wall, hammering it gently into place. Several empty spaces where he'd chipped around it were evident, but that couldn't be helped.

Timothy scooped up the mortar and brick remnants from the cobbled floor with his bare hands and flung it over the side of the pit. "The caretaker said there's no further work to be done here and no more visitors," Andrew said as he helped his companion, "and this weekend the bulldozers will push the earth back over the ruins. We must pray that for the next few days, no one else comes into the pit or jars that roundel loose. What I'd give for a little bit of wet cement!"

"Let's go, Andrew. Our luck has held, but it won't forever." Timothy hoisted himself up out of the pit, followed by Andrew. "We've got what we came for. Don't look inside yet, let's get out of here first." In a few minutes they were back in the car.

Andrew looked at the box with its ornate Tudor rose clasp. "I still find it difficult, Tim, to comprehend that more than four hundred years ago I also held this in my hand. Can you imagine anyone's reaction if I should tell them that?" He laughed. "I almost don't believe it myself."

He undid the clasp and took out a small ball of red velvet. "It's not even damp! I thought it might fall apart"—he spoke, almost to himself—"beautiful color, excellent condition . . ."

"Andrew, you're sounding too professional! For God's sake, open it up!"

The velvet folds fell away; and there before them, shimmering in the dusky light inside the car, was Queen Catherine's golden pomegranate. "The Nonsuch Lure." Andrew smiled. "There it is, Tim—hundreds of years old and oh, so beautiful! How I wish Chloe had seen it!"

For it *was* beautiful. The golden color only emphasized the warmth of the diamonds, emeralds, the tiny flashing rubies and sapphires so intricately set into the precious metal. The diamond at the tip was large with a blue-white brilliance almost blinding as Andrew turned it around, to spark the gems' facets of color. "No wonder the queen and her mother loved it. Do you think it has any magical properties?"

"I'm a medical man, Andrew"—Timothy laughed—"and not supposed to believe in magic." He held out his hand for the bauble. "But who knows? If a curse can linger throughout the centuries, perhaps an evocation for good—such as this little clump of gold and jewels—can also exert a force that's benevolent. I don't know. Even if it actually possessed no power or force of its own, the very fact that people have *believed* it did would give it some power. Now may I ask what you intend to do with it?"

"I'm going to take it to Cuddington House and photograph it and the portrait also. It seems that's all there'll be of the lady for me to take back to Williamsburg." Andrew mused. "Odd, but ever since I found those things in the attic, I thought I, too, might meet a Chloe Cuddington. I've sensed

—same as you—that this is all part of a larger scheme of things. But for what? To exorcise that maniacal force at Nonsuch? I can't believe that. In a few days those trenches will be filled in, and in a year there won't be a trace of the excavations. People have walked around there for years—only Julian was ever hurt. I still feel, somehow, that this little adventure hasn't ended, but I have little excuse to remain."

Timothy accompanied Andrew to his room, for he was anxious to examine the Lure leisurely. Andrew placed it on a table where the lamplight played on the perfect curve of the golden fruit, embedded with flashing gems. "It's a spell binder."

Timothy turned it carefully. "Each new side is completely different. Can't you see how even a queen would be enamored of this? How old d'you think it is, Andrew?"

"Isabelle was mid-fifteenth century, and Father Felix told Thomas it had been in the Spanish queen's family for a long time. That's got to be five hundred years or maybe even six hundred."

Andrew busied himself with the camera equipment. "While you're here, old man, give me a hand with this. I was going to ask the luscious Rosa or the unflappable Harry to assist me, but this will save me the trouble. I think we'll shoot this portrait from the wall, then move it to different parts of the room. The light is stronger in several places—it's almost too bright during the day."

Gently, the two men lifted the heavy frame from the wall and set it between the windows. The shades were pulled against the light that came in from the brightly lit Strand, and Andrew quickly and efficiently snapped several shots with his own lighting equipment. "Now let's put it on the other side of the room. That's fine, Tim, give me a hand. Oh, watch out!" In his eagerness to help, Timothy had backed up against the table holding the golden pomegranate. It lurched to one side, then careened toward the end, and without thinking, Andrew dropped his side of the heavy frame and grabbed the clump of gold just before it fell. The frame, too heavy for Timothy to grab and hold upright by himself, crashed to the floor. There was a sharp sound of wood splintering while Andrew swore loudly and both men turned to see what damage had been done.

"Rosa Caudle will have my head and she'll be justified," he muttered, looking at the split frame. "My God, what's this?" He held up a small roll of parchment, neatly tied with a black velvet ribbon. "Tim, I don't believe this. Look! It just fell out of the frame—it must have been inserted somehow." He peered into the frame's jagged edges, and there, easy to see, was the split section of what had been a neatly hollowed-out part where the rolled-up parchment had been hidden.

"I'll be damned," Timothy said puzzled. "Open it, Andrew, for God's sake, and let's see what it is." Carefully, he leaned the portrait back against the wall, relieved the shattered frame had not harmed the canvas.

Already Andrew had taken the parchment to the nearest light and was smoothing out the sheets. They were as fresh and springy as the day they'd been inserted in the frame. Glancing through the pages of small, neat and dark handwriting, he said, "It hasn't faded at all—incredible! But, of course, there was no moisture or light inside the frame. The wood really acted as a preservative. It's a document of some kind—here—it's called 'A Defence of My Beloved.' " Quickly, he ruffled through the pages to the end. "Tim! It's signed 'Bartholomew Penn. September, 1568.' 1568? That's more than thirty years after Thomas ended his memories on the tape. D'you think this might tell us what we want to know?" Andrew peered closely at the handwriting. "Old Penn wrote a good hand, it's quite legible—d'you think we could make it out?"

Timothy took the sheets, amazed at their resilient strength. "This is quite legible. If this had been written by Henry the Eighth some forty years earlier, you'd have had to have it deciphered. But his children were taught a different hand, and all wrote quite legibly. Penn was of that generation and, being an artist, I would think he took pains. Yes, I think I can read it." He looked through the pages quickly. "I think this is going to answer a lot of your questions, Andrew. Supposing you let me start?"

Andrew was nervous. Did he *really* want to know what Bartholomew Penn had to say? Then the sweet, deep gaze of Chloe Cuddington met his, and again that feeling of being transported into the portrait with her swept over him. He clutched the Lure in his hand, suddenly opening it up and holding it toward the portrait. "Here it is, my girl," he said quietly. "You never actually saw it in your lifetime. But here it is . . . safe. And it will be kept safe, just as your Thomas promised." For a moment he felt his eyes mist over and felt more foolish and nervous than ever. "Read on, Tim," he said, settling himself in an armchair. "We've got most of the pieces of the puzzle right here. There's the portrait and here's the Lure. Now maybe old Penn can fill in the rest."

Timothy adjusted the light near his chair and, in a low even voice, stopping only now and then as a word puzzled him, commenced to read from the parchment sheets.

Bartholomew Penn's Narrative

A Defence of My Beloved

This is a portrait of my dearest wife which was painted in July, 1536, before our marriage.

Her name was Chloe Cuddington. She was the daughter of Sir Richard Cuddington and Lady Elizabeth of Cuddington. Surrey, whose land was taken by King Henry VIII in exchange for the Manor of Ixworth in Suffolk. The family moved from Cuddington in mid-autumn 1536.

The last few weeks in Cuddington and the beginning of their new life in Suffolk were bitter and unhappy because of the death of Brother Thomas of the dissolved Merton Priory. There was, consequently, a scandal of which my dear wife was accused of being a witch or at least of possessing devilish powers. I am convinced that only her friends in Surrey, her influential family and her own stout defence of herself saved her from what might have been a horrendous fate. It makes one wonder how many other souls as gentle as my Chloe's have suffered a tortured death because ignorant minds cannot or will not try to understand? Chloe once told me that the only person—other than her parents and myself—who had understood was her childhood friend, Brother Thomas.

I am persuaded that in years to come as this portrait passes from generation to generation, a false story of Chloe Cuddington Penn and Brother Thomas—and the last few weeks at Cuddington—may grow larger than the actual facts merit. Therefore, I wish to write the truth. I do not trust these words to be kept in my desk or in a portfolio or letter-box; such a testament might be too easily lost or suppressed. But if, as I think, the portrait will survive, then these words over which I have laboured and the manner in which I have secreted them will, I vow, be received as the Will of God dictates. They may even be discovered at a time when they will be most needed and welcomed.

My own view of this story is, I accept, colored by the fact that Chloe Cuddington was my beloved wife. But I am convinced that the facts I tell are true, for she did not lie. This is why a defence for the dearest and rarest creature on earth is necessary and right.

I will start at the beginning.

I met Chloe Cuddington shortly before I undertook a commission from her uncle, Sir James Cuddington, to paint her portrait. This was done midsummer, 1536, and it is one of the finest I've ever completed. I say this with true modesty: my wife's beauty made it all possible. Not only her physical attributes, but the shining brilliance which emanates from the goodness of her soul and spirit.

We were not married then, although—I hope I am not immodest—I was aware she would not be averse to any suit from me. She was gentle and receptive and, at the same time, withdrawn. There was, seemingly, a part of her which was untouched, sealed off from all outside influence, as though she had determined the condition herself. That was to be so all the remainder of our days. But in time I understood what it was . . . and sympathised.

I took this portrait to Cuddington during one of the last weeks the family was there. They professed themselves very pleased, and in due course, Chloe asked her parents that I also paint their portraits. She sparkled as she said this, her eyes friendly and sweet. I knew she wished me to accompany the family to Suffolk. Her parents immediately agreed, and I felt more joyous and happy, for we would be together for many weeks. A long time later she told me that was what she had wanted.

Now I write of the incident that—many, many years later—still pains me and fills me with grief. It was a grief that I know my dearest wife lived with until the end of her days.

Her greatest childhood friend was Brother Thomas of Merton Priory. Thomas was almost as a member of the Cuddington family and held in great affection by them. He was an exceptionally handsome young man . . . one of the few holy brethren that I can truly say possessed a noble spirit and a lofty idealism, which showed in every line of his bearing and person. A most unusual young man. I think it would have been a great challenge to have committed his likeness to canvas. There was something about him I have never seen in anyone else—ecclesiastic or other—that may have defeated any artist to reproduce. One cannot create a nobility of the spirit—that belongs to God.

On one of our last days at Cuddington, Brother Thomas came from Merton bearing a beautiful *Book of Hours* which he and the other monks had made for Lady Elizabeth. Sir Richard and I had been to Ewell and on returning saw Chloe and Brother Thomas talking with Hurst, an undergardener on the estate, who had left Sir Richard's service to work for the King's Surveyor as a labourer. He was shouting and threatening them with a clenched fist. Sir Richard was all for taking a whip to the man—but he quickly left when he saw us. We all met back at the manor, and Brother Thomas, after presenting the *Book of Hours* to Lady Elizabeth, went on to the church upon which spoliation had started.

We were in the Hall having a simple meal—the plate and much of the furniture having gone ahead to Suffolk—when Domino, the head gardener, burst in upon us. He was hardly lucid, but crying loudly, tears running down his cheeks, "Oh, come sir! It's a terrible thing; Oh, come quickly, good sirs . . . I think the boy is dead. . . ." I can remember the fear in my loins as we all ran, quickly, out the gate toward the church. I will never know how, but Chloe actually reached there first. I think it truly unnatural she should have accomplished this, but it seems she sped on feet that hardly touched the ground. Her face was very white, and she kept crying, "Thomas, Thomas. . . ."

She had been there only a minute or more when we all arrived right behind her. She was on her knees, her face twisted with grief and—was it rage? The monk's body lay in the chancel of the ruined church. His gown was torn, a sandal missing . . . truly, there must have been a great struggle. But now his poor battered face gave little indication of it, such a pummelling he had received. But my dearest Chloe held that head with its gashes and blood seeping from its wounds as if it were the most precious thing in the world. She held it to her breast, kissing the matted hair and crooning, "Oh, beloved, oh, Thomas, do try . . . don't go, my darling . . . oh, Thomas." She spoke thus for several moments and then, miraculously—and I think all who witnessed this tragic scene would agree (for we were a silent stunned lot)—the man rallied briefly. I think she verily willed him back from the dead, for his body (Domino later told us) had been as one lifeless, when he'd discovered it. She wiped the ravaged face with her skirt and smiled into the pain-filled eyes, her tears making clean little rivulets on the bloodied skin. "Thomas, do try," she repeatedly begged.

The man could not speak, but I know he heard. While he could say nothing, there seemed to be great communication between them. I know that everyone who witnessed this felt she'd received an answer. She kissed the man's face and said in a voice I will remember until the day I, too, am dead. "Thomas, I love you. This was not meant to be . . . this was not to be your fate. I know . . . I know, my darling. . . ." She rocked him as if he were a babe. "But, Thomas, we will be together . . . oh, my darling, we *will* be together . . . even if it takes until the end of time."

The man's eyes closed, and we thought he was slipping away when a great commotion occurred behind the wall. As our eyes were all on the grievous scene, Domino had seen Hurst behind a part of the gutted church wall. He'd slipped up behind the man and clutched him, shouting as he did so. Immediately, Sir Richard and I accosted the man, who was also bloodied and gave every evidence of having received a beating himself. Sir Richard struck him a great blow across the face, cursing him for the coward he was, saying he'd see him swing from the highest tree for what he'd done. Verily, I thought he might kill the man himself, for he was so overwrought. "Come and see, you swine, what you've done. Come and see your devilish work." He thrust the man in front of the dying monk and Chloe.

My dearest girl looked up and saw the dirty figure. Never have I been so wondrously impressed by her great fortitude. The tearful face became almost calm, and she still cradled Brother Thomas' head as if it were a precious jewel. "Hurst, you evil demon," she said in a quiet voice, "see what you've done! For what? What did you wish to know? What could he tell you? You've killed him, you devil, and if I could relinquish this beloved burden for a moment, I would arise and kill you with one blow!'' There was a deathly silence for a moment; it almost seemed as if her spirit were raging a war with his. ''But I will not, Hurst. I will not commit a sin such as you've committed today, *and for which you will pay for centuries to come*. I curse you, Hurst. I curse you with the fear of God in my heart and joy there, too, for the suffering that will be yours. For the Kingdom of Heaven—where this beloved man of God is going—will be forever denied *you*, Hurst! May you wander, lonely, desolate and exiled, always from any human spirit, with all the horrors and suffering of the lonely, the damned and the exiled, upon your spirit. You are cursed, Hurst, forever! Go away! You sicken my sight.''

Her words—and the power behind them, which struck us all as dumb—had reached Brother Thomas, and through a veil of suffering, he saw his murderer. It is difficult to believe when I say there was a look of total forgiveness in his eyes, but it is so. But if it was, my wife's curse was more powerful than the monk's forgiveness. And there seemed to be little penitence or remorse in Hurst. He stood there, belligerent, sullen, almost completely unaware of the magnitude of his crime. As if in answer to the curse and the monk's forgiving glance, he muttered, ''I will find out, Brother Thomas, what you would not tell me today. You'll tell me someday. For we will meet again. Oh, yes, we will meet again. . . . I will wait. You have not undone me forever.'' Sir Richard became so angry at the man's words that he bound his hands and committed him to the tithe barn under guard until the sheriff came for him.

It was in the days that followed that the scandal erupted that was forever to cling to my wife's name. If it bothered her, she never allowed it to show. Impatient, yes—angry perhaps, but never concerned. It was as if she knew that by paying attention to such scurrilous rumours, she would only demean herself. ''Any gifts I have I was once told I must use for good,'' she would always say, ''I have never perverted them . . . the rumours are nonsense. . . .'' I verily believe she never realized the danger she was in—or cared.

The scandal commenced when Hurst attempted to shift the blame. He said that my dear Chloe had lured him, encouraged him and then cast him aside. Anyone who knew her, of course, knew the folly of his charge, but there are many dark minds always ready to believe the worst. He said she possessed powers which made him do her bidding. He cast doubts on her integrity and dishonour on her name by accusing her of dabbling in the black arts and of seducing a priest. He pointed to the curse which she'd placed on him when Thomas lay dying and said he'd had to protect himself from the priest's attack when they met in the church. Thomas had refused to tell him where something important had been buried and said my darling knew of it also because she'd seen it in a dream—another example of her occult power! He recounted instances of which I was unaware, they having occurred before I met her, when ofttimes she had told her father or a villager—even a doctor!—that something might occur, that someone would live (or die). And whatever my dear girl prophesied usually came to pass. The villagers—mostly all—were sympathetic, defending her since she'd often cured their animals of illness or disease. But a few of the ignorant or suspicious spread rumours that the animals were really her "familiars" and of the devil and that my darling girl was . . . a witch! And that Thomas, who had known of her devilish gifts, had kept silent about them. From this long distance in time, it all sounds childish and superstitious. Yet at that time it was frightening the way the rumours spread and the story grew.

In the end what really did my darling untold damage was the curse she'd placed on Hurst. Those same ignorant ones in Cuddington who were only too ready to deem Chloe a witch were sure Hurst was also of the devil. And there they may have been right. The man had a foul reputation in the village as a drunkard and petty thief. He'd tricked many, beaten others—for he had a superior strength for one so small—and in general built up much ill-will towards himself. Two nights after Thomas' burial, he was taken surreptitiously, gagged and bound, from the cellar of the sheriff's house. At Cuddington church he was strung up on a beam over the chancel and hung. His body was seen there the next morning by one of the king's workmen, who ran for assistance in removing it. When a group returned, the church was on fire, and they could do nothing. It took a long time to burn as the crowd watched. Sir Richard came—the only one from the manor house—for Domino had been so distraught at Thomas' death, he'd taken to his bed. As he watched, Sir Richard said, "It's too good an end for the abomination he was." At that point the swinging corpse was consumed by the flames, and I know I will tax credulity if I say that Sir Richard, the most practical of men, later told me it almost seemed that the man's soul returned as the body burned. He looked at Sir Richard and laughed. This, of course, only lent credence to the story that Chloe was a witch—that her curse upon the gardener had provoked his own death—that the two of them were bound to dark powers and that Satan had then come for his own and that Hurst had not died. It was always said after Nonsuch Palace was built that the chancel site, later covered by the inner court, was haunted.

I weep as I finish this, for the following days were sad for everyone. Thomas was buried in Ewell churchyard, and Chloe lived through those weeks afterwards as if she, too, had been committed to the soil. I understood then, as I had not understood before, that sealed unapproachable manner of hers. She had dearly loved that honourable man of God. And he had loved her. But they had respected his vows and gone their separate ways. Later I told her of my deep admiration for their integrity. It was a feeling which grew with the many years we shared together.

For we did marry. I went to Suffolk and painted her parents. Each day Chloe and I grew closer—the new surroundings helped. The tragedy even bound us together. I could talk with her as I had never talked with anyone else and she with me. She readily admitted her love for Thomas and said, "It will never die, Barto." I do not believe it ever did—or ever will. But there are many kinds of love and the most joyous day of my life was when she said she loved me, too, and would honour me with her hand. Sir Richard and Lady Elizabeth—concerned for their daughter who had become almost a ghost of her former self—gladly gave their blessing, and we were married late in 1537 and went to London. While searching for lodgings, we lived at Cuddington House, and after several weeks Sir James asked us to make it our permanent home. I was to instruct young Richard, whose talent was genuine, while Chloe would act as hostess and chatelaine for the beautiful old house which was one of the showplaces of the Strand.

A whole new life opened up for us. Often her parents visited us. They rarely spoke of Surrey and never ever returned there. They said the Manor of Ixworth was handsome and profitable; the king had been generous. But I know Sir Richard never had the feeling for the land that he had had in Surrey.

That was the past and the story of my dear wife's tragedy and the explanation of what she called her "gift from God" which has been so misunderstood. One reason I write these lines is that it will not be misunderstood in the future. Once Chloe said she'd considered it a "taint." But someone she loved had said it was no such thing, but an act of spiritual grace. I am sure that someone was Thomas, and I bless him for putting her mind at ease.

And now I write of happier times! For I pride myself we *were* happy together. I knew there would always be that sealed part of her nature which would not be mine. But I didn't care. For was I not the most fortunate of men otherwise? Even in her withholding, my wife was the most generous, loving and gentle person. One instance will suffice to tell:

As I have said, her parents refused ever to go see what the king had built at Cuddington. Nonsuch Palace, it was called, and it was, verily, "as there was none such in the land." For months in London, my wife also refused to go. But eventually, as commissions came my way, I was honored by the king to paint and gild the work of a master carver, Nicholas Bellin from Modena, who was to create giant figures which would adorn the outside of the palace. It was an impressive commission. And it was a tribute to my wife's understanding that she promised to accompany me to Nonsuch—as it was then called—and live with me at Sparwefeld, the little cottage which was now empty since old Domino had by then died. Chloe often said his death was as much Hurst's responsibility as if the man had killed him, too. The cottage was hers for life, after which it would revert to the Crown. But I am getting ahead of myself.

The first day at Nonsuch we found the palace almost complete except for the outside ornamentation. It was, I am sure, a difficult time for my Chloe, but she marvelled at what the king had wrought. How to describe its wonders? Its rolling elevation, leafy groves, wooded hillocks. Two gatehouses, one of which has an arched entrance, leads to the royal court. Over this a beautiful clock with golden chimes and figures of the zodiac. Statues are everywhere—in the gardens, walks, bowers and placed between projecting windows. In the Privy Garden an eagle stands on a lofty arch, a pinnacle is topped with a pelican, and another is graced by a phoenix. There is a pyramid and a prancing white horse on either side. Through a circular plane there is a grove dedicated to the venerable goddess, Diana, where skilled topiary work, sandy walks and countless young fruit trees are evident. There are streams, open woods, a sumptuous Banqueting House, delightful promenades and sanctuary for the deer, fowl, birds and other animals.

Yes, we both marvelled. There was no indication of where the manor house had been, except for Sparwefeld, and by taking our bearings from there and from recognising several venerable old trees the builders had spared, we later placed it just outside what the king called the "wilderness." Often she and I picnicked there among the beautiful trees and shrubs with the myriad birds she said were probably from Sparwefeld. She said the "wilderness" was the nearest thing to what the land had been before the king changed it all. Each subsequent stay made her time there easier, and within a year, she was as much at home at Nonsuch and Sparwefeld as she was at Cuddington House.

Only one thing she would never ever do. By sighting the distance from those she recognised, she would never walk near the site of the fountain in the inner court. She said it covered the chancel of the old Church of St. Mary the Virgin where Thomas had been so brutally attacked and from whose beams Hurst had disappeared in flames. On one of our first visits she spent some time near the kitchen, asking a servant where the wine cellar was. He gladly pointed it out to her—a doorway leading down several steps to a most commodious area with a large soakaway in the center. The king has stocked it with the finest of French and Flemish wines. It was most impressive with its rough walls which, Chloe said, came from Merton Priory. She especially showed me an old Norman roundel she remembered distinctly as being above the Priory gate.

The years passed happily. God ordained we would have no children, and while this was a disappointment to me, my wife did not appear so afflicted. "It just was not meant to be, my dear," she often said. But such deprivation was little in comparison with all she gave. She could be joyous and gay, wise and good—and such loving company! I was the most fortunate of men and if, indeed, I had not known it myself, I never lacked for those who so informed me! Her beauty grew with the years; London gave her an aura of sophistication at which her parents marvelled when they visited. The Nonsuch panels were a great success, and I became quite the vogue working in many great houses in the country and in London. James Cuddington introduced us to the court, and Chloe quickly became the confidante of young Princess Elizabeth, who at times—depending on the political climate—lacked friends, especially during the difficult years when her sister Mary was wed to the Spanish emperor. But Chloe never denied her loyalty for Elizabeth and, though she was nearly seventeen years older than the princess—who was wise and mature beyond *her* years—they were great companions. Who could have foreseen that Elizabeth would one day become queen? When that blessed day arrived, she paid great honour to Chloe Cuddington Penn by making her a lady-in-waiting. I have, many times, seen the queen sitting in the Hall at Cuddington House, a lovely, radiant red-haired creature I shall one day paint, enjoying a respite from the court. There she and my dear wife would sit and drink wine and listen to music or read poetry together. Or they might sit and, like two schoolgirls, eat rich comfits and nuts, throwing the shells into the fire and laughing like two sprites through it all.

Queen Elizabeth was very indulgent of Chloe Cuddington Penn, and it was this indulgence which led to her name being associated with the controversial Dr. Dee. The queen loved

Nonsuch and often visited there. Chloe, a lady-in-waiting, would have to go also. But early in their relationship, Chloe asked that she be excused from accompanying the queen on her walks. Elizabeth rose early every morning and walked her beautiful grounds in search of exercise. Chloe said she would entertain her and wait upon her at Sparwefeld; she would attend her in the bedchamber or Great Hall. But she must *not* walk in the inner court, and she told the queen the Banqueting House made her ill. She explained how her old home had been near the site, and the queen, understanding, shouted one of her great oaths and said since her father had been such a taking man, she, herself, could be a giving and forgiving queen.

Yet, for all her affection for Chloe, the queen said the situation might be misunderstood and she would look the fool for indulging her lady-in-waiting. So she asked Dr. Dee, whom she held in the highest regard, to come to Nonsuch. There Chloe told him her story. Dee, thanks be to God, understood. He told the queen my wife was finely wrought, with great spiritual gifts, and should not be made to go where she felt uncomfortable. If the area near the dragon fountain was distressing for her, she should remain away. Chloe later told the queen and Dee that the fountain had been built over the chancel area of a church pulled down under desecrating conditions. Dee convinced the queen that Chloe was honourable in her determination to avoid it. Unfortunately, this was cast about the court in a furtive fashion. There were still people living in the vicinity who remembered the horrible episode of Hurst's death and, with little better to do, recalled his accusations of witchcraft. The whole episode was revived for several months, and Chloe's continued refusal to discuss it only lent credence to the affair. Finally, the queen made it known that any references to her cherished lady-in-waiting would meet with firm recriminations, and the stories ultimately died down. She said that Chloe must do as she wished at Nonsuch, but she must not deprive her of her company. So Chloe came and went as she pleased—avoiding the spots which held too much heartache and possible danger—for all the years she spent at the palace.

But if this bothered my darling, she gave little indication.

She remained her loving and sweet self, winning over many friends at court. By that time her cousin Richard had grown to manhood and, under my tutelage, gave every indication of becoming a superb artist. This pleased her very much; she almost looked upon the lad as a child of her own. When her Uncle James passed away, he left the house to Richard, who insisted we continue living there.

It was many years later that she told me of Queen Catherine's Lure. I think she had a premonition perhaps that her time on earth was limited, although there was more than a year left to us. I well remember the night at Sparwefeld as she was lying in my arms and, in the sweetness of the moment which still makes my heart ache to recall, she told me the story of Father Felix's burial and of the Lure. I then understood her interest in the wine cellar.

I write now of my darling's end. It is only two years since this has happened, but the wound is still fresh in my heart as her beauty and goodness are still alive in my mind. It was a peaceful end, occurring when my darling had not quite attained her fiftieth year. No one would have guessed her age, for that silver hair remained always beautiful and her face was virtually unlined. Her figure was that of a girl. It was her beauty as much as her spirit which made the queen like to have her around, for Elizabeth's beauty depended more on artifice and habiliment, and she always insisted on being surrounded by rare beauties.

The queen's doctor who attended my dearest wife was never able to tell me exactly what she died of. She was not ill very long. It was almost a spiritual languor, a slow wasting away of her spirit as well as her will to live. She took to her bed in our room at Cuddington House, lamenting that she was too weak to go to Sparwefeld. Once more, she said, she'd like to see a Surrey spring, but we had to be content with the greenery of Durham House yard and the Southwark shore. Often I carried her to the summerhouse in the garden in the back and we'd watch Richard paint or I'd work in the flower beds. She was so light in my arms.

At the end she seemed to run a slight fever and lay in our bed, her hand so thin and almost transparent. She spoke of the past, of the beautiful Surrey hills surrounding her home and how she and a boy named Thomas had ridden over the land which would one day be hers. "It was a lovely time, Barto," she'd say. "I've been a most fortunate woman. I've had Thomas, and you . . . and the queen. Always I shall remember you all . . . and my parents . . . and Domino." Her parents had long since died and left their estate to Richard, who also inherited the title. "He'll have children," Chloe had said. "He should have this house and Ixworth and Sparwefeld." Shortly after the queen had come to the throne, she made over Sparwefeld to the Cuddington family for ever, which had much pleased Chloe. There was a ceremony in the throne room to which the whole court came. "We Tudors are a grasping lot," Elizabeth had said in that strong clear voice as she handed Chloe a parchment from which dangled the royal seal, "but we can be giving to those we love." And as she embraced my dear wife, both had tears in their eyes.

But I return to the last scene. It was twilight, and though she was comfortable, my wife's face was more flushed than usual, and I persuaded her to take a little wine. I held the glass to her lips, and she lay back on the pillows, that beautiful hair spread in disarray such as I'd seen it in our more intimate and loving moments. "Barto. . . . You are so kind . . . so kind," she whispered, "thank you for loving me." She turned her face to the wall and I sprang to grasp her by the shoulders, almost willing that she not leave me. She turned to me, her dear face almost smiling. "You must let love go." Again her eyes closed, and she seemed to sink in my arms. And then something happened which strains belief, but I do not lie. She seemed to give a great sigh, almost as if her soul were leaving—or being taken—from her body. She lay passive and still, and I thought she had left me. Tears were pouring from my eyes onto her cheeks, and perhaps their gentle wetness revived her. But I think not. It was something else, and it was not of this world.

I do verily believe she had almost left her body when, suddenly, her eyes opened wide. It was like a miracle, but I realised at once it was not this world she was gazing upon—it was the next. And her expression was wondrous! "So beautiful," she whispered, "so beautiful . . . such light . . . it almost hurts my eyes. Oh! Oh! I cannot believe it to be. . . . Oh, it is! Oh, Thomas, I'm coming. . . . Wait, my darling!'' Her thin arms seemed raised almost in benediction, and I realised she was opening them to receive someone. For a moment my mind did not grasp the import of her words. *Thomas?* It had been well over a quarter of a century since that tragedy; rarely had he been mentioned. And suddenly, *I knew*. I watched her sadly. Her eyes closed as if in great joy, as if the glory of the scene facing her were too much. Her thin arms clasped around her body as if she held someone to her, and then, quietly, she simply stopped breathing. I knew then she was gone. But wherever she was, *she was not alone*. This was a great consolation to me.

There is no more to this story. Except that this woman I loved—seen here on this canvas in the first flush of her maidenly beauty—who was dearer to me than life itself, must always be protected. I have wrought her beautiful body with paint. There is no way to protect the beauty of her soul, except to explain those incidents of a long-ago time, one now almost forgotten, when her name was besmirched with foul accusations, of which there was not one iota of truth. This portrait, which hung at Nonsuch for a time when the queen was there, was returned to the family at Chloe Cuddington Penn's death. Elizabeth ordered the whole court into mourning and took to her bed for days, so bereaved was she by my darling's passing. Now that it is mine again, it will surely pass to future generations of the family, for Richard, I am sure, will have many descendants. So I write this story as it actually happened—and secrete it well—for the time when my wife's name may again be assailed with false innuendos. It is the truth from one who was there.

BARTHOLOMEW PENN

September, 1568.

Chapter Nineteen

The room was quiet as Timothy laid the last parchment sheet on the table and looked out the window. "And now, Andrew, we *really* know," he said softly. "That was quite a fellow your Chloe picked for herself." He took a handkerchief from his pocket and blew his nose loudly. "Quite a fellow."

As Timothy read, Andrew's eyes had been on the portrait, while his mind was busy evoking Chloe throughout the remaining years of her life without Thomas. He felt depressed and saddened; he looked almost haunted. "Tim, what would be the word for it? Soul mates? That sounds overly dramatic to me. Yet certainly Thomas remained her great love, but Bartholomew seems to have made her happy—in his way."

"I think—no, I'm *sure*—that Chloe and Julian-Thomas were soul mates. We have to use that for want of a better word! *They were destined to be together*." Timothy paced around the room. "But we all have free will in our lifetime on this earth. Thomas chose the church. Then the Lure was placed in his care. Lastly, Hurst interfered in their relationship, becoming violent towards the end. Everything stood in the way of the realization of their love. Julian's life was cut short just when he could have been with Chloe. That force at Nonsuch—the Hurst force, whatever you want to call it—seems to have been compelled by the power of Chloe's curse to remain there . . . forever. Just as she said, lonely, exiled, damned to hell and utter isolation, waiting only to exert that murderous energy whenever the spirit of Julian-Thomas was near. Twice he won—by killing. But you were too strong for him, Andrew. That exorcism broke the curse and sent him . . . somewhere. If it's freed you, it's also freed him. There was a Karmic link between you, Chloe and Hurst—perhaps a carryover from a *previous* lifetime we know nothing about—that's lasted over four hundred years. High time it was broken! Four hundred years may seem a long time to us, yet it's nothing but a second as time is counted in the infinite. It's taken that long to bring about this retribution for Hurst and, let's hope, an opportunity for *you* again. With someone named Chloe. . . ."

"That's what kept occurring to me *before* we read Bartholomew's wonderful 'Defence.' God, how I myself would like to have met the man! Thomas knew what he was doing when he urged Chloe to accept him." Andrew's mind was still filled with the tremendous tale Timothy had read.

"The only reason—the *only* reason I can now see for your being brought here, Andrew, is that you are finally to meet your young lady. Or it might have been predestined that you perform the exorcism of Hurst. He had 'served his time,' shall we say, and was fated to be released. But it's all over now—there's nothing to keep you from searching for your girl." He rose, glancing at the portrait as he did. "She shouldn't be difficult to recognize if you see her," he said dryly as he let himself out the door.

Andrew picked up the parchment sheets to tie them together again. He'd show them to Rosa Caudle in the morning and arrange for a new frame for the portrait. Tired as he was, however, he wrapped the Lure carefully in its red velvet and returned it to the little box. And then, drawn to the sheets again, he sat down to read once more Bartholomew Penn's moving words of his life with the wife he'd adored.

The following morning, while shaving, Andrew tried to recall his frame of mind when he'd arrived in England. Was it only a month ago? What an arrogant, self-centered, shallow ass he'd been! Sleep had been difficult, for parts of Thomas and Julian's taped words kept recurring. Their memory of making love to Chloe—who'd returned their ardor with such passion—had kept him tossing and turning. There had to be a meaning to this whole incredible experience, and what was it worth if it didn't bring him into contact with the same radiant creature—one who'd give some meaning to his life? For he now recognized his incessant traveling, his insistence on all his creature comforts, his selfish approach to women had been nothing but an escape from facing the reality that there wasn't one particular person on earth who meant a great deal to him.

The thought was still in his mind as, briefcase in hand, the Lure safely in his pocket, he left the room, deciding suddenly to descend by the stairway instead of the lift. Just as the Cuddingtons did so many years ago, he thought. Slowly, walking down the wide stone stairs, he wondered: How many times did James, Chloe, Richard and Bartholomew use these very stairs? Dusty now, few people ever came that way. And what room had she died in?

At the foot of the stairway, he noticed the little plaque with the history of Cuddington House on the wall. Taking the lift each day, he'd hardly noticed it after the first reading. Now he glanced at it again, noting how each little item tallied with what he and Timothy had learned in the last several weeks. *Was it only weeks?* He felt he'd lived a lifetime and then almost laughed outright at the thought: he had lived *several* lifetimes! Then, suddenly, words leaped out at him. "In exchange for the Surrey property, Sir Richard Cuddington was given the manor of Ixworth in Suffolk, where he died in 1567 *and where his descendants still live today*."

Andrew felt as if he'd been hit by a thunderbolt. "*And where his descendants still live today.*" Of course! There it was—plain as anything could be. He could have seen it daily for more than a month but had noticed it this morning only because he'd taken the stairway. That *had* to be it. It was his—and her—last chance.

Suddenly, *he knew*. With that calm elation he now recognized as certainty, he knew that at Ixworth he would find a beautiful, slim, silver-haired creature named Chloe Cuddington. . . .

Andrew bounded to the desk, the Lure jiggling in his pocket. Rosa Caudle smiled at his inquiry. "In Suffolk, sir? Well, I'm sure I don't know. You see that branch of the family and this—well, we've had no communication in years. It's been a long, long time, sir—before I was born!

They stayed up in the world, and the Cuddingtons at Sparwefeld and here—they've always had to work for a livin', sir. No, I'm sure I wouldn't know anything about the Suffolk Cuddingtons. I never even *thought* about them, truly." Then she smiled at Andrew. "I know what you're thinkin', sir. It just might be! Why don't you give it a try? I'm sorry I didn't think of that myself . . . that resemblance. It's a shame we've let the relationship die, sir, but that's the way it is. Way back, of course, the families were close, and we're all sprung from the same seed, but they'd be very different from us today, sir, Harry and me."

Andrew leaned across the desk, astonishing himself, and kissed Rosa loudly on the cheek. "Rosa," he said, watching that delightful pink cover her face, "if I find in Suffolk what I *think* I'm going to find, I don't think there will be *anything* different from the young lady upstairs—and she won't think you're all that different either! She probably doesn't even know there are Cuddingtons here."

Rosa clasped his hand. "Good luck, sir! And bring her back here if you do. . . . Oh, wouldn't it be nice to see her . . . for real?"

Within the hour Andrew had rented a car from a Piccadilly showroom and was en route to Ixworth. Once outside the mainstream of London traffic, he gave himself up to the beauty of the English villages, lunching quickly at Bury St. Edmunds, directly across from the high monastery gateway. He thought how Thomas would have loved it. Continuing his journey, he reflected: what are you going to do when you get there? Barge right into her home and say, "Where is she?" What'll you do when you see her—confront her with the whole story? At which point she'll probably call for help, think you're a lunatic and have you tossed out!

Two hours later Andrew passed a small sign, IXWORTH. No longer a village, he noted, but he could see the remnants of its village days. The Market Cross was still in the center, and cheek by jowl with later Georgian and modern buildings were several black and white Tudor dwellings. Built by the time Sir Richard had arrived, he was sure. Straight ahead was the

King's Head, with the stern, unrelenting face of Henry VIII swinging on the signboard. Andrew realized how thirsty he was. And disheveled. If he hoped to meet his Fair Lady of Four Hundred Years, he might need a bit of what Rosa Caudle called "freshening up."

Moments later, combed and washed, he stood at the bar savoring a pint of ale and a generous plate of sandwiches. He asked the barman the way to the manor house.

"Sir Richard's? Right down the street, sir, turn right—down the next right—out a bit along the river. Then you'll see the wall which goes along the front. Bit built up there now, sir, but you can't miss it."

Andrew thanked the man, paid his bill and left. He felt better for the food and drink, yet he'd never been so nervous in his life. Catching sight of himself in the car mirror, he almost laughed aloud. His brow was drawn in anxiety and—perplexity? Well, he consoled himself, you're on an unusual expedition, the most remarkable you've ever had! It was a comfort that he didn't feel foolish, only *certain*.

Following directions, he drove slowly down the street, wondering how Richard, Elizabeth, Chloe and Bartholomew Penn had felt the day they'd come this way for the first time. The roadway was, obviously, what had been the main road then; there was no place for any other. But instead of a paved roadway with the usual traffic signs, a pub and a tearoom, what would they have seen? Beautiful open country. As he drove along, in between houses and shops, he could see vistas of fields, large clumps of trees, a stream that might once have been a river—it would all have been Cuddington land. Four hundred years had made a difference, and as the barman had said, it was a little built up. Somewhere, sometime, someone had had to sell some land. He felt better for the thought. A title was enough to combat; he didn't wish Sir Richard to be Croesus also.

Ahead was a small church, in essence pure Norman with later commendable additions. Andrew felt that strong urging he'd learned to trust to go inside. He parked the car and, ducking his head as he went under the low doorway, entered the musty building. It was larger and brighter than he'd expected and, luckily, empty. Straight ahead was an imposing monument—a large stone white angel, standing almost on tiptoe, its vast wingspread silhouetted against the stained glass window, dimmed by the dust and pollution of the roadway outside. Beneath the angel he could see three burial plaques, their ancient brasses worn with time and, he suspected, rubbings which the curious had taken for permanent relics. One was imposing. A man, curiously familiar, and a small, lovely woman, both in Tudor dress, knelt facing each other, their hands clasped in prayer, their robes arranged gracefully around them in eternal alabaster. Andrew looked at the man's face. It was square, with a deep cleft in the chin, with sharp, winged brows over widest eyes. Chloe had surely been her father's child. Andrew read the inscription:

> Here lieth buried the bodies of Sir Richard Cuddington, Lord of the Manor of Ixworth after the suppression of the Abbey which he had of a conveyance from King Henry VIII in exchange for his Manor of Cuddington, now called Nonesuch, in the County of Surrey, and his wife, Elizabeth.

Andrew could not decipher the dates; he'd been away from his Latin too long. His attention was further drawn to the two adjoining vaults and brasses.

> Here lieth Chloe Cuddington Penn, cherished wife of Bartholomew Penn, born May 10, 1516, died September 6, 1566, at Cuddington House in London. Beloved child of Sir Richard and Lady Elizabeth Cuddington.

Fifty years old, Andrew remembered. She had been a long time without her Thomas. . . . He turned to the next brass:

> Bartholomew Penn, beloved husband of Chloe Cuddington Penn. A Sergenat-Painter to His Majesty, King Henry VIII, and decorator of Nonesuch Palace. Born Amsterdam, Holland, March 3, 1515. Died November 9, 1568.

Only several months after he'd written that stirring defense of his adored wife, Andrew realized and felt his eyes smart. *You were not without your Chloe too long, Master Penn, only two years.*

His reverie was interrupted by a scratching noise, and he realized he was no longer alone. Quickly, he stepped behind a pillar, resentful of the intrusion. A clear voice rang out. "Come along, Richard, do! Don't lag, child. . . . We haven't got all day. Set up your things right here—I think you'll be able to do the angel quite nicely. Is this all right?"

Andrew stood, rooted to the spot. It was a woman speaking, and she was garbed in the shapeless trench-type coat, the "mac" so beloved of the British, with a woolen tam-o'-shanter over her fair hair. *That hair*. . . . Andrew felt a clutching at his innards, for nowhere had he ever seen hair like that except in Chloe Cuddington's portrait. He pressed against the pillar, excited and apprehensive. A child, perhaps eleven or twelve years old, came into view, carrying a sketching pad in his hands. A handsome child, reminding Andrew of someone. Then the thought hit—suppose it was *her* child? Richard, she'd said. That's something he hadn't counted on. She might already be married, and this could be her child.

Andrew stayed behind the pillar while the boy spread out his materials. The girl had her back toward him as she helped the child off with his coat. Then, straightening up, he could see the pure profile, turning now, so almost three-quarters of her features were visible. He noted the strong line of the jaw and the merest hint of the deep cleft in her chin. Her dark eyebrows and lashes were vivid against the ivory skin and the colored light that streamed in from the windows. The blond hair was a close-cut cap about her head. Other than that, she was identical to the portrait. Taller, possibly, than he'd imagined she might be, which was hardly surprising. The human species had grown by many inches and pounds in the past four hundred years.

Andrew remained in the pillar's shadow, feasting his eyes on the loveliness he'd memorized, still unable to grasp the fact that here was the girl he'd dreamed of in the flesh. He longed to approach her and say, "Look here, you and I know each other very well. Please believe me, my darling, and don't think me an utter fool. If you'll just give me time, I'll tell you the whole story."

But for the moment, he merely stood there, awestruck at Chloe Cuddington incarnate. Slowly, she walked beneath the windows, her small feet neatly shod in low-heeled pumps, her legs slim and beautiful. Andrew thought with quiet humor that he had one advantage over Julian and Thomas—they'd never seen her legs! She seemed familiar with the church, stopping to straighten an altar cloth and poke among a vase of flowers set in the baptistry. She moved gracefully and—Andrew sought the word—*proudly*. Just as Julian had said.

He wondered what he should do. If she kept walking as the child worked, eventually she'd come upon him hiding like an idiot behind the pillar. He wanted to rush and take her in his arms and ask if she knew him. And how would that appear? Take it easy, he told himself. Don't blow it now—there's a lot riding on this first impression. But what could one say to this Girl for All Seasons? That she *has* to like you or else four hundred years of love, tragedy and waiting have all been in vain?

Only a few feet away, she stopped near the Cuddington burial vaults. Her face was hidden in the shadow cast by the angel's wingspread. He thought she was about to return to where the child was sketching when she said quite clearly, "You don't have to stay behind that pillar. The church is open to everyone."

Andrew's jaw dropped, and he stepped out into the dusty light, feeling stupidly foolish. The child looked up briefly to see who she was addressing. "I was afraid to startle you, that's all," Andrew said. "I thought I'd keep out of sight, and you'd go right on out. Then, instead, you stayed. I didn't know." . . . He was sounding like a nincompoop, rattling on like that, but so amazed was he at her sudden appearance and her words, he could think of nothing else to say. It wasn't the way he'd planned it. He'd hoped to be very much in command of the situation. Instead, it appeared to be the other way around.

And then she smiled, and Andrew could only hope he

didn't look as ecstatic as he felt, for he'd never seen Chloe Cuddington smile. So used was he to that level, piercing gaze that the sudden crinkling of the large dark eyes and the relaxing of the wide mouth over strong white teeth astonished him.

"That was considerate of you, very. I saw you from across the street when you parked your car. I was going to leave Richard here while I did some errands on the High Street. I came in . . . because . . . it seemed to me for a moment you were someone I knew. Now I know I was wrong. You're an American?" She held out her hand. "Welcome to Ixworth."

"I'm Andrew Moffatt." He took the strong slim hand, delighting in its warmth. "Yes, I'm an American. But one very much at home in England. I've spent a great deal of time here."

"Well, welcome again, Mr. Moffatt. My name is Chloe Cuddington. This is my nephew, Richard!" Her voice took on a stern timbre. "Mind your manners, Richard. At least look up and say hello!" The boy raised his head and smiled graciously, nodding in their direction and then went back to his sketching. "He's an absolute nut where his art is concerned. We humor him, however, for he's actually very good for his age."

"You live in the manor house, Miss Cuddington?" Andrew hoped he sounded properly surprised. "Odd—that's where I was bound when I passed this church. And never can I resist a small ancient country church."

"You were coming to the house? What on earth for?" The strong, winged brows were questioning arcs. Well, now, thought Andrew, there's the rub. What could he say? Then, smoothly and glibly, he heard himself explaining, "I wish to see the portraits by Bartholomew Penn which I understand are there. I was interested in his tomb, here." He nodded in the direction of the burial vaults. "I've seen quite a bit of his work in London and understand you also have some." *Well, thanks, Bartholomew!* Andrew was relieved.

"Why, yes." Chloe's voice was pleased, yet her face bore a puzzled expression. "You're sure what you've seen are authentic Penns? In London? We've tried for years to find more. I understand he was quite productive, in his day, but

Christie's and Sotheby's haven't had any in years. We've a standing order."

My darling, Andrew wanted to say, you haven't had a chance because they're all hanging on the wall of a sweet little Surrey cottage that's over six hundred years old and belong to two charming and lovable older people who really don't know much about them except they've always been in the family. But you're going to love them—and they're going to love you. And so am I. . . .

"I've seen some in a little place near Nonsuch Park." He got no further, for Chloe had turned to him, her features pink with excitement.

"There are some Penns at Nonsuch? That might be where the family once lived. It's a long time ago, Mr. Moffatt, and you wouldn't be familiar with it. It sounds like a story made up for the unsuspecting tourist. But I think an ancestor of mine owned the land there."

"And King Henry took it all. Every last parcel and built Nonsuch Palace. Yes, Miss Cuddington, I *do* know the story! I think maybe I know it even a little bit better than you!" He saw her excitement turn to amusement. Now she's thinking I'm just another brash American, Andrew decided, but he didn't care. "You own Sir Richard and Lady Elizabeth Cuddington, I believe."

"Well, it's amazing you should know, but yes, actually we do. They're considered Penn's finest."

Andrew wanted to say that wasn't what Penn himself had thought. Penn's finest is against a wall in Cuddington House, its frame split, its glorious canvas untouched, and it's of you, my darling. . . . He must have been gazing intently, for she said, looking a bit confused and bewildered, "You're sure we haven't met before, Mr. Moffatt? You seem to know so much about us, I thought. . . ."

Suddenly, for the first time, Andrew felt confident. "Yes, we *have* met before, Miss Cuddington. But it's been a long time, and I wouldn't expect you to remember. Do you think you might show me the portraits?"

She hesitated for only a moment. "Oh, well, if you say so. But you'll have to tell me sometime, for I don't remember. It must have been quite a long time ago." She smiled and held out her hand again. "Come along then, Mr. Moffatt, and see the Penns. We English must be neighborly to our cousins across the sea! Richard, we're going back to the house. Mind you come home directly you're finished, d'you hear?" The child waved absentmindedly, absorbed in his work. As he went by, Andrew glanced at the drawing, intrigued. The child had done extraordinarily well and was completely engrossed.

Outside, there had been a quick shower, and as they emerged, the moist weak sunlight caught them unaware. Chloe took off the tam-o'-shanter and shook her fair hair which shone with crystalline brilliance. "That's better," she said, laughing as she turned to face him. Andrew caught his breath. The smile died on her lips, for there again was that intense, forceful light in the man's eyes. "We've met before, you say. Odd I can't remember. But that's the reason I went into the church—because I thought you were someone I knew. How long before you're going to tell me, Mr. Moffatt?"

"That depends, Miss Cuddington," Andrew replied, taking her arm purposefully as they walked along the High Street, "upon several things. But we have a good deal of time and mustn't hurry. It'll all come out one day. We can afford to wait." He smiled into the great dark eyes raised to his. "However, if you insist on an answer, I'll tell you when the time is right. And that may take . . . forever. Until, let's say, the end of time?"

Chapter Twenty

Timothy Hodge read the letter from Andrew with great satisfaction. It was postmarked "New York City," where the Moffatts were closing up his apartment, preparatory to taking up permanent residence in England. Less than a month had elapsed since he and Andrew had found Bartholomew Penn's stirring "Defence," yet in that time Andrew had discovered Chloe, married her and brought her to Cuddington House. Rosa Caudle and she had taken one look at each other, embraced warmly, and together they'd all gone to Andrew's room, where she'd seen the portrait which might have been of herself.

"It was a moving moment, Tim," Andrew wrote. "I haven't played the tapes for her yet. It may be months—or years—before I do. But she's 'our' Chloe and my dearest wish is that you love her, too. I don't see how you can help it. When we return, we're going to live at Cuddington House. Soon, Rosa and Harry will want to retire, and I'm going to ask to buy it and we'll 'restore' it—properly. Already, they're talking of leaving Sparrow Field to the only remaining family member they know. Somehow it's all falling into place, and Chloe is back where she belongs—or soon will be. She *loves* Sparrow Field. She couldn't believe the Penns when she saw them. It has been as magical a time for her as for me. We can't wait to see you when we return, which will be very soon."

There'd been no time for Andrew and Timothy to discuss anything at first, so busy was everyone with passports, packing, marriage licenses and planning. More than once as he commenced reading the letter, it had occurred to Timothy that Andrew hadn't mentioned the Lure. But then, at the bottom, had been a " 'P.S.' " "Speaking of magic, read the London *Times* carefully each day now. They'll be making an announcement soon."

The announcement had been made that morning. Timothy picked up the *Times* from his desk to the marked article entitled "Important Acquisition at British Museum."

"An anonymous donor has made a handsome gift to the British Museum of an exquisite and rare pre-15th-century ornament in the shape of a golden pomegranate. Reputed to be a possession of Isabelle of Castile, it was brought to England as part of the dowry of Catherine of Aragon, Henry VIII's first wife. From the time of her exile and death, however, the provenance of the jewel is extremely hazy.

The anonymous donor, who is thought to be an American, gave strong testimony that the pomegranate was genuine and had been discovered during the recent excavations of Nonsuch Palace, constructed by Henry VIII in the 1530s. As interest in the palace has been very great, discovery of the pomegranate has been opportune. Therefore, Museum officials have placed the object on display in the Main Rotunda, where a small especially constructed and lighted display case carries the identification of *'The Nonsuch Lure.'*

The display will continue indefinitely, although the Nonsuch excavations themselves have been filled in for several weeks."

As he left the office, Timothy felt a strong urge to see Nonsuch once more. In moments he was in his car, heading in heavy traffic southward toward Ewell. Less than an hour later he stopped briefly at Sparrow Field's gate, thinking what it might become when Andrew and Chloe Moffatt ultimately owned it. Without any doubt, he knew the first thing Andrew would do would be to plant a beech tree in the center of a restored circle, and somewhere beneath it would be a bench. . . .

A few moments later, he parked outside the gates and walked slowly down the long treelined drive toward Henry

VIII's outer court, on past the site of the clock that Julian and Chloe had marveled at in their imagination, toward that demon-haunted area near the old chancel. It was dusk, and he could envisage a monk and girl together in the "wilderness," where the old fishpond had been. In his mind's eye, he could see that same monk and a tall blond man hurriedly bricking up a wall in an area where the king would later store his wine. And where even now a holy man slept in eternal peace, undisturbed and undefiled.

But how Nonsuch had changed! Now there was nothing but new turf, raw and pale, covering the filled-in trenches. Great trees, descendants of those which had graced Cuddington village and the manor house park, soughed softly in the twilight. The caretaker's mobile home was gone, and the park now appeared smooth and undisturbed. In the coming spring it would be newly seeded and lush, and soon no trace would remain of the proud palace of Nonsuch, buried now, probably forever. It was no longer a place of magic, black or otherwise. Now it was only a green park, where tomorrow people would come to picnic and walk, to lie in the sun and read their newspaper. Perhaps a small boy might even fly a kite. . . .

Timothy walked back to the car feeling satisfied and, oddly, complete. As the great gate closed behind him, several lines flashed into his mind, and he wondered if the Bard had ever seen Royal Nonsuch:

> ". . . be cheerful, sir.
> Our revels now are ended. These our actors,
> As I foretold you, were all spirits and
> Are melted into air, into thin air:
> And, like the baseless fabric of this vision,
> The cloud-capp'd towers, the gorgeous palaces,
> The solemn temples, the great globe itself,
> Yea, all which it inherit, shall dissolve,
> And, like this insubstantial pageant faded,
> Leave not a rack behind. We are such stuff
> As dreams are made on, and our little life
> Is rounded with a sleep. . . ."